Chapters: a Novel

Brian M. Slator

Copyright 2012 Brian M. Slator

～～～

License Notes

I0667173

This book is licensed for your personal enjoyment only. This book should not be re-sold. If you would like to share this book with another person, please purchase an additional copy for each recipient. Thank you for respecting the hard work of this author.

～～～

ISBN-10: 0985994711

ISBN-13: 978-0-9859947-1-6

ISBN 978-0-9859947-1-6

9 780985 994716

90000>

～～～

Dedicated to all the people who in some way inspired me to write this book, to Liz Macaulay who saw me through to the end, and especially to those few who couldn't stick around until I finished: Rich Ferguson, Jim Lafky, Andy Laugel, Kate Schmidt, Helen Slator, Mike Smith.

~~~

Table of Contents

~~

Chapter 1

When the guys graduated from high school in 1970 it was normal they would all leave home and move in together. Book had serious interest in college, study, and learning. Ace and I were both fed up with school and going through the motions. And Hack had zero inclination but needed a place to live.

We found a slummy rented hole near campus – warped, water-stained hardwood floors, peeling wallpaper, broken plaster – the usual sort of place.

There were still elm trees in Minneapolis then. We had one in front and two in back. There was a garden plot and a picket fence, and behind the house a tarpaper garage with broken gunny-sack windows and a sagging door.

Four years would pass before the manslaughter back there.

The house had five cubicles advertised as bedrooms, a grease crusted kitchen with brown linoleum that turned out to be cream colored after fifty or sixty moppings, a dank basement replete with a cranky oil burner, and no storm windows.

But the price was right.

Ace arranged for the lease and we all agreed to take it, sight unseen, happy to have a place at all. That's what you did in those days – you finished high school and you moved out of the house.

Among the many shocks my system received that summer, one of the largest, and farthest reaching, occurred the day we moved in.

Her name was Rexee' and it turned out she had been living in our garage for two weeks.

Hack and I were carrying a sofa into the house when she came around from our rented backyard, a dripping paint roller in her hand, wearing desperately short cutoff shorts slung low on her hips and a diaphanous, threadbare men's undershirt that didn't conceal her braless applesized breasts or their peachy nipples, or cover her navel or the lustrous unblinking eyeball tattoo on her honey tanned shoulder.

We had never seen a woman with a tattoo before.

There was avocado paint in her long, lager colored hair and a wispy down covering her coppery, bowed cowgirl legs. She was barefoot and smoking a short Camel cigarette, holding it like a sailor, pinching it with plum colored fingernails. When she spoke she had a habit of cocking her head to one side and looking out of the corner of her eye.

She said, "Can either of you beefcakes help me set up some fucking scaffolding? I can't hold both ends and work the screwdriver too."

(<o>)/(1.2)\(<o>)

Lily of the Alley stepped back from the reeking trashcan with a golden plated chain in her fist. She was not deceived. It was a bauble, not a treasure, and the catch was the catch was broken. There are no Eldorado's in the alley, just Lily and her loco motives.

She eased down her shopping bags, sat on an overturned paint can, and idly dropped the chain into one of her bags. Reaching into the other for her tobacco tin, she popped it open with a chipped thumbnail and picked through the butts and stubs looking for smokeable length.

She lit one, careful not to set her matted, stringy hair on fire.

A blade of morning sun cut the dirty brick wall at her back and she leaned into it savoring the bitter blue smoke.

(<o>)/(1.3)\(<o>)

Hack and I were sitting on the Web House porch enjoying a sunny Wednesday morning in June, two summers before the Bicentennial. A mug of coffee for each, the morning paper in a mound at my feet.

It was the morning of the manslaughter, though we would not know that until later.

"What kinda bird's that? Crane or what?"

Hack, whittling with a little yellow knife on a two foot length of two by four, glances overhead and says, "Heron."

He clarified, "Great Blue Heron."

I watched it circling lazily, head curled between its shoulders, long slender pointed beak, narrow head, bare stork-like legs trailing straight out behind, gliding in big spirals only occasionally beating its wings.

"Majestic, ain't it?" Hack squinted at me.

"No kidding," I said, "What's the story? They live in the slough?"

"Yeah, they build big nests, out of sticks and grass, high up in dead trees."

"Not too blue, are they?"

"Not really," he shrugged, "You can see it a little better up close."

"Fish eaters?"

"Yeah, fish, frogs, I guess … saw one hunting once – I was moving real quiet near shore and it was knee-deep in a backwash."

He paused, in a momentary reverie, and then looked to see if I was still listening.

I was. He went on.

"It just stood there, real still, not movin'. I watched for a long while, easy – and just when I made to leave, it snaked its neck out, faster than anything, splashed in the water and came out with a fair-sized chub."

He shook his head, "Fast – quick on the draw, real sudden."

"Faster than Ace, with his Fanner Fifty?"

"Yeah," Hack smiled, "even faster than that."

We sat. Hack whittled. I daydreamed.

Hack nodded to himself, "Don't see 'em over this way much."

"But – funny for birds," Hack whittled on, "they live in colonies together. Sometimes two, three nests in a tree, and twenty or more in a bunch."

He added, "I asked Book, they call it a rookery."

"A rook?" I said, "Like a gypery?"

"You could say that," he nodded, smiling, "a rip-offery."

I watched Hack shaving wood in long sure strokes. He was surprisingly dexterous for a hulking and heavy-knuckled guy. The morning sun was warm on my arms and the smell of damp grass made the coffee taste sweet.

We sat. We basked. He carved. I daydreamed.

"How's your back Skate," he asked, broaching a tender subject.

"Swell", I said, deflecting him," What's the carving?"

"Gun butt for my flintlock. I don't like the one they sent."

5

"Dan'l Boone, eh? – the rippinest, roarenest, fightenist man the frontier ever knew?"*

Hack pauses his labors and says, "Are you picking on me?"

Hack had been assembling a black powder musket from a kit. And while firearms of any type tended to make me nervous, I never gave him any flak. Muskets aren't like high-powered rifles or anything, and they have a certain historical interest. Hack was always fiddling, fixing, or making something anyway.

I picked on him from time to time, in friendly fun.

I ducked his question, shrugging, "Habit, I guess. Black on white. No offense."

He paused for a moment, squinting at me some more, then went back to what he was doing.

I closed my eyes, and continued idly reviewing a story I was working over. I wasn't too pleased with it, but there were a few nice lines – Nun puns.

(<o>)/(1.4)\(<o>)

He arrived home from the doctor's having narrowly avoided being killed in the process. The experience moved him so much that he got a pen and wrote, "Kelsey came in from patrol having narrowly missed being hit by a shell. The experience moved him so much that he got out his little notebook, sharpened his pencil on his bayonet and wrote, "Rico came in after the strike demonstration had turned into a riot having narrowly avoided being beaten to death by an enraged Pinkerton. The experience moved him so much he filled up his fountain pen and wrote, "Farley arrived back at his puptent as the sun set over Gettysburg having again narrowly avoided a blast of grapeshot. The experience moved him so much he put a fresh nib on his pen, opened his inkwell and wrote, "Three-fingered Mordecai hunkered down by his campfire and daubed at a claw mark on his neck having narrowly avoided being mauled to death by a bear. The experience moved him so much that he tore a blank sheet out of his Bible, pulled a porcupine quill from his rawhide shirt and with HIS OWN BLOOD wrote, "Nathan returned to his New England farmhouse after firing some shots heard round the world and having narrowly avoided being shot as a traitor. The experience moved him so much that he got a piece of parchment and his goose quill and wrote, "Miles returned to the stockade after a day of clearing timber and nearly being crushed by a falling tree. The experience moved him so much that he opened his journal and wrote, "Sir Francis returned to his cabin after narrowly avoiding being swept overboard in a gale. The experience moved him so much that he opened the logbook and entered, "Sebastioan the Abbot returned to his monastery after having narrowly avoided being trampled to death by a team of Roman horses. The experience moved him so much that he opened his illuminated manuscript and inscribed, "St. Erile returned to his cell after being beaten nearly to death by a jealous husband. The experience moved him so much that he got out his wax board and stylus and scratched, "Whoo, that was close.""""""""""""

(<o>)/(1.5)\(<o>)

When the notice arrived, it caught Skate by surprise. He wanted to believe their elm was invincible: immune to the Dutch Elm disease decimating their boulevards. And now, after standing up to it for hundreds of years, their giant faltered just in time for the Bicentennial.

A city crew was coming to cut it down and chip it into sawdust, the biggest elm in the area, and the last on the block to go.

Skate posted the notice on the kitchen bulletin board and made his lunch.

Down the back steps he could hear Hack snoring softly.

Hack worked nights driving taxi and slept downstairs through midday. Before sleep he usually spent the dawn hours kicking around down by the river, then slept, and spent evenings, as we all did, at the Web, our house.

Ace and Book both worked regular jobs and, when the notice arrived, Skate was working part-time at the library, by Book's good offices.

(<o>).[].(<o>)

The evening was unusually warm for early May. Book was taking his turn at the dishes while Ace and Skate talked and pretended to garden. Ace had spotted some windmill parts in the dump and wanted to organize an expedition to retrieve them.

"For the Bicentennial," Ace argued, "it's upon us, we need a project."

But Skate's natural apathy was in full force, on top of which he doubted Ace's fixation with alternative energies would ever save any real money. So Skate was hedging with intent to shirk; Ace was cajoling with intent to persuade; both of them knowing it was forgone. Skate always went along.

Out front, Hack was standing on the sidewalk staring up. Skate had seen him there a few minutes earlier. He was still there when Ace noticed him.

"Check this," Ace said, hoe in hand, "another statue to lethargy! Feigning catatonia to avoid marginally honest toil."

Ace talked like that sometimes.

Skate walked out front and looked up, following Hack's gaze. Their elm was looking haggard, worse than he'd realized. Like most stricken elms, theirs had kept a lot of foliage while giving up to random spots of yellow and partial baldness. Their tree was a giant, and a little unusual in that the bottom two-thirds were still fairly lush, while the top third had sustained the most severe losses. It looked bald, it looked bad.

Skate couldn't see anything much, and climbed the front steps.

"Hack?" he said, "Lose something?"

Hack kept looking up into the tree.

"I'm almost pretty sure," he said, "There's a female heron roosting up there."

Ace heard them as he walked up and said, "How do you know it's a female?"

Hack gave a typical sort of reply, for him, shrugging, "By looking at it."

Book walked out from the porch, drying his hands.

"And what, precisely," he said, "do you mean by roosting?"

"I mean," Hack said, "with a nest nearly built, and looking to lay."

They all crowded around where Hack was standing, craning their necks to catch a glimpse. There wasn't much to see.

7

Skate said, "What's she doing here, Hack? The aerie you showed me is miles up-river."

"A couple three, anyway," Hack said, "sometimes they get mites in their ears and it drives 'em batty. Maybe her flock drove her off."

Hack gestured haltingly, as though he had no idea.

Skate noted this oddity but said nothing.

"Anyway, if she's due soon she'd need to nest somewhere," Hack added, "and this is the highest point around."

This last was a statement of true fact and could not be disputed, their elm was the biggest for many miles – so they went to the dump and scrounged.

(<o>)/(1.7)\(<o>)

It was a Bicentennial June Monday and Skate walked home from the Library to make lunch, as usual – thick slices of dry and unchewable whole-grain bread topped with oily, nasty peanut butter and brown lettuce, all from the food co-op down the street. As he turned the corner onto their formerly shady residential street he was struck by how vacant the neighborhood looked with so many elms gone; and he was particularly aware of how bad their own elm looked. The top third of the tree was almost completely bare now, and from a distance and the right vantage point, the heron's nest was clearly visible – nestled in a crook just below the point where the foliage disappeared and the naked branches were exposed.

(<o>).[].(<o>)

A tangled mass of twigs and sticks, as big around as a truck tire, and held together by some miracle of nest building physics, the heron nest is an unlikely looking structure, more like pick-up sticks than wicker engineering.

Even at the two-thirds point in the tree, their nest was at a height of at least 80 feet. Their elm was over ten stories tall, and three of them could not link hands around it at the base. Theirs was a big granddaddy elm – nobody knew how old it was, but upwards of 200 years was a reasonable guess.

Their tree was a seedling when the Declaration of Independence was being signed, and a sapling when the Constitution was being drafted. In its prime it was a king-hell super tree, massive and stately, the tree you would want to be, if you were a tree. It had survived the deadly winter cold, and the furious summer tornadoes, the simmering summer heat and the periodic droughts that Minnesota endured over the decades. Through all this it stood tall and survived.

But the Dutch Elm beetles were killing the elms, foot by foot, yard by yard, and street by street.

There was no cure for Dutch Elm disease. Like 18th century treatment for gangrene, there was only one idea, the best idea, the best idea – amputation. In this case that meant dropping infected trees before they could infect other trees. As a treatment, it was crude and rude, but the only known cost-effective course.

(<o>).[].(<o>)

At ground level, Skate could see there was trouble starting. Hack had his back to the elm trunk with his arms folded.

Skate knew this posture – since grade school – Hack was digging in over something.

Facing Hack, with his back turned to Skate, was a heavy man wearing a white hardhat and 'City of Minneapolis' printed across the back of his khaki coveralls.

"You better believe I've got a right to remove that tree," the man was saying, "the property owner was formally notified and given due notice. You're the one's got no rights – no right to prevent me and my crew doing our job."

Seeing Skate walk up, Hack said, "Do you know what this man is talking about?"

"I'm afraid I do. The notice is pinned up inside," Skate said.

There was an armada of city equipment in the street. Two orange city pickups idled across from the house, and a huge equipment truck with a crane and a 'cherry picker' basket was parked just down the way. A dozen men stood idle or waited in trucks as the three of them decided the future of the elm and its tenant.

"Notice or no," Hack shook his head, "I told you. There's a Great Blue Heron up there, injured and nesting on eggs. No way you cut this down."

"This ain't up to you, or me either," the foreman said, "if you don't move I'll call the police."

"Surely there's other trees that need cutting down," Skate said, hopefully, "can't you by-pass this one until the chicks have hatched? How long can that take?"

Skate looked to Hack.

"Three weeks until they hatch, but another eight weeks before the chicks can fly and take care of themselves."

Skate looked at the foreman and could see he was a hard-boiled egg. One of those bosses who would chew a man out for being late to work on a Monday morning, and still hold it like a grudge on Wednesday. A man who fixed his plans and gave them over in stone, and then whipped his men to see they came through and didn't make a liar out of him. A man with a vein throbbing on his forehead and big hammy hands that looked ready to tear into Hack for good and all.

Hack stood with his arms folded.

The foreman briefly thought about taking a physical approach to the problem – sweeping Hack out of the way and doing the job while this other punk wailed about the injustice. But as he looked over the big one, he thought better of it. The kid was standing pat, solid and calm, and looked to be composed of spun steel.

The foreman thought he himself was pretty tough, and the littler one was nothing to worry about – but this bigger one would be a total whomp-ass handful, and he simply did not want to find out how tough the big kid was. Playground rules pertained – the big kid looked tough – and you didn't 'try it' unless you were willing to find out 'how tough' – and the beating that might entail.

Skate said, "Ten, twelve weeks – that's not so long."

"Fuck you," the foreman said, speaking to Skate and not Hack, "that's into September – no way, no goddam way in hell."

"You'll have to wait," Hack said.

"We'll see about that," the foreman swiveled.

"Lazlo!" he shouted toward his truck, "get me the chief on the radio."

In the truck, Skate could see, a frail looking and skittish man jumped in his seat and grabbed at the dashboard.

The foreman looked fiercely back in the general direction of the giant elm.

"We'll see," he said, and then turned and walked away.

While the foreman was walking back in his truck, Skate stepped forward (having backed away while the foreman was yelling at them).

Skate felt a twinge in his lower back, suddenly aware it was sore.

"Shit, Hack," he whispered, "didn't you see the notice? I put it on the bulletin board."

"Yeah, I saw it," Hack said calmly, "that's how I knew to keep watch for these guys."

"They're going to call the cops, you know."

"Can't help that," Hack shrugged.

"It'll take some time though, I guess," Skate fumbled through the truth of it, calming himself, "I'd better go and make some calls myself."

"I'll be right here."

(<o>).[].(<->)

A small crowd had gathered in the street.

Book left work and was out front chatting to Hack who, true to his word, stood his ground under the elm.

The foreman sat in his truck with the frail and nervous Lazlo, gulping at a thermos of coffee and talking into his radio with mounting vehemence.

The foreman did not know it, but Lazlo was a State Champion chess player with steely nerves in chess game situations. However, in this format, Lazlo was a quivering mass of anxiety, which the foreman did not know either, such was his ambivalence towards the quivering Lazlo's feelings. He was indifferent to the emotional well-being of Lazlo and pretty much everyone else.

The foreman ordered all his men into their vehicles, where they chatted and listened to tinny city vehicle AM radio until mid-afternoon. They ran out of conversation as the sun slowly crept across from where it was before to where it was now.

For the men on the crew this was an afternoon off work – an event that seldom occurred – not with this foreman's tendencies. Most of them were secretly pleased to see him angry and frustrated. They savored his exasperation. A few of them, more senior, viewed the scene with dismay, knowing the foreman would ultimately take his spleen out at their expense. He was that kind of boss.

(<o>).[].(<->)

Across the way, this year's pack of College Joes were out in surfer togs and reflecting sunglasses, lounging on lawn chairs with an open cooler of beer and a blaring stereo pressed up to their windows. This group was more or less indistinguishable from all the others – every new academic year, a new group rented the houses around them.

It was a college neighborhood.

Every sunny summer day they gathered – as they were gathered now; with the same general indolence and preoccupation with campus sports and college girls – the surfer ethic supported by Daddy's checkbook. Year after year the same – only the faces and the music they broadcast to the neighborhood ever changed. This year, the Bicentennial, it was a mixture of Fleetwood Mac and Springsteen, with hit albums on the charts.

(<o>).[].(<->)

Skate made his phone calls.

Book checked out of the campus Library and was home in minutes.

Ace took off work too, and was inside on the phone, shaking things up – first were calls to the Society for the Prevention of Cruelty to Animals, the Audubon Society, the Humane Society, and the Department of Natural Resources.

Then to a few friends.

Ace was a master at rallying the troops. He was our agent for extroversion.

"Look man, can you stop over this afternoon? We've got a situation developing here and we could use some bystanders. ... Yeah, well see, I've got some more calls to make. Stop over and I'll tell you all about it. ... Right, bring some friends, and a camera if you've got one. Okay, later."

Now he was on the line with a reporter from WCCO, the NBC flagship station for TV and radio in Minneapolis.

"That's right, a Great Blue Heron, you know they're kind of rare. ... Right, we've adopted her, she's pregnant and can't ... that's right, we've named her 'The Constitution of the United States'. Yep, you've got it. Hold on a second."

Skate was standing by in their little telephone alcove overlooking the side yard and Rexee's garage, looking up phone numbers and assisting. Ace covered the mouthpiece, trying not to laugh.

Skate wept.

"Oh, man," Skate quailed, "The Constitution? I don't know."

Suddenly his back was paining him. When Ace got too ebullient, Skate sometimes got paranoid.

"It came to me in a flash. It's perfect. Us, the Web, the valiant and patriotic defenders of the Constitution of the United States, fighting the good fight, standing up to the system, mixing it up against the MAN!"

"This guy is eating it up," Ace waved the receiver with both hands, "I've just got to keep a straight face."

Ace turned back to the phone.

"You still there? Good. ... Yeah, that's right, a diseased elm and home to the Constitution of the United States – they want to cut it down and over-turn the Constitution. We're expecting the police, and a crowd is forming. ... A mob? No, I'd say we're still definitely in the pre-mob stages – but a demonstration is looking highly possible."

Ace listened, checking his watch.

"Look, I've got to let you go, are you gonna send someone down here? ... Okay, don't wait too long – a situation is developing."

Ace hung up as Patrick walked in the front door – lean, red-headed, and dressed for work in tan pants and a white, short-sleeved shirt.

"What's happening, boys?" Patrick said, "Hack is out there stalwart and standing fast for the environment, like that time we were going to tip that barrel of industrial jelly into the river, remember that?."

"Oh," he added, "and the Pigs are just pulling up outside."

"Not just the environment anymore," Skate said, rubbing his lower back, "Ace upped the ante. Now we're defending the Constitution of the United States."

Patrick smiled, eyes wide, "Far out. What's the plan?"

Seeing the police arrive on the scene as Patrick said, Ace was already moving outside, but stopped and turned.

"Paddy me boy," Ace said, "Do you still have your protest supplies in the garage?"

Patrick shrugged.

"Skate, help him look would you? We could use a few signs when the cameras get here."

Ace turned to the street. Skate and Patrick headed back to where Rexee' lived.

(<o>)/(1.13)\(<o>)

```
Great Blue Heron
Ardea herodias Linnaeus

IDENTIFICATION
Length: 97-137cm (38-54in). The Great Blue Heron is a
large, dark blue-grey bird having a white crown, cheeks
and throat. A black stripe on the side of the crown
merges into a long occipital crest. The neck is grey
with a violaceous tinge on the back and sides, and is
striped black and white underneath. The back is blue-
grey, the sides blackish, and the belly grey and white
striped. The thigh feathers are a distinctive chestnut.
The bill is yellow with a dusky culmen. The irides are
yellow, the lores dull green, and legs greenish-brown.*
```

(<o>)/(1.14)\(<o>)

Skate walked out into the gloaming darkness with two mugs of coffee.

The police arrived, four squad cars, taking positions at each end of the block. Their first official act was to order the volume down on the surf-rat fraternity stereo. With calm and civility restored they turned off their blue car-top flashers.

The foreman did not know it yet, but he was on the losing side for this work day. Hack did not know it either, but he had won the day. There was enough of a commotion, and enough of a crowd, the police were not going to let anything decisive happen as the sun was setting. In this case, their whole agenda was to keep things cool. Indeed, half the men remembered this address from that thing before – that thing with the black dude.

(<o>).[].(<o>)

Of all things, university area police are best at crowd control. A decade of anti-war demonstrations taught them well: turn up on the scene, establish commanding positions (usually on the perimeter someplace) that allowed for easy and rapid escape, and stand by. Getting into the middle of things at the wrong moment often just made things worse; and with mass media on hand, making things worse was a bad career move.

That deal in Madison Wisconsin had made a difference. Patrick was there.

(<o>).[].(<o>)

"I was just there to observe," Patrick told them once, "My protesting days were coming to an end. So I was sitting back from the action, watching from a tree limb on a nice old oak. The students were chanting against the war, some speeches were delivered, the usual sort of thing. In the middle of this, I saw uniformed police moving through the crowd, just walking into the mob and then standing or leaning in amongst everyone, offering no threat, just standing around.

But from up where I was, I could see they were 'taking positions' equally spaced through the square.

Then, a signal must have been given, because without any provocation they all took their billy clubs out at the same time and started beating the absolute shit out of anyone near them. It was coordinated among the cops, although they denied it later, and it was total panic and mayhem among the students.

People were running from one cop, right into the billy club of the next one over. Tactically speaking it was beautiful.

From a human point of view it was an absolute horror. Cops were fiercely beating young guys, and knocking the crap out of young girls. Mostly people were just out sunning themselves, listening to political speeches. When the cops started swinging, chaos ensued.

One small group of football players and wrestlers fought back, after a girlfriend was clubbed, and drove one of the cops back towards my tree. I'm happy to say they knocked him to the ground in a bloody pulp, and I jumped down and kicked him in the ribs before we all scattered."

"There was an investigation afterwards," Patrick said, "and the police were exonerated – the violence was caused by the students and 'outside agitators' in the official report. But everybody there knew different, and the firestorm of protest led to changes. After that, there was a higher cost to being a Pig."

Patrick stopped there, and took a big gulp out of his Bloody Mary

We nodded.

Right.

Patrick always got worked up towards the end of a story. Was he actually there? Yes. Did he actually jump out of his tree? Probably. Did he actually kick a downed and bleeding cop? Get out of town. Patrick? C'mon.

Still, the backlash of the Madison protest made a difference in how things were handled in these latter years.

Approaching the Bicentennial, the war was over and the cops were pros. They were there for crowd control and to keep the cool.

(<o>).[].(<o>)

Skate walked out front, handed a mug to Hack and said, "How you holding up? You want a chair?"

Hack shook his head, "Better to stay on my feet."

Skate nodded, "Ace is pissed about the media. He figured to keep things cool, and you safe, with some exposure."

Hack murmured, "Eight million flashers in the Naked City."

This was originally Ace's line, and it always made Skate laugh.

Hack looked at his watch, "I'm going to need some relief here in a few minutes. Can you stand in for me?"

Skate said, "Sure – all coffee and no pee makes Hack a full boy."

Hack smiled, "Yeah, that too; but it's feeding time."

Hack glanced up, "I've got a delivery to make."

Skate gaped, then shouted in a whisper, "You FEED that bird?"

Hack shrugged, "Twice a day, what do you think she's been living on all this time?"

Skate didn't answer.

Filling in for Hack daunted him. He tried to imagine a single situation he could handle as well as Hack, and nothing practical leaped to mind. An algebra test, maybe, or a world war two trivia contest, perhaps. Otherwise, Hack was the big quiet presence that Skate always wanted to be. When things got hairy, Skate would wish for Hack.

Skate looked up and down the street, apprehensively, feeling another sharp twinge in his back, "Where are you going to be?"

"Hovering," Hack glanced up again, "like your guardian angel."

(<o>).[].(<o>)

The city crew was still parked out front although "quittin' time" was well past. The foreman had been around from vehicle to vehicle with the same benediction.

"You're off the clock, there's no overtime. But I'm staying right here and we'll drop this sucker at midnight if we have to. You can do what you want."

They all knew this was true. They could leave – and carry their foreman around, on their backs, until they died or screwed up and got fired – or they could hang around and see what happened.

One man, new on the crew, took the chance.

"Chief," he said, "I can't stay. This is my wedding anniversary, I've got restaurant reservations, and if I don't go home my wife will kill me."

The foreman didn't say anything – he didn't even scowl. He just nodded and shot a look to every other man there, and then he stalked off. The men all knew what it meant, and no one said a thing. This new guy's wife couldn't kill him now, not if he left – he was already dead, as far as this job was concerned.

(<o>).[].(<o>)

It was dark when Hack opened Book's second story window.

He stepped from the window sill of Book's upstairs bedroom onto the solid limb that stretched from their elm alongside the house. On a breezy night this limb scraped paint off the siding and lulled Book to sleep.

Tonight this branch led upward as Hack, dressed in black with a small wicker catch basket over his shoulder, and an unlikely looking fencing mask over his face, stepped out and over to the tree.

Skate would not have seen Hack's move except he was anticipating it – it was that fluid and that dark. But he saw the motion, glanced up quickly and then looked away again. Skate didn't want to call attention as Hack slowly and smoothly moved up, about six stories vertically, towards the nest.

The street was half full with people in the deepening twilight, standing in small groups or milling around. No one saw Hack, and nearly no one saw Skate's glance. Most people were distracted by the timely appearance of the WCCO Channel 4 News van, which just then pulled into sight and stopped by the two north-end police cruisers blocking traffic onto the block, the intersection nearest the house.

(<o>).[].(<o>)

"Ace!" Skate called, a little shrilly, "we've got a TV crew."

Inside the Web house, protesters leaped to their feet.

"Far out!" Ace cried, scrambling off the sofa, "get the pickets in place! Now! Now! Everybody, grab your signs! Move!"

(<o>).[].(<o>)

The stand-off had dragged on for hours.

The pals and hangers-on had assembled in response to Ace's call. But there is nothing more slow-moving than a summer stand-off, so singly and in pairs they had wandered into the house to escape the heat. Giving the appearance of a protest is hot, thirsty work, in June, and somebody had arrived with a case of cold beer.

When the television crew arrived the 'protesters' were mostly inside, having a cold one. Skate was the entire protest at that moment, maintaining his lonely vigil on the sidewalk in Hack's place.

When Skate gave the alert, Ace and the protest crew boiled out of the house . Most held a nicely lettered signs on a stick, with slogans like "Save the Constitution!" and "Hell no, the elm don't go!" and "Give me herons, or give me death!" and Patrick's least favorite, "Elm trees are made in the shade!"

The pals and hangers-on quickly formed a conga line of protest in front of the house – as though they had been there all along – with Ace leading the parade in a tight circle, up and down the blocked-off street.

Book came by and handed Skate a sign saying, "Motherhood Uber Alles!"

Skate put it aside with distaste.

There was a nice level of artificial energy forming, as the protesters, fueled by beer, and reliving their recent anti-war youth, took up a chant for the benefit of the cameras.

Ace had rehearsed them, waiting for the media, and working out two versions: "Save a tree, save the planet," and "Hey, Hey, Hey! Elm Tree, Stay!"

Neither of these had tremendous panache. But, Ace reasoned, they were working under time stress, and handicapped by beer. Plus, Patrick had taken all the good slogans for the signs.

The city crew stayed in their vehicles, the police stayed at each end of the street, and the camera crews set up to record the event for the 11 O'clock News.

Skate, at the base of the tree, resisted the impulse to look up and see how Hack was doing. He hoped the tumult in the street would keep attention focused there, and let Hack do his business undetected.

(<o>).[].(<o>)

Hack's move from house to tree was covert but nonetheless detected. First by the reporter who, sitting up front in the news van, was one of the few people on the street not looking at the news van when it arrived. This reporter, alert to new scenes, and very good at his job, saw Skate's one furtive glance and followed it up to where Hack was ascending.

The reporter called into the back of the van, to a camera man,

"Set up fast and track up that tree – someone is climbing around up there."

Delmar followed Skate's glance too, and caught the motion, black on gray and brown, of Hack's climb.

Delmar followed Hack's ascent, but not from the street level.

Delmar was in the alley, behind the Web house, on the sloping roof of the garage across from Rexee's. And Delmar wasn't following Hack's progress through a camera lens either. Delmar followed Hack's climb through the pinhole sight of a lever-action Winchester 75.

(<o>)/(1.23)\(<o>)

From fourteen thousand feet you see blue smoke and clouds, a chimney poking through the haze and herons circling in the west. At steeple level dirty rooftops tarred with gravel slant toward the boulevard. A battered taxi on the northbound waits for uptown traffic, blinker amber winking, rolling past the stop. Just under treads the sewer grate says Minneapolis.

In Annie's Diner near the corner, eggs are sizzling on the grill. The point on Ace's pencil snaps just midway through sixteen across. He laughs : STRESSFRACTURE was the phrase.

Ace watches Annie neatly slip the coffee pot away. Not hard to look, a slim shape in a greasy uniform; a bulky apron tied at waist, a hairnet over walnut colored braids. She pops her hip against a sticky drawer and slides a number two along the counter top.

The pencil sails past Lily dozing on a stool.

"Don't break this one," she nags and smiles, "or you're cut off for good and all."

He stops the skidding pencil with his wrist and fakes disdain. They play this little 5 A.M. scenario, and kid around, enjoy the vacant diner, come awake and plan their day. For years he's been the first one through her door. For weeks they've been adjusting to romance. Last Friday he moved in.

The taxi stops out front and in walks Hack. His wallet chain swings silver with his gait, the cab keys pinched in heavy hand, bruised knuckles, oily boots, blond beard, a frayed jean vest and smiling round his eyes.

"Good morning Hack," says coffee pouring Anne.

"And howdy Annie. What's the schedule Ace?"

"The lad strikes ground in half a spin, we leave in ten and grok him at the gate. Through baggage claim and traffic, hitting Doogan's right at happy hour."

"Okay," sez Hack, "troop transport at the action ready set. You got some roughage Anne? A bellyful might save me after Doogan's gets a grip."

(<o>)/(1.24)\(<o>)

Patrick slid onto a barstool and rested his weary head on his hands. Red curls lodged between his fingers as he pressed his rusty eyeballs with his palms. Calvin slipped a Bloody Mary double between his elbows and beneath his nose saying nothing. Patrick meditatively stared into the glass, admiring the pepper speckled ice cubes with the bovine rumination of the thoroughly exhausted man.

It was six A.M. on Wednesday, happy hour at Doogan's.

He said, "Thanks Cal," knowing another stroke had already been noted on his tab, and Cal could give a damn whether he was grateful or not. The score got settled payday, twenty-six times a year.

Old man Sutter was sitting in his personal booth, blindly surveying the latest racing form and chewing an unlit stogie. He made occasional notes on a napkin, sipping his tumbler of brandy and hawking up lungers into a Styrofoam cup.

The next booth boasted the bloated girth of Fat Henry who peered with thin interest at a well worn copy of yesterday's newspaper. Henry slurped from a shell of beer that he ponderously refilled from his private pitcher. Dressed in the soiled white uniform of a hospital orderly, Henry looked like nothing so much as the great white whale with his face tinged pink and his blubber heaving. He delicately drank from the ridiculously small glass and filled and refilled it, moving with the casual grace and studied indifference of the resignedly obese.

Calvin resumed his usual station at the far end of the bar. His sleek, thin black back gently rippled as he dealt a hand of gin to young Remo who was gathering the cards in his arthritic claws when the back door opened and the guys walked in.

(<o>)/(1.25)\(<o>)

A one act play in several scenes:

Scene One –

The lights come up on the interior of Doogan's Bar; a dimly lit, crummy little dive like so many others. Center stage is dominated by a pitted Prohibition era bar; a scuffed brass rail along the bottom and a featureless spittoon at each end. There are some dusty "top shelf" liquor bottles behind the bar and a cloudy mirror on the upstage wall in back of it.

On a level two steps down from the bar are a line of four or five small, cheap, Formica tables with a few chairs around each. At the far right is a beat-up, coin operated pool table and an equally beat up jukebox.

Standing at the audience-left end of the bar is Calvin, the whipcord-thin, black bartender/owner dealing cards to Remo, a young, unkempt white man with critically arthritic hands dressed in Army surplus fatigues.

Two of the audience-right tables are occupied: the farthest right has Old man Sutter, who is absently perusing a racing form and making notes on napkins. He drinks brandy from a tall tumbler and coughs with emphysemic violence, spitting into a cup; the next table has Fat Henry, an enormous man dressed in a stained white orderlies uniform. Henry has a pink face and pours tiny glasses of beer for himself from a glass pitcher.

At the center of the bar a thin, red-haired young man sits with his back to the audience, slumped over a fresh Bloody Mary – he is the picture of fatigue.

It is Six A.M. on Wednesday – Happy hour at Doogan's.

The audience left door opens and three men enter.

In front is Ace, short, wiry, and blond with a spring to his step wearing a leather, fleece lined, flying jacket. Behind him is Hack, big and bearded, wearing greasy denim jeans and vest; and then comes Skate, average height, weight, coloring and stature, wearing an old, brownish corduroy jacket.

=#=#=#=

Ace
... and here we are again gentlemen, the tavern nearest to the center of the civilized world. So close, in fact, that a distinction need hardly be made.

Patrick
(swinging around on his barstool)
Oh! How you talk.

Hack
Howdy Cal. Remo.

Patrick
Skate, you're back.
(They are all obviously glad to see each other)

Skate
Well said, Patrick, nice pun. Meanwhile, I've been up all night on an airplane, this is evening to me; who's having one? Hack?

Hack
I been driving all night, I'm due.

Patrick
I'm fresh, you can buy the next one.

Ace
Innkeeper! drinks for my friends. And gents, I move we desist with all this peasant banter, adjourn to a suitable enclave, and proceed with the next order of business.

Patrick
Does Annie serve Sanka, Ace? Ever heard of it?

Skate
You drinking Ace? And is Book about?

Ace
(to Patrick)
You speak in strange tongues, pale man, I know not what you say.
(to Skate)
I knew I'd fall in with a bad crowd. I've got the day off, en-toy-or-lee. And yes, I called him from the airport, and his myopic countenance is imminent.
(They each take a bottle from Calvin, no glasses, and sit around the center stage table.)

18

          Skate
Anything developed since Monday?
(They look wordlessly back and forth)

          Ace
No image, no vision, no nothin', no how. I've been asking
around, and trying to find a clue. Nix. Nothing in the wind,
nothing on the lines.

          Skate
(to Hack)
How's your rib?

          Hack
Tender.
(he flexes his left arm)
Tender and juicy.

          Skate
You track around at all?

          Hack
Yeah, but no sign to speak of. The garage back of Rexee's had
it's roof fall in, looks like, and Tiger never came back.
That's about it. Nothing on the ground, that I could find.
(he pauses)
Rexee' is pissed

          Ace
Nothing more understandable, nothing more predictable.

          Skate
Strange, though. Mighty strange.
(shrugs, pauses, and shrugs again).
And the next order of business?

          Ace
Old news, new news, what's news. The medical news from Mayo?

          Skate
They report that I'm presently alive, but the condition won't
last indefinitely. How're things with Patrick?

          Patrick
Working the night shift again. Not much going on. You know
Carol is having a baby?

          Hack
(laughing)
Really! who's the father?

          Ace
Who's the mother?

          Skate
No, somehow you "forgot" to mention that. When's it due?

          Patrick
Late July.

          Skate
Next month! You close-mouthed bastard!

          Ace
Yowzer! A yankee doodle, Bicentennial bambino.

          Hack
The Web's first legitimate child. Nice goin' Pat.

                Patrick
(blushing)
It was easy.

                Ace
Shows what you know.

                Skate
Yeah, congratulations Pat. We've got to buy baby clothes.

                Patrick
Baby clothes?

                Skate
You poor simple fool. This is a baby, it needs clothes -- tiny
little clothes.
(Skate looks around the table, knowingly)
You're counting on Carol to take care of all this, I'm
guessing.

                Patrick
(sheepish but defensive)
Well, she's done it before, I haven't.

                Skate
What fools these mortals be.

                Ace
Indeed. And Hack, What Ho?

                Hack
Decided to ease out of the cab business. You know my uncle
left me those acres up in the woods -- the home farm. Mine if
I pay the taxes. I'll clear a spot, build a cabin and go to
ground.

                Ace
Leaving the Web?

                Hack
Leaving the house, I guess, eventually, yeah.

                Skate
How're you going to live?

                Hack
There's a few dinero in the bank and I got my seaplane rating
now. There's always a little cash in flying supplies in to
berry pickers.

                Skate
A cabin, Hack? I mean, a rifle butt is one thing, but a cabin?
Plus, a few dinero? A cabin, that's a lot of berry-pickups.

                Hack
Ya, well, I seen it done. There won't be any trouble there.
And bucks, hell; most of the materials are laying there on the
property. I felled the timber last summer, it'll be seasoned
and ready by now; needs to be stripped though. The caulking is
waiting down in the clay bottom, the shingles are in a stand
of cedar that I have to clear anyway. All I really need is a
ton of plywood, some fixtures and a lot of bull labor. (he
pauses) You guys are all invited.

                Skate
Sounds good Hack, really.

Ace

No kidding, it's perfect. I was just thinking last night --
here it is, past Spring and no one has planned any
Bicentennial projects.
(He speaks accusingly towards Skate)
My windmill project never got off the ground
(Skate shrugs)
Except Patrick of course.

Patrick

Me? Bicentennial projects? Imperialist madness.

Ace

Yes, yes. Meaningless acts to commemorate our great nation's
200th Birthday. Everybody's doing it. All over the country
people are planting flowers, cleaning up parks, picking up
litter.

Skate

One guy has vowed to hop nineteen hundred and seventy-six
freight trains.

Ace

Yes. And it behooves us as the hardcore, central cadre of the
Web to plan some suitably nostalgic act of total inanity on
which we can all someday look back and wonder whether we had
all lost our minds.

Skate

Very well put. Any ideas?

Ace

None yet. Patrick, as usual, has preceded us. Carol's
Bicentennial pregnancy is perfect, just right. As the great
white father told us to go forth and be fruitful. And Hack!
Zounds! A project in the true, time honored pioneer spirit. My
kowtows to both of you.

Patrick

I was serious about the Sanka. You should look into it.

Ace

(to Patrick)
There you go again, speaking in tongues. Is that Dominican you
speak? Or Franciscan?

Patrick

Jesuit, flat out

Ace

Jesuit? Eye-eee. Never Jesuit. In nominee spiritu sancto.

Patrick

You doorknob. You never did learn your Latin. It is "In
Nominie Spirito Sanctus."

Hack

Oh, for the love of Mike

Patrick

You mean, in god's name

Hack

Yeah, that too.

        Ace
(turning to Skate)
But what of Skate? What plans for the gentle bard?

        Skate
(Thoughtfully)
I've just been turning that over. Number one, I'm quitting my
job. That, I decided months ago. Then, I'm going to write the
book I've been carrying around in my head. And third, if Hack
goes for it, I'm going to move up north into the woods and
help build a bicentennial log cabin.
(Pauses)
What say Hack?

        Hack
No problem, no sweat. I got that little trailer up on the land
already. You can settle in any time you want. And I could sure
enough use the help. But I couldn't pay you.

        Skate
Pay! Don't CHARGE me, is all I ask.

        Hack
That's a deal. Maybe first we could build you a little shack
down by the water, to write in I mean. Maybe pay you that way;
give you a little green acre or so.

        Ace
That would be acre "Verdus in Nominie Spirito Sanctus"

        Skate
(ignoring Ace)
Don't worry about it Hack; and I won't either.

        Ace
Plots hatched, Deals struck, Webs woven, right before our
wondering eyes. That's what the old network is all about.
(he raises his bottle, as if to toast, everybody ignores him)

        Patrick
Skate, what's your book going to be?

        Skate
Uh, well Pat, it's kinda hard to explain. It'll be ...

        Ace
A filthy Bicentennial Bestseller filled with livid passion and
smutty goodparts?

        Skate
Nooo ...

        Ace
Oot with it laddy.

        Skate
Alright, alright, but keep it quiet okay. Don't let it leave
the Web. I don't want some scum stealing the idea out from
under me.
(The others say nothing, waiting. Skate warms to the subject
as he goes along. He's been thinking about this a lot.)
Okay, right, the idea is this: I'm going to write a book of
fiction called "Well-Versed". The title is from an eight
stanza street-poem that I wrote last year. The first four
verses are the start of the book, then the body of the project

                            22

is a collection of stories, poems, anecdotes,
characterizations -- and the final thing is the end of the
poem. So the body of the book is like the "middle" of the
poem, see, and all the various things in the middle are then
woven together into a story line.
(There's a silent moment while Skate lets this sink in)

    Hack
(Whistles softly through this teeth)
Sounds like a headache to me.

    Patrick
How long you been working on this?

    Skate
(Shrugs)
Coupla years, coupla lifetimes. I don't know.

    Ace
Didn't you show this to Rexee'? What's the story about?

    Skate
Yeah, well, I should know by now it's bad luck to say too
soon.

    Patrick
Can you tell us the poem?

    Skate
Little bit I guess:
(He closes his eyes and leans his head back; then tapping on
the table in bebop time recites).
Man with an earring ain't always a faggot.
Lad taking welfare is more than a maggot.
Don't look at me, man, you said it first;
It don't hurt to be well-versed.
(He stops and looks from face to face. Nobody speaks. He goes
on)
Raged down some roadways and had some bad spills.
Pursued some devils and eaten some hills.
Loved by a legion but ending up cursed;
It don't hurt to be well-versed.
(pauses, goes on, tapping the table with vigor)
Said hello and goodbye to some lovers and friends.
Came up real fast with emotional bends.
Reeling with feeling but sounding rehearsed;
It don't hurt to be well-versed.
(Skate ends here with a flourish).
There's more, but I don't want to mess with my luck.

    Hack
It sounds real good Skate, like a song.

    Skate
Yeah, I guess it is, in a way. I live in daily fear that some
glitter-rock lamebrain is going to use "Well-Versed" as an
album title or something.

    Ace
Skate, if nothing else it'll make a damned fine Bicentennial
project. I'm so inspired I'm going to break one of my personal
rules and buy you all a drink.

> Patrick
> I'll have a pint of cognac, please, and bag of beernuts.

> Hack
> Case of beer for me, thanks Ace.

> Skate
> Same here Ace, and ditto.

> Ace
> (turning to the bar)
> Calvin my good man; what are the chances of starting up a
> bartab here?

> (Blackout).

(<o>)/(1.26)\(<o>)

diaria -- 1.0 -- 7/12/76 -- Somewhere west of Minot

diaria get it. it's like a diary i'm keeping but really
i'm just blowin it out my ass. not everyone will find
that funny, or as clever as I do.

meanwhile, i'm sittin here at this trusty word processor
thousands of bucks worth of electronic wizard jim-jams
and like my good friend tom sez "if this typewriter
can't do it, then fuck it, it can't be done."*

there's a couple things should be addressed here: like
what it is i'm doin and what it is i'm pretendin to do.

at root i'm tryin to tell a story. and that'll get done
no matter what else happens. the interest lies in the
way i get it on. here comes details of fictional
methods, knowin what's been done, how and when, and
tryin to lash together somethin that's different both in
method and madness or structure or lack of same.

one of the things we need then is a theme or two or
more.

another thing is a time frame or two or more.

and then characters, situations, episodes, events et
cetera to make it a FICTION, a ripping good yarn.

so it becomes my job to provide some of this stuff. and
if you don't mind i'll be stoppin like this from time to
time, just to explain what's goin on and see if yer
still with me.

another item, evidence of handwaving and eccentricity,
is the didactic (educational) stuff that i'll
periodically be dunning you with. some of which will be
filtered in the form of legitimate criticism and
explications of this thing that has come to be known as
contemporary fiction, or metafiction, or reflexive
fiction, or self-begetting fiction, or surfiction, or
experimental fiction (although some in the fabulation
biz frown on that last term -- I can't tell why) and
some of it will be of other ilk.

and so you get a combination of fiction and criticism, fact and fancy, and the line drawn between hard or impossible to see. f'rinstance i'll be quoting passages from critical works and the effect is that i'll periodically have to FOOTNOTE the references and quotes that i'll be stealing; perhaps making this towards the first footnoted novels ever documented.

there's more to say, lots more, but there's no need to wear it all out at once.

one thing. though -- james joyce has a long twisted discussion in one of his books* that compares different modes of literary expression. to him there is epic, lyric, and dramatic in that order.

epic where the authors voice speaks to the reader.

lyric where the authors work speaks to the reader.

dramatic where the characters in the authors work speak to the reader.

we'll have a little of each, a little of something else, and a few instances where we can't tell just what in the hell is goin on.

If you got this far, well, stick around, we're in this together. that's how i see it.

(<o>)/(1.27)\(<o>)

Mounds of debris on every point, ashtrays overflowing, candle guttering in a cracked saucer, balled up clumps of unlined paper pouring over the lip of a shopping bag trashcan. Exhausted bard slumped in a tawdry chair snoring, heavy coffee mug dangling from a limp index finger, television in the corner showing snow and giving off sausage sizzling white noise.

Bard belches, coffee mug shakes loose falling onto empty beer glass shattering it. Bard leaps awake, scared shitless; then settles nervously back into chair gouging gravelly eyes. His back bothers him.

An image flickers on the TV. screen, he stares startled, blinks, it's gone, blinks, it's back. No sound, no white noise, no nothing. Eagle eye view of a city in a mist, zooms to building top level, zooms to street level hovering over a taxi. In a diner, two people, man and woman, cabbie enters. A blinking eye. Cut to a saloon, four or five people, three more walk in. Cut to a bag lady smoking.

Bard leans forward, what is this? No credits, no audio, no clues. He's interested.

A collage of visuals; kids on a playground, J.F.K., Rome, the Kremlin, the Lafayette Escadrille, library shelves, a '57 Chevy, a prairie sunset; kaleidoscopic, prismatic snapshots of faces and places, pedaling furiously past, fast and faster. Madness. Stopping suddenly on a long still close-up of an icecube. With pepper on it. In a Bloody Mary.

Dissolve to a tenement. Moving day. Summer sun, pretty girl, seen before, elm trees everywhere. Old footage. The bard is riveted. Fascinated.

The frame freezes. Slowly an upper and a lower eyelid enter from the top and bottom of the screen. They inexorably converge. Pause. The one eyed monster winking.

The bard awaits expectant. The eyelids tremble. The bard sits poised. The eyelids gently open. Meeting eyes to eye. A message gradually appears on the screen in crystal letters. It says :

To Be Continued ...

(<o>)/(Endnotes 1.28)\(<o>)

1. Boone, Daniel, NBC Television Series (1964-1970). 20th Century Fox Television. Broadcast 'in living color'.

2. James Hancock and James Kushlan, The Herons Handbook (New York: Harper & Row, 1984), p. 50. (Based on "The Herons of the World," 1978)

3. Tom Robbins, Still Life With Woodpecker (New York: Bantam Books, 1980), p. 3.

4. Joyce, James, Long Twisted Discussion on Epic/Lyric/Dramatic Voice. In "A Portrait of the Artist as a Young Man" originally published in book form by B.W. Huebsch, New York, 1916.

Chapter 2

The night seemed soft to Hack as he moved along Book's branch towards the elm's trunk – but he felt a slight unease too, as though the air were too rich and too dark.

He could feel the chub fingerlings flopping and writhing in the basket against his side. For three weeks he had netted them (illegally) in a river pool and stocked them in Book's fish tank.

Then twice a day, just before dawn and just after sunset, he climbed up to her.

She refused at first, snapping and flapping to drive him off. She had nearly taken his eye with her long knife-like beak. But Hack persisted, borrowing Book's fencing mask to protect his sight, and offering her live fish until finally hunger won out over fear and pride, and she took what was offered.

Hack had lied.

The chick was already some weeks old, the normal three to four week incubation period shortened presumably because the mother, unable to fly, nested full time.

Hack told no one.

A mother nesting with a fragile egg would stand less disturbance and so would be left in peace – a mother with a chick could more easily be captured and transported.

Hack knew this and wanted to prevent it. After three weeks of twice-daily feedings he felt a certain bond with both mother and child, and a certain paternal responsibility. They were his – his to take care of, and he could not do that if they were hauled off to some animal shelter or incarcerated in a zoo.

Hack moved easily upward. He had already made this trip forty times and knew every handhold. Elms are cake to climb once you get past the base and into the branches.

Reaching the lowermost branch on their giant was a struggle from the ground, even for Hack who could stuff a basketball with both hands, but getting on from Book's window made the whole thing easy.

He pulled himself into position near the nest.

With his back to the Web, and both feet planted in secure crotches, his hands were free and he could swivel at the waist to dodge beak thrusts, which still occasionally came, and which came with such terrific speed that even he was hard-pressed to avoid them. Usually, he had learned, she "telegraphed" each thrust with a twitch, so he was mostly ready when they came.

Hack spoke to her, softly and calmly, as he reached into the basket for a fish. He kept a wary eye on her slender S-shaped neck, coiled to strike as it naturally was. She seemed nervous tonight, perhaps distracted by the extra noise and unusual level of activity on the street. She had an odd looking habit of fidgeting around the nest, hampered by her damaged wing, and an eerie way of moving her entire body while keeping her eyes steady, fixed and immobile. Everything moved except her eyes, which were yellow and sharp – deadly and predatory.

Hack tossed the first fish onto the nest in front of her. The fingerling flopped once, arching itself into the air, before she struck – catching it crosswise then flipping her head and wolfing it down in a rapid series of crunching gulps. The chick, fuzzy and ugly, reached up and pecked it's mother on the underbelly, then tilted back slightly and opened its mouth. The mother leaned over then and disgorged partially digested fish fragments into the chick's waiting mouth. Hack immediately threw a second fish and the process went on.

On the third fish the mother regurgitated the offal in front of the chick, onto the nest, rather than directly into the chick's maw. The baby struggled to scoop up the remains, but managed it finally. Hack guessed that was some Heronic rite of passage while a chick was maturing. He tossed another fish.

Hack was so absorbed with this scene that he failed to notice what went on below him.

(<o>)/(2.2)\\(<o>)

Tiger felt hot and uncomfortable. His skin was prickly and every hair on his body was trying to stand up. He had been sitting on the grass in the Web backyard.

Before that, he stood with the protest, held a sign, and drank some beer. But he shrank from that, and wandered, as he tended to do, to a quiet place – the backyard in this case, where he found a sunny spot on the grass near Rexee's garage.

As the sun went down, and the shadows crept toward him, he backed up to stay in direct sunlight; until finally he was sitting next to and behind a lilac bush, pressed against the garage wall. Surrounded by fragrant shrubbery, all he could see was a narrow band of backyard and, if he craned his neck, a small garage across the alley.

But he was starting to feel hot and uncomfortable, temperature rising – his skin seeming to twitch and writhe over his body.

So Tiger lay over onto the cool earth and pressed his face into the dark soil. This felt good and now, as he lay there, he could see nothing but the roof of that other garage across the alley, and the moon rising behind it, almost full, as daylight faded.

Tiger lay on his side and smelled the soil.

He recalled an old "Rawhide"* installment where Gil Favor, the trail boss, went out on a picnic with some woman and Gil, tired of droving cattle and looking to settle, fell to his knees and picked up a pinch of soil and then, dabbing soil to tongue said, "This land is as rich as butter – you'd just have to drop seeds here and stand back."

Tiger's face was, by this time, laying flat with his cheek against the cool buttery ground. He turned his head and touched his tongue onto a clod of dirt near his face. This soil was nothing like butter, and he spit and drooled until the grit and the taste was gone.

Still, it felt nice to lie on the cool soil and smell the earth – it soothed him a little. He could smell damp loam and hear the evening sounds: people talking on the street out front, gravel crunching under someone walking down the alley, and the faint croaking of the heron high overhead.

Silhouetted to him, and no one else in the world, Tiger could see the shoulders and head of someone lying prone on the garage roof across the alley,

28

their antennae pointing up toward the heron through the gathering dark, as though trying to receive a message – or send one.

In the alley, between the opposite garage and where Tiger lay, a frail figure stood with one arm up – not like a salute but like the Spiderman about to shoot some web – arm extended, wrist bent back, thumb extended but middle fingers bent down. An old, stooped woman who seemed, from where Tiger was laying, to hover a few inches above the ground.

(<o>)/(2.3)\(<o>)

```
re-cur-sion
\\ re'kerzhen\\ noun [LL recursion-, recursio, fr.
recursus (past part. of recurrere, to run back, return)
+ -ion-, -io -ion--more at recursive definition]: SEE
recursion.*
```

```
recur-sive definition
\\ re'ker|s|iv\\ noun [recursion + ive]: a definition of
a function permitting values of the function to be
calculated systematically in a finite number of steps;
esp.: a mathematical definition in which the first case
is defined in terms of one or more previous cases and
esp. the immediately preceding one. a recursive
definition of the factorial is given by
0! = 1 and (n + 1)! = (n + 1) X n!
a recursive definition of oatmeal is given, in the first
case, by a box with a man on the cover and, in the
subsequent cases, by that man holding a box of oatmeal
which, in turn, has a man on the cover who is holding a
box of oatmeal.*
```

(<o>)/(2.4)\(<o>)

The reporter approached Skate with an imposing directional microphone and the second cameraman. The first cameraman was across the street, as ordered, trying to find an angle to film Hack up near the nest. Skate eyed the reporter with suspicion, but his attention was mostly on the cameras – one across the street and one approaching with the reporter.

"What's your man doing back there?" Skate, taking the initiative, nodded to the first camera.

The reporter ignored the initiative and the question and looked up, "Channel 4 news. What's your man doing up there?"

(<o>).[],(<o>)

The first cameraman had found a spot, finally, on the porch steps of a house four doors down across from the Web. He had a clear image of Hack, the nest, and the Constitution of the United States.

It was dark but, through the viewfinder, he could see the big guy reach into his basket and dangle a fish briefly and then flip it into the nest with his wrist. It looked like a wary dance from this angle, the bird sometimes snatching forward without warning and the big guy recoiling to avoid her.

(<o>).[],(<o>)

Clouds were gathering overhead and the sun was past setting; and yet the heat seemed to be rising and the air was very still.

Tiger was also very still, under the shrubs against Rexee's garage, laying against the cool soil and trying to tell if he was suffering bum-rush hallucinations or seeing the real world before his eyes – it seemed very real, but Tiger was never sure.

Delmar lay very still, on the inclined slope of the garage roof across from Rexee's – his breathing was very steady as his finger tightened on the trigger of his rifle.

Skate stood very still, at a loss for words and desperately trying to think of some way to stall, some yarn to spin. His mind was a blank and he wished Ace or Book or anybody would come along and divert the reporter facing him.

The first cameraman stood very still, squinting through his lens because, though he couldn't be sure in this light, it seemed as though there was some other movement at the edge of the nest. There was a man, there was a big bird, and there was maybe something else.

The crowd in the street was suddenly very still, since many of them had seen the cameraman training his equipment up the tree, and human nature was to follow that gaze, and besides it was becoming too oppressively hot to move.

Hack was very still, warily guarding against the heron's next thrust, and the Constitution of the United States was momentarily still, her neck coiled into that graceful "S", prepared to strike as always, as was her nature to do.

(<o>).[],(<o>)

And then several things happened in rapid succession.

(<o>).[],(<o>)

The Constitution of the United States snapped her head forward and Hack swiveled to avoid her.

Delmar's rifle fired, the bullet passing through Hack's shirt and taking a stripe of skin off a rib before striking the Constitution of the United States at the base of her long elegant neck and killing her dead.

The shot ringing through the neighborhood seemed to set off an immediate reaction, as a bolt of lightening arced down from the thunderhead above, and struck the power pole on the nearest corner with a clap of thunder 50 times louder than the rifle shot. Every light bulb on the block blazed brightly and went out. The entire neighborhood was plunged into darkness.

A jagged bolt of what looked to Tiger like green electricity shot from Lily's palm up to Delmar's garage roof sniper spot. And before Delmar could ratchet his rifle to squeeze off another round, the garage roof collapsed under him and he fell, unconscious, onto the concrete slab inside the empty garage.

(<o>).[],(<o>)

To Skate, already keyed up into an unbearable state, each explosive report seemed to touch another open bleeding spinal nerve as he jerked, right-left-right, impulsively shying away from each, like a thoroughbred on steroids.

Then, when he heard something tumbling through the branches directly above him, he thought Hack might be falling. His impulse to break Hack's fall

30

was equaled by his fear of being crushed, and he couldn't see anything from where he stood.

In the end, Skate just twitched in place, his back shooting pain up his spine and his fright and flight reactions canceling, until the Constitution of the United States, as limp as a washrag and as dead as a stump, landed at his feet with a sickening and bloody "thumpch!"

There was a moment of pure, liquid silence as Skate gaped at the Heron corpse, the whole scene recorded by Channel 4.

Then all hell broke loose as Ace and the protesters, plus a crowd of others boiled onto the front yard of the Web, shouting and cursing and waving their arms in the darkness, as the clouds riffed on the lightening and an unholy downpour commenced.

(<o>)/(2.10)\(<o>)

It was three summers before the Bicentennial, on a very hot day, and Hack and Skate had carried groceries home from the local market (the House of Rip-off, as it was known to all, an appellation coined by Ace that nearly everyone in the neighborhood quickly adopted). As they walked into the yard they could see Rexee' was lying out on a blanket in the back, reading and sunning herself as she often did on sweltering days.

She was talking to a man who stood over her. He was tall and his hair, while dark, was cut very close and showed white on the sides of his head. He was wearing military leftovers: combat boots, camouflage pants, a military green t-shirt and, improbably considering the heat of the day, a khaki vest. He stood with the posture of someone who took himself very seriously, and he was talking to Rexee' with an intense and almost fierce look. Rexee' was looking up at him, but stealing glances at her book, a sure sign she was bored (Skate knew this behavior first-hand, and watched for it now, whenever he talked with her).

Skate and Hack went inside to start putting groceries away. But first, Hack leaned out the kitchen window, which faced the backyard, and called through the screen,

"Yo, Rexee', we've got your stuff."

Rexee' got up from her blanket but, before she started into the house, she made a point of taking leave. The man in combat green had made a small move toward following her in, and she clearly didn't want that. Skate couldn't hear what was said but, after she turned her back, Skate clearly saw him look past her, toward the house, with what looked like anger and irritation on his face.

Rexee' came in the back door and into the kitchen. Hack was smearing an immense dab of peanut butter onto a slice of grainy co-op bread.*

"He a friend of yours," Hack asked.

"Shit," she said, "I doubt that guy's GOT a friend, unless it's attached to his wrist. You know him?"

"Seen him around," Hack said, "and he looks familiar from somewhere. He roams the neighborhood at night sometimes, and he drinks at Doogan's once in a while. Remo knows him, I think."

Rexee' nodded, "Yeah, well I've got my doubts about that character, too."

"Remo's a good head, he just takes a pragmatic view," Skate said, "What's this guy have to say?"

31

Rexee' looked out the window, "Who can tell. One minute he's talking about street crime, how the "Africans" are ruining this country, and sleeping with all the white girls, and ruining the economy because they won't work, and yet at the same time, through some perverse logic, making it more difficult for the rest of us to get jobs. The next minute it's the environment, and how it's too late now, and it can't be saved, so why avoid nuclear power, and what's the use of limiting nuclear weapons when all-out war is inevitable anyway."

Skate whistled, "You two have wide-ranging exchanges."

Rexee scowled, "I got that out of about three 7-minute lectures, much of which are repetitious. He also believes in "survivalism," living off the land like insurgents when the nuke-down happens, a universal military commitment for all, men, women, children, the halt and the lame. The liberation of South-east Asia, the War in Viet Nam, the spread of communism in this country, the domino theory, and the return of the fucking international gold standard."

Hack was smiling around a mouthful of peanut butter and bread, "Did he clue you into tax resisting too?"

"Probably," she answered, "I can't remember. I just wish he'd peddle it elsewhere – he's around to badger me every time I step out the door."

"Who knows, Rexee'," Skate said, "maybe it's love."

(<o>)/(2.11)\(<o>)

What Lily of the Alley sees, she sees in stereo: not double vision, more like second sight. Her hearing is 3-D and sense of smell comes through her fingertips. Her taste is in her mouth, but sharpest is direction sense; she knows which way is up.

As Lily legged it down the lane her feelers were in phase. She heard a water droplet falling from the slanted gravel roof and saw it splashing on a pipe before it met the ground. An ant was loudly dragging moss across a concrete slab. Some bird was erking on a ledge and plucking fluff to line a nest.

She poked a trashcan freshly packed with trash and smelled the fetid scent of coffee grounds. A lonely pint with half a shot of gin was underneath. Her sense of timing told her now is now. She tossed it back and wiped her lips with wrinkled shawl, then dropped the empty in the can.

Three-story cracked brick alley walls on either side and underfoot red cobblestones with concrete oozing from the seams. Some scummy puddles, soaken litter, cans and bottles, rusty drainpipes, peeling paint, a spider crawling on a dripping faucet as the smell of fresh made doughnuts rumbles under Anne's back door.

The crone is in her element. Undreamt of riches lurk on every side and Lily has no problem getting on. In fact, she thrives. Her clothing and most victuals are as found. Then sometimes, like just now, a bit to drink. And Annie, lovely lady, helps her out.

When Lily turns the knob and totters in, a smiling cookie greets her with a cup. The countertop is wiped as Lily takes a seat and Annie says, "Good morning Lil."

" 'ave found a chain that you might like."

It's Lily's way to pay. But Annie doesn't see the point; a woman gets to such an age, and lives as rough as Lily does, and never says too much at all, deserves some gratis grub once and again.

They make a funny pair. Young Annie bright and lively, smiling, talking, listening, cooking, banter back and forth. A softly throbbing flush below her collar and a gentle aching in her thighs from Ace's love embrace – her eyes get shiny when she steals a moment to recall his heated, gentle, probing, urgent force. Her mouth is dry, she licks her lips.

And Lily, old and dry as mummy dust, can see an orange aura in the room and smell the love sweat bubbling on Anne's breath.

"E've 'ad a man," croons Lily softly smiling at Anne's shock and loss of voice; the dart of flat unvarnished fact provoking heated blood that climbs up Annie's throat and cheeks. A rosy glow, a guilty flush, a thrilling rush of juice and sap, as Lily cackles musically and says, "not 'ard to see."

(<o>)/(2.12)\(<o>)

I was aware of Effie long before we met. She had a second floor room in a house across from us, and she was pretty enough that I noticed her right away. Her landlord had upgraded the building, so her room actually had a fairly nice plate glass window facing our street. One day walking by I looked up to see her looking down.

I waved up and she waved back.

Another time I found myself ahead of her in line at the House of Rip-off, and we chatted. I actually lingered on the corner a bit to see if she was walking back towards our block, but she came out and went the other way without seeing me. I think I saw her briefly at the surf rat kegger, but she was with some other girls, and we didn't speak.

Effie and Delmar had moved into the neighborhood at about the same time, which I maybe should have taken as an ominous coincidence, but I never did.

Effie was short, and soft, and just a little plump, but she had a nice easy smile, long straight blond hair, and a short, soft, womanly profile. She had nice legs and an hourglass figure. I liked her before we met.

(<o>)/(2.13)\(<o>)

A place like Doogan's can sometimes seem to have a life of its own. The cycle of business and customers lends a certain personality, a rhythm and a respiration. The early morning crowd is generally the same: a mixture of broken down alcoholic wrecks like old man Sutter, disability cases like Remo and guys off the graveyard shift like Fat Henry and Patrick.

Happy hour, from six when the doors open until ten, tends to draw long-haul truckers in from a night of driving and worn out working girls in from a night of hustling. Occasionally customers of these types arrive separately and leave together.

There is a regular set of middle aged business executives that have a couple of belts before facing their demanding bosses and the upstart junior execs beneath them that snap at their heels in the competitive frenzy of youth. These same executives invariably return to "have a few" at lunch and then again to "have a few more" before going home to face their demanding wives and frenzied upstart children.

One morning an executive regular, Dane Telmah, confided to Skate, "Son, there is only one sure way to succeed within the corporate structure. The method is both simple and time-honored and I will now impart it to you – for free."

He paused and gulped his bourbon press, cleared his throat for effect and continued, "The secret is to make YOUR boss look bad in the eyes of HIS boss. If you do this often and skillfully enough you will soon have your boss's job. This is how I got my present position and also how my boss got his."

He finished his drink and collected his change from the bar, fortified again against the slings and arrows of outrageous fortune hunting.

"But don't spread it around," he laughed grimly, "it might hurt sales on my forthcoming book."

He had, in fact, written a book entitled TO BE A SUCCESS OR NOT* and it sold quite well. He moved into a Florida condo and never again drank before the cocktail hour. Skate's autographed copy still sits, unread, on his bookshelf – right next to his Bible and a dogeared copy of FEAR AND LOATHING IN LAS VEGAS.*

(<o>)/(2.14)\(<o>)

The fraternity house around the corner from the Web was a beer-drinking frat.

We knew them first from one summer night of debauch shortly after we moved in, where they broadcast surf music to the neighborhood through giant speakers blasting from their windows. It was some sort of cheesy Hawaiian luau party. The whole neighborhood was invited. It was a block party. A party that we skipped, alas.

However, from that day onward Ace referred to them as the "Surf Frat", which if you say it aloud comes out, "surf rat". They were the surf rats to us from then on.

(<o>).[].(<o>)

This was one of those summer nights at the Web: the night of the great window fan debacle, and the surf rats were having a kegger.

We did not skip this one.

It was a hot night, and we boys were all camped out near the keg.

Patrick was talking to a librarian friend of Book's, an older woman in her early thirties, who was saying "There's room for outsiders on the inside, don't you think?"

Her name was Carol, she had two kids, and Patrick was clearly smitten.

Ace was talking to Bonaparte, a roly-poly black guy, and a grad student in Theatre who lived nearby. Bonaparte was one of those guys, half an artist and half a street thug, who worked fairly diligently, but cut loose with a bender whenever the stresses got to him, which was fairly frequently. He had the round smooth face of a cherub, except for a Prussian style dueling scar down the side of his face – a puckered slash that gave him the appearance of a hired killer. On this particular day the sun was just going down and Bonaparte was already wobbling.

Rexee' came along with us, as she occasionally did. She was leaning against a picnic table in her summer uniform, extremely short shorts and a practically see-through undershirt and no bra, with a beer in one hand and a cigarette in the other. Hack and Skate were standing with her, although not talking about much. A guy in military camouflage pants and a military green t-shirt filled a beer mug. It was a pewter metal mug, and it was attached to his belt with a silver chain.

Rexee' studied the figure, and when he turned away from the keg she said, "What's with the hardware, Slim?"

"Green River!" he answered, "we fill the cup, and when we drink, we say GREEEEEN RIVER!"

He tossed back the mug, opening his throat and draining it.

"Yeah," Rexee' said, "okay."

"It's a battle cry," said the pseudo-soldier, "from the patriots of the Revolution...and a drinking, ... a drinking, ..., a drinking pledge ... to honor ..."

He paused, a mistake with Rexee' impatient on a hot night.

"To honor what?" she challenged him.

"There was a kind of man," he improvised loudly, "that went his own way, and traveled the lonesome prairie. He was a loner, a lone wolf, and a hero, and a spirit of independence. He was a cowboy."

He raised his mug.

He shouted, "GREEEEN RIVER!"

He drank.

"Yeah," Rexee' said, "so?"

"They're mostly gone, the cowboys," he said, "but the spirit passed to the truckers. They drive the roads. They go their way. They drive that long highway and only answer to themselves."

He raised his mug.

He shouted, "GREEEEN RIVER!"

He drank.

He turned back to the keg, and re-filled his mug.

Skate could see that Rexee' could see that this was nowhere. She looked as languid as ever, but she was ready to step off.

"The truckers own the road," he was back, refilled and starting to repeat himself, "and they do what they do what they do. They represent something. Something we've lost."

"Okay, sporto," Rexee' said, "I'll take your word for it."

"But the truckers, the old-timers, are dying off," the guy went on, "and they've passed their heritage to the next wave. Now it's the bikers. These are the knights of the highways and the byways. These are the last real Americans. GREEEEN RIVER!"

Rexee' sauntered past him and re-filled her beer cup, leaving them alone with this guy. They stood there, waiting for her.

35

Skate was lost, not knowing what to say, and not comfortable with the silence.

"What's your name?" Skate said.

"I'm the watcher. GREEN RIVER!" he drank, "I stand against the putrid stench."

"Yes, okay," Skate said, emboldened, "you're the stench stander. But what's your name?"

"I hear your question," the guy said, aggressively, "and I hear your quailing. And I hear the disrespect. You don't fool me."

The guy was, by this time, leaning into Skate's face, and snarling.

Skate realized his back was paining him, through the beer, but he stood his ground, mostly because he was backed against the table with nowhere to go.

Rexee' slipped back into her spot on the table, and broke the escalating mood.

"Yeah, sure," she said, more casual than the situation seemed to call for, "but what do we call you, cowboy?"

And this broke the moment, which had the guy starting into a stare, and he took a half-step back.

"GREEEEEEEN RIVER!" he drank, "people call me Delmar."

(<o>)/(2.16)\(<o>)

The surf rat event was a billowing success. Neighbors came from blocks around and crowded the yard, and into the alley. The first keg was quickly drained, and the second was well on the way. The 'rats' recognized the potential for profit and sent for another barrel.

It was one of those summer nights: so hot and humid the beer seeped right through your skin. You could stand around and pound it down and sweat it out without ever needing to urinate. There was lightening in the air while we rode the night train.

Skate saw Patrick and Carol stepping off, hand in hand. They never came back.

Ace and Bonaparte were discussing theater and film. Ace had a lot of opinions on these subjects, and Bonaparte had started too early – he was not keeping up too well. There are guys who seem to cope just fine, up to a point. Then quite suddenly they are shit-faced and out of control. Bonaparte was one of those guys.

Meanwhile, Delmar had fixated on Rexee' and was doing his best to keep her attention. His politics came out right away.

"There's no sense protesting nuclear power," he was saying, "there's no point."

He was losing the advantage. Rexee' knew a lot, and could speak at length on subjects that interested her. But she didn't have much interest in current events, or politics, or sports. These topics didn't bore her exactly, but they held no interest. She wasn't ignorant either, as she was capable of the occasional incisive observation, but none of this could hold her interest for long either.

"What's to protest?" she said, "it's nuclear, it's powerful, it's out there."

By this time she was just turning his words, and not really speaking to him. Next she would be backing away and going home. He did not get this. He persisted.

"My point exactly," replied Delmar, "the planet is already screwed up beyond redemption. Preventing a power plant isn't going to prevent the inevitable."

But Rexee' was already looking around for someone else to talk to in the crush of humanity surrounding the beer keg.

Delmar stepped closer.

"You and me should leave here," he half-whispered, "this pond is getting crowded with scut, and I've got a place where the water is cool."

"This beer is pretty cool too," Rexee' side-stepped, "and I'm with these guys."

She nodded to Skate and Hack, who were standing nearby.

They both heard what she said and briefly locked eyes, knowing what it meant. There was no universe where Rexee stuck around with them if something better came along. And there was no circumstance where Rexee' needed anyone but herself to blow back an unwanted suitor. She shut them down on her own, with a cutting word and a dismissive shrug, and they'd seen her do it any number of times. Skate had watched her do it to him, personally.

She was asking for help. Not a scream, but a whisper. For all her cool and composure, which was considerable, she had detected a predator and was throwing out her lifeline.

Delmar, meanwhile, considered his odds. The smaller one, Scratch or Screed or Skeet or whatever his name was, was no problem. Delmar could give him a leg sweep and an elbow and he'd be out for the night. The bigger one, Hack, who he recognized from somewhere, was something else: a spool of coiled steel. Delmar could do him, he was confident, but it would get nasty. He could take them both, he was sure, but the woman might not see it the right way.

"They won't mind," he said weakly, knowing it was over, "it's a hot night."

"Yeah, I know," she said, holding out her cup, "Get me another, would'ya"

Delmar looked at the cup and stewed a bit. He was trumped, and he knew it. There was no way this was going to work out like he wanted, with her in his apartment – and there was no way to save it. He decided to salvage his offensive instead.

He took a menacing step forward, causing Skate and Hack to tense just the littlest bit. He leaned over to a point his face was just inches from hers.

"No," he snarled, "I don't think so."

Then he swung his pewter mug at her head like a like a vicious right hand punch, stopping an inch from her head, sloshing beer onto her face and hair.

And he screamed spittle into her face, "GREEEEN RIVER!"

Then he turned to the alley and stalked off, spraying gravel with every step.

(<o>).[].(<o>)

The three of them stood there – Delmar was gone.

Hack was cool, the moment was over. He knew it was a fake punch from the way it was thrown.

Rexee' was cool, the bastard had left, which was what she wanted. A little beer on her back on a hot night was nothing to be alarmed about, and nothing new.

Skate was shaking and his back was throbbing. The mock-punch was still registering and the whole thing was already over.

The rest of the party hardly noticed. It was a late-night drunken kegger, and a little beer was spilled. Nobody commented.

Delmar disappeared down the alley, and Skate was still processing his energized flight/fright response. His back was in spasm. He could not move.

Besides, now that it was done, he was struggling with the after-image. As Delmar was throwing his "punch", with no time to respond except to shrink, and while he, Skate, was frozen in the moment, it had looked like Rexee', rather than flinching from the blow, had raised her chin to meet it. Against everything that seemed normal, she had thrown herself subtly forward, rather than back.

Skate loved her more than ever. He couldn't say why.

(<o>).[].(<o>)

Shortly after, Abel the sculptor was standing with them, mostly talking to Skate. They knew Abel from school, where he was a wrestling and football jock but, in one of those stereotype-breaking confluences, also very smart, something of a mathematical wizard. Abel had, towards the end of their senior year in high school, started branching out.

At one point he and Skate had worked on an 8-millimeter animation. Skate clicked the movie camera in single shot mode, popping off a few frames at a time as Abel daubed thick wads of paint onto a canvas in a kind of Van Gogh slap-dash corn field. The idea was to mate this with a voice over, Skate reading a Carl Sandburg poem.* The effect was poetry proceeding as the painting emerged stroke by stroke.

Since graduating Abel had kicked around, first enrolling at the University of Oklahoma as an engineering student on a wrestling scholarship, but quickly losing interest in technology and feeling boxed in by wrestling, then switching majors in a dizzying sequence, ending up in the art program, until finally dropping out and coming home to the Upper Midwest.

"They had a big athletic facility," Abel said, "and a system where they would pull in these movable walls, to subsection the floor space, and the wrestling team had one of these areas. Then the wrestling team pulled in more movable walls, so each of the classes had it's own space, subdividing further."

"So you were working out in a cubicle," Skate offered.

"Yes," Abel said, "so one day I came in, and I realized the campus was a box around the athletic center, which was a box around the athletes, with walls around the team, with more walls around individuals."

"Uh," Skate said, "a box within a box within a box within a box."

"Yes, recursive damnation, so I quit and came home."

"Green River," Hack said.

"Exactly," Abel nodded.

(<o>).[].(<o>)

In those days you could move into an old shop-front in the warehouse district just north of downtown Minneapolis for not-too-much, and a few arty types were setting up their garrets there. Abel rented an old bread store with a big picture window for a studio. He was also taking classes at the "U" at the time, although this would be ending soon.

"Levi Strauss is the guy," Abel said, "a European."

Skate raised his eyebrows, "the blue jeans guy?"

"No," Abel smiled, "a genius."

Linguistics, went the explanation, moves towards psychology. And anthropology subsumes linguistics, in a movement towards conceiving all thought in terms of linguistics. Abel talked about signifiers and signifieds, where words signify thoughts and blobs of carefully placed paint signify a landscape. He maintained that the idea of illusion and reality rested in the stripping away of signifiers but somehow maintaining the signifieds.

"Green River?" Hack asked.

"Exactly."

(<o>).[].(<o>)

"What you mean by that!" Bonaparte was shouting, "why you pullin' that shit?"

Ace and Bonaparte were still camped by the keg, despite the crush of humanity, but at this point Ace was retreating before the rage of the emperor.

"Be cool, man," Ace was saying, "I'm just heading out, that's all."

"I thought you were alright!" Bonaparte was upset, "I don't need to take this racial shit from you!"

"What?" Ace was standing, open handed, and baffled.

"You know what you said," Bonaparte shouted, "now I guess we know where YOU stand. This is where it comes out! This is the shit I live with, every day, all year long. You're part of it now. You're out there too!"

He had worked himself into the fighting crouch of his youth. He was ready to rock and roll.

"Man," Ace said, baffled, "what is this?"

Bonaparte was wobbling, his eyes glazed over, with a shrill edge to him. He had focused on Ace, and he was furious. Ace was not a fighter, but Bonaparte was, and Ace was about to get pounded.

Suddenly, out of the gloom, Book walked into the picture, himself with a beer glass in hand. Book wedged himself into a position between Ace and Bonaparte.

Book was round and soft, not a fighter either, but he was also big, and could be immovable when he chose to be. He was a bifocaled blockade.

"No fighting," Book said to both, "no fisticuffs. It just won't do."

"You," Book said sharply to Ace, "I think it's time to go."

"Bonaparte," Book went on, "He did not say what you think he said. This is over, and we're going home."

Then Book swept his arm around Ace and guided him away from the keg.

"Sorry, man," Ace said over his shoulder, "no offense."

(<o>).[].(<o>)

"You okay," Skate said to Rexee'.

"Yeah, but I've got to wash this beer out of my hair."

"Hack?" Skate asked.

"Finest kind," Hack had read all the M*A*S*H novels, "I thought he was sizing up the point of your chin. Until Rex walked back and chilled him."

"Yeah, well," she said, "he wants everything he can't have."

Book drew Ace over towards where they were standing.

"It's time to go, I think," Book said.

"What in the hell just happened?" Ace asked.

Skate assumed the question was about Delmar.

"Bad days at Black Rock,"* he said, "axe madness in the heat."*

"Well," Hack laughed, "a little cooler than that, actually."

"I don't mean that," Ace wailed, "I mean just now with Bonaparte."

"As near as I could hear," Book said, "you were ready to leave and said 'See you around like a doughnut', and he took it like a racial slur."

"Yes, that's right," Ace said, remembering, "I was trying to get away. I guess I'm insensitive."

"Truer words," Book said, "let's get the hockey puck out of here. The night has grown old."

(<o>)/(2.22)\(<o>)

A one act play in several scenes:

Scene Two –

An hour has passed, it is 7:00 a.m. The guys: Hack, Patrick and Ace are still sitting at center stage. Skate is standing at the center of the bar with his back turned. An older man in a business suit is leaning against the right end of the bar with a tall mixed drink. An attractive young woman in a gaudy, revealing dress is sitting at the far left table nursing a cola. A couple of guys in work clothes are sitting with Fat Henry. Old man Sutter is offstage in the men's room.

When the lights come up Skate turns around with a tray of drinks and delivers them to the table.

=#=#=#=

```
    Skate
Here goes men. What say we try and go for bicentennial beers
before closing time.

    Ace
An alcohol overdose in the great American tradition of
excessive consumption.

    Hack
Be a helluva bar tab for poor Ace.

    Patrick
Stimulate the economy though.

    Skate
(laughing)
While depressing our neural motor functions.
```

Ace
And inflating our ambitions while recessing our sensibilities.

Hack
Sounds good to me.

Ace
Wait, for poor Ace? Oh no, every man for himself.

Skate
(after a pause)
Where do you suppose Book is shelved?

Patrick
We could page him.

Hack
He's probably still in the rack or bound up on the dumpster.

Ace
Leaf it to me. Cal, can I make a call?
(Cal nods and Ace leans over the bar to audience right,
retrieving the phone. As he begins to dial the front (audience
right) door opens and a heavy man in a short sleeved white
shirt and thin tie wearing thick glasses enters and stops
directly behind Ace.)

Book
Hello.

Ace
(pretending to speak into the phone)
Hello, Book?

Book
Yes.

Ace
Get your bibliophilic butt in gear. We can't call the meeting
to order until you make the quorum.

Book
I'm imminent.

Ace
Expedite you effete intellectual loafer; the bard awaits.

Book
Buy me a drink and I'll be there before you can turn around.

Ace
(hanging up the phone)
Buy him a drink he says, surely he knows
(spinning suddenly and pointing at Book)
that it's HIS turn to buy.

Book
I'll have coffee …

Ace
Unacceptably weak tea.

Book
… with a shot of brandy.

Ace
(summoning Cal)
Done.

        Book
(Book sits at the table)
Hi guys, lovely morning to sit in the dark.

        Skate
Nice to see you Book. How's it?

        Ace
(with a coffee mug)
Book has fallen in love with a word processor. Can't keep his
hands off her.

        Skate
Nice rhyme.

        Hack
Sounds like the pickle slicer.

        Book
What's that?

        Ace
A tired old factory joke.

        Book
The allusion escapes me.

        Hack
Well, this guy goes to work in the pickle factory and sees a
sign says "Don't slip yer schlang into the pickle slicer" and
of course he's not gonna but finally he can't resist and he
slips his schlang into the pickle slicer.

        Patrick
(playing the straight man)
And then what happens?

        Hack, Ace, Skate, the guy in the suit, the two working
guys, Fat Henry and the whore
(in unison)
She got pregnant.
(Much laughter)

        Ace
Congratulations Book, you're the last person on earth to hear
that joke.

        Book
(deadpan)
I don't get it.
(More laughter)
My, things are lively here.

        Patrick
Only since you arrived.

        Book
Bien sur. But of course. How are you Skate?

        Skate
Patrick's having a baby.

        Book
Really, when?

        Skate
Next, get this, next month! He "forgot" to tell us.

        Book
What a communist.

    Patrick
I could have sworn I told somebody ...

    Book
Told somebody! What is that? You're not communist, you're a,
a, a …

    Ace
Book sputters.

    Book
You're a, a, you're a, … goddam Protestant!

    Ace
Oh, man. You didn't have to say that, did you?

    Hack
Let him up Book, for gawd sakes, he's sorry, can't you see. He
has remorse and contrition.

    Book
I should think so.
(wags his finger towards Patrick)
Let's never let this happen again, shall we?

    Patrick
(tapping his chest)
I am heartily sorry for having offended Thee, and I detest all
my sins.

    Book
I should think so. (mutters) Protestant.
(long pause)
Meanwhile, Skate, how you doing?

    Skate
Good, good, a little tired, a little tipsy, but generally
relaxed; what's a word processor?

    Book
New gadget - like a typewriter with a computer memory. We
finally got one at work and I'm training in.

    Skate
Useful?

    Book
More convenient than functional. How's the writing coming?

    Ace
Speaking of word processing.

    Skate
Great guns. I'm at it all the time.

    Ace
And still waiting to make his first dime.

    Pat
Another unfortunate rhyme.

    Skate
Look Ace, the overwhelming likelihood is I'll never make that
dime. Doesn't matter, not right now. I just want to write.

Ace

Everybody wants to write my son. The world is glutted with unpublished manuscripts. Hell, my uncle's next door neighbor wants to write - he's a plumber. My dentist wrote a Sci-Fi novel for cripes sake.

Skate

Really appreciate the support Ace.

Ace

No offense friend, but reality dictates that the organism demands nourishment.

Book

Meaning a man must eat.

Skate

(mildly heated)

Don't feed me the reality crap - I know more about that than all you pimples combined.

Patrick

Too much, man, let it all hang out.*

Hack

Easy Skate.

Skate

Alright, yeah, it's cool; but for the time being I prefer to deal in terms of fantasy.

Book

(after a pause)

I read about a guy in Boston who's going to sit on a flagpole for nineteen hundred and seventy-six hours.

Hack

What for?

Patrick

About, uh, carry the two, uh, eighty days.

Skate

You could go around the world in that time.

Book

It's a radio promotion.

Patrick

More selling of the Bicentennial. The Buy-Sell-tennian.

Hack

I saw someone's been paintin' the fire hydrants downtown.

Book

What color?

Hack

All colors. They're paintin' 'em to look like little people with big noses, or just red, white and blue.

Ace

Save us from this crass conventionality. The Web must do something more fitting, more apropos, more ...

Patrick

(sarcastically) Patriotic?

Ace
Vile term.

Book
The last refuge of the scoundrel.*

Skate
So this bunch will feel right at home.

Book
They're talking about forming a human chain on the 4th of
July. People holding hands all the way across the country;
along Interstate 80 I think.

Hack
There's a lot of sweaty palms.

Patrick
Hell, a coast to coast line of bumper to bumper traffic would
be more like it.

Ace
Ever the cynic.

Patrick
You should talk.

Ace
But seriously folks - we need ideas, plans, projects of epic
dimension, tasks of monumental proportion, something truly
bigger and better ...

Skate
Or smaller and better ...

Ace
Whichever the case may be.

Book
We'll have ample opportunity; the Bicentennial extends for
seven years, until November 1983.

Patrick
You must be kidding!

Ace
It's true, we're commemorating a long dragged-out period of
civil unrest.

Patrick
And a long dragged-out history of interfering in foreign
countries, exploiting the working class, stealing raw
materials from underdeveloped nations, military intervention
in places we don't belong, imperialist foreign policies,
oppressive abridgements of personal liberties, with poverty,
disease and hunger in our own country, and where guys like
Rockefeller and Nixon send the children off to war, and don't
even pay taxes.

Book
Well, my, yes, that's pretty much true.

Ace
Coming out of our shell a bit are we?

Patrick
Yeah, yeah. But, it just infuriates me to think of the
disgusting hypocrisy this country is capable of. Self-

45

aggrandizement -- while really this country has got more to be ashamed of than proud of.

    Book
A ringing indictment, not altogether unfair.

    Hack
I dunno.

    Ace
Extreme to a slight degree.

    Skate
A little bit extreme, Ace?

    Ace
An extremely insignificant degree of extremity. Here's an idea. Lets go get an American Buffalo, dye it red, white and blue, then take it around on the state fair circuit billed as the …

    Skate
No, don't say it.

    Ace
Yes, yes,
(pauses)
the Bisontennial.
(all groan).

    Book
A monument is always nice.

    Patrick
Such as?

    Skate
Something along the lines of the sphinx would be about ideal.

    Hack
I think it's been done already.

    Book
But you know, it's still uncertain who built the thing, when or why. Myth has it that it was patterned after an even older construction that pre-dates any other cultural or historical record.

    Ace
No one even knows who built it?

    Book
Nor why.

    Skate
I have a theory.

    Ace
Do tell.

    Skate
It's a message from a dying civilization on the correct way to live. A simple expression of the basic, earthy, central and most important things that mankind needs and yet finds so easy to forget.

    Patrick
Particularly here in the fatcat Bicentennial year of our lord 1976.

                Skate
Feature it -- you want to leave a message that will be
received without the need for a spoken or written
understanding; a symbol easily recognized on a level beneath
language. How can you get it over, make it last and make it
understood?

                Ace
All breath is suitably bated.

                Patrick
Talk about shells.

                Book
My, I'd build a Sphinx. But what, I'd wonder, would I be
trying to say?

                Skate
Well, it's elementary really. The instruction is this: live
every moment of life with the body of a lion and the head of a
man.

                Patrick
(Whistles satirically)
Heavy.

                Ace
A little obvious isn't it?

                Book
Not to me.

                Hack
And the source is unknown?

                Patrick
Unknown? -- the worlds most published poet?

                Ace
Naw, that's anonymous -- different guy.

                (Blackout).

(<o>)/(2.23)\(<o>)

diaria -- 2.0 -- 7/20/76 -- roadside south and west of
Laramie

in real life rexee' was a grad student in american
literature and a part-time employee at the university
hospital x-ray center. naturally, because she had a way
of seein thru the bullshit of life, and a penetrating
way of lookin at things, we came to call her x-ray
rexee'.

i was writin at the time and one day nerved up enough to
ask her to read some. she got thru about two pages of
the first one and put it down, lookin at me perplexed.
why she asked are you tryin to write like a fuckin
romance poet? i admitted i didn't know what that meant,
bein in some confusion over the terminology.

she sed it didn't matter a shit anyway, they were long
buried. then she told me to fergit this crap, she called
it, and get into the 20th century for cripes sake.

47

then she read me some passages out of a book of literary
criticism. went like this:

"In the fiction of the future, all distinctions between
the real and the imaginary, between the conscious and
the subconscious, between the past and the present,
between truth and untruth will be abolished."* then
this:

"Thus fiction will become the metaphor of its own
narrative progress, and will establish itself as it
writes itself. This does not mean, however, that the
future novel will be only "a novel of the novel", but
rather it will create a kind of writing, a kind of
discourse whose shape will be an interrogation, an
endless interrogation of what it is doing while doing
it, an endless denunciation of its fraudulence, of what
IT really is: an illusion (a fiction), just as life is
an illusion (a fiction)."*

she grabbed another book and read a marked passage:

"Its central protagonist a novelist and its central
action the conception of a novel, the self-begetting
novel is supremely reflexive. ... Like slapstick farce
in which the side of a building collapses to expose a
demure gentleman at his bath, the self-begetting novel
deliberately lays bare all its working parts."*

"This I call Surfiction. However, not because it
imitates reality, but because it exposes the
fictionality of reality."* and this:

"The experience of life gains meaning only in its
recounted form, in its verbalized version ... "*

then she wrote out about ten books for me to read and
told me to get lost. a writers gotta read, she sed.

(<o>)/(Endnotes 2.24)\(<o>)

5. Rawhide (television series) NBC, 1959-1966.

6. Webster's Standard American Heritage New World
Dictionary of Inert Phrases and Little Used Words
(Minneapolis: Clean Jerk Curl Press, 1976), p. 1976.

7. Ibid. p.1976

8. Food Coops were collectives that bought bulk
products, like natural peanut butter in five gallon
tubs. You brought your own containers, and volunteered a
few hours a month, and in exchange you got healthy
natural food at bargain prices.

9. Telmah, Dane. TO BE A SUCCESS OR NOT. (Minneapolis:
Clean Jerk Curl Press, 1976), p. 1976.

10. Thompson, Hunter S. Fear and loathing in Las Vegas;
a savage journey to the heart of the American dream,

Illustrated by Ralph Steadman. [1st ed.] New York, Random House [c1971] 206 p. illus. 22 cm.

11. Sandburg, Carl (1918). Laughing Corn. In Cornhuskers. Henry Hold and Co: NY

12. Rock, Bad Days at Black (1955). Metro-Goldwyn-Mayer (MGM)

13. Dostoyevsky, Fyodor, that short story about the unbearable heat with the roommate sharpening his axe in the last paragraph

14. Hombres, The, "Let It Out (Let It All Hang Out)" 1967. (Cunningham; McEwen), Verve Forecast

15. Johnson, Samuel (1709-1784), the classic Classicist. On the evening of 7 April 1775, is rumored he made the famous statement, "Patriotism is the last refuge of the scoundrel."

16. Raymond Federman, editor. Surfiction : fiction now and tomorrow, 1st ed. Chicago : Swallow Press, [1975] 294 p. ; 23 cm. p. 8.

17. Federman, p. 10.

18. Kellman, Steven J. The Self Begetting Novel (New York: Columbia University Press, 1980).

19. Raymond Federman, editor. Surfiction : fiction now and tomorrow, 1st ed. Chicago : Swallow Press, [1975] 294 p. ; 23 cm. p. 7.

20. Federman, p. 7.

Chapter 3

The entire street converged on the elm, and on Skate, even as a furious pelting rain began to fall. The police cars at each end of the block descended on the Web with blue lights flashing. Questions flew back and forth between the police and Skate, the reporter and Skate, among the crowd, and finally to Hack who managed to climb down under his own steam, only to get placed under arrest for illegally discharging a firearm within city limits, lack of a weapon notwithstanding.

The second cameraman who had been standing by the reporter when the "shots" were fired (almost everyone recalled hearing two, or even three), had flinched almost as badly as Skate, and his film was worthless as evidence. The first cameraman, more of a seasoned pro, flawlessly recorded the entire tree-top scene in an inconclusive and murky gray on black, with a brilliant flash of white masking the key frame – enough to prove Hack had indeed been in the tree and something, possibly a set of bagpipes, tumbled to the ground afterwards.

The pounding rain discouraged most of the people, and when the first police car left with Hack in the back, the rest of the crowd went home. The corpse of the Constitution of the United States was wrapped up in plastic and departed in the trunk of a second police car. The incident was barely mentioned on the late night edition of the Channel 4 news: a story without good film is hardly a story.

Ace and Book went downtown to bail Hack out of jail and had to wait around for him. The police insisted on taking him to the emergency room and having his rib bandaged. After that was a quick hearing and $200 bail (fairly steep for the day), and they were all back at the Web before midnight.

(<o>).[].(<o>)

They were sitting around the kitchen: Ace, Skate, Hack, Book, and Patrick, who was soon to be overdue at work.

Book had brewed a pot of excellent Jamaican Blue Mountain coffee, and they were trying to figure out what in hell happened, when Rexee' walked in after a night in the bars.

"What in the fuck went on out here," she said, "the yard looks like Napolean's Third Army came through."

Rexee' looked ravishingly European with her dark honey colored hair hanging down her back, wearing a black shift with big wild yellow flowers printed on it. She carried a black umbrella with a very sharp looking pointed tip. She had given up smoking Camels and instead carried a curved clay fisherman's pipe – which was lit. She had never shaved her armpits in the time they had known her, after the European fashion. To Skate, raised in the upper Midwest fashion, she was the only woman he could imagine that that would look good on.

They filled her in on the events as best they could. Book offered her coffee, but she got the Jim Beam down off the refrigerator and poured a belt into a Burger King Bicentennial give-away glass instead.

"You are shittin' me," she finally said, "shots fired? What the goddam hell?"

Hack looked thoughtful, "I don't know, Rex. I was facing the street, so I guess it came from back towards your place."

Rexee' was calm, but looked a little pale.

"Delmar," she hissed.

"C'mon, Rexee'," Skate said, "you think he's stupid enough to get out and immediately start in at fucking up his life again?"

"No," Rexee' said levelly, "he wants to fuck up OUR lives."

(<o>)/(3.3)\(<o>)

This is the story of the guys. The guys in all their different guises and their friends and contacts that came to be known as the Web. It began in a Catholic grade school because of, and despite, the peculiar flavor of education found there. Kennedy was president, John XXIII was pope, John Glenn was just back, television was divided amongst Westerns, espionage variations and glorifications of World War II; and the Communist Russians were very, very scary. And a group of guys with nothing in common but proximity in time and space and a Catholic background started hanging around together. It was 1963, at the tail end of the Fifties in Minnesota.

Timothy, because he was tallest then, and the most mature, and because he had already shown signs of possessing a clear organizational mind and because then he had dreams of becoming a fighter pilot, adopted the name "Ace". His heroes were Richtofen and Rickenbacker, but a fear of heights grounded him and he did all his flying in his imagination which was, then, better than any of ours.

Benjamin loved reading, facts, figures and statistics. He knew things by the thousands, but even as a kid lacked energy and adopted sedentary habits. Walking, which we all did in massive amounts, and chess, which mainly only he enjoyed, were the limits of his exertion. He wore thick glasses, played piano when his parents forced him, wrote poetry that he'd recite to us in a rich monotone while we roamed the neighborhood, and always, always had something to read when our conversations would drag or bore him, which they often did. We called him "Book".

Jackson Hackney had so many names that none of them really stuck until years later. We called him "J", Jack, and "Ack". School and sports held little interest for him; he liked machines, gadgets, toys and gizmos, working with his hands and hunting and fishing in the woods. He was a chubby kid in those early years but grew into a great, hairy-chested giant. He started driving cab in high school and we naturally came to call him "Hack".

Patrick was always Patrick. Tall, painfully thin, quiet and reserved, he crawled into the Web by sheer weight of constantly being around. A good student with a shy sort of humor he just hung in there so much that it came to be expected.

And me, I was the new kid on the block. Mom, Dad and I had just moved from another part of the continent and I had a funny accent. I was a little shy too and at a loss until I gratefully fell in with the guys. I read a lot then, but not facts like "Book". Rather I'd read adventure stories, wilderness stories, pioneer stories, dog stories, war stories, horse stories and old west stories – action fiction with young boys as heroes; with just enough history thrown in to keep events in context. So I could close the books and daydream about being there.

Fiction was all I cared for and almost all I'd read on my own. Occasionally I'd write absurd, poorly plotted little stories and salt them away, never showing them to anyone.

I'm still doing that.

And since I was half-athletic, had fair balance, found that games came easily and played hockey, the guys took to calling me "Skate". My back problems didn't start until later.

But this is history, where it started with the guys. The point to this prolix narrative has several other focii; like the eye of the fly perhaps hundreds of focii. There's the symbolic end to the symbolic revolution, the boomerang of progress, the mystery of information, the climb of time, the life of the imagination, the inspection of the mysterious, the modern mythology, some optical illusions and paranoid delusions, multiple contusions, various confusions, fictional reality, and realistic fiction – with just enough history thrown in, real and imagined, to keep events in context.

(<o>)/(3.4)\(<o>)

Skate had terrible jitters as he followed Hack and Ace back towards Rexee's garage apartment, and his back was fully paining him. He could not get the image of the dead Heron out of his head – laying there at his feet, at the base of the elm, bleeding out like a slaughtered jock.

Book and Rexee' followed behind, as the group scouted the terrain to see if Rexee's place was safe.

That was when they found Tiger. He was laying in the dirt alongside the garage, slowly curling and uncurling from a fetal pose, like an infant stuck and trying to swim through mud. The lilac bush in front of him shook a little every time he uncurled, as they gathered around him and watched under Ace's flashlight beam.

"Tiger," Ace said, "buddy, is that you?"

Skate's eyes darted around the black shadows of the yard. The streetlights were back on, but the moon was dimmed by cloud cover. He could hardly see a thing and his back was killing him.

Rexee' held the flashlight as Hack and Ace reached under the lilac and pulled Tiger out by his rigid arms. They stood him up, his purple tie-dyed t-shirt looking like a grimy target of irregular concentric circles, the knees showing out of his jeans, his hair wildly matted with mud and twigs, one of his testicles peeping through a worn hole in his crotch. He was covered in wallow but his eyes glowed. He stood on his own and, when Hack and Ace let go of him, he went as rigid as a tree.

"She reached," he muttered, "and the antennae was retracted."

"The signal," Tiger added, "was clear, and green."

Ace looked at Rexee', then spoke to Tiger.

"C'mon, buddy," he said, "what are you doing out here?"

Tiger shook, as though he were being electrocuted, and said, "It's done now."

Then Tiger slouched into a feral crouch and started walking. He moved alongside the house and out into the street. When he crossed into the middle of the road he turned abruptly and walked up the center, where the stripe would be, past their elm and out of sight, toward the city. Skate followed him to the corner of the house and watched as Tiger walked to the intersection and turned, still in the middle of the road, off towards whatever Fate had planned for him.

(<o>).[],(<o>)

Rexee' had given Hack her keys and, by the time Skate got back, Hack had the door open and the lights on. Ace and Hack looked around inside while Skate and Book waited outside with Rexee'. Patrick had gone to work – he was on nights.

The apartment was judged safe to enter, but Rexee' was clearly unsettled at the thought of a lurking Delmar.

"Thanks boys," she said, "anybody care for a nightcap?"

It was still a little short of midnight, so they all piled in. Book went back to get his Joe DiMaggio Mr. Coffee pot and the Jamaican Blue Mountain it had brewed, and he and Ace had whiskey-coffee. Hack had straight coffee and Rexee' had straight whiskey. She'd been working on the Jim Beam in their kitchen after a full night in the bars. She was half lit.

Rexee' arched her brows toward Hack, "You're not planning on working tonight are you?"

Hack glanced at the ceiling and shrugged.

"Fish gotta swim" he said.

"As if you know anything about fish," Rexee' laughed.

"American fish," said Hack, "I don't keep good score with foreign fishes."

"I'll say." she sniggered.

"We had fish dinner the other day," Hack explained, "and I ordered haddock, whatever that is. She had the shad. I thought. But they switched our orders."

Rexee' laughed, "He only thought he had haddock."

"And she knew they were switched," Hack nodded to Rexee', "and didn't say anything. For a while I thought we had the same thing."

"So," said Book, "you mean…"

"Yep," said Hack, "I had my heart set on haddock, but instead I had shad."

Rexee' and Hack were laughing out loud by this time.

Skate looked pained.

Ace and Book looked at each other and shrugged – a private joke.

Then they remembered they had jobs to work in the morning. After a day of confrontation and confusion, all nervous energy was drained, except for Rexee', who seemed to want everyone to stay and talk.

Hack sat on a stool and started to lace up his workboots. Skate noticed they were already in the garage, Hack had not carried them in. Rexee' watched him for a moment, almost maternally, then turned to Skate.

"Who was that shithead in the dirt out there?" she asked.

Skate had slumped into the corner of her couch where the pillows lay.

"Tiger," he said, "a friend of Patrick's, I think. He got some bad acid on a hot night."

"Yeah," Hack said, "the night of the 'Who' concert – orange barrels."

"So he never came down," Ace added, "but he seems to be harmless."

Rexee' looked mildly startled.

"What," she asked, "do you fuckheads know about acid?"

Ace looked at her calmly, "It was the summer of '71, Ex-Ray. The whole world was into it."

She didn't actually like the nickname, but usually hid the fact.

"It's true," Skate nodded, "we were pretty much dead anyway – it didn't matter."

"Yeah, well," Ace said, "I'm pretty much dead now, too. I've got to split."

Ace and Book got up to leave together. Book carried his coffee pot and said, "Hack, I'll make another pot on my way upstairs, for your thermos."

They trudged out the door – Book the very picture of spent weariness, and even Ace's fabled energy at low ebb. Book disappeared into the house, and Ace headed down the road in the same direction as Tiger, but on the sidewalk, toward Annie's.

(<o>)/(3.6)\(<o>)

Hack had thought he had had haddock.

But she had known Hack had had shad.

Then, confused, he thought that he had had that that she had had.

That meant that Hack had thought that he had had that that he had thought that she had thought that he had had and not that that he had thought that he had had.

But Hack had had no haddock, Hack had had that shad.

(<o>)/(3.7)\(<o>)

When Tiger thinks about himself it's sometimes Polaroid: the image isn't clear at first but then develops over time. He has a spotty memory for what has gone before and tries to think about himself as though he has no past. But pictures sometimes fill his mind that he cannot control, and voices speak in faded words that he can't quite make out.

He used to be a normal kid, or so it seems to him. But then his parents died aboard a Douglas DC-3 that hit the ground exactly as his daughter died while being born. And when his wife heaped all the blame onto his battered psyche, and sold the car, and kicked him out, he never felt the same again.

So later, when he saw the "Who", it was the best he'd felt in months and something in him wanted that, to stay in that pure moment from then on. So he quit caring for the things that went before and brought him down and stammered on instead. This meant he couldn't be the man who shaved his face or washed his clothes, and meant he couldn't pay his rent or work a job from nine to five.

And once you've broken with that norm, that things should be just so-and-so, it's not that hard to give it up and let the whole thing fade. And now it's been so long that he just doesn't try to cover up. He lives between his ears and sees the world in black and gray. He never plans or thinks ahead, but lives the moment as he waits to see what will develop next. When Tiger looks around the world he sees in Polaroid.

(<o>)/(3.8)\(<o>)

"That damn tree is dead for sure this time," said her Father, so loud and near her ear that it startled her. And so, in fright, she slammed the refrigerator door REALLY HARD. She saw him standing in the hallway wearing his baggy weekend overalls, his expression turning as he made out the small jar of maraschino cherries in her hand. On the table behind her stood a platter of rich chocolate cake and an open ice cream tub, and a bag of pecans, and an aerosol can of whipped topping, and a squeeze bottle of chocolate sauce.

He turned on his heel and pushed out through the breeze-way screen door, back toward his workshop in the detached garage by the alley. She watched him go, relieved he had not really confronted her so early in the day, and sat down at her traditional place at the table, Father, Mother, Daughter arranged for the evening meal. For a moment she paused and surveyed the confections, then she glanced at the wall clock: 8:15 AM. Then she shrugged imperceptibly and fell to her task thinking, "the breakfast of champions."*

(<o>).[],(<o>)

Annie's mother had planted the tree. It was a frail, struggling, willow-like thing, planted in honor of Anne's birth, that had never blossomed or really come into its own.

Year after year it had existed in the margin, threatening to die, but never quite doing it, and yet hardly maturing after its first few seasons. Annie identified with it sometimes.

Annie's mother had died – long ago, before she could remember. Now her father said her tree would die for sure; and her father was hardly ever wrong. There were times, like right now, that the idea of death didn't seem even remotely frightening or scary to her. Death, or anything else, didn't seem like much of anything, either good or bad. To let it all go might be right. Why fight?

Annie finished her breakfast and cleaned up the kitchen, mechanically as she always did, through rote memory and habit. She really would have liked another serving of ice cream, but she resisted. But then, when she saw her father pull out of the old garage and drive down the alley, she got the ice cream out and ate several large spoonfuls straight from the container. She had checked her weight that morning, and it was disturbingly high – this had depressed her, she supposed, and made her more hungry than usual and crave for sweets.

(<o>).[],(<o>)

Annie is a victim of the well known self-fulfilling prophecy where, as the weight goes up, the esteem goes down, and the appetite goes up, causing even more eating and more weight: a prophets version of recursion, often called a "vicious cycle."

(<o>).[],(<o>)

The next day was a beautiful sunny Sunday. Annie went to church, saying a rosary in her Mother's memory. She didn't attend very often, but more than her father, who only went for Easter. She walked down their back alley, and when she entered the backyard the sight of her poor stunted tree moved her to fill a watering can and sprinkle the tree's trunk. For a 19 year old willow it was truly a pathetic sight, hardly taller than she, yellow where it should have been green, and no bigger around than her wrist.

A willow tree that old, she thought, could be as big around as her waist, even as lumpy and obese as she felt today. As she stood there, she had the sudden urge to get her father's axe and put an end to the fragile dwarf. Her father might get mad, but he'd said himself it was sure to die soon anyway.

She had just about resolved to do it, when she noticed a green shoot on a branch near her face. Hidden amongst the pale and wispy yellow leaves, a dark green bud had sprouted. She looked around for more, and found a few, distributed here and there among the dried twigs that passed for branches. Her tree was making an improbable bid for survival. Annie forgot about cutting it down, but dismissed the growth from her thoughts – it was probably some kind of desperate pre-death fling; like Rory, the hamster she had owned for a few weeks when she was eight years old.

(<o>).[],(<o>)

She had gone to the pet store with her father and, looking into a dimly lit cage full of hamsters, had chosen Rory because he had gotten up from the corner, curious and aggressive, and had come up to the front of the cage while his many siblings slept in their mound of cedar shavings. Once they had taken him home, Annie had tried to play with him, but Rory's aggressive nature made him a difficult pet; especially to someone timid and unfamiliar with animals. Rory nipped, and Annie couldn't muster the courage to handle him very much at all.

Rory had fallen ill later, and lay panting and feverish, snapping when she tried to hold him. Her father gave Rory water from an eye-dropper, but soon the hamster lost interest even in drinking. At this stage Rory was too spent to even nip. But now, when Annie picked him up, for just the second or third time ever, she realized he was far too hot. And then, an hour or so later, when she looked in on him, Rory was up on his feet. She called her father and watched as Rory, very stiffly, and with red burning eyes, moved toward the front of the cage. She moved to pick him up, but her father told her not to.

"He's got a fever, Hon," he said, "he doesn't know who you are."

Half an hour later when she looked, Rory was laying stiff in the middle of his cage, dead.

"But I thought he was getting better," she wailed.

"It happens that way sometimes," her father told her, "when a sick animal is about to die they'll seem to get better for a bit. But it's like they use up the last of their energy all at once."

Her father suggested they might go and get another hamster. But Annie didn't want to, and he didn't insist.

(<o>)/(3.13)\(<o>)

I was aware of Effie long before we met. I'd watched her walk past our house, her long straight yellow hair bouncing in rhythm with her stride.

She and her roommates moved into the neighborhood about the same time as Delmar, three years after us. But while we were cutting loose from our families and flexing our new liberties, they appeared to be taking things very seriously and following their parent's plan – studying, hosting dinner parties, studying, cleaning the apartment, studying, and studying.

One time, though, I saw them, four young women of mismatched shapes and sizes, like a crazy set of model train components all built in different scales, and they were pushing a garage sale sofa along the sidewalk, huffing in unison and shrieking like sorority sisters. Then, tipsy with exertion, they stopped in mid-block, sofa on the sidewalk, and sat down on it to rest. To them, this was REALLY WILD!

(<o>)/(3.14)\(<o>)

Skate needed some supplies from the record store one morning, so he went into Doogan's to wait for it to open. The place was empty except for Fat Henry, so Skate sat in Henry's customary booth to chat. At this point they knew each other only slightly.

Everybody knew Henry worked in the hospital. He came in every day wearing scrubs. Besides, you didn't need to be around him long before you'd hear him complaining about his job: Henry's favorite topic.

Skate was in a period where he was "collecting" stories.

(<o>).[].(<o>)

I been workin' the hospital for eight years now, and believe me, there's plenty of stories to tell about a place like that.

One time I was sweepin' outside maternity; ya know, the place with the glass window for all the proud papa's to come and gawk at their new tax deduction; and I seen this little arm comin' from outa one the cribs sorta twirlin' in the air. This little arm rotated for a bit and the little I.D. bracelet on the little wrist came off and flipped into the corner of the room.

Old Flo, who was in sanitation for those rooms hobbled in just then and seen the bracelet in the corner. She went to get it and seen there weren't one but two little bracelets layin' there. So Flo picked 'em both up and just kinda stared at 'em for a minute.

Then, quick, she looks around to see if anybody's watchin' and me, I've got my back to her, watchin' her reflection in the window opposite. She hides the little bracelets in her hand and starts lookin' through the cribs., there musta been twenty of 'em, and pretty quick she finds a kid without, so she picks a bracelet and sticks in on the kid. Then she finds the other one and sticks the other bracelet on it.

Flo had no more idea of which belonged to who than I did; but suppose she figured – and was so stupid I'm not sure she even could figure – that it was easiest to just slap a bracelet on a wrist and let fate handle the rest. Besides her odds were 50-50, whether she knew it or not.

Now I don't know about you, but I'm one of those people who always figured I was raised in a family of strangers. It never seemed that I woulda even known my family except that I was born into it, and after seein' that, well, who's to say who's related to who, and how we got into the family we got into.

(<o>)/(3.16)\(<o>)

I closed my eyes and idly reviewed a story I was working over. I wasn't too pleased with it, but there were a few fine lines – Nun puns.

Hack and I were sitting on our porch enjoying a sunny Wednesday morning in June, just after sun-up, two summers before the Bicentennial. Hack was just home from work, and I was up early – back pain pushing me out of bed as the sun came up.

A mug of coffee for each, the morning paper in a mound at my feet. Hack was whittling with a little yellow knife on a one foot length of two by four, working on a musket stock.

"Ya hear Rex rollin' in this morning?" Hack asked.

"No."

"About five, right after I got home. Big spade carrying a whiskey bottle and her recitin' Wordsworth at the top of her lungs."

"Mm."

Hack got a big charge out of Rexee'. They had an easy rapport and he could joke with her. They were comfortable together, I think, because he never considered her in romantic terms. Rexee' respected anyone she couldn't seduce.

Which is why she didn't respect me.

I ached with lust, and then hated myself for mooning puppy-like around her. My stomach was always turned to jelly and I couldn't help staring with fascination at her smooth brown legs.

I was a joke, and a sap, and a coward. I was embarrassed for myself at many levels.

I'd heard her come home alright, laying in hot agony in my bed. I don't think reciting from a Romance poet was intentionally cruel; Rexee' was just a little thoughtless, and sometimes loud, where I was concerned.

She thought me an inferior writer and a nuisance when I asked her to read my absurd, poorly plotted little stories. She obviously disliked reading them, but took great pains telling me exactly how lousy she thought they were. She gave me an entirely new insight into the meaning of the word 'rejection'. The axiom that an author is his own worst critic was never true in my case.

"She ever talk about me to you?"

"Naw, Skate, not really."

Hack's kindly face wore a troubled expression. I knew he was holding back. The day before I'd overheard her call me a pain in the ass. I don't know why it is I go on these fishing expeditions. Something in me craves punishment, I guess. Do rats crave traps?

The heron breezed overhead again, swooping in beautiful silent arcs. I could make out a line of darker feathers skirting the long white line of its underneck.

"Why you suppose she and Ace are so cold?"

"I dunno. They get along alright. Probably too much alike."

Just then there was a tremendous crashing noise from behind the house and Rexee's voice climbing to a furious screech.

"Stop that! STOP THAT YOU BASTARD!"

Then a series of whip-crack like noises matched by pained grunts, followed by a snapping sound. Hack and I exchanged bemused, worried looks.

Then we heard a thick, black, male voice bellowing, "YOU WHAT HOE!"

We were familiar with commotion from back there, and learned to ignore it. But this seemed different.

And then we heard Rexee's strangled cry for help.

I was momentarily frozen by indecision. Hack was not.

Hack was magnificent.

He jumped up and beat feet around the corner while I struggled out of my chair. His moccasins threw gravel. He reached Rexee's chipped green door and turned the knob. It was locked and without a pause he kicked splinters off it. It didn't fly open though until I, running full tilt boogie, unable to stop, threw myself into it, and through it, flying full-face into the concrete floor.

A black man with thickly muscled shoulders and a heavy gold wristband had Rexee' pinned against the wall with his hands around her throat. They were both naked. Rexee's moist pubic hair glistening like a new penny, the black man's sharply defined buttocks twitched as he shouted.

"I ain't no slave for whippin'!" he was rhythmically knocking her head against the wall with every fierce word.

His eyes bulged in yellow fury until Hack, running right over me, poked a sharp left into the guy's floating rib, provoking a whoosh of hot air that Hack choked off with a stiff open handed uppercut to the man's throat that convinced him to let go of Rexee and fall backwards onto the floor. There was a broken green splinter of bamboo tomato stake on the floor – apparently Rexee's misguided weapon.

She was sobbing and trying to catch her breath as I scrambled to my feet. My left arm felt broken where Hack had stepped in his rush to combat.

"Son of a bitch," Rexee' gasped, "Son of a bitch was going to piss in my rubber plant."

"Okay Rex," Hack handed her a long silk robe, "It's alright."

I watched as the little mound of pink flesh under Rexee's navel disappeared beneath the silk. The black man squirmed on the floor; it looked like he was having a little trouble breathing, but he seemed to be okay. The fight had been slapped out of him.

The morning sun was shining through Rex's battered door, hanging by one twisted hinge. Rexee' slumped into her wicker chair and I was dumbly observing the cut of light crossing the black guy's chest when a shadow suddenly stepped into the doorway.

I turned and saw Delmar, our demented cross street neighbor. He wore nothing but khaki shorts and unlaced combat boots. There appeared to be blood smeared on his belly and he carried an extremely evil looking rifle aimed at the man heaving on the floor.

"Did this black scum rape this woman?" he hissed.

And before I could think he squeezed off a short burst, raking a dozen slugs across the guy's chest and neck.

The sharp reports were painfully magnified by the confined space of the garage. The black guy was dead before the echo died. His twitching corpse hardly bled. I was surprised at that. I'd never seen a dead body before, much less an execution. It happened so quickly that I was shocked out of reacting. It seemed unreal, somehow, dreamlike.

Hack, whose back was turned, spun into a low crouch, his fright/flight mechanism still in gear. He was about to charge the door.

Rexee' let out a muted wailing moan, an unearthly sound.

I was dumbstruck immobile, out of touch – but Delmar was calm, almost casual. He pointed his rifle at the ceiling, resting the stock on his hip. Silhouetted in the door he had an almost mystic look to him. He had a small smile on his lips and seemed peaceful and proud of what he had done. Through his cotton shorts I could see he had a partial erection.

There was what seemed like a very long pause before Delmar rasped, "Anybody got a smoke?"

There was a pack of Rexee's Camels on the floor near a whiskey bottle next to the bed. I shook two loose and tossed him one. I lit the other one. It was the first one I'd ever really smoked. I felt somehow I needed it.

Hack gently touched Rexee's shoulder saying, "C'mon, let's get out of here."

He had to help her walk; she was badly shaken and still heavily drunk.

We filed out, following Delmar who'd turned on his heel and wordlessly marched out the driveway; the hardware on his rifle lightly jingling with each stride. He did not look back and, honestly, it didn't seem like he even remembered what he'd done anymore, as I later testified. It was somehow all beneath his consideration. Just another chore.

And it was a macabre scene. We three, Hack, Rexee' and me, stepped out into the brilliant summer morning, a beautiful day, but with a warm black corpse on the concrete behind us. Delmar stepped stiffly away from us, a military man, Rexee leaned on Hack and sobbed drunkenly, and me chilled to my core, still trying to make sense of it.

Then we heard a hollow rasping squawk and looked up to see a heron just floating, wings outstretched and feet dangling, softly coming to land in the top of our big granddaddy front yard elm.

"Something must be wrong," Hack stated the obvious, "Heron don't land here."

"It's a mother," Rexee' put in, "looking to build a nest for babies; the American Dream."

She was wide-eyed, shit-faced, traumatized, and on the verge of mumbling. Her hair was hanging in knotted amber ropes, the silk gown clinging to her damp body.

I suddenly loved her very much, knowing we'd never make a pair.

"The American Dream," she said, "the American 'merican 'merican Dream!"

Hack helped her to my chair on the porch.

I watched them move and eyed the heron for a moment. It glared at me, balefully, with intense yellow eyes. It did not appear to be looking to build a nest. It appeared to be looking at my eyes for food.

Hack and Rexee' were mistaken. It would be another two years before our Elm became a Heron home.

My back was killing me.

I went inside to call the police.

(<o>)/(3.17)\(<o>)

A one act play in several scenes:

Scene Three –

Another hour has passed, it is 8:00 a.m.

Hack, Ace, Book and Skate are still sitting at center stage. Patrick is offstage in the men's room.

=#=#=#=

```
     Hack
Skate, I've been meaning to ask you -- what's a street poem?

     Skate
It's just a poem written in the language of the streets.

     Book
And characterized by bad grammar and incorrect usage, ala
Dylan.

     Ace
And as in the phrase, "I can't get no satisfaction."*

     Skate
Nothing too unusual about a sub-culture developing its own
language, is there?

     Ace
Not at all. My grandmother was a flapper in the 1920s and
would trot out strange expressions all the time when she was
drinking.

     Book
Like 'twenty three skidoo'?

     Ace
Yeah, but funny stuff too, like 'You shred it, wheat'.

     Skate
It wasn't that long ago that all good things were 'fab'

     Book
And later, good things were 'groovy'.

     Skate
And before that, they were 'solid'

     Ace
And the black man was a negro, until later he was colored,
then for a brief while 'spade' was cool, and then African
American, and now he's black.

     Hack
Things that used to be hot, are now cool

     Skate
While females were dames and broads, then girls, until they
became chicks, and later progressed to … what, females again?
```

        Hack
Babes.

    Ace
I don't think so.

    Book
I wish I knew.

    Ace
I wish you knew, too. Then you could tell me.

    Book
Maybe we can ask Rexee'

    Ace
I doubt she'd know

    Skate
I doubt she'd tell you.

    Hack
Tricky, ain't it? Saying the wrong thing? I think the secret
is to say it as if you don't mean nothing by it. Then it's
just words.

    Skate
Yeah, just words, that's the thing.

    Hack
Well, what's your secret?

    Skate
I wish I had one.

    Ace
That great American philosopher, John Wayne, in that great
American organ of culture, Playboy, said "never insult someone
unintentionally."*

    Skate
Truer words were never spoken.

    Ace
Wait, help me, does that mean, logically, those words are
true. Or there are more true words, but nobody said them
because they're obvious. Or wait, …

    Skate
You've been hanging around with Book too much.

    Hack
Speaking of words.
(speaking to Ace)
What did you say to Bonaparte that day?

    Ace
I don't remember, honestly, nothing.

    Book
I remember. We were leaving and you said, 'see you around like
a doughnut' and he drunkenly perceived it as a racial slur … a
bummer.

    Hack
What a night that was.

Ace

Never to return again, I hope. I was caught flat-footed, with the head of a lion and the body of a man.

Hack

That's how it works for me, most of the time.

Skate

The verbal go mute, and the meek inherit the earth.

Ace

Something like that.

Book

You better look out when that day comes. I'll be taking names and collecting albums.

Ace

Gawd, I wish you'd let that go.

Hack

And bitchin', you remember that? It's a bitchin ride, it's a bitchin deal. Who was that west-coast doorknob?

Ace

That was no doorknob, that was Skate, fresh back from one of his motorcycle sojourns.

Skate

(sighs)

Yes, I adopted some west coast slang, in an attempt to illuminate you clodhoppers. This failed.

Ace

Like a lens, you are. A focal point to culture.

Skate

(sighs again)

I regret some of my old school pictures, too.

Book

Pictures in your photo ALBUM?

Ace

Book, I beg you, let it go. I lost your album. I bought you a new one. Please make peace.

Hack

But he borrowed an original, numbered, White Album on white vinyl with photos enclosed, and personally autographed by John Lennon, right Book? And replaced it with a, what'cha call …?

Book

A what'cha-call "imitation", is what'cha call it.

Ace

Collectible dreck, manufactured nostalgia, opiate of the masses, dross for the dump. I'm sorry Book, I really am. I don't know where it went, or what happened to it. But it's not like I sold your birthright.

Book

My, my, my. Standing in the rain for an hour to get an autograph. Where's the value?

Ace

I swear, again, I'll make it up to you. There's more where that came from, I'm sure. Plenty more. Puh-lenty.

        Skate

We live in times of plenty -- much plenty. While I was in the
hospital I talked to a woman who believed the Baby Boom
generation is the most significant thing to happen since the
invention of contraception. She claimed the huge numbers born
in those years will affect everything from the environment to
the space race in a way that nothing else will, including the
atomic bomb.

        Hack

I just heard about that. That's us right?

        Ace

The baby boom? Yeah, everyone born in the forties and fifties,
I guess.

        Book

Technically, between 1946 and 1964.

        Skate

She maintained that the Viet Nam war was a conspiracy against
the Baby Boom, to keep population levels in check. According
to her, we are the largest group of people in history to reach
maturity simultaneously.

        Book

That last is, technically, true.

        Ace

Patrick will love that. He's been looking for a conspiracy to
get pissed off about.
(Patrick has emerged from the men's room and is standing
behind Ace)

        Patrick
(sitting)

Not true. You pricks conspire against me every time I take a
leak and that doesn't piss me off in the least.

        Ace

That's because we're your friends, we're not like the others.*
Skate, what ward was this woman in? She didn't, by any chance,
have her sleeves laced around behind her back, did she?

        Skate

I think she was visiting. I met her in the gift shop.

        Ace

Yes, of course -- and what did you bring us?

        Skate

Memories. You know, they've got a museum at Mayo, filled with
bizarre artifacts. One thing on display was a piece of wire,
an inch long at most, that they took out of some guy's chest.
He was mowing his lawn and ran over an old chunk of guy wire.
Through some quirk of fate it sailed up and hit him next to
the heart. He was short of breath but didn't even know he'd
been wounded until the following Monday when he had an X-ray
taken. Apparently he lived.

        Book

The Baby Boom hypothesis has one interesting feature: there
has never been a generation with so much competition within
itself. And our birth year, 1952, is the biggest of them all.

64

        Patrick
And a Year of the Dragon in the Chinese calendar, don't
forget, mystical and potent by itself -- many Chinese timed
conception so their kids could be just like us.

        Book
All true, and this creates an unnaturally acute shortage of
resources.

        Hack
Resources?

        Book
Oh my, you know, careers, mates, consumer goods, housing.

        Skate
So that explains it.
(The stage right door opens, admitting a shaft of light that
silhouettes a female form. Rexee' walks in the back door of
the bar. She is small and attractive, not classically
beautiful but with an assured manner and a graceful sort of
poise. She is wearing a bright yellow blouse with brown canvas
shorts and wooden sandals. She has a brown canvas book bag
over her shoulder and her long hair is piled up and tied on
top of her head. She crosses toward them at center stage,
picking up a chair one-handed and carrying it with her. She
stops behind their table and they move aside so she can sit
down. She sits in the middle, between Hack and Skate, at
center stage.)

        Rexee
Explains what?

        Skate
Explains why "I can't get no satisfaction."

        Ace
But he tries, and he tries and he tries and he tries.

        (Blackout).

(<o>)/(3.18)\(<o>)

diaria -- 3.0 -- 8/13/76 -- sturgis

one of the amusing gambits in the authorial bag of games
is the shifting point of view. stories are told by a
teller; right, but the teller needs a frame of
reference, a vantage point. now, tradition dictates a
single teller with a consistent point of view. but
tradition don't buy much on this corner.

part of point of view is person. third person is pretty
common; y'know -- he said or she said or sucking his
teeth, he put down his pen. second person is fairly rare
and hard to sustain, altho i've heard its easier in
french due to their grammar. one example that springs to
mind is from fourteen thousand feet you see. first
person is pretty popular in autobiographical fiction or
any tale told by someone relating events as they happen
like in huck finn and me, i was the new kid on the
block.

narrative methods can vary too -- there's what's called
omniscient where the teller is completely outside the
story observing events and even reading people's minds;
and then there's the narrator that is also a character
in the book, sometimes major, sometimes not.

for 100 years now, tho, the line of sight will slip from
one person to another and some authors, devious
bastards, will tell the story thru so-called unreliable
narrators. this really mucks the water. a reader doesn't
know WHO to believe, if anyone. the point, i suppose, is
exactly that: ya rarely DO know who to believe -- that's
one of the givens.

here in metafiction land we don't go in for that sort of
thing; at least i don't. as my buddy hunter sez, "we're
your friends ... we're not like the others."* of course
i'm not sure i believe HIM -- but you can rely on ME.

no, really.

as a final word, fer today at least, on the topic of
person; there's some stuff that resists easy
classification or to which the subject just doesn't
apply. ya don't, fr'instance, speak of the point of view
in a play; ya just don't. and pieces like this (where
the narrator isn't telling about anything so much as
talking to the reader, directly into yer face, so to
speak) don't really have a category either. it's an old
gambit; henry fielding worked it out centuries ago,* but
since HE didn't clap a literary term onto it, I might
try -- maybe we'll call it zeroeth person.

(<o>)/(3.19)\(<o>)

Sucking his teeth, he put down his pen and minutely inspected a curved
mote of dust that seemed to be hovering a foot from his face. Clods of words on
the desk, thrown from a shovel, sprayed on the puddle that lay in the way.

He flinched and the mote that had perfectly lain on the origin of his eye
came loose and floated down the parabolic slope of his retina. Fighting to catch
it in focus he batted his eyes and made it all worse. The mote escaped at a
velocity proportional to his efforts. The harder he tried to see it, the harder it
was to see.

(<o>)/(Endnotes 3.20)\(<o>)

21. Vonnegut, Kurt, Breakfast of Champions. 1973,
Delacorte Press

22. Jagger, Mick and Keith Richards (1966). (I Can't Get
No) Satisfaction. ASCAP.

23. Wayne, John (1971). Playboy Interview. Playboy
Magazine. May. Volume 18, issue #5

24. Thompson, Hunter S. Fear and loathing in Las Vegas;
a savage journey to the heart of the American dream,

Illustrated by Ralph Steadman. [1st ed.] New York, Random House [c1971] 206 p. illus. 22 cm. P.4.

25. Ibid

26. Fielding, Henry. History of the Adventures of Joseph Andrews and of his Friend Mr. Abraham Adams, written in imitation of the manner of Cervantes, author of Don Quixote (New York: Rinehart, 1948). Originally published in 1751 by Henry Fielding (1707-1754).

Chapter 4

When Ace and Book had gone into the night, Rexee' disappeared into her bedroom and left Skate and Hack sitting across from each other.

The apartment did not have interior walls, it was a converted garage. All the living areas were defined by temporary artifacts. The bedroom wall was nothing but a drapery and, in fact, all the different living areas were defined by tapestry and carpetry rather than lathe and plaster.

The living room was an old 1950s style coil-of-cord rug surrounded by a sofa and two easy chairs. The kitchen was a long thin carpet against the counters running along the wall, and the bathroom was a walled-off corner big enough for a toilet and a shower cabinet. Nearly half the garage had been partitioned off with floor length drapes, and that enclosed Rexee's sleeping chamber. Skate had been back there only twice: once to help fashion a scaffold in 1970, and then again in 1974, at the front end of Delmar's sentence. Skate looked for old blood stains on the concrete floor, but there were none. They had been scrubbed and worn down to nothing in the two intervening years.

The garage had been built about the same time as the house, sometime during the First World War, so it was really a garage and a half: enough room to park a car but with plenty of space for a workshop and storage. It had been converted to a livable space at some point, probably in the 1960s, by sealing up the garage door and calling it an apartment (it had the basic plumbing and an oil burner now converted to electric heat from the beginning – Rexee' had the shower installed herself).

Ace maintained the architect had been Norwegian.

"Who else," he argued, "would build a garage with a bathroom."

The place also had Norwegian insulation, in Ace's phrase – that is, none at all, up until Rexee's first winter night there. She found frost spots on the walls and an icicle forming on the shower head that morning.

She came over and showered in our house that day.

"A fucking icicle," she said, "can you believe that shit?"

The next day the landlord had insulation material blown into the walls and ceiling. Rexee' saw to that.

The guys avoided the landlord by taking care of things themselves. Rexee' worked him like ratchet, and got what she wanted, when she wanted it. That was Rexee'.

(<o>).[],(<o>)

Rexee' turned on her bedside lamp and changed into her night clothes. Skate struggled with his eye movement.

Her naked silhouette was perfectly outlined on the flimsy drapery and he wanted to stare at her feminine form, but Hack was sitting right there, so he didn't. Hack didn't seem to notice.

When Rexee' came out she was wearing a pale yellow kimono with a split up the thigh and large black birds flying around her torso. She walked over to the kitchen counter and put away some dishes and then turned around.

"I suppose," she said, "you guys have to go?"

Hack pulled himself out of his easy chair.

"Yeah," he said, "duty calls."

"How about you," she asked Skate, "can you stick around for awhile?"

This was new to Skate, and he didn't answer immediately. Usually Rexee' was throwing him out of here, not asking him to stay.

"I guess so," he nodded.

Hack looked at Skate, "I'll be by about 5 a.m. then, to pick you up?"

Skate blinked, and then it dawned on him; the Mayo clinic, he was flying to Rochester in the morning.

"Yes," Skate said, "I'll be ready. With today's events I'd forgotten."

"Say," he added, "are you okay to drive? I didn't see you sleep today."

"Two hours ago I was dogged," Hack answered, "but now's my usual work time and I feel fine. Besides, I'll bet Book's coffee is real, real strong tonight."

"Chewy and delicious," Skate nodded.

Hack looked at Rexee', "I'll check in with you when I get back, if your lights are on."

"Okay, handsome," she said, "I'll see you then."

Hack walked out with his moccasins in his hand, looking as big as a mountain and as nimble as a goat. Rexee' poured some whiskey into a tumbler and sat in the chair Hack had just vacated.

"You want a drink," she said, "help yourself."

Skate lay on the overstuffed couch and contemplated her. He had to admire her, he couldn't help it.

Here was a woman, clearly afraid or at least genuinely nervous about the looming shadow of Delmar in the darkness, and yet still with enough moxie to be inhospitable.

On one hand, she clearly wanted company in this dire hour (and many people, in this situation, would concede that enough to offer and make a drink for you). But she didn't have enough 'give' in her for that. Or else she was simply falling back on old habits, as people will do. Skate couldn't see which it was, and wished he could. She put her chin forward, that much was clear.

On one level his problem was simple. He wanted her, he wanted her forever, but he wanted her to be nice to him – like she had been to Hack before he left. He viewed this as simple, sexual and primeval.

But he needed her too: as a friend, and as a mentor. He valued her, and though she rarely betrayed her feelings, he knew it was mutual. They had already been through the worst and the best, and they knew each other very well.

She was a link into the world of literature, and he desperately wanted to impress and please her at that level. But he couldn't make her a friend first – it had to be a sexual relationship that turned into friendship – it just couldn't work out the other way, he knew that much – she didn't sleep with her friends. This left him bereft.

"So, why is it Rex?" he said, hanging it out there.

He had her attention, but she didn't speak, so he went on.

"Why is it, after all the time and the truth that has passed between us; why is it we don't sleep together?"

She didn't seem the least bit startled by the question, which disappointed him a little.

"I don't sleep with my students," she said, "and I don't sleep with my friends. And you're not the sort of man I collect."

"And Hack is," he observed.

"Let me ask you a question," she deflected, "how do you like your shower, hot and hard, or warm and soft?"

"I don't know," he answered, "warm I guess."

She nodded, "That's what I mean. I need a hot, hard shower – nothing else will do."

(<o>)/(4.3)\(<o>)

Skate had been to his mid-morning class, a baffling Shakespeare lecture about deconstruction into signifiers and signifieds – he hardly caught a thing. Then he stopped into Doogan's on the way home for a beer and some reflection. Now, as he navigated the sidewalks towards the Web, he saw her far ahead, standing on their corner – short, blonde, plump.

He collected himself, in case she was still there when he walked by.

He expected this to be another miss. Like the time he waited outside the House of Rip-off – she went west, and he went east. But just in case, he steeled himself for the encounter. He lit a cigarette, to sooth himself – and to look cool.

She was still standing there when he ambled up.

"You lost?" he grinned.

She turned, recognizing him and smiling, "No, I think I can find my way."

She held up a key, "My friend wants to borrow my old bug, later, but asked for the key now."

"Uh?"

"Yes, as she drives by in another car, in a big rush, late to an appointment."

"Ah."

"We do these things sometimes. Her crisis becomes my emergency."

"I have that too," he said, thinking of Ace, "we also serve who stand and wait."*

"Here she comes," Effie nodded up the street, "frantically late and urgently in motion."

"Yeah," Skate replied, "I have that too."

A rusty brown Chevy Impala pulled up, billowing blue exhaust and pounding like a Harley. A freakishly thin woman leaned over to shout out the passenger side window.

"I can't stop," she howled, "the battery is dead and the alternator won't charge. If I turn it off, I'll need a jump to get going."

Effie shrugged and stepped forward with her car keys.

"Here you go, Mary," she shouted, "when do I get this back?"

"I've got the thing in Monticello, then I've got to drop that stuff in Stillwater, and then I've got to dump this piece of junk back near here. Then I need to grab your car, do that other thing in Osseo, and then get to dinner with my Mom. I'll be back here after supper. Okay?"

"Not a problem," Effie backed away, "drive safe."

The car pulled into the street, barking like a Sherman Tank and blowing dark smoke.

"She know her way around?" Skate asked.

She turned to look at him, "Oh, yeah, she's from around here."

"She'd better be," Skate said, "from here to Monticello, to Stillwater, back here, then out to Osseo and back, all before supper?"

"Mary is frantic and anxious, but she can drive like a banshee and rarely misses a commitment. She's never on time, either, but that's just something we come to expect."

"Yeah, I'm like that."

"Maybe you'd make a teacher then."

"Me?"

"That's what Mary does," Effie went on, "over at the U. Biology. They say she's very good."

"Don't know much By-all-o-gee."

"Don't know much about a Science Book?"*

Skate laughed, "Yes, that's right."

"So," she ventured, "what are you doing now?"

(<o>).[],(<o>)

They were at Doogan's, the day after "the event", two summers before the Bicentennial.

"You're taking classes," she said.

"Here and there. I've got Shakespeare now."

"What's your major?" she asked.

"I'm a firm, firm, undecided."

"How's that going?"

"It's okay. They let you take two years before they force a choice."

"So you're shopping."

"Yeah, I guess."

"Me," she said, "I commit. I choose a major, and then I pursue it with full vigor."

"How's 'that' going for you?"

"Great. I've committed to four majors already," she sipped her beer, "and I'm thinking of changing again."

"It's a means to an end, I suppose, but not for me."

"Why's that?"

"Decisions are a problem, sometimes," he paused, rubbing his lower back, "I'm cursed with 'unlimited potential'"

"You poor boy."

He put on a doleful face.

"I'd go to the counselor, and take test after test, and they'd all tell me the same thing: 'you can do whatever you want'. This started in grade school."

"Must be nice."

"No, it's not actually nice. It's a plague. It's back on you. You seek a little direction, and you get optimism and indecision instead."

"They didn't want to limit you."

"Yeah, well" he shrugged.

71

"Tortured soul, Leonardo type figure?"

"Ah, see, no. If I was, I wouldn't get that you're pulling my chain right there. I'm in a much sadder notch. Over the thresholds of the standardized tests, in the airy percentiles. Which means the counselors won't 'limit' me."

He paused to light a smoke.

"But in a group of the really smart guys, like the giant brains who turn up here at the U. in Shakespeare for example, I'm among the dumbest ones. Today's lecture?"

He shook his head and exhaled tobacco smoke, "I don't think I understood any part of it. I could not catch the thread at all"

"You're the dumbest of the genius class. How I pity you."

"I'm marginal. That's the thing," he laughed, "Oh! how I suffer!"

"Actually," he went on, "my grandfather would tell you what I am is somewhere between a wastrel and a ne'er-do-well."

"What my father would call a 'hippie dirt-bag'?"

"Pretty close, yup." he agreed, "but I prefer reprobate."

(<o>).[],(<o>)

They had settled into a booth at Doogan's after Skate explained this was his "easy" day – a class in the morning, and no library work scheduled.

It was a Tuesday/Thursday summer school class, and he routinely walked home from lecture, stopping at Doogan's on the way to do a little reading and note taking.

This day, he had done that, and then picked up a babe on the way, and detoured back to the bar with her.

It was the Thursday after the shooting, the massacre in Rexee's garage, and Skate had considered skipping class. But he didn't know what else to do, so he followed his pattern.

She shifted uncomfortably in her chair.

"I wanted to talk to you about the murder," she said.

"It seems like only yesterday," Skate murmured.

"It was, wise guy, is that funny?"

He shuddered, "I've never seen anything like it, and never hope to again."

"I was out there, you know," she offered.

"Yeah, I thought I saw you, but the events took over the day."

"You want to talk?"

He tried to laugh.

"You already opened me up like a can opener. I'm sitting here spewing hidden thoughts about test scores and counselors, and everything else that leaps to mind."

He stopped.

"I'm jangled, to tell the truth. I don't know why I'm talking."

He took a long drink from his beer, and waved to Calvin for another.

"You didn't see," she said, "but I watched my freaky neighbor coming back. So I crossed the street and looked into that apartment. I saw the body."

She bobbed her head.

"I was afraid to look," she went on, "but your buddy was heads down with that drunken bimbo, who was retching by then. So I just walked right by. I'll never forget it."

"Rexee' is her name, and she's a friend," Skate shook his head, "and I've been trying to forget. But after leading the cops back there, and answering questions all day, and then leading more cops back there later."

"Yeah?"

"Yeah, I don't know. I feel almost anesthetized. Seeing the body lost it's edge. Maybe that's sad to say. They covered him up with a police blanket."

He took another drink.

"Seeing the murder, the spray of bullets past my head, that's what I can't get rid of. Every time I close my eyes, that's what I see. I re-live it"

"You sleep much last night?" she asked.

"Not whatsoever."

She nodded, "Me neither."

(<o>)/(4.6)\(<o>)

By the time the guys moved into their first house things were altogether different. Nixon was president, Paul VI was pope, Neil Armstrong had taken the big step, television heroes tended to be doctors, lawyers and cops; and it was our own military-industrial complex that was scariest. It was 1970, the late sixties in Minnesota.

That first summer set a rhythm for the next few years.

What started as a cheap roof for seedy students evolved into a crossroad wayside colony for progressive pilgrims: such a collection of tramps, vamps, scholars, hustlers, loons, castaways, runaways, vagrants, chiselers, losers, boozers, heroes, zeroes, queeroes, workers, shirkers, mystics, saints and sinners as we (so green) had never known.

Nobody knows when it started exactly, but sometime in the 1970s we started talking about ourselves, and thinking about ourselves, as THE WEB – an interconnected network of acquaintances and friends that spanned intellectual disciplines, political sensibilities, social structures, economic groups, racial backgrounds, and religious training. We were the Web, and we knew everybody. Or, if we didn't know them, we knew somebody who did. Or we knew somebody who knew somebody who did. We lived in the Web House, equidistant from everything.

Geography was fundamental.

The house itself was situated at the center cleavage point in a piegraph of the city. We lived in the focal point, the eye of the storm, the center, as Ace was fond of saying, of the civilized world.

The wedge to our west was the campus: spacious, verdant and manicured. The various disciplines of knowledge neatly compartmentalized by building and department: Chemistry next to Physics and opposite Philosophy, with a library in the middle – Book's bower.

North and east was the factory district: asphalt and concrete, light industry, warehouses, scrapyards, the dump, and wholesale outlets, the centers of production, blue collar hourly workers, lunch buckets and hardhats, noon whistles, truck drivers, union shops, semi-skilled employment, and Annie's Diner – all Ace's area.

The downtown section of the city was immediately to the north and west: glass and steel, parking ramps, busy sidewalks, busy streets, hustle and panhandle, tall crumbling edifices, urban dwellers, white collar salaried workers, shopkeepers, lunch counters, street cops and centers of corporate power – Patrick's portion.

To the south lay the slough and beyond it the Mississippi River: surrounded on three sides by old man river, ignored by developers (due to unsuitable soil and the firm grip of the Army Corp of Engineers who technically controlled it), the slough was marshy untamed swampland, hardwood forest thickly undergrown, sanctuary for small game and hobo derelicts, obscure winding trails, mossy rocks, leafy carpet, loamy soil, Great Blue Herons, and underground springs bubbling from split jointed granite – Hack's haven.

And just up the road was Doogan's Bar – a dimly lit, crummy little dive like so many others – a varied clientele, a sanctum of familiar faces, Formica tables, a juke box, a pool table, a sandwich kitchen, and nothing to recommend it. The pit into which I fell.

(<o>)/(4.7)\(<o>)

In the fifties the guys had been cowboys. They sat on Saturday mornings, and after school, and they watched and learned. Not conscious study so much, but a form of immersion. They devoted so many of their waking hours to adopting the cowboy way that, by the time they were twelve, they each could have written a Masters thesis on western and cowboy lore – thousands of hours of instruction were delivered through the television during their formative years.

From Bat Masterson they learned to go into a gunfight with the sun at your back; that way the other guy had the sun in his eyes. They learned from Wyatt Earp that a six-shooter should only be loaded with five bullets, to keep an empty cylinder under the hammer and prevent misfires. From Rawhide they learned you hold your lariat out of the water when you cross a stream to prevent it losing it's limber, and also how to end a stampede by riding out in front and leading the herd around in a big circle until they got tired. From Roy Rogers they learned it was safest to lay down in the face of a stampede of horses, since they'll jump over you, but they also learned countless times that a cattle stampede will crush you. Roy also taught them to always mount a horse from the left side, unless of course you were in a hurry in which case you could leapfrog onto a horse's back from straight behind if you get a running start.

From the Lone Ranger (actually Tonto) they learned the plains Indians had a sign language, so different tribes could communicate (they only learned one sign, though, the upraised palm, accompanied by the "How!" which was apparently the universal Indian greeting). They also learned that Indians communicated complex messages across long distances with smoke signals. Gene Autry showed them how, when you're in a bar fight, you can block a wild right hand punch with your left forearm, and then punch back with the same hand. Most cowboys blocked with their left and punched with their right.

Kit Carson showed how, if you were being chased by a gang of bad guys, you could, if you were far enough ahead, jump off your horse where they couldn't see you, then throw your lariat over a stump or boulder at about knee level. Then, by hiding across the road, you could pull your rope taut like a tripwire and drop the whole gang on the ground as they rode full speed into your rope and pitched headlong onto their faces. This gave you enough time to get away.

Paladin taught them the gunfight should always be the last resort.

(<o>).[],(<o>)

The general rules applying to guns and fights and gunfights, chases, ambushes, and other protocols, according to Saturday morning and after-school television.

In a gunfight, the bad guy always draws first. A good guy waits until the bad guy makes the first move, then draws. If a good guy gets shot, it is always in the shoulder, almost always the left shoulder. If a bad guy gets shot, it is usually in the hand, and sometimes in the gun, which knocks it out of his hand. If a bad guy shoots someone in the back, they invariably die – back-shooting was something only bad guys did, and it was always lethal. Bad guys don't usually bother counting their shots, so they are often surprised when they run out of bullets. When a bad guy runs out of ammunition, they always throw their gun. Good guys never do that. If a bad guy has a clear shot at an unarmed or unsuspecting good guy, the chances are excellent they will miss or their gun will jam.

When someone is shot in the arm, you dig the bullet out with a knife, assuming there is no doctor around. When someone is shot with an arrow, you have to push it through, break the arrowhead off, then pull the shaft out. When someone is bitten by a rattlesnake you cut an "X" over the bite with your knife and suck the venom out; this only takes a few seconds and recovery is usually immediate and complete.

If a good guy is chasing someone at a full gallop, they can often shoot them out of the saddle with their six-gun, by carefully aiming, usually hitting them in the shoulder (this is an exception to the back-shooter rule listed earlier). If a bad guy is being chased they can try shooting back behind them, but they never hit anything and it's a waste of ammunition. A good guy will almost never bother shooting backward when being chased on horseback, it's a waste of ammunition. When a gang of bad guys or a band of Indians attacks a stage coach the first person shot is always the guy 'riding shotgun', by someone riding on horseback at a full gallop. The guy riding shotgun rarely gets a shot off, and when they do, they almost always miss. The passengers on a stage coach can often manage to shoot a great number of hostile attackers, though.

In a barfight, breaking a chair over someone's back will rarely faze them. However, hitting someone on the head from behind with a pistol barrel always knocks them unconscious. Bad guys always throw the first punch in a fight, which is always a wild right and always blocked with the left. Kicking is completely unfair in a fight, and only the worst bad guys resort to it.

Good guys know a lot more shortcuts than bad guys. Their horses are always faster. However, a gang of bad guys or Indians will eventually overtake a stagecoach, even if a good guy has taken the reins. The exception is when the driver has been shot and the reins have fallen. Then, the procedure is to jump onto the back of the lead horse and drive from there. You will always get away if you do this.

When a bad guy waits in ambush for a good guy, their first shot will always miss, giving the good guy a chance to take cover. Good guys never ambush people. Another word for ambush is bush-whack, also less common, dry gulch. Special note, if a group of Indians shoots at you and runs away, you should not chase them as they will often be leading you into an ambush.

When bad guys are staying someplace, it's called a hide-out. When cowboys are staying someplace, it's called a bunkhouse. A string of horses is called a remuda. A cowboy's rope is called a lariat, which is used to lasso things: horses, cattle, and bad guys. You throw a lariat by twirling it over your head, never underhand. Food is called grub, but a rolling kitchen is called a chuck wagon. You can cook withoutn't salt, and you can cook withoutn't flour, but you can't cook withoutn't water.

Cowboys ride horses, Indians ride ponies. When you're tracking someone, you can always tell it's an Indian because their horses are unshod. Indians are good scouts and trackers, but the best are white men who have lived with the Indians. You can't track people across rocks or at night, unless you're a very, very good tracker. Often, when tracking, you will find little strips of cloth in the bushes, letting you know you're on the right track. You can tell if a group of riders are approaching by laying your ear on the ground to listen for hoofbeats. If you're tracking someone, you can tell how far you are behind by feeling the ashes in their campfire, although a very good tracker can tell just by looking at the tracks. If you're lost in the desert without water, you can get moisture from a barrel cactus. When bad guys run out of water, they toss their canteens away; good guys rarely do this, and they tend to conserve water better, too.

(<o>).[],(<o>)

It was a rainy summer afternoon and we were stuck inside watching an anonymous cowboy movie on television. The hero was on the run, being chased by a gang of bad guys. He rode up to a stream and stopped to look back, the bad guys were not in sight. So he stepped his horse into the stream and walked it to the left, staying in the streambed.

Little Ricky Pawlowski was sitting with the boys, and said, "He should get going, they'll catch him."

Ace rolled his eleven year old eyes and said, "Come on, Ricky, he's hiding his tracks. They can't track him through water."

"I just hope he's going downstream," Book said.

"Of course," Skate answered.

Next scene, the hero steps his horse back out of the stream and ropes a sagebrush, throwing overhand, of course, and then dragging it behind him as he rides off.

"What's he doing?" Ricky asked.

"Pay attention, Ricky!," Ace snapped, "he's covering his tracks."

"Oh," Ricky said, embarrassed.

(<o>).[],(<o>)

Ace had a Mattel Fanner Fifty with "shootin shell" plastic bullets and greenie stickum caps. He practiced his 'quick draw' until he was pretty good. He also had an authentic looking Winchester 75 repeater rifle with a lever action that would jack a plastic bullet out of the breech.

Book had an equally authentic looking rifle, except it had the big-loop Rifleman version of the lever.

Patrick had the rare and covetable sawed-off shotgun from Wanted Dead or Alive, but the holster was broken.

Hack had a wooden carbine that his father had carved for him out of a two-by-four with his jig-saw.

Skate had a plastic rifle and, the newest acquisition, the Mattel Derringer Belt Buckle, which was a little silver one-shot pistol (also with "shootin shell" plastic bullets), that could be clipped into a big imitation silver belt buckle. Once you cocked the derringer, and placed it in the buckle, and set the little switch, you could fire the gun by pressing your belly outward. It was perfect if a bad guy had you with your hands up; you could gun him down by surprise.

Of course it only worked if they, the bad guys, hadn't seen the Mattel Derringer Belt Buckle advertised hundreds of times on television. The boys had all seen the ad, so there was no surprise factor left to it. Still, it was pretty nifty, and it actually shot a plastic bullet, like Yancy Derringer, very nice. You rarely took the bullets outside though – too easy to lose.

The movie was over, the good guy prevailed, and without too much singing, which was generally viewed as the weakest part of any cowboy movie.

"What should we do?" Ace asked.

The rain had ended, although the sky was gray. The grass was wet.

"Let's play guns," Skate said.

(<o>)/(4.11)\(<o>)

It was the fall of 1968. The guys were in the first few weeks of eleventh grade. They were at a high school dance, held in the auditorium of Our Lady of the Snows.

Oteye and the Klang were playing. A band of fairly talented local musicians – white high school boys who covered Wilson Pickett, Sam Cooke, Sam and Dave, James Brown, and the tunes of the other occasionally high tempo soul singers. For a slow-down break, they gamely belted out Otis Redding, Barry White, or Lou Rawls.

The Catholic School dances were famous for frolic. Rather than being heavily supervised, the opposite occurred.

Public high school dances normally had teachers and football coaches patrolling the perimeter, lurking like herons, looking for trouble, and nipping it – separating young teens who seemed too amorous, on one hand, or too aggressive, on the other. Most fights at public school happened in the parking lot after class, or in the parking lot after a football game.

There were seldom fights at public high school dances. They were more frequent at the Catholic venues.

The Catholic School dances were supervised by the occasional parent or college aged student home for a break. The priests and nuns would rarely show up, and then only for a moment early in the evening. As a group, then, the chaperones were ill-equipped to intervene, with little or no moral authority, and largely unsure of themselves. The Catholic School dances were always more rowdy and they usually had a better band, so they attracted a bigger and more varied and active crowd, and from farther away.

The far north side was mostly white, and a public high school dance was always limited to the students and their guests: mostly white. But a Catholic School dance cast a far wider net: kids would come from all over the north side, and even from across the river, over Nordeast. This put Italian kids with German kids with Polish kids with Protestant kids with Catholic kids. And sometimes it put white kids with black kids. Like if Oteye and the Klang were playing.

And, everyone was there for the same reasons, in roughly this order.

Listen to the music and dance, often into a musical frenzy.

Attract members of the opposite sex, usually with the intention of cementing a burgeoning relationship, but quite often with the intention of discovering somebody new.

See and be seen.

Find a fight.

(<o>).[],(<o>)

Skate had gym class with Gus Garrison, two years in a row, so they knew each other. They played on the same volleyball team and slogged around the field on the mandatory Presidential Fitness 600 yard run.

Gus was an extraordinary physical specimen, like Hack – someone who could play almost any game with extreme ease and high skill, and without any preparation or practice. Garrison was a guy with all his molecules in place. Extraordinarily strong, light on his feet, with super-quick reactions and a natural rhythm.

Garrison could do anything – but for the exception that he was worthless in basketball, and he simply could not ice-skate. He had not learned.

He was average height, but heavily muscled with a thick neck and big shoulders.

Gus had matured early, so in junior high he was a man among boys, a real monster. He was already, in 9th grade, the father of an illegitimate child, and starting his testosterone-fueled male pattern baldness.

Skate could never say why they hit it off, but they did. A lot of kids avoided Gus because of his background and his reputation. A lot of kids were simply afraid of him. To Skate, who had moved in relatively recently, Gus was something of an open book. They were both outsiders in some sense. Skate because he was new. Gus because he had broken every rule of common conduct, and he was the suburban high school version of 'shunned' as a consequence.

They started talking, Skate and Gus, because their gym lockers were next to each other. They kept talking because they realized they had things in common. Skate wished he had Garrison's courage. Gus wished he had Skate's brains.

Skate was no Hack as a physical specimen, but he could handle himself. He could run, and he could hit, he could wrestle, and he could skate. Never the best in class at anything, but above average in almost everything.

Garrison would have been the best at nearly everything, but he rarely tried.

Gym class meant nothing to Garrison. School kept him out of juvenile detention, that was it.

He was in that category of guys who could fight – seriously fight. When he was twelve or thirteen, he battled the legendary playground bully, Lou Granifaldi. Granifaldi was years older and significantly bigger, and he almost tore his ear off, but Garrison, instead of submitting, fought back, choked him off, and walked away with blood streaming down his neck. Granifaldi lay on the ground, moaning.

After that, Gus was one of the few who never had to fight again, because he had already created his legend. He was so tough that by 10th grade he was a schoolyard king, untouchable. Through high school a lot of guys might have grown bigger and stronger, football players for example, but nobody – I mean nobody – messed with Garrison.

(<o>).[],(<o>)

Well, except that one time in gym class when big-body-builder Steve Janosich, hyped up on first-generation steroids and full of himself and his muscle tone, confronted Gustafson like a boy-child, saying "Let's fight! For fun!"

And Gustafson faced the man-boy, and closed his hands in imitation of prayer.

"Get ready, goddamit," Janosich shouted.

"I am ready," Gus said, quietly, like a Kung Fu master with a secret.

So Janosich launched himself at Gustafson with little warning but in a clumsy assault. Gus moved a little bit sideways, then punched Janosich in the face, hitting him on the side of his forehead, with tremendous force and a cafeteria fork bent over his fist with tines extended.

Gustafson could have killed him, and probably would have, but the metal landed too high on his skull, and there were too many witnesses. Lucky for Janosich, who was twice the size but half the man. He went down like a rag-doll and just laid there bleeding a bit from the scalp.

(<o>)/(4.13)\(<o>)

Annie got up and made ready for work. When she came downstairs she saw her father had already left, early, as he often did on Mondays. She sighed with relief and opened the freezer thinking, "breakfast of champions," but stopped, and on an impulse, walked out into the backyard. The green shoots were still there, a little bit larger and with a few new ones starting.

Annie splashed a little water on the trunk, for luck. Then she went back inside and had some toast and a big glass of orange juice.

So it went on.

The tree gradually became a green thing, rather than a yellow-brown one. The buds gave way to shoots, and the shoots gave way to tiny delicate orchid-like flowers. And these flowers transformed themselves into sweet and impossible fruit. At the same time the tree took on at least a foot of new growth and its trunk even seemed to swell by an inch or two. Annie checked on it, and gave it a splash of water, every morning before she decided on what to have for breakfast. Toast and juice had seemed fine for a while now.

One day Annie came home from work and found the fuse for the kitchen had blown out during the day. She replaced it, something she had never done, but only seen her father do, and checked the refrigerator. Most of the food was salvageable, but the ice cream had melted into a creamy pool. She wiped it up and threw the carton away.

That evening her father complimented her cooking, something he very seldom did, and then told her she was looking very attractive lately, something he had never done before.

Annie told him he needed a new prescription for his eyeglasses.

That June was the hottest anyone could remember, and July was even worse. Annie watered her tree, a splash every day.

When the tornadoes came, no one was surprised. The storms swept through the seven county area, as they did from time to time during muggy summers, felling trees and knocking over power lines. One twister touched very near their house and, while it did very little damage beyond tearing a few shingles away, it ripped Annie's' tree out of the ground and hurled it into the sky. She never found out where it landed.

It also dropped a power pole onto her father's car – while he was in it, driving home.

He wasn't harmed by the impact, it landed over the hood, and the raw power that ran through the body of the car did not effect him either, since his tires were touching the ground.

But he didn't know that his car was "live" until he got out, cursing the damage to his cherished automobile.

Then he killed himself.

He turned to shut the car door after he was out.

The instant he touched the metal, his body formed a fatal circuit, and he was electrocuted dead.

As they say, he never knew what hit him. He died at the speed of light.

(<o>).[],(<o>)

Annie grieved. She was devastated – there was no one, and no thing, left in her life. She buried her father and went on, but without caring for herself. She plodded forward, through the Fall and the Winter that followed. She even lost a little more weight, but in the wrong way, and for no real reason beyond self-neglect.

That Spring was particularly fresh and pleasant. And one sunny Sunday, on her way to Mass, Annie passed through the back yard and noticed a frail green shoot sprouting from that torn spot in the backyard lawn. Without giving it any thought, she got a watering can and gave the sapling a splash of water. And though she knew it was her imagination, it seemed as though the sprout had grown an inch or so by the time she came back from church.

And that is how Annie came into the Web.

She dug her roots into the community by using her father's insurance money to buy the little diner her father frequented on his way to work. She sold the house too, and moved in over the business. Very little of her previous life came with her when she moved: some photos, some memories, and a strange potted plant that bloomed with orchid-like flowers and impossible fruit.

She ran that establishment with good grace and good cheer. And when Ace first laid eyes on her it was a beautiful sunny Sunday morning, and they got to be friends.

(<o>)/(4.15)\(<o>)

"What'd ya make of that guy?"

"Delmar?" Ace whistled a long sliding note through his teeth, "lunar landscape."

"Yeah? You think?"

Ace and I were mowing the lawn, a miserable thankless job we always put off too long. We were near the end of our fourth year and still no one stepped forward on a regular basis. Ace could only talk me into helping when it just could not be put off any longer. Catholic guilt gets things done, which is why it has survived the centuries.

All we had was a push mower, before the days when power mowers were the standard. This was a handle with curved blades that worked well when the terrain was flat and smooth, and when the grass was low, and caused heavy exertion and copious sweat whenever it was otherwise, like every time we used it.

In other words, we put off mowing because it was a stone drag. But when we finally got around to it, the grass was so high, we endured a stone cold drag, which is one level worse.

We stopped for a drink of water and sat on the front steps in some shade. I'd noticed some movement in the second story window across from us and wanted to put off the mowing.

"I repeat, what is with that guy," I said, pointing my chin up to Delmar's apartment.

"You ever talk to him?" Ace asked.

I shook my head.

"You wouldn't ask that if you had," Ace twiddled a coin across his knuckles while we loafed, a W.C. Fields trick from the film festivals.

Book walked out with three cold glasses of Tang.

"I heard you mention our neighbor," he said, "he reminds me of that kid at Cub Scout camp."

There had been a Jamboree up in Elysium when they were boys.

"Why does everything happen to me?" Ace leaped to the memory, "that kid?"

"No! You think?" I said, "didn't that kid end up down the river* or something?"

"The same one where the moose attached their car, wasn't it?" Book added.

"That was the same kid?" I asked Book.

"I'm asking you," he said, shrugging.

Skate could see where the sun was burning them shirtless.

"Oh, that's interesting," Skate said, finishing his Tang, "He dropped his ice cream cup, or something, and almost cried about it. You think that is THIS guy? Too much."

"Yeah, I am thinking so," Ace was nodding his head, sauntering over to the lawnmower, "I doubt he would remember us though."

(<o>).[],(<o>)

For a second Skate was in the Principal's office with his parents and Sister Monica. It was 1963. They were all looking at him, with a question in the air. How did he get these answers? Why was there a zero on his homework paper?

Skate looked from face to face, his heart pounding. His parents looked angry. Sister Flavian, the principal, looked angry too. Sister Monica* cast him a bland glance that disguised a smirk.

"I didn't pay attention," Skate quailed, "I was being lazy."

"Explain this answer," Sister Flavian said sternly, "how did you get 15 times 15 is 44? This should be easy for you."

Skate looked at the paper, and his mind raced, but he had no answer and no rationale.

"I just wrote down a number without thinking," he lied, "to get it over with."

Sister Flavian exhaled. This was a big disappointment to her. A top student was falling by the wayside, probably because of problems at home, as so often occurred.

She looked to the parents, sitting there dumbfounded, and stabbed a needle into them.

"This boy needs discipline, and that is something that starts in the home. Are you prepared to set this straight?"

Skates father got to his feet. He had been called away from work for this meeting, and he was both angry and embarrassed.

Sister Flavian continued, "We do not tolerate this. The public school is where this sort of thing goes on."

"This will not happen again, Sister," Skate's father declared, "you have my word."

Sister Flavian bobbed in stiff-necked agreement.

"You are correct, sir", she said, "this will not do."

In the early 1960s the Catholic Schools were burgeoning with students, and you applied to get in. Not everyone was accepted.

Skate's parents were children of the Great Depression, as all our parents were. There was never a question of taking your child's side in a school-related issue – the teachers and the principals were right in what they did, you assumed that, and you supported their decisions.

Skate's mother marshaled her courage, stood up and said, "Are we free to go?"

Sister Flavian nodded stiffly, and they filed out of the room.

Skate got to his feet and slank out of the room. He looked to Sister Flavian, and saw nothing in her face. He saw a look of profound disappointment in his parents. And he glimpsed a smirk of triumph from Sister Monica as he turned to go.

As he trudged down the steps behind his parents, Skate felt a rush of relief. He had gotten through without the truth being revealed, and for that he was profoundly grateful.

It would be hell at home for a while, but that was okay.

He was not in real trouble – they did not know the truth.

(<o>).[],(<o>)

Ace was our public relations wing, our people dealer, our agent for extroversion. He was the outgoing one, made friends easily, and was on a first name basis with the whole neighborhood within a month of our arrival in the summer of 1970, four years before.

He was just one of those people, a likeable sort, on the small side, quick, always moving, always thinking, good at turning a phrase, and with enough time to stop and chat with anyone. He gave off good energy and was easy to like. And he was a damn shrewd judge of character.

"Strikes me as a guy on that hard brittle edge."

Ace lit a cigarette.

"He told me once he was a grad student in Physics when they jerked him into the Army. And, it was truly creepy when he talked about it. He claimed he saw a lot of combat – and he loved it."

"Christ."

"Yeah, no kidding. Another guy I met knows him. Said dear Delmar liked it too much and got a psycho discharge out of it – section 8 – and never actually saw combat. Now he's living off disability – the government dole. That pays his rent, I guess, and he spends his time preparing for the crunch."

"The crunch? Meaning what?"

"The crunch, you know, the crunch when the global nuke-down starts, and the system falls into chaos, with anarchy prevailing and bands of wild urbanites are roaming the streets in search of food. You know, the nuke-down."

"Ah," I nodded, "of course – the nuke down."

"He's a survivalist, this year's trend – a year's supply of dried food and a cache of hardware to defend it.

I had never heard the term 'survivalist' until that moment. But it was the early 70s and new terms were commonplace.

"Survivalist, seriously?"

"Deadly. If you ever feel the need to get your skin crawling just go talk to the guy. Hates blacks, hates jews, really hates commies and harbors deep resentment toward anyone left of Hitler."

"Ah, okay, I get it," I said, "like George Wallace."*

"Yeah, sort of" Ace said, "but deeper than that."

"I've always thought he looked kinda familiar," Ace said, "from the old days, maybe. I dunno."

"I don't know if I see it," I answered, "or maybe I do, and I'm hoping you're wrong."

"Yeah, well," Ace said, "I'm often wrong."

Skate nodded eager agreement.

Ace stubbed out his smoke.

"I s'pose we should get to mowing, then," I said.

"Yep," Ace allowed, hoisting himself off the steps, "I s'pose."

(<o>)/(4.18)\(<o>)

A one act play in several scenes:

Scene Four –

It is a little before 9:00 a.m. and the bar is crowded with truck drivers in work clothes and businessmen in suits. Most of the booths and tables are full, and there is very little standing room at the bar. At center stage the six are sitting at one table and are arranged as before: Patrick, Ace, Skate, Rexee', Hack, and Book.

=#=#=#=

Rexee'
So what are we the guys upon for drink?

Hack
Losing it early.

Rexee'
Okay, and whose turn's up to buy?

Ace
Ex-Ray, it's always good to see you. I'm pretty sure it must be yours.
(Rexee's turns and waves until Calvin acknowledges her)

Calvin
What'll it be, Rexee'?

Rexee'
A round, there Calvin, and a Bloody M.
(Rexee' turns back to the table)
Now, any sign of our Dream bird?

Hack
None.

Ace
Perfect, it's the Bicentennial year, the Constitution of the United States is dead and the American Dream has vanished. There's a theme for you Skate, you could write "the Grim American Novel."

Skate
What are you talking about?

Patrick
Weren't you told?

Skate
I repeat the question.

Ace
The lad has been incommunicado.
(To Skate)
You didn't call or anything, and I didn't try to track you down.

Book
It's true, Skate, we talked it over and decided not to disturb you.

        Skate
Will anybody be answering my question soon?

        Ace
Hack, you want to take this one?

        Hack
Well, (pause) basically, (pause) I lied to everybody when I
said the heron had an egg about to hatch.
(long pause)
She actually had a chick up there.

        Ace
And . . .

        Hack
And she didn't just happen to choose our tree. I found her
down by the river one morning, her wing practically cut off,
and I brought her home, nest and all.

        Ace
And then . . .

        Hack
And then I made out to everyone that she couldn't be moved.
(By this time Hack has his head down on the table, buried in
his arms).

        Ace
(solemnly)
Jackson did a very bad thing -- he told his first fib.

        Hack
(Nods into his arms).

        Skate
Unbelievable. You found that bird on the ground?

        Hack
(Nods again).

        Skate
And you found her nest, and climbed up and got it, then hauled
it all home to the Web, and climbed our tree, and put it all
up there?

        Hack
(Nods).

        Skate
Jesus, what a bitch that must have been. Who knows about this
besides us?

        Ace
Just us -- Web family business. But I keep wondering why,
Hack, you chose that tree when you knew it was going come
down.

        Hack
(Raising his head)
I didn't, I mean, she was up there three weeks before that
notice came.

        Book
That explains it. I was wondering myself. But with three weeks
before the notice arrived, plus three more weeks before they

came to cut it down. The chick was nearly two months old by
the time of the 'events' last Monday.

Hack
Little less I think, but yeah, about that.

Rexee'
So what the fuck took place?

Ace
Yes. Well, the day after the death of the Constitution of the
United States, the city crew was back, bright and early to cut
down the tree.

Book
They were there before I left for work.

Ace
Yes, and who else is there, but Hack, again, with his arms
folded, saying "woodsman, spare this tree."

Hack
I'd barely got back from taking you to the airport, and they
were setting up to cut it down. I didn't know if the chick
could take care of itself, so I decided to hold them off.

Skate
That same foreman in charge? He must have gone ape-squat.

Book
My, yes. He was enraged.

Ace
So Book calls me up, and I take another day off work

Skate
Calls you up? Did you call in sick?

Ace
I was at Annie's. I called in sane.
(pause)
Anyway, then the scene starts developing: the cops turn up,
the crowd starts forming, the media is alerted. We dub the
chick 'the American Dream' and Patrick turns up after work in
the morning, and starts making more protest signs.

Skate
The Web defends the Constitution of the United States, until
it is killed, and then moves on to protect the American Dream,
I get it.

Patrick
It's another hot, muggy day, so tensions are rising nicely.

Book
And the crowd is a lot bigger, due to carry-over from the day
before. I counted roughly 200 people on the street.

Ace
Then, just as the stand-off is getting underway, and the WCCO
news team arrives on the scene, we hear croaking and squawking
and barking from the elm.

Rexee'
A real cacophony -- non-musical.

Hack
She was hungry. I didn't get up and feed her that morning.

Ace

And then (pause) she flew away.

Skate

She flew away?

Patrick

That's right. Don't you love it. With a crowd assembled, and a confrontation in the works, the Bicentennial on the horizon, the people taking to the streets and …

Book

(interrupting) With the Constitution of the United States dead …

Ace

(interrupting) … and with chaos under the heavens, the situation is excellent, and civil disobedience is in full flower …

Patrick

(nodding) … the American Dream … just … flew away.

(Blackout).

(<o>)/(4.19)\(<o>)

diaria -- 4.0 -- 9/1/76 -- memphis

there's some standard themes in metafiction and some parallels to be drawn from elsewhere -- things that frequently pop up. reams of critical stuff has been written; i'll try to boil it all down a bit.

the big thing, major issue, is in trying to represent reality somehow. reality meaning how the world really is. fiction is a way of doin that -- by tellin a story that never really happened in such a way that the truth of things are revealed.

how can you get to that when yer dealin from a deck of imagined cards? weel, its like this -- a fiction, even tho it never really happens, can get at the reality of stuff even better than a history can. history is just the story of what went on thru the eyes of some observer; and it's really easy for someone to see what they want over what they don't. some wisenheimer, voltaire maybe, sed "history is a pack of tricks we play on the dead."* anyway it's possible for there to be more truth contained and transmitted by a fiction than can be found in some histories that might be mentioned.

as rexee' pointed out to me once: "The real thing, then, is God's world. The world of the fabulator is different. And the difference, the artifice, is 'part of your point'. The fabulator's attitude toward life is elliptical. By presenting something that is like life but markedly different from it, he helps us define life by indirection."*

there's nuthin too new about this reality quandary,
believe me. virginia woolf went thru an entire
speculation, back in the 20's or 30's, about some woman
in a dark brown overcoat. the question, she asked, is
how does a writer get at the reality of a person just
from lookin at 'em? ya see a woman on a train but how
much can you really say about her? the important thing,
the reality, is what goes on in her head -- what she's
really like. sayin that she's dressed in brown and needs
a wash doesn't cut it. ya gotta get into her head. and
even gettin into her head don't really cut it either.
she might be a raving lunatic or a vegetable or
completely out of touch with herself.

this dilemma is faced by fabulators and reporters alike.
people like hunter thompson and tom wolfe try to write
about what's goin on in the world; but just tellin
what's observable doesn't make the nut. so these guys
get in there and make themselves part of the story. they
become figures in their own journalism, characters in
their own fictions.

thus tom wolfe tells the story of the merry pranksters
and hunter thompson tells the story of the hell's angels
and norman mailer tells about somethin else and ya come
to realize that they couldn't have said and done and
seen and witnessed everything they've reported; but it
doesn't really matter because they're givin you a
picture of what transpired that's more IN THERE than any
so-called straight journalism could be. as my good
friend hunter sez, there's " ... an obligation to COVER
THE STORY, for good or ill."*

these guys, by the way, have come to be known as gonzo
journalists; and tho the term isn't used, yer modern
fabulists could be considered gonzo novelists becuz alot
of times you'll get a fiction where the author includes
himself as a character who is writing a fiction. this is
often called the reflexive element of metafiction. the
classic example is the novel, by gide i think, about a
guy in prison who is writing a novel about a guy in
prison who is writing a novel about a guy in prison who
is writing a novel about a guy in prison who is ...
well, you get the idea.

I never read this, Rexee told me about it.

gide, of course, was in prison when he wrote it. in
mathematics this phenomenon is referred to as recursion,
a function that defines itself. and there's a recursive
interpretation of history too, you've maybe heard the
saw about history repeating itself. Same difference.

(<o>)/(4.20)\(<o>)

Bard on a blanket, toasting. Hot fun in the sun in Como Park, feverish with a summer cold, sitting in the shade he freezes.

Rays cook him to a crispy turn. Half baked.

Not Tiger, a fully roasted nut.

Bard shifts to keep the shade of his head over his journal, blinding inspiration otherwise, blinding nostalgia in any case. Bard rests his head on his journal, for direct data transmission. If only the damn thing would write itself, like a well-manned kayak, it rights itself.

What's up? Seems to be the question.

If every camera lies, why do we trust binoculars?

In the age of the cowboy, there weren't many girls, have gun, will travel, the old western koan, he wore a cane and derby hat, they called him bat.

What else? Sturm and Klang, again, and a hard sad rain.

(<o>)/(Endnotes 4.21)\(<o>)

27. Milton, John (1608-74). "They also serve who only stand and wait" English poet, author of "Paradise Lost", from his poem "On His Blindness". Quoted in "Straw Dogs" (1971) ABC Pictures.

28. Cooke, Sam (1959). Wonderful World (Don't Know Much). Keen Records

29. "Down the river" in Minnesota is a euphemism for the Correctional Facility for delinquent boys in Red Wing, MN which is located on the banks of the Mississippi in the southern part of the state.

30. In the catholic church, nuns take the names of saints. Saint Monica and Saint Flavian are patron saints of "disappointing children".

31. Wallace, George: American political figure (1919-1998), governor of Alabama, famous for bigotry and being paralyzed, and committed to a wheelchair, after surviving an assassination attempt in 1972.

32. Voltaire, a prolific French weisenheimer, AKA François-Marie Arouet (b. November 21, 1694 - d. May 30, 1778).

33. Scholes, Robert (1979). Fabulation and Metafiction (Urbana: U. of Illinois Press), 222 p. ; 24 cm p.76.

34. Thompson, Hunter S. Fear and Loathing in Las Vegas: A Savage Journey to the Heart of the American Dream (New York: Fawcett Popular Library, 1971), p.5.

Chapter 5

Delmar felt an itch on the tip of his nose.

He tried to reach up and scratch, but his arm would not move. He opened his eyes and saw there was a yellow-jacket wasp on his proboscis, and when he flinched and recoiled from it, the wasp quickly stung, twice, and flew off.

Delmar shrieked and tried to claw at his face, but again nothing moved. He was shocked at the sound of his shriek, which came out like the croak of a corroded hinge, or a dying heron. Then Delmar realized he was lying in a pile of rubble on a concrete slab, with one arm underneath his chest and the other pinned by his thigh. He was mostly facedown, in a small pile of boards and plaster, and he had no idea how he'd gotten there.

His nose hurt like hell, and two red-purple welts were already rising. Delmar shifted and rolled until his arms were free, then he pulled himself sitting upright and tenderly touched his nose.

What had happened? What the hell had happened?

Delmar was in a small dimly lit building. He could see a rake and a car tire leaning against the wall, and a shelf over them with a watering can and some empty jars. There was a door beside that. Overhead were bare rafters and a naked lightbulb, and directly above him there was a big hole in the roof … the sky was blue.

He tried to get up, but his joints were locked. He imagined this was how rheumatism must feel. Slowly he gathered himself together, heaved himself upwards, and struggled onto his feet.

His head felt light and giddy and his mouth was very dry. Gawd, he was thirsty.

He half-stumbled to the light, caught himself against the door, and gazed out a small glass pane.

It was a non-descript yard behind a non-descript house, but he spied what he wanted – a garden hose.

He paused a moment, trying to be vigilant and wary, but his thirst was overpowering. He looked over his shoulder and realized he was in a one-car garage, and then he went out.

The house looked lived-in, but empty at the moment, like no one was home. He clasped the hose and turned the faucet – and stuck the hose directly into his mouth.

The first water was warm and brackish, from sitting in the hose, tasting like plastic and mold, but he hardly cared. He pumped water directly into his throat without swallowing, like opening the gullet for a chub, or a carton of chocolate milk. Then he let some pour out onto the grass until it ran clear and cool. Then he drank some more – as much as he could hold.

Delmar began to recall events: the roof, the rifle, the shot, the lightening. That was all he remembered. Had the lightening hit him? He didn't know. How long had he been laying there? He didn't know that either. His nose hurt like hell, with two wasp stings, and even with a bellyful of water to slake his thirst, he now realized he was hungry, very hungry – very, very hungry – ravenous.

His stomach lurched, and a gallon of brown water retched out onto the grass. He felt stomach acid burn his nostrils as he fell to his knees and vomited again – another bucketful of spume out his mouth and his nose.

He felt like shit and he was pissed off about it.

His nose burned, his chest hurt, his joints ached, his bowels churned, and Delmar, as cranky as a black bear and as savage as a wolverine, wanted to find something helpless and kill it. And he wanted to eat, huge ravening helpings of anything, it didn't matter. Gawd, he was hungry.

Delmar turned to go and feed his hunger lust, but he stopped, vigilant and wary, and went back into the garage. It took a short bit, but he picked through the boards and shingles until he found his rifle: the short barreled Winchester 75.

He pulled it out of the wreckage and slipped it into the scabbard he had fashioned in the lining of his camouflage pants. With his military vest pulled down to conceal the rifle butt, the weapon was hidden, although the barrel reached his knee and interfered with his walking a little.

It didn't matter. With his weapon in place he felt better. Now he just needed to find something to kill and eat. Gawd he was hungry.

(<o>)/(5.2)\(<o>)

Delmar stumbled around the corner and down the block. He stopped at the first building he knew had food: the House of Rip-off. He walked straight back to the freezer section and tore open a box of ice cream sandwiches. This is when he noticed, for the first time, that his hands were black.

He wolfed the ice cream in huge bites and swallowed without chewing. And as he chewed he remembered the night cream used to blacken his hands – and his face – before his last patrol. He tore into another ice cream sandwich – and ate it on the way to the checkout counter. Gawd he was hungry.

He had several more in the crook of his elbow as he approached the cashier.

The college kid behind the register had been watching him eat, and now looked at him with wary suspicion.

"That'll be a dollar-seventy-eight with tax," the clerk said.

Delmar sensed fear.

He realized suddenly what an imposing figure he cut, with his face blackened and his military gear, camouflage outfit, flak vest, utility belt – he felt like a goddam warrior. He stood still for a moment, to let his presence wash over the cowering plebe, then reached into his pocket for some money.

Nothing, no cash.

His pockets were empty – he had been on military patrol – military protocols pertained – no coins or keys to jingle and give away his location, no identification to give away his identity in case he were captured – no pictures or personal mementos of any kind. And no money.

He stopped fishing in his pocket as his eyes landed on the stack of morning papers laying on the counter. The headline said, "Tall Ships Prepare for Harbor Gala," and the paper was dated Wednesday.

Wednesday! – he was sure his latest patrol had been on Monday.

"Shit," he said.

Then he turned abruptly and walked out the door. He'd go to Doogan's, he thought to himself, and have beer, and maybe sandwiches. A man could live on credit in Doogan's. As he left he heard the voice of the clerk calling after him, but he ignored it.

Delmar tore open another ice cream sandwich and walked on.

(<o>)/(5.3)\(<o>)

A one act play in several scenes:

Scene Five –

It is just after 10:30 a.m. and the crowd in the bar has thinned.

Most of the patrons have either gone to work or home to bed, but a few people are still standing at the bar with their backs to the audience.

At center stage the six are sitting at one table and are arranged as before: Patrick, Ace, Skate, Rexee', Hack, and Book.

=#=#=#=

```
    Rexee'
So, what are we talking about?

    Ace
Poised for a new topic. What's new wit'chew.

    Rexee'
I've been looking forward to this, it's the first time you've
all been collected together. I wasn't there, so what I want to
know is: what in the hell happened Monday?

    Book
Whatever do you mean?

    Rexee'
Do I need to reach over there and slug you? You know what I
mean. Shots fired, herons wasted, and no useful explanations.

    Book
Monday, let's see, Monday. Hmm.

    Rexee'
I am lining up your chin. You know that, right? Come on!

    Ace
Before you lay him to waste, which he prolly deserves, I can
tell my story in about three sentences. I was on the phone,
with someone in the Biology Department at the U, totally
engaged. Then there was an explosion in my ear, and I dropped
to my knees. I think some juice came right out of the
receiver. It felt like someone had taken ice tongs to the side
of my head. I got up and ran, totally disoriented at first,
looking for a foxhole. Outside, there stood Skate, groatless
and up to his ass in newscasters and heron corpses. End of
story.

    Book
I was in the bathroom downstairs. I heard three distinct
sounds: pop, BANG, crack -- the second by far the loudest.
Then the lights went out and I finished my business in the
pitch dark.
```

Hack

Me, well, I dunno. I only really heard the lightening, and that nearly shook me out of my tree. She offered to peck me, I moved, and felt this bite on my side. I thought she'd, uh, impaled me, and I almost lost my grip. Then, when I looked up she was gone, and the cops were moving in. I didn't know she was shot until I got down.

Rexee'
(Speaking to Skate)
What about you?

Skate

I was facing off with that reporter, trying to hide the fact that Hack was up the tree. Of course, he walked up and the first thing he asked was why Hack was up the tree. I was looking for a rock to crawl under, and then, like Book said -- how'd that go?

Book

Pop, BANG, crack!

Skate

Yes, thank you, exactly, pop, bang, crack. Then I hear something tumbling through the branches and I think: ohmygawd Hack is falling! But before I can even respond to that, the Constitution of the United States is lying at my feet, croaked.

Rexee'

With a bullet in her.

Skate

Croaked, like I said, a bullet maybe, but dead as dead can be.

Hack

Yeah, with a thirty-ought-six slug in her, like from a small deer rifle.

Rexee'

And that's what ran along your rib?

Hack

(shrugs) I guess so.

Rexee'

And what about that fruitcake? Has anybody seen him?

Ace

Tiger? Yeah, what about him, Patrick? You talked to him lately?

Patrick

Pretty tough to talk to Tiger anymore. Why?

Ace

We found him laying in the dirt afterwards, groveling in the gravel, and couldn't get a coherent word out of him. Apparently he'd been back of the house the whole time.

Patrick

Doing what?

Ace

Doing God knows what Tiger does. We got him on his feet, and I said "Tiger, buddy," and he walked off, into the night, down the middle of the road.

Rexee'
What a fucking fruitcake.

Book
He said something, but it was spacy, like he does, "The beacon
beamed" or something. You know how he talks.

Skate
(Raising his beer bottle)
Makes sense to me.
(Skate shakes his bottle, noticing it is now empty).
Anyone ready for another?

Rexee'
IN A MINUTE!
(she is angry)
Why am I not getting the answers I need? There was violence
done outside our doors -- weapons were discharged, and no one
can tell me a thing about it, or give an explanation, or a
reason, and I need that, I need some answers!

Ace
Yes, answers would be nice. I'm telling you Rexee', the word
is out, the sources tapped, and nobody has heard anything. All
drums are silent.

Hack
I looked around out in the alley, but I didn't see anything in
particular. No shell casings or anything.

Patrick
It could just be random violence, you know. Some gunslinger
with his head full of glue, or even a practical joke that went
wrong.

Skate
It might even have been Tiger, I suppose.

Patrick
Doubtful. He's lost, but he's not mean, I don't think.

Book
Then what did happen?

Patrick
I don't know what the mystery is. It is 1976 and We've got a
quarter million trained fighting men roaming the country,
mostly with chips on their shoulders, back from the war and
finding nothing around worth doing -- no welcome home parades,
and no jobs. Probably another quarter million convicted felons
on the street, out on parole. And the rest of us aren't
exactly that stable either -- most of us are outlaws of one
type or another, at least in our hearts. Nixon saw to that.

Book
Nixon? What was HE doing in the alley behind the Web?

Patrick
C'mon, Book. The war drags on, ended but not over, and
everybody knows they're just pawns in some stupid
international game, and practically everyone agrees that we
were going off into rice paddies because Nixon didn't do his
job. He can't settle the conflict, so he throws cannon fodder
at it. That's us. And the law says we have to go.

Ace

And a lot of people said, 'hell no, we won't go.'

Patrick

That's right. And it put us outside the law. It put us in conflict with our parents, our teachers, the church -- it put us in opposition to a lot of the stuff we'd been raised on. And once you're out there, outside the norms, it's not that hard to go the whole yard. I mean, hell, the nuns used to shriek about commies in the same tone they used to shriek about sex and drugs.

Ace

And rock and roll.

Skate

Yeah, you're right, the law didn't mean as much. The law was tear-gassing people in Chicago, and shooting people dead in Ohio, and fixing to send us all over to Viet Nam. I remember it well. We were told that L.S.D. would cause us 'chromosomal damage' -- whatever that means, and nobody cared.

Hack
(nodding)
We were pretty much dead anyway -- it didn't matter.

Ace

And by the time we were up for it, the country was coming around against the war, and nobody wanted to be 'the last soldier killed in Viet Nam' least of all me.

Rexee'
(rising from her chair)
What in the fuck does that ancient history have to do with what's going on now? That war is over! Do you know his two years are up? That bung-hole, fruit loop, fag-bait, trash is out of prison? He's been out for two weeks, I checked. He's walking around out here, God knows where, with a hard-on for the bunch of us. And you fuck-heads are talking about random violence and the Catholic Church! There was nothing random about this.

Book

But what is to be done?

Rexee'

Oh, that's great. What is to be done? You two just tell me you're leaving town, off to Elysium and Mother Nature. Holing up like turds, you pricks are leaving me to deal with Delmar by myself. How am I supposed to do that? What is there to prevent that leech? He's out there, and he's armed, and he can attack us whenever he chooses and disappear afterwards without a trace. What good are you?
(she doesn't cry, but she's close to it).
(a figure, dressed in army fatigues, moves forward from the shadows at the back of the bar -- it's Delmar, he has been listening)

Delmar

They're shit. So are you.

        Skate
(gives a yelp, and starts to laugh)
Perfect. Perfect timing.

        Delmar
(to Skate)
What's so funny? What are you laughing at? Something funny?

        Skate
You are.

        Delmar
Outside. Get up. Outside. Let's go. I'm going to crush your
chest, you asshole. Let's go, douche bag, outside.
(There is an empty stool at hand against the bar, and Delmar
flings it, backhand, across the room. After the crash there is
a moment of silence; no one moves).

        Ace
Skate, ask him if he wants to fight.

        Delmar
Screw you, you prick. I'll take care of you when I'm finished
with him.

        Book
(clearing his throat).
Do you want to fight?

        Delmar
GET UP!

        Ace
Well, then, just stick your head up your ass, and fight for
air.

        Patrick
Or look, you can join the Catholic Church and fight for Jesus.

        Remo
(sitting at the end of the bar).
Haw! Fight for air, that's funny.

        Delmar
Screw this.
(Delmar reaches under his vest and starts to draw a short
barreled Winchester rifle out of his pant's leg. Hack springs
to his feet and lunges at Delmar, gripping him on one wrist
and by the throat. Hack quickly pushes Delmar to the bar and
bends him over it backwards. Calvin, meanwhile, produces a
baseball bat from behind the bar and moves behind the two of
them. He doesn't strike, but just rests the bat on Delmar's
forehead. Everyone freezes, no one moves.)

        Calvin
(Mildly)
Should I crush your skull?
(There is a moment of tableau, then Rexee' moves over from
where she has been standing and, with tremendous chorus line
form, kicks Delmar full in the crotch. Delmar gasps and
crumples, Hack lets him go but neatly slips the rifle out of
Delmar's pant's leg and lays it on the bar.)

        Rexee'
(Screaming)

Come around here again, you filthy murdering fuck, and I'll
cut your nuts off. Do you hear me, you scum? The next time I
see you I'll castrate you and shove your balls down your
throat.
(Delmar can only moan and hold himself. The front door opens,
and a young man walks in with a policeman.)

    Clerk
(Pointing at Delmar, on the floor).
That's him, officer. That's the man.

    (Blackout).

(<o>)/(5.4)\(<o>)

By 1974 'the sixties' were almost over in Minnesota. Nixon gave up being
president and turned it over to Ford (from "tricky Dick," according to Ace, to
"Dick's doof"). The war was still going on (until the fall of Saigon, April 30,
1975), but many American troops had been pulled out, and the draft had ended,
in 1973.

Television, like much of the rest of the country had started to polarize, and
the new catch-word was "quality programming," which meant a new dimension
of the class system was evolving according to personal viewing taste: a certain
kind of person watched "socially relevant" situation comedy, another kind of
person watched whatever else there was.

At the Web we hardly watched any television at all.

By 1974, two years before the Bicentennial, the streets had calmed
considerably. There were fewer people hitch-hiking than before, and fewer
people that just hung out on the corners and in the bars.

There had been a huge mass of directionless souls on the streets in those
early days, many of whom were hangers-on to the Web, making up our social
fabric in the early 70s – the list from before – the tramps, the vamps, the
scholars, the hustlers, the loons, the castaways, the runaways, the vagrants, the
chiselers, the losers, the boozers, the heroes, the zeroes, the queeroes, the
workers, the shirkers, the mystics, the saints and the sinners.

The people on the scene. The usual gang of idiots.*

But by 1974 this had started to change. Many people, tramps and vamps,
settled down and simply got work; many others, scholars and hustlers, moved
away, into the countryside to raise food and kids, or back into the universities to
finish up; the loons and castaways stayed where they were, but discretely; the
runaways went home; the vagrants, chiselers and losers, mostly joined the
boozers; the heroes stuck around, defending the Constitution of the United
States with heronic might; the zeroes remained incalculable and indivisible; the
queeroes came out; the workers worked at rising above and getting better work;
the shirkers never changed, they just shirked in new contexts; the mystics and
the saints found Jesus in their everyday lives, dropped out of the Hari Krishna
and started going to Mass; the sinners continued their pattern but with remorse;
and some just sort of faded away, like Tiger.

The war and the draft aren't really part of this story – not in the nasty
hammer manner you'd think for a story set in these times.

Although, in another way it loomed over everybody and effected
everything.

By the war I mean Viet Nam, of course, and by draft I mean conscription: the notion that the young male members of a society can be plucked out of their lives and sent to war, whether they want to go or not, and whether they believe in the cause or not. The idea here is that citizenship entails responsibilities: paying taxes, obeying laws, killing enemies – whatever society happens to demand.

The draft was run on a lottery, which was supposed to be fair. In our nineteenth year our birth dates were drawn from a barrel on nationwide television. It was made known that the first 125 dates (over 1/3rd of the total) would mark the people to be drafted, of which the first 80 or so (just over 1/5th of us) would be likely to see combat.

Our odds were slightly better than some others because we were born in 1952, a year of the dragon in the Chinese system of counting, and a leap year, which meant there were February twenty-niners in the pool. With 366 days in our pool instead of 365, we had exactly a 0.273224043715846994535551912568306 percent better chance of slipping the draft. Two point seven tenths of one percent, a better discount than Fast Eddie would give you on a pound of weed. We were, as a group, truly blessed.

After our lottery day, the draft no longer loomed over everybody, just the remaining draft-bait and, as it turned out, none of us went. We knew some people who were supposed to go, but didn't, on various grounds, like mental incapacity, conscientious objection, or hearing loss. We knew some people who did, and some of them saw real combat.

Some others went, but spent a lot of time in Saigon and at barbecues on the beach – I've heard these called themselves "rebs", rear echelon bastards.

No one we knew beforehand was killed, we knew a few wounded – although what counts for a wound is open to discussion. A couple of people we knew were never the same as before they went – their eyes had been opened to fear and death, and they didn't feel the same about things anymore: they no longer cared about some things, and no longer cared as much about some other things. There was lightening in the air as they rode the night train.

We did, however, get to know a lot of people after they were out of the service. Remo was one of those.

(<o>).[],(<o>)

We were a sort of 'after school club' – the sixth grade kids Sister Monica let stay after school. This was my first school, and my first Sister Monica, before we moved. There was me, Pat Lockes, June Duvies, and one or two other kids. Like Tom Piwers who was good at math and played sports. The idea was we would work on our homework assignments and watch the latest technology in education: closed-circuit TV. We were a mix of good and bad students, and before long we were all striving to curry favor with the good Sister.

The good sister was large, wide, and wrinkled. She used to stroke us affectionately while we did our work. She let me look at my school file once, which was full of test scores and teacher comments. My permanent record.

As the year progressed, she started leaving the math answer sheet out where we could see it (the answers to the homework sheets she sent home every day). This was a lot of difficult division problems with fractions, and some word problems. Some of us started 'sneaking' the answers, but she knew, and soon we were all doing it. After a while it was just blatant cheating. She saw this happening, but it was an activity to which she did not object (if you were a good student, like most of us were).

Pat Lockes was not a good student, and he was made to do his own work. He was a beautiful boy with a tough-guy swagger, but he was not mentally swift. Sister Monica would spend a lot of individual time with him after school.

One day Sister Monica approached me as I was filling out the math worksheet from her master copy (yes, flagrantly cheating). I looked up as she walked over, and did not even pretend to cover up. This had gone on so long, none of us gave it much thought any more.

I stopped writing as she walked up, expecting her to say something. But she did not speak, instead she just reached down and picked up my left hand from the desk. She held my hand between both of hers. I was eleven years old, she was huge. As my hand disappeared between hers, I was struck by how it felt sort of leathery, sort of papery, like a pair of foolscap oven mitts.

She just held my hand for a few moments and let it go. Then she went to the front of the class and talked about her favorite obsession, the interpretation of the role of the witch in "The Wizard of Oz" which was her favorite film, and the subject of a research paper she had written on her own initiative.

This pattern was repeated several times. Sister Monica would approach me as I was cheating, and would hold my hand in hers – for longer intervals each time – then go speak to everyone from the front of the class, making everyone look up from what they were doing.

Then one day it happened. She approached as I was cheating on my homework, as usual. She took my left hand in hers, as usual. She looked at me wordlessly for a moment, as usual. Then she pulled my left hand towards her and laid it on her right breast.

There was a moment of unreality, as I copped my first feel through layers of Benedictine Habit.

Without thinking, I pulled my hand back, yanking it away from her grasp.

She looked at me, silent but a little hurt, it seemed to me. And I realized for the first time that she had us each situated so she could approach us with her back to everyone else. Nobody had seen her hold my hand all these weeks, and nobody had seen what just happened.

Not a word passed between us and I thought it was over.

The next day, Sister Monica left her answer sheet out for me to copy, as usual. However, the question asking for the product of 15 by 15 was filled in with 44, which I copied without looking. Indeed, every question was wrong, and I got a zero for the homework.

The next thing I knew, Sister Monica raised an alarm and I was in the Principal's office with my parents, trying to explain why my answers were so cock-eyed. Luckily I was able to lie my way out of it.

I never had to tell how I cheated off Sister Monica's answer sheets, and I never had to tell how I touched her breast for a moment. I never had to tell about the after school club, and how we all copied answers, except for Pat Lockes.

99

Then we moved away, and I went to a new school where I met Ace, Book, Hack, Patrick, and that gang.

I was really lucky that way and never really got in trouble for all the bad stuff I did, cheating and lying and so forth. And, since we moved, I never had to talk about it either. Much later I heard that Tom Piwers developed a debilitating stutter. I thought that was strange, since he was one of the 'leaders' in our class when we were younger. As a young boy, Tom was confident and self-assured, a pretty good baseball player and easy to talk to.

I guess something happened to change that for him.

(<o>)/(5.6)\(<o>)

At Hallowe'en the kids go out and collect pillowcases of candy. After two weeks all the good stuff is gone and the half-empty bags lay around the house. The day after Thanksgiving the bags disappear. The kids don't even notice.

At Christmas the stockings are hung by the chimney with care. Santa fills the stockings with candy, taking great care that every kid's stocking is filled from some other kid's pillowcase. After one week all the good stuff is gone and the half-empty stockings lay around the house. Long before Groundhog's Day the stockings have disappeared. The kids don't even notice.

An Easter basket is hidden under each bed. The Easter bunny fills the baskets with candy, taking great care that every kid's basket is filled from yet another kid's stocking. After a couple of days, all the good stuff is gone and the half-empty baskets lay around the house. Soon the baskets disappear. The kids don't even notice.

At Hallowe'en a big bowl appears by the front door and baskets of candy are tossed into it. As other people's kids come to the door this candy is given away by the handful. Meanwhile, the kids go out and collect pillowcases of candy. After two weeks all the good stuff is gone....

(<o>)/(5.7)\(<o>)

Skate and Effie worked through several beers and a few too many topics.

Back at the Web house, there was a vigil going on. It was Thursday, the day after the 'event', and Book took the day off work to sit and tend to Hack and Skate.

Hack spent the Wednesday much as Skate had, answering questions and recounting events for reporters and police. He did not go to work, and sat in funereal reverence through the evening, tending to Rexee' who was barred from her own house until the police declared the crime scene open, which was not until the next day. She slept on their couch, on and off during the day, under a heavy feather comforter manufactured by Hack's grandmother Zelda, many years before.

The police woke her up for questioning, several times. Skate and Effie were also questioned.

Delmar was questioned, back in his room, and arrested for murder.

(<o>).[],(<o>)

Thursday morning, after the police blockade was lifted, they moved as a group into Rexee's to clean and straighten.

Ace, who came home from work on Wednesday when he'd heard the news on radio, also skipped work Thursday. He took charge of mopping the bloodstains and disinfecting the area. He was good and thorough about it, a good German, to Rexee's relief, and saw that nothing of the blood and gore remained.

Skate had Shakespeare and left them to the cleaning, while he trundled off to class. Hack and Book stood by, helping, sort of.

Skate was on his way home after Shakespeare to participate in the disinfecting when he encountered Effie on the street. They detoured back to Doogan's.

(<o>).[],(<o>)

"We should go," Skate said, "we're cleaning the crime scene today, and I should be there."

"We should go," Effie said, sipping her umpteenth beer, "but I want no part of any crime scene. We should go home and have sex to forget."

Skate flushed, flustered, but managed small humor.

"You mean sexual intercourse, with each other?"

"Yes," Effie nodded, without flush, fluster or humor, "that's what I'm talking about."

"Okay," Skate said, "I'd like that."

(<o>).[],(<o>)

By 2 PM on Thursday the cleaning was done, and all evidence of crime and massacre had been expunged.

Rexee' had bundled up every piece of fabric, clothing and rugs, and Book had laundered them all. She and Ace had scrubbed and scrubbed, floors and walls. Hack had moved furniture and helped out.

Finally it was done – no trace remained.

They stood and looked at each other, a moment of clarity, work done and nothing to do. They needed to continue, but did not know how. Until Hack's inspiration.

"Food?" Hack asked.

"Definitely," Ace answered, exhaling with relief, "the organism demands nourishment."

Rexee' was still hung over, and did not think she could eat. Book and Hack were ravenous.

"Skate should have been back by now," Book said, "let's hold on, and go someplace together."

(<o>).[],(<o>)

Skate and Effie left Doogan's and wobbled down the road.

Skate tried to sober up as he walked the line. It was a time to be straight. Sex in the afternoon after many beers required a certain decorum. He hoped to be equal to the task, and was sure, with his reservoir of sexual energy, that nothing could go wrong.

They turned the corner, she and he arm in arm, passing the front door to Delmar's and walking up to Effie's porch into her apartment.

This put them almost directly across from the Web house, with their backs to the garage, just as Ace and the crew came out of Rexee's carrying buckets and mops.

"Yo! Skate!" Ace called across.

Skate stopped and turned.

"We're going to eat. Where you been?"

Skate waved across the street to them, unwilling to stop lest a bubble be burst.

"You go," he hollered back, too loudly, "I'll see you after."

He turned to Effie, saying, "okay?"

She nodded and gripped his arm to keep him walking.

"Food later," she said, and guided him up her porch steps.

(<o>).[],(<o>)

Ace was slack-jawed.

"You see that?" he asked aloud to anyone listening, "that boy has been to the bar, and now he's off to get trimmed."

"Looks like it," Hack agreed.

"While we scrubbed hemoglobin, tissues and fluids off concrete!"

"Looks like it," Hack restated.

"While Book did how many loads of diseased laundry."

"He had Shakespeare," Book shrugged, "besides which he's useless at laundry."

"While I'm standing here, starving, with buckets in my blistered hands."

Rexee' popped Ace crisply on the shoulder with a closed fist. She threw her weight into it – her punch had snap.

"Zip it, Timothy," she hissed, "you weren't there. That's exactly what that boy needs."

Ace favored his aching arm as they watched the door on Effie's house shut behind the new couple.

There was a moment of silence.

"Food?" Hack asked again.

"Definitely," Ace answered.

"Yeah," Rexee' added, "I'll try that."

Book nodded, "It's just what this bunch needs."

(<o>)/(5.13)\(<o>)

Skate sat down with old man Sutter, collecting stories.

"You stink," Sutter said.

"Yeah, sorry, I was over on campus watching the protest. The students had the street closed, and a barricade. The National Guard showed up and lobbed tear gas into the street."

Skate took a long drink of beer.

"I saw it on the TV," Sutter said, "looked like a bunch of pissants."

"Yeah, well," Skate wanted to finish, "from where I stood, there was only one way back, and that was across the street. I had to run through a plume of smoke, and it sprayed my leg like a skunk."

"Yeah?" Sutter was barely interested.

"Yeah."

They sat awhile. Calvin brought them a round.

"You in the military?" Skate ventured.

"Twice."

"No kidding."

"Yeah."

(<o>).[].(<o>)

Bill Sutter was a product of his generation. Born in the twenties, raised in the thirties, slogging across France in the forties. A rifleman in the infantry, he had come ashore in one of the early waves at Omaha Beach. Then, for the next year he walked eastward, across France, through Belgium, and into Germany. He and his platoon had been shot at, and had shot back plenty. He'd learned how to find landmines with his bayonet, and how to throw a hand grenade, and how to tie a tourniquet.

One day, while probing through a field looking for mines, his unit was attacked by Germans crawling up a road ditch. He threw a grenade into the ditch, but a quick-witted German tossed it back. It landed ten feet to his right, close enough to kill him for sure. But it landed directly on a land mine, both grenade and mine detonating together.

The force of the mine explosion, aimed primarily upward as they were, lifted the force of the grenade explosion, so mostly it went over him.

That was his explanation for it, anyway.

"I was almost dead twice," he said, "at the same time."

So rather than being killed, twice, he got away with an eight inch shard of hot metal embedded in his thigh. This is where the tourniquet skills came in handy.

He laid there for a long while as the battle raged, until the Germans were forced to withdraw, and a path through the landmines was cleared, and the medics could come and lug him away.

He got eighteen weeks of medical leave for that. Then he rejoined his unit in Belgium, and continued walking (now with a slight limp), the rest of the way into Germany.

(<o>).[].(<o>)

After the war, Bill Sutter kicked around like many of his generation, trying to find work and get back to normal. He took advantage of the GI Bill, and went to college, eventually ending up in medical school. By the early 1950s he was in his thirties, a veteran and a doctor, and working in the University hospital. He bought a Harley like fringe lunatics did in those days – not a badge, or a statement either – an edge wish. War changes people.

"Things were pretty good," he said, "but somewhere in the fifties I took a left turn."

Bill got involved in Socialist politics, which was not that unusual in Minnesota at that time. While the country at large was mostly dreading the Communist menace, there was a long standing left-leaning tradition in the upper Midwest, going back to the days of labor strife and farm unrest in the Great Depression.

One thing led to another, and in 1959 Bill Sutter found himself in Cuba, fighting with Castro, trying to bring down the Batista regime.

These were muddled political times. Many in America viewed the Castro forces as freedom fighters in a war against oppression and poverty, much in the tradition of the American Revolution whose bicentennial was about to be celebrated.

Others viewed Batista as a stabilizing force in the region and a good ally to America. A friend to business, and to mobsters, Cuba was a playground for the rich, with a seemingly happy peasant native culture filled with song and dance.

Later it was clear that American interests supported both sides of the fight. This was when American hegemony* began to finally unravel. The 'beat poets' started it, but the 'cubanistas' drove the final, unrecoverable wedge.

Skate was hearing this biography in muddled political times – while Vietnamese peasants armed themselves against American soldiers, thinking of themselves as freedom fighters.

(<o>).[].(<o>)

"You KNOW Castro?" Skate said.

"Yeah, well I was a Major, and he was Generalissimo of the armed forces. We ate at the same table, let's say."

Skate was leaning forward, "So what's HE like?"

"A bastard and a ruthless genius. He knew what he wanted, and he knew what he was doing the whole time. That's why so many of us left. It pretty soon came clear he was working everybody against the middle. So when he went commie and linked up with Russia, some people were surprised but nobody was shocked."

"The nuns said that was his big betrayal, that he double-crossed everybody with that – even the church."

"Well, yeah maybe the U.S. State Department was shocked. But I guarantee you the CIA was not. Besides, I was with him on many a Sunday, and I never saw him go to church."

Skate whistled, "You know, that undoes about half of everything I learned in Catholic School."

"Well," Sutter said, "I can't help that."

(<o>).[].(<o>)

Bill Sutter moved back to Minnesota and got his old job at the hospital. His days of politics were over. His days of drinking began. By the time the guys knew him, he was fifty-five years old but he looked seventy. His role in the hospital had been reduced over the years until finally he was little more than a curmudgeon* to the medical students and a ghost in the hallways.

A short time later there was a story in the paper about the hospital staff threatening to strike over a wage increase. Skate asked him about it.

"You care?"

"Not really," Sutter said, "I can barely drink what I make now."

(<o>)/(5.18)\(<o>)

Skate stepped away from the shed corner and hopped backwards into the nightshade. He froze in a crouch and listened, slowly swiveling his head. Hack was off to the left, a couple of lots down, waiting for Book to lumber past: not a problem. Ace was closer, probably in that spot he liked between old man Lawson's house and Ricky Pawlowski's garage. He would be looking forward, probably, also not a problem. Peter Pawlowski, Ricky's little brother, was on one knee with a plastic rifle, trying to peer around the corner of Taranto's house, but his toy plastic combat helmet was bumping against the wall and pushing down into his eyes.

Skate had seen him there from two houses down, and had worked his way through the deep end of the backyards to a point directly behind the kid. Peter was looking towards the street, hoping someone would come along that he could shoot, and hoping nobody would come up behind him. He was about to be disappointed. He was a good kid, but not that good at guns.

Skate was crouching in the shade of a tree that stood between him and Peter, the shade caused by the streetlight at the corner in front of Peter. This was a trick he'd recently taught himself; a bold trick actually, as it was a variant of "hiding in plain sight", using a natural camouflage and lurking without cover. On a dark night, if you stayed low in the shade, you were practically invisible. If you were quiet you could walk up the shade like a tightrope, and somebody like Peter, with the streetlight in his eyes, would never see you. The only thing to go wrong was if you made a stray sound.

Skate inched forward in the sanctuary of his shade until he reached the base of the sheltering tree. Then he aimed his wooden carbine at Peter, paused to savor the hit, and yelled "Pow" into Peter's direction.

Peter spun around, startled, and Skate said "you're dead, kid."

"Pow," Hack said, a foot from Skate's ear.

"You too."

It was Skate's turn to be startled. Hack had moved up on him, silent as he could do, from the left. Skate slumped, defeated, and looking to his RIGHT, he saw the blunder. The moon was up in that direction, and his shade trick was undone by the silhouette from the side.

He wouldn't make that mistake again.

(<o>).[].(<o>)

We played 'guns'. We played all the time. From the moment that hide-and-seek got tired, in about second grade, we were at it. After school we played 'ball', whatever was in season: baseball or football mostly. After dinner, as the light dimmed, we played 'guns'.

The rules changed from time to time, usually as Ace thought of some new wrinkle, like capturing a flag, or what not. But the game was simple: we ran around the neighborhood with toy weapons and shot each other. It was the best game.

We were all about the same age, and lived within a few doors of each other. There were several other kids our age, and many more just a few years younger. It was that kind of neighborhood: young families in cramped post-war housing. The adults, probably to preserve any hope of sanity, would "send the kids out to play" after dinner. Every day. And away we'd go, usually to play guns.

Sometimes we chose teams. Sometimes it was every man for himself. Ace was fairly average at guns, Hack was a lot better. Book was hopeless. Patrick was okay. I was the best.

(<o>).[].(<o>)

Skate had flanked Ace. They had both come around to the back of Lawson's from opposite directions and surprised each other. Ace ducked back to the corner and waited in a crouch. Skate, meanwhile, had bolted AWAY from the house, across one yard and sharply into the alley. Then, as Ace collected himself and started forward to hunt him, Skate doubled back down the alley and waited for Ace to cross his line of sight. Ace was doing well, for him, working the cover and staying in the dark, but Skate saw him pass. Then, once Ace had gone by, Skate moved into position behind him, and started a hunt of his own.

From there it was pretty easy. Ace had assumed Skate made a simple retreat. He worked his way into an advantageous spot, and positioned himself, quite cleverly, under the bower of a low-slung fir. Skate would not have found him, except he watched him choose the spot from his vantage point, behind. Ace was waiting there, sniper-like, when Skate moved up behind him. Skate got on his belly and inched into position, but there was no clear shot, even from just a few feet away: Ace was that well hidden.

Finally, Skate worked himself within a few feet, keeping himself under cover all the while.

It was funny, actually.

Ace was prone, with all his attention focused forward, looking and listening with his every fiber. Skate was prone too, just a little behind him, and to the side, and out of respect for the tenuousness of the shot, even at close range, given Ace's good cover, fired three times.

"Pow," he said, "Pow, Pow."

Ace reacted like he'd touched a live electric wire. His body jolted and flinched, much as though he'd been shot.

"Christ," he said.

"You're dead," Skate replied.

(<o>)/(5.21)\(<o>)

Oteye and the Klang were halfway through a high-speed set, and the dance floor was packed. Skate was standing up front with Hack, watching the band work their instruments. They were mostly white suburban guys, but the bass player was a thin black guy with amazingly long thin fingers – Willie something. He was all over at bass.

In those days, most bass players played with two or three fingers strumming like they were walking their fingers over the strings. This guy sometimes played bass with a guitar pick, like Paul McCartney, the first time they'd seen that for themselves.*

After a while, Skate circled the floor towards the back of the chapel/gymnasium. They sold cold soft drinks in back for a dime, and with all the people and the warmish night, it was starting to get pretty hot on the dance floor.

Skate liked to dance, and there were plenty of dances where he'd spent the entire time on the floor. Hack and Ace hated to dance, and they routinely spent the entire night up close, directly in front of the speakers, listening to the music, feeling it in their chests, and watching the musicianship of the band.

Skate got his ten cent soft drink in a soft paper Dixie cup. Then he wandered back along the side of the dance floor to watch a group of black kids dance.

Whether it was racially centered or not, the white kids generally learned to dance by watching the black kids. The black kids had established the smooth arm-waving, foot sliding, head-nodding style that everyone was now doing.

Except this black group – they were doing a new thing – like stepping in place – except with an uncanny off-the-beat rhythm. They seemed to be doing everything late, behind the song. It almost looked bad, except they were consistent with it, and they were all doing it together.

It was a fascinating scene to Skate. The entire floor moving with the music, except this little group moving against it. Skate tried to catch their rhythm by jigging a little bit in place, off to the side by himself, but you could only do that for a minute or two before calling undue attention to yourself.

He resolved to talk to them about it during the next break, which was something he was capable of doing. Skate was an earnest seeker and didn't mind talking to strangers as a junior in high school, if the situation seemed to call for it. Besides, he was well enough known on the dance floor, and one or two of the black group were familiar to him, by sight at least. Meanwhile, he watched, which was how one generally learned to dance a new move. There was no way to ask for a lesson and remain cool in high school, it did not work that way.

Out there near the black group was Gus Garrison, who Skate noticed was already master of the new style. Just like Garrison, Skate thought smiling, anything physical was just too easy for him, from running to throwing to archery. Garrison could pull it off without trying, and there he was again, honking on the new moves that Skate couldn't even quite see yet. He laughed in Garrison's direction, and got a small wave back, and headed back to the drink stand for a ten cent refill.

"You think something's funny?" a voice snarled in his ear.

Skate wheeled around, startled. It was a tough looking customer in a leather coat, with two thugs behind him. The guy wore a Bogart-style fedora, an odd affectation in those days, and he had a chiseled Italian looking face, with a sharp nose and thick brows. Skate didn't know him or his pals, but had seen them earlier from across the floor. They looked like guys to stay away from, and he had.

"I saw you out there, laughing at my friend Gus."

The guy was standing uncomfortably close, and Skate instantly saw this could quickly turn bad.

"I know Gus, he's a pal of mine."

The guy grabbed a fistful of the fabric of Skates shirt, high on his shoulder.

Skate stood his ground, afraid to flinch – his back gave him a little pain just then.

The guy was strong.

They were the same height, eye to eye. The guy was lifting Skate off is feet. "You need to come outside with us, and we'll see what's so funny."

Just then the band stopped playing. The dancers started to clear the floor. The guy pulled him forward by his shirt.

Skate was in sports, and in good condition. He could run a mile in under five minutes.

But he was fifteen years old, and this guy appeared to be in his twenties.

Skate moved his feet apart, ready to try and break free and run if he could. The dancers were clearing the floor, many headed towards the back where Skate's drama was playing out.

"Go and ask him," Skate croaked, his throat suddenly tight.

His back had a sharp twinge of pain as he arched against the guy's grip. Skate could see Garrison, still in the middle of the dance floor – not heading this way, just lingering on the floor.

Skate knew he was free of this – if only Garrison would just walk up and say something. He expected that to happen, and in the interest of trying to maintain a little internal dignity, was in the process of planning a 'move'. Not to fight back, which could turn out badly for him – but to break free at the right moment to make it through.

His plan, so far as he had one, was to wait until Garrison was walking their way, and then throw his arm over the guy's wrist and drop to his knees, breaking the grip. The hope was to be free of the guy's grip for the few seconds it would take to back away, and let the scene sort itself out.

In a vacuum, it was the sort of defiance that could lead to a swift beating. But in this situation, it might just allow him to retain a shred of self-respect and back away at the same time with his skin intact.

Just then, "Salt" Peters ran up, breathless. Peters had been around since grade school, and he was now one of the tough-guy hangers-on that mostly just loitered out at the park smoking cigarettes.

"There's a bunch of niggers in the parking lot, looking for a fight. Tell all the white guys you know."

Peters ran off.

The guy let go of Skate's shirt and turned to his pals.

"Let's go," he said, and turned towards the exit. He'd apparently forgotten about Skate.

When the guy moved away, Skate could see Gus Garrison was now standing just a few feet back. Their eyes met.

"Friends of yours?" Skate asked.

Gus shrugged.

"I'd stay away from them, if I was you," Garrison said, "they're rough."

(<o>).[].(<o>)

The fight in the parking lot did not come off.

None of the guys had gone out to participate, and neither, it turned out, did Garrison. Book, who lived across from the school, and never went to the dances, reported there were police cars in the parking lot before the band stopped playing. The small crowd that went out to fight or watch were ordered off the school's property and told to go home. The dance was cancelled at that point, and the Klang never played their last set.

Garrison's tough guy friends never came around again. Skate never saw them after that.

(<o>)/(5.23)\(<o>)

When walking over to the dump you pass a trestle on the left. You scramble up between the footings, coming out below the tracks, then crawl another twenty feet until you find the massive drainage pipe. By hunching down a little bit you walk right under northbound tracks and find yourself inside the dump. It beats the climb you'd have to make to get across the razor wire fence.

Utopia to Ace. He makes this journey twice a week.

"Behold the treasure at your feet," he says.

The dump is like a playground to the boy. He knows it like the inside of his gloves. He loves it like a Heron loves to fish.

"I never cease to wonder at the stuff that other people choose to throw away," he says, "What fools these mortals be."*

The Web became a kind of mad museum for the stuff that Ace brought home, a funky landfill of gimcrack and dreck, collected with an eye to the surreal.

… a yellow English teapot with a matching doily; a heavy iron kettle and a set of blacksmith's tongs; toy soldiers in a metal western fort; a greasy stovetop caddy, for spoons, shaped like a human tongue; some matchbox cars; some cook books; some blankets from an army surplus store; the lenses from a telescope; a fishing tackle box with lures; a set of Barbra Streisand disks (he took those back); a carton full of heavy cardboard tubes; a jewelers loop; the works from a grandfathers clock; the hubcaps from a Cadillac (for ashtrays of the finest kind); a gasmask; fourteen hockey pucks; some picture frames; a yard-tall cardboard Eiffel Tower with a plaster frog inside; a tinwork model of a wacky looking service station; a box of flimsy leather working gloves; a rusty railroad switch lock; no end of bookshelf parts; a set of folding chairs; a shopping cart (we used this to haul stuff).

And Ace was the curator of this mass. A man with eyes designed for art, he crafted spectacles for us, with Barbie dolls embracing robot cars, and Christmas dioramas filled with leering sheep. He hung a junk art gallery one time, and mounted pegboard for the kitchen pots to hang.

He took us to this place time after time, to scavenge what was there and bring it home. It was our ritual. We saw a lot of stuff and hauled it home.

(<o>)/(5.24)\(<o>)

```
diaria -- 5.0 -- 9/15/76 -- winston-salem

tragedy is a literary concept and, in the literary
business, is a technical term. it comes down from the
greeks, or before, and denotes a situation where an
exalted person falls from greatness into oblivion or
obscurity. the greeks had no drama that featured the
common man, and the tragic tradition has followed that
lead. shakespeare, for instance, wrote great tragedies
```

like hamlet and macbeth, but always about kings or
princes who had it all and then blew it.

so stories like "death of a salesman"* or "the glass
menagerie"* are not technically tragic, no matter how
they seem, because the characters are not exalted to
begin with. there are those who argue that these ARE
tragic because the characters labor under delusions of
grandeur, and when these delusions are shattered it is
true tragedy, but this is a minority position.

this sort of literary distinction leads one to question
whether the term "tragedy" is useful anymore. for
instance, in the bicentennial decade the story of nixon
qualifies as tragedy while the story of remo does not.
this makes little sense to me, but that too may turn out
to be a minority position.

a lot of people have come out in defense of nixon. after
all, they say, he didn't do anything much more serious
than petty larceny and still he got crucified -- plenty
of others did the same or worse and it was just business
as usual. nixon, by this logic, got a raw deal.

the story of nixon reminds some others of the story of
al capone, aka scarface, the mobster and racketeer of
prohibition era chicago. this guy was responsible for
dozens of murders and tons of lesser crimes from
smuggling to prostitution to gambling -- none of which
he was ever convicted for. capone went to prison for
income tax evasion because he couldn't account for his
lifestyle in terms of the income he reported -- he never
paid for his real crimes. this guy, by the way, was an
extremely powerful person, royalty after a fashion, so
when he died of syphilis in obscurity (if not poverty),
his life's story might qualify as tragic, at least under
some interpretations.

nixon, on the other hand, went under on account of some
petty bribery, questionable campaign practices, and
lying about it afterwards -- little of which was ever
proven, and all of which he was pardoned for later (by
ford, his hand-picked replacement for president). and
none of which, to the thinking of many, were his real
crimes. nixon was elected in 1968 after promising to end
the war, nixon was RE-elected in 1972 with the same
promise: to end the war. in the meantime a total of
about 55,000 guys were killed, hundreds of thousands
more were wounded, and nearly everyone was screwed over
by it somehow. nixon lied, and it cost a lot of people -
- that was his real crime. the one he never paid for,
and never could.

so is nixon a tragic figure? you tell me. after all, he
got away with it; he never has, and never will, and

never could, pay his debt to society. he was exalted i guess, but he only fell as far as retirement to his plush ocean-side estate and then he died.

(<o>)/(5.25)\(<o>)

Skate was sitting on the Web house porch pretending to read on a cloudy Saturday morning, just days after the homicide event. He took this position, hoping to catch sight of Effie. He had not seen her since the day of sex, which ended only yesterday but seemed longer ago.

He did not know her last name, he realized, and did not have her phone number. So he was reduced to surreptitious surveillance in hopes of spotting her. So far, no luck.

The sex had been very, very satisfying, and the sleep afterwards rehumanizing. They played naked in the afternoon for hours. Then as darkness fell, they had fallen too, into a total coma, both of them catching up on missed nights sleep.

The next morning they romped again, casually and languorously. Then Skate went off to change his clothes, still the ones he was wearing when they broke down Rexee's door on Wednesday, to work his Friday shift at the library

Effie planned to drive home to stay with her family that day.

"I'll be back in a few hours," Skate said, "I'll look for you."

"I should be going before then," she said, "assuming Mary brought my car back."

"Okay," he kissed her, "I'll look for you anyway."

"A couple of days," she grimaced, "is about all I can stay at home. I'll be back soon."

He looked at his watch and pulled on his pants.

"I've really got to go," he said, "it's bad when I'm late to work, and I do that too often as it is."

"Later, lover," she smiled at him, "I'll look for you, too."

(<o>).[].(<o>)

That was Friday.

Skate pulled his shift at the Library, and when he got home her lights were out and her bug was gone.

He tried to get back to "normal" – reading Shakespeare and working on things like the garden and the yard. But all he wanted to do was hang out with Effie, and so he kept a lonely vigil through the weekend, hoping she would come back.

But the weekend passed, then Monday and Tuesday too. No sign of her.

He tried to read, but his eyes glazed over. He tried to write – same thing.

Rexee' moved back in – ensconced in her lair.

Everybody else worked on Friday, and things were settling back to normal.

Ace organized a trip to the dump, but there was little worth salvaging.

(<o>).[].(<o>)

They did the usual weekend things.

Ace herded them all (Book, Hack, and Skate, waiting to hear from Effie) to an 'art opening,' on Saturday evening, but there was little enthusiasm. Rexee' went along, sticking to the group, as she sometimes did. But the art was bland and the food table was below average. There was free wine, though, and they all helped themselves. Still, there was a pall over events, and they found themselves back at the Web house by mid-evening.

"Doogan's?" Hack asked.

And they went for a while.

They were sitting in silence, with the Saturday crowd jostling around them, and Rexee' broached the topic.

"Do we need to talk about it?" she asked.

Nobody spoke, until Book filled the silence.

"I don't think it's a 'we' thing so much. I think it might be a 'some of us' and 'some of you' thing."

Hack was nodding in agreement.

Book went on, "I wasn't there, and I only want to talk about it as much as 'some of you' do. That's you, Hack, and Skate."

"Same goes for me," Ace added, "I don't want to NOT talk about it, because I'll talk about anything that helps. But I don't want to be pushing to talk about something if it doesn't need to be talked about."

Ace looked at Book, "Am I getting this right? They were there, we were not, and I'm afraid the long silence is just because of that. They need to talk, and we're holding something up."

Ace looked around the table.

"You get me?"

Rexee' had not been talking, but she took this opportunity.

"I don't know about anything, and I don't want to talk necessarily, but I know the thing that's bad is secrets, and that they are what can poison things. I read a statistic the other day, that 90% of marriages that suffer the death of a child end up in divorce."

She took a drink.

"Right now, I can't stand the idea of divorce. So I want to talk about things as much as they need to be. You guys mopped the blood off my floor, and I can't think about how to thank you. I can't imagine why anybody would do that."

"Sorry about that," Skate offered meekly.

"You're exempt," Hack said pointedly, "I was checking the angles, and when Delmar wasted the dude, the shots cleared your head by about a foot."

"I suppose that's right," Skate said, "although I hadn't thought of it. I was still on the ground."

He laughed,

"Laying there, nursing my arm, where you stepped on me, you bastard."

"I felt that," Hack said, "I almost tripped. That was you?"

"Hell yes, who punched in the door? Not you. I was the instrument of that. Flat on my face. No skill, no grace, but apparently I can plow through a door when I feel the need."

He pointed to his bruised shoulder, "Hockey practice."

Ace said, "You should have worn a helmet more."

Skate got up from his seat, and turned his back to the table. Lifting his shirt sleeve, he displayed a round black bruise on the back of his arm, covering his triceps.

"I'm lucky you didn't break my arm," he laughed, "you bastard."

"When the door blew in," Rexee' said, "it was like the light of heaven. He was big, and he had me pinned, with a grip on my throat. And he had murder in his eye. I was about to black out, and I'm SURE he was going to kill me."

She looked around the table.

"I was at his mercy, and there was no mercy there. I've never been so helpless. I don't like to think about it." She took another pull on her beer, "And then the door blew open."

"That was me," Skate said, "flat out, head first, avon calling."

Rexee winced, "I didn't actually see you at first, he had my throat. The first thing I saw was light, then I saw dark, I think, and the next thing I saw was Hack."

Hack was shaking his head.

"I never hope to see anything like that again," he said, "that guy had you by the neck, and all I could think was to break his grip."

"I saw that, from the floor," Skate said, "a sharp left and a hard right, and he was on his back, sucking for air."

"Then there was a shadow in the doorway," Skate added, "and I don't actually remember everything after that."

"Oh, I wish!" Rexee' said, "I have been playing this back and forth like film through a movie projector. I see this over and over when I close my eyes. Suddenly Delmar is amongst us, and I cannot figure it anymore. He takes us out of our world."

"I know what you're talking about, a little bit," Hack said, looking at Rexee', "I was looking at you when the shots were fired, and by the time I got around, the one guy was already dead, and the other guy had his rifle, Delmar had his rifle pointed at my face – I could tell he was glazed over. He was one trigger-pull away from burping all of us."

"Then Skate gave him a cigarette," Rexee' said, "and that cooled him out. I'd almost forgotten that."

"I did?"

"Yes, you goof," Hack said, "and you lit one yourself, from Rexee's pack."

"You owe me a cigarette," Rexee' laughed, "you bastard."

"Two I think," Book interjected, "according to my calculations, he owes you two."

(<o>).[].(<o>)

They were in the midst of a surging Saturday night crowd, with traffic in and out the door, and music blaring on the jukebox. They had a table in the corner to themselves amongst the madding crowd: Ace, Book, Skate, Hack, and Rexee'.

They were talking about the 'event' and Skate was nicely wired, with a half a head of beer, and his skin on alert as he re-lived it. He could remember the whole event like a filmstrip, a series of frozen images, and the sound of bullets slapping into prone flesh were the thing that haunted him.

"Helpless," he said, "that's a word I keep hearing myself say in my head."

He looked around the table. They all seemed to be looking past him.

"I blew through that door like a Sherman Tank. I feel good about that. And Hack stomped over me to the rescue, like the Russian Army through Lithuania. That's good too. But, as I lay there, I could see Delmar, and there was a moment where I could have done something. But I was frozen. I could have said 'NO', but that never came out. Nothing did."

He took a drink.

"I could have maybe knocked his knees out from under him, or done something, but it was over before I knew it. And I did nothing."

A soft hand landed on his shoulder, and a soft voice said, "Can I say something?"

Skate, reliving the event, jumped from his chair into a tortured crouch. Then he lost his balance trying to turn, and fell awkwardly to one knee beside his chair.

"Easy, boy," Hack said, helping him up, "you got the heebee jeebees."

Skate, pulling on Hack's grip realized Effie was behind his chair.

He was overwhelmed by regret and relief, and did his best to recover.

"Oh, hey, I've been looking for you."

Skate realized he was panting, and tried to stop.

"Sorry," Effie said, "this is the wrong time to sneak up on people, I'm realizing."

Hack pulled a chair over, and Effie sat down between him and Skate.

Ace did his thing.

"I'm Ace," he shook her hand, "and this is Book, Hack, and Rexee'. Skate, I'm thinking, you know already."

"Hi everybody," Effie said, smiling stiffly.

"Everybody," Skate said, "this is Effie. Effie, this is everybody."

"I live across the street," Effie said, "from your famous hippie house."

"Hippies!", Rexee' snorted, "these guys are hippies like, like, Moose are Reindeer."

"My," Book said, "that's almost a regional reference."

"If we were in Lapland," Ace countered.

"Like Camels are Horses," Rexee' answered, "like foul are fair, like Cranes are Herons, like butch fag dikes are ballerinas."

Rexee' was out of breath.

"Like, hey," Effie said, "horses eat it."

"Fuck a red duck," was all Rexee' could think of.

Hack looked at Book and started to laugh. Ace joined. Skate was laughing too.

When everything is stupid, all you can do is laugh.

"So," Rexee' said, "are we talking now?"

"Yes," Effie said, "I think so."

(<o>).[].(<o>)

"I don't know what's right," Effie said, "but I took a class, and the people, Viet Nam veterans, who don't do well, are the people who are closed off and can't talk about things."

She looked around the table.

"I don't know if that applies, but I think it might. It's the helplessness, I guess"

"It's a college class," Ace said, "how could you go wrong?"

"Any number of ways," Rexee' said, "you bastard. You work your factory jobs and look down your anti-intellectual nose at college education."

"Well," Ace sniffed, "it's not for everyone, is it?"

"Oh, wait a minute," Skate said, defensively, "what are you picking on her for?"

"Besides," Book added, "you took your share of college classes."

"Ticket punching," Ace said, "that's what college is. Going through the motions until you get your grade, then more motions until you get your degree. Pay your money, do your time, and get you ticket punched. Voila!"

"You're the most ridiculously cynical bastard I've ever met," Rexee' said.

"Ridiculously, religiously cynical," Book added.

"Deliciously, devoutly cynical," Skate said, "with whirling fervor."

"Dominican," Hack nodded.

"Wait a minute!" Ace said, "why are you all picking on me?"

"You make yourself a target," Effie answered, "and you get your throat pinched."

(<o>).[].(<o>)

They talked it over.

They all knew Delmar in one way or another, and all had a tale to tell.

None of them had a story to tell about the dead man, not even Rexee'. He was dead, that was all.

Rexee' then Hack, and then Skate, told what happened that day, as they saw it and remembered it.

It became clear that Rexee' did not remember much. The night before, yes, drinking and bringing the guy home with her. But the morning of the event, not so much.

She felt guilty, though, it was plain. She could have done something different. She could have avoided the whole thing. And having friends who would help clean up the gory mess, made it better and worse at the same time.

"I'm stuck on how to repay you guys, for saving me, and sticking with me," she said, "I feel like I owe a debt. I don't know what to say."

Book cleared his throat, "I am reminded of the day my little brother was born. My mother had terrible labor, and suffered through a terrible birth. After a while we all got to go in and see her. My father was almost crying, looking at his poor battered wife, my mom, and he just reached out to hold her hand, with tears in his eyes, and he said 'Thank You'. I felt like crying myself."

Book stopped, took off his glasses, and wiped his eyes.

"'I know' was all my Mom said."

There was a moment of silence, then Hack looked at Rexee'.

"We know," he said.

Rexee', the toughest chick they knew, started to cry. They had never seen that.

"I know," she sobbed, "I know you know."

115

(<o>).[].(<o>)

Hack draped his arm over Rexee's shoulder until things settled down,

He had an action tale to tell: scream, run, kick, bam, bam. But his back was turned when the fatal shots were fired. He missed that completely.

Skate had it all in mind, though, like a slide show he could rerun with perfect clarity over and over, forward or backward, up to a point. He told it in detail, and in Technicolor, as well as he could.

(<o>).[].(<o>)

Later they were chatting amongst themselves.

"You're back?" Skate asked Effie, "I've been watching your door."

"I'm in the same place you are," she said, "processing a murder."

He nodded.

"I went home, planning for a couple of days. But there was no comfort in it, that's all."

"Home and hearth." he answered, "I should have done the same, but it never came to me. I guess the Web house is my home now. That's where I go when times are tough."

She touched his arm.

"We should go home together when you're done here."

Blood rushed into his chest, and his groin, and he felt a swell of emotion.

"We need to stay, though," he looked around the table, "until this is worked out some more."

She nodded and sipped her drink.

"It's a process," she said quietly so Ace wouldn't hear, "we all need to work through it."

"Is that what they said in class," Skate said.

"Yep," she answered.

(<o>).[].(<o>)

They sat together and told their tales.

Then Calvin cleared out the bar and sent them away. They walked together down the street, aiming for the Web house.

Ace and Book went in. Book went to bed, and Ace left again for Annie's. Rexee' retreated to her garage, with Hack as protector until his taxi shift started. Skate and Effie went across the street to her place.

(<o>).[].(<o>)

Sunday morning, early – Skate and Effie lay in bed.

"What 'chew feel like doing today," she asked him.

"I was thinking of taking a ride," he said, stroking her thigh, "want to come?

"Didn't we just do that?"

Skate laughed, "Yes, we did, I meant a motorcycle ride."

"Sounds fun," she said, "where to? Anyplace special?"

"I was thinking New Orleans," he studied her reaction, "or maybe L.A."

She didn't hesitate.

"Yeah, okay," she said, "Let's go. Let's just pack and go."

"That's what I was thinking. You got any money?"

"Maybe a hundred dollars."

"Me too. That'll do," he said, "Let's see how far it takes us."

(<o>).[].(<o>)

Skate crept into the Web house, early morning, and was packing clothes into a small sack. Book came by, on his way to the bathroom, poked his head in, and saw what Skate was doing. His eyes narrowed.

"Going somewhere?" Book asked.

"Taking a ride," Skate shrugged, "with Effie."

"Back soon?"

"Couple weeks, couple months. I dunno," Skate answered, "probably not forever."

"Well, okay," Book said, "I'll tell everyone."

Book held up his hand, like a traffic cop.

"You remember what your parents used to say, 'write if you get work'."

"Don't worry Book, I'm coming back."

"Well, don't forget to write…."

"You know it."

Book turned to face him, "I don't just mean 'drop us a card from time to time'"

Then Book went to the bathroom, and Skate went to get Effie.

(<o>)/(Endnotes 5.36)\(<o>)

35. Magazine, Mad. American humor magazine, founded 1952.

36. Hegemony -- leadership of one nation over others.

37. Johnson, Samuel, (b. 1709 - d. 1784) an English literary figure, author of a famous dictionary -- 'curmudgeon' is believed to be a 'made up' word, coined by Sam Johnson to describe himself -- a recursive definition.

38. Shakespeare, William (b. April 23, 1564 - d. April 23, 1616) a famous English playwright.

39. Arthur Miller, Death of a Salesman: a play in two acts (New York: Dramatists Play Service, 1952).

40. Tennessee Williams, The Glass Menagerie: a play in two acts (New York: Dramatists Play Service, 1948).

Chapter 6

Skate met Effie on the sidewalk. She carried a suitcase.

Skate laughed.

"Here's the thing," he said, "on a motorcycle you want soft bags. That way we can pack things so you can lay against them. There's room for one backpack on the seat, and one over the back fender. That's it."

"Your bag is on the seat," she said, "why not just put my case on the fender, and let's go."

Skate sized it up, and saw it might work. Besides which he wanted to move on down the road – without loss of energy or enthusiasm, or too much thought, either.

"Yeah, okay," he said, "let's do it."

"But next time, young lady," he wagged his finger in mock remonstration, "you bring a SOFT bag. None of this tourister luggage stuff."

She played along.

"Luggage never again," she said, "down with duffel from now on."

(<o>).[].(<o>)

They were on the road and Skate immediately felt the thrill of it.

Moving through the country, no real plans, no destination, and what happened – it happened. He was living the dream and he knew it – a tankful of gas, straddling a humming scoot, an open road in front of him, a pretty girl on the seat behind him, a couple hundred dollars in hand, and nowhere to be and nothing that needed doing – except do what they were doing – and move it on down the road.

(<o>).[].(<o>)

They made their way across on I-94 to St. Paul and got on Highway 61 heading south down the river. Skate had briefly thought about fleeing to the northwoods, as he tended to do, but decided to veer away, like Monty Python,* to the south and "something completely different."

Within an hour they were following the river down through Red Wing, site of the shoe factory and the famous boy's reformatory they'd all been taught to fear as children.* After that, they were free, clear, and on their way.

They passed through Wabasha and Winona, then stopped for a break in La Crescent after three hours of riding. They were in a gas station near a rest area that overlooked the locks. Boats were being raised and lowered, according to their aims.

Effie looked tired.

"How you doing" Skate asked, "holding up?"

Effie shrugged and smiled serenely.

"I'm doing okay," she said, "doing what I want to do, and being where I want to be."

She gazed into his face.

"How 'bout you? Having second thoughts?"

"My life is a series of second thoughts," Skate answered, "but I'm on the road, and loving it. I'm where I want to be, too, and I'm glad you're here with me."

She nodded.

"We're at a choice point," he said, "we can go west from here on the interstate, and head across the great plains towards the mountains. Or we can go south, down the Mississippi, and aim towards New Orleans."

"What do you think?" she asked.

"There's lots of factors," he said, "south is a much more interesting ride and we get to New Orleans in just a couple days. West is the historic American choice, and the mountains are awesome, but it's a lot of flat emptiness between here and there, and a lot longer trip to see the historic Pacific Ocean."

He shrugged.

"Either way we can end up in California if we try hard enough. It's just a lot of miles and a lot of time, and a lot of wearing dirty laundry in between.

"Stop," she said, "you make it sound too romantic."

Skate laughed.

"I've done it both ways," he said, "but it's 1974 now. Maybe this means I do it different this time."

"You didn't mention East," Effie said, "what about the historic Atlantic. I'm pretty sure it's closer than California."

"East!" he blurted, "back east? Never thought of it, don't see it."

She looked at him for a moment.

"Then," she said, "the river's the thing. That's what I say."

"God said to Abraham, kill me a son," Skate recited.

She smiled, "Abe said, Man, you must be putting me on."*

He nodded and smiled. She knew her lines. This was a good sign. They gassed up and headed down highway 61, towards whatever might actually be there.

(<o>).[].(<o>)

"Shit," he said, and shut off the engine.

"What's the matter?" she asked.

"It's a metal mesh bridge," he said, "I hate these things."

They were about 250 miles out of Minneapolis, following Highway 61, way east of the Mississippi and about to cross the Wisconsin River into Boscobel, Wisconsin. With gas stops and traffic they had been riding for about 6 hours.

"The problem is, what?" she asked

"These bridges," he answered, "built during the depression, are made of metal mesh. The bike slips and slides across them, and there's this feeling."

"What feeling?"

"Like your slip-sliding across a cheese grater," he grimaced, "I have nightmares about these things."

"You start across," he went on, "and the bike starts to fishtail, and you get this sense that you're barely holding it upright. There's a weird mush in the handlebars, like you're on icy rice."

He shrugged.

"I've never fallen down on one of these, but it always feels like I'm about to."

"You can do it," she clapped him on the shoulder, "just wait for a minute, and then we'll take it across real slow."

119

"Yeah," Skate said, "we make it through this and find something to eat, yes?"

"I'm starving, and there's food over there, I bet. Let's move."

(<o>).[].(<o>)

"That WAS weird," she said, on the other side, "Back on this end of the motorcycle there is this feeling like when the car has no traction on slush. I felt like we might go sideways and fall over at any point."

"Yeah," Skate said, "I haven't figured out how to take those yet. Fast is scary, slow is scary. I opt for slow. You okay?"

"I knew you could do it," she said, "but I'm ready to eat for sure. Like maybe we sight see and rest up after we eat. But we eat first – immediately would not be too soon"

"It's been a good day," she went on, "and maybe this was the bridge to tomorrow."

(<o>).[].(<o>)

Boscobel Wisconsin, birthplace of the Gideon Society and home to the Unique Café. They had burgers and pie, and then walked arm-in-arm up and down Main Street after, to digest.

"I guess we're on the road," she said.

"Looks like it," he nodded, "the stuff of movies and short stories."

"Question is," he added, "do we press on into the darkness, or find a place to hunker down for the day?"

"I'm not in a rush to get somewhere," she answered, "and we're both running on adrenaline and enthusiasm. Maybe this is a good place to stop and take stock."

"You mean," he smiled, "to pose the existential questions?"

They sat on a bench in the late afternoon sun in a little park by City Hall. There were railroad tracks to their right and a crummy little tavern across the street.

"What day is it?" she asked.

"This would be," he paused, "um, let's see, the murder was on Wednesday, I went to Shakespeare and we hooked up on Thursday. You took off for home on Friday, and then found us in the bar on Saturday night. So this is Sunday, June 23rd, 1974, the year of our Lord."

"What happens if we disappear for the summer?" she asked.

"I flunk Shakespeare, I guess. And maybe the boys get up in arms about the rent. I miss a few days work at the library. That's about it. You?"

"About the same," she said, "I'll drop the classes, owe the rent, and miss the paychecks. Same deal."

"Okay, that's the planning. What about today?"

"I'm fried with decisions and planning. Let's get some beer and groceries, and find a place to camp. We can hit more road tomorrow."

He looked at her in studied wonder.

"You know," he said, "that's the best idea I've heard since the Agnew resignation.*

"I'm a logical positivist," she said, "I have good ideas from time to time."

"Head of Man," he laughed, reaching for her, "and body of lion. It's good."

(<o>)/(6.7)\(<o>)

Ace and Hack worked their way down the low iron railing on the west side of the playground, scuffling along in an easy stroll. Skate and Book, with Patrick in tow, had started out near the basketball hoop and wandered north through the littler kids, looking everywhere except over towards Ace and Hack. They were angling towards the door in the elbow of the "L" that school formed on their side of the schoolyard.

It was a brisk March day in 1965 – lunch hour at Our Lady of the Snows. The guys were in seventh grade.

With the cold air, there were few kids out to play. The older girls that stayed for lunch would linger inside and visit or read. The younger kids were often kept in if the sun wasn't shining. The boys their age tended to play rough games of tag or king of the hill, if there was a decent snow bank to fight over. This day, relatively nasty with wet cold, the playground was mostly deserted.

But caution was needed. There could be kids, or worse yet nuns, looking out over the playground. There could be nosy neighbor ladies looking from across the street.

Stealth was required – it was an age of spies.

They planned these missions in the seven-to-nine minutes it took them to wolf brown bag lunches and chug half-pint milk cartons. Ace was the master of this, he could tilt back his head and open his throat and simply pour the whole carton down in under four seconds. They timed him.

This day was to be the culmination of several scouting trips. They were planning to pop the hatch.

Ace and Hack arrived at the school doors. Skate's trio huddled back several yards, where the edge of the building gave them a clear view of the street. They watched for cars, and for pedestrians.

Skate carefully scanned the street, up and down. The coast was clear.

Ace and Skate locked eyes. Skate pumped his fist slightly, against his body, blocking so only Ace and Hack could see.

That was the signal – the mission was a 'go'.

Hack, seeing this, casually leaned back against the school door 'bumper bar' and Ace slipped past him into the building. Hack eased the door shut, staying outside on look-out while Ace scouted inside.

First, to the right a few steps, to see the auditorium was empty. Then he reached into the gloom near the janitor's doorway and pulled out the empty milk crate Skate had hidden there earlier in the day, after his milk carton deliveries were over. This was the 'prop' Ace would use if there was an unexpected nun in the hallway.

"I found this outside, Sister," the story would go, "and thought I'd better bring it in."

Then back along the hall, prop in hand, stopping to crane his neck around the stairway and, seeing the steps were clear, continuing down the hall to the corner where he could look up the interior of the long side of the "L".

Hack could see Ace through the door for most of this. Counting to five, he leaned back against the door again until he could see down the hall to where

Ace was stationed. Ace pumped his arm twice, like pulling an imaginary train whistle, the sign for "clear". Hack quickly passed the sign on to Skate, and then ducked into the doorway himself.

While Skate stayed behind to continue the watch, Book and Patrick walked excitedly over to the door and pushed through. Meanwhile, Hack had swept up and around the stairway corner where he stationed himself on the landing. From there he could listen for footsteps coming from above, and still see Ace in the hallway below.

Once he saw Patrick and Book about to go inside, Skate took a last keen look around and moved towards the door himself. Ace retreated from his corner and Hack descended the stairs, and they all met in perfect unison just inside the door where they'd started. Clockwork so far.

The next objective, after the rendezvous, was right in front of them: the janitors doorway under the stairway. It was heavy, metal, and painted black.

Mr. Taranto didn't lock it when he went home for lunch.

Ace carefully placed the milk crate back in the shadows, then pushed through the heavy black doorway, followed by the others, with Skate last, shutting it behind him QUIETLY.

They were in.

Down a short set of steps, they were in an equipment and locker room: dark, with a single, bare, low-watt bulb. Through another door, and down another few steps and they were in the boiler room, smelling of oil and heat. Then, another small room, barely larger than a closet, with boxes and jumble and, behind a crushed box, the prize: a metal half-door, no more than waist high, with a heavy metal handle.

Ace crouched and worked the handle, careful not to disturb the boxes around it. When it opened far enough, he scrambled through and disappeared into the dark. The rest followed. Skate last, pulling the door shut behind him QUIETLY.

They were in a low crawlway aiming west. Some yards ahead was dim light from above. They stayed on their feet, able to walk without getting on hands and knees by stooping at the waist and scuttling forward.

At the crawlway's end, Ace stood and hoisted himself through a manhole-sized opening and up into the pale light.

All followed.

They were in a dead space built into the side of the school where it met the church.

The whole complex was actually a "T" shape when viewed from fourteen thousand feet, but with fencing and so many off-limit areas, their school experience was limited to the east-side upside-down "L" of the "T". On that other holy day of the week, their church experience was limited to the west side "L" of the "T". Today, as several times before, they had crossed the "T". Indeed, their scuttling tunnel work had moved them the length of the west end of the top of the "T". In other words, they had traversed from the altar to the baptistery, as they had done in reverse every Sunday for years, but only this time, UNDER the floor of the church.

Ace gave the hard fist sign, meaning "freeze". It was time to listen.

They crouched, like watchful deer, scanning for the sound of movement inside the church. They were in a very narrow, very tall room, a sort of utility closet inside the walls of the church. They could see gray concrete, and plaster squeezed through lathe. And they could see ladder rungs against the far wall, leading up to a hatch, three stories above their heads.

They were in a place where nobody went, and where they were most definitely not supposed to be. There was silence, but they listened with total occupation for sounds of danger.

Ace was satisfied of temporary safety, but he pulled the "freeze" sign again, and then pointed to Hack. Hack pulled a coil of stiff wire out of his pocket and put it in his teeth like a pirate, then hoisted himself onto the ladder and swarmed three stories up to the hatch, new as a penny and quiet as a dime. He was remarkably light for a heavy kid.

Hack stopped at the top and hooked his elbow through a rung, then he folded out his wire and started fishing in the seam of the hatch. They had been here twice before. Once retreating when they found the hatch was locked, and a second time to fiddle with the latch and see if it would open. Hack had determined that a loop of wire might slide through and jimmy the mechanism.

It only took him a minute, which seemed much longer as they waited.

Then, Hack had it.

They waited quietly, a disciplined patrol, while Hack pulled himself up out of sight. Then they lined up at the ladder when Hack re-appeared and gave them the "clear" sign.

Ace stood at the base of the ladder and held each one until the ladder was clear.

"One by one," he whispered. Two people on the same ladder was too many.

When everyone else was up, Skate offered to let Ace go first. But Ace waved him through. Ace didn't like heights, as everyone knew, and he would put it off as long as possible – until he could no more.

Skate scaled the ladder and pulled himself through the hatch.

They were in the steeple!

What a kick.

There was a pointed roof and a low slanting wall, and, improbably, a locked door to the right. There were louvered slits on two sides, and by peeking through they could see the roof of the church in one direction and the church-side street in the other. But only barely, as the slits were at an angle for ventilation, not sight-seeing.

When Ace came puffing up the ladder and through the opening he hissed "Holy Shit."

This broke the silence and they entered into excited whispering.

"Where's this go?" Patrick wanted to know, trying the knob on the locked door.

"When's the last time anyone was up here?" Book wondered.

"Where to now?" Hack asked.

Everyone looked to Ace, but he was gasping in relief, like a walleye flopping on the bottom of a boat. Ace had a lot of nerve on the ground, but not at the top of a three-story ladder. He didn't want to go further, and he didn't want to go back, either. Ace had a thing with heights. Ace was spayed.

"Let's savor the moment a bit," Skate said, taking sympathy, and looking around to the group.

The scene reminded him of an episode from "Combat"* where the squad lounged in the loft of a French barn. It was time for a smoke and to await the next mission: Moose, Sarge, Cage, Doc, and Kinch with his B.A.R. But nobody dared bring a cigarette to school.

(<o>)/(6.8)\(<o>)

The nuns. They were Dominican at Our Lady of the Snows. They wore long black robes in layers, and had a tight-fitting headpiece of stiff white cotton that enclosed their face like a ski-hood and continued to a circle of stiff white that gave them the appearance of having their heads served on a platter.

We feared them, we dismissed them, and we were mystified by them.

Most were old and wizened, with deeply lined care-worn faces. A few were younger, and a couple might have been pretty in civilian clothes. Some of the younger ones were capable of laughter, but most were not. Some were sympathetic to teenage angst, but most were not. They were stern disciplinarians

They taught us history and composition and math and science. They taught us religion; Oh! how they taught us religion. Non-Christians never baptized went to hell. Protestants went to hell, too. Babies who died without sin went to Limbo. Offering up pain could help release souls from Purgatory. There were two kinds of sin: venial and mortal. You memorized the first sixty questions in the Baltimore Catechism to get First Communion; another 100 questions for Confirmation. Your soul was like a milk bottle. A venial sin put spots on the milk, and bought you a term in Purgatory. A mortal sin turned the bottle black, and you were sentenced to Hell. Until you went to confession, which wiped the bottle clean – luckily for us.

The priest got most grace from the Mass, then the altar boys, then the choir, then the congregation. Certain sequences of repeated chants could earn a plenary indulgence. The rosary was powerful, the Catechism was to be memorized, the Pope was infallible, and marriage was a sacred bond. Divorce was more than a sin: it excommunicated you. Priests and nuns were in the habit for life: no exceptions.

And they taught us Catholic politics. War in opposition to Communism was righteous. The Communists and the Nazis were the same; and if there might be technical differences, their effect was the same. Sacrificing your life in battle was the quickest way to heaven, especially if you went to confession right before.

We feared them. We plotted against them. We believed every word they said.

(<o>)/(6.9)\(<o>)

After Skate had taken what he considered to be sufficient abuse from Rexee' over his delicate, contorted short stories he decided it was time to move on. He started his street novel: Well-Versed. He took to spending his evening hours and his weekend mornings alone in his room, gazing out his window or leaning back in his chair with closed eyes working, he promised himself, on his novel.

The guys worried awhile, when they finally noticed his new habits, since it came without any of Skate's characteristic announcements or pronouncements.

"You think he's onto something?" Hack asked one evening, the question floating above the forum for anyone to spear.

Hack was cleaning corrosion off a crusty, unidentifiable piece of metal he'd brought home from the slough; chipping away with a penknife over a piece of old newspaper, an array of probes and pointy-things around his spot on the round table.

"Could be," Book murmured.

He was imagining Thucydide's account of the Athenaeum siege of Crete* and could only offer part of his mind at the present. He was learning Italian.

"I just hope to shit he stays on it until this week's Johnny Walker is aged. I could use about 12 years off."

"Ex-Ray, Ex-Ray," Ace countered, "a little compassion for Dostoyevsky's twisted soul."

It made her cranky to grade Freshman themes.

Ace was, by far, the most cynical of them where Skate's writing was concerned. Even Rexee', who was mercilessly critical, could sometimes find a word of encouragement, although she loathed Skate's moist grateful puppy glances when she said anything even remotely optimistic.

But Ace was oblivious.

"My old man's next door neighbor wants to be a writer too," he'd intone sarcastically, "and he's a plumber."

To Ace, who tended to view life with mystic fatalism, you were either a writer or you weren't, an artist or not. One was born to a calling and had it all through life; like the nuns said: ordination, marriage, or single – the vocations.. You didn't look for the American Dream to sprout peacock feathers and you didn't work yourself into being a writer. Ace loved Skate, with a brotherly sort of protectiveness, and he knew Skate like he knew himself: stubborn, intelligent, and hard-working

Skate was all that, Ace knew, but there were no peacock feathers hiding up Skate's ass.

Since the day Skate had pronounced them, each and every, members of his "editorial board," and had passed them carbons of his latest diamond, Skates twisted soul had been an open joke and source of mockery among them.

Hack read with an eye to plot. He often misunderstood words and phrases, had no literary perceptions to speak of, and usually just didn't get it. The stories disappointed him because nothing much ever "happened" and he had no basis, then, on which to judge. He'd hand them back with an embarrassed shrug and say "I liked it Skate, really, especially the part where he spilled the coffee on himself," or something of the sort. Hack was careful to be somehow complimentary and brief. He admired Skate for his determination more than anything, but was too pragmatic to really see the point.

Book was non-committal. His mind tended to make comparisons to the classics, even where no comparison existed. He neither praised nor buried but said something like "It reminded me of Borges," or "of Fitzgerald," and refused to elaborate. He'd ask pointed questions like "What are your themes?" and Skate, embarrassed, would admit he had none, or would try to make some up on the cuff.

Skate found the two of them both encouraging and infuriating.

Rexee' was savage. She was Ghengis Khan with a blue pencil. She ripped him for style and usage, punctuation, run-ons, fragments, clumsiness, vagueness, vacuity, and everything else. She just wished he would quit and leave her alone. She was forced to admit, however, that his punctuation was improving.

Ace would avoid even reading, refusing to encourage such foolishness and, often as not, would slip them under Skate's door like a borrowed bath towel, unsoiled and without comment. He wished Skate would climb down out of his tree and face facts.

(<o>)/(6.10)\(<o>)

It was one of those summer nights at the Web.

Book was hunched in the corner of the stereo alcove, pressing his headphones into the sides of his skull and twiddling the knobs on his newest audiophile gizmo. He was humming softly to himself as beads of sweat were dripping off his nose. Hack was lounging on the ratty couch, a hairy bear wearing nothing but infeasibly short cut-off jeans and holey leather moccasins, flipping through a tattered coffee table book on pioneer buildings – something Ace had fetched up from the dump. Skate was heading down the stairs when Ace walked in with a beat-up window fan.

It was one of those Minnesota summer evenings when the air is so hot, moist, and heavy that talcum powder forms clots on your hands, matches do not like to light on the first strike, and the exhale of a panting dog feels cool. In other words, it was Minnesota miserable.

But, as Hack liked to say, "at least the bugs ain't bad yet."

"Let's try this, then," Ace said, and hoisted the fan onto the bike room windowsill.

The window was open almost all the way, but not quite enough to accommodate the fan, so Ace tried to one-hand it upwards. But it would not move, so he tugged down a bit to free it, and it shot down, almost closing. And when he tried to raise it again, it was stuck near the bottom.

Skate got in there to help him. But, of course there was clutter on the floor under the window, so they were working at arm's length, and of course the window was now firmly stuck in it's distorted old-house frame channels, and of course the glazing was cracking out, under its umpteen layers of old lead-based paint, and of course the window frame itself was separating at the corners because the frame itself was just as old as the house.

So when Ace leaned over to lift the window, it went up a barely an inch and stuck again. And when he reached under and yanked, the window moved only a hair, and jammed a little more. And when he grabbed the top and pulled down, it refused to budge.

126

Now Skate leaned over, supporting himself with one hand against the wall, and reached under the window saying "together, then." And the two of them strained upwards against it. To no effect.

"Alright, let's try down, on three."

And now the window would not move at all.

By this time they are both running with sweat, and the feeble breeze they had, when the window was mostly open, has been stopped altogether. They are both leaning over at the waist, one hand under the window and the other propping themselves against the wall and Ace is trying to hold the fan in place on the window sill, holding it up, and in the way of their work.

"Jesus fucking Christ on a crutch," was one of Ace's favorite expressions.

"Jesus fucking Christ on a shit-stained, cock-sucking, fag-bait crutch," he expanded.

Skate was starting to lose his temper too, but Ace went first.

"Who is the bung-hole that left this shit here?" he started, and kicked at the boxes on the floor, "who's bleeding bung-hole crap is this?"

He kicked harder, attempting both to vent his spleen and slide the boxes out from underfoot. No shortage of temperament at the Web.

"Hey, easy with that."

These particular boxes happened to be brimming with loose metal parts that Hack was saving for some unknown purpose; and now Hack was on the floor trying to pull the boxes away from the wall, but unable to slide them between the bikes and the boys, who were leaning in place and blocking the way.

"I got it Skate," said Ace, "back out of the way."

So Skate let go of the fan, and pushed back a step, while Hack dragged the boxes, which were on a piece of carpet fabric, which Ace had planted his support leg on, which pulled Ace's feet out from under him, which brought him to his knees under the window sill, and dropped the fan to the floor, causing a strut on the fan motor to snap.

The fall disabled the unit – busted until it could be disassembled and repaired.

"Shitty fucking death!" was another of Ace's favorites.

"Shitty fucking cock-sucking whore-bait scum-suck ... DEATH!"

Normally, Skate would have been cursing too by now. But Ace was so far into it, it was almost too funny.

"Ace," he said mildly, "I guess death would be too good for him, yes?"

"Bung holes," Ace moaned, still on his knees, "I'm plagued with bungholes. You are all a bunch of bungholes. This is an association of bungholes."

Ace gathered his one last ounce of rage, shouting "This is a bunghole's club. This is a mother-fucking cock-sucking bungholes club, and you are all charter members."

Skate looked at Ace, and then over at Hack. Hack looked at Ace, and then over at Skate. Book had heard the commotion through his earphones and was standing in the background, looking at Skate and Hack, who were looking at him. Nobody laughed, although the temptation was overwhelming.

Patrick walked in the front door.

"Hey guys, the surf-rats are having a block party, and they just tapped a keg. Who's up for a cold beer on a hot night?"

(<o>)/(6.11)\(<o>)

Remo was a veteran.

Four years earlier he had a motorcycle accident, after surviving two tours in Viet Nam. Swerving right after a rainfall to avoid a pair of horseback riders Remo rolled his shiny new Harley Sportster through a barbed-wire fence and straight into a granite outcrop. He lay in the ditch for nearly an hour with a broken jaw and massive head injuries. For two days his life was in question, but on the third he began responding. He suffered a major concussion and remained in a coma for almost two months.

No one who knew Nestor Remopilovich very well was surprised to hear of his accident. Once he came back from the war, he was an accident about to happen.

Known as Remo to his friends, he had the worst driving record imaginable. That he had purposefully driven into the ditch to avoid killing a horse was not remarkable either. His co-workers smiled at that detail.

Remo was blond-haired, blue-eyed, and well-liked. The short, stocky Russian peasants' son was a seeker of life. As a Marine in Viet Nam he had volunteered for Recon. Strong willed and independent he was good at it. Receiving the Silver Star for bravery he was sent home for a cut on his hand that became badly infected. The cut resulting from an encounter with the tomato slicer in the mess hall while serving K.P. duty for some minor insubordination.

Remo returned home to enroll in the University but quit to indulge his hobbies, which were fast sports cars and motorcycles (as attested by his driving record), jumping out of airplanes and underwater diving. Remo and his brother were some of the first para-sailers in history: driving madly across frozen Medicine Lake in their junked-out truck, with 200 feet of nylon rope towing a rider, wearing an Army surplus parachute harness, skidding along the ice feet forward until pulled airborne. It was 1972, they made the papers.

He was bright and affable, loving to tell outrageous stories about Viet Nam ("a Siberian Tiger jumped right across our campfire," he once claimed, with an earnest face. We shot it, and skinned it, but the Lieutenant took the hide, there was nothing we could do), or of his latest adventure. Sometimes these were pedestrian ("I needed to reset the calendar on my wristwatch back, before the leap year, so I pinched the stem in an electric drill and spun it in high speed reverse … it burnt out the mechanism after about six months"), or some crazy sequence of mishaps with cars and meetings and missed opportunities, usually colored by heavy drinking.

Remo had a pet Tarantula he let roam free over his body, walking around with it on his shoulder, nuzzled to his ear, like a pirate with a parrot. He tinkered with sports cars and raced motorcycles. He had a Harley-Davidson Sportster, tuned to a turn, that he claimed could beat a rice-burner in any gear (Skate rolled his eyes at this fabrication). Remo hosted parties in his attic, which had been painted black, and hung with dayglow posters: a nude silhouette, an orange man with an 'afro', the side of Dylan's head with electric hair. There was a "black light" hanging from the ceiling and a strobe light operated by a switch on the wall.

Skate could attest, there is nothing quite like watching a Tarantula walk up your arm towards your jugular vein, moving in starts and jerks while a strobe light turns the scene into something surreal and carnival.

(<o>).[].(<o>)

That all changed after the motorcycle accident – the head injury.

When, after nearly six months, he returned to work, Remo was a different person. The concussion was severe, impairing his speech, slowing his thought processes, and retarding his movements. His hands, which had once been dexterous enough to assemble a Holly carburetor or an M-16 in the dark were like blocks of wood by comparison. His speech was slurred and difficult to understand. He walked clumsily, like a robot with alternating twitches and jerks. Worst of all, his thinking was very slow, his memory shot.

Most of what he knew about his job had been forgotten, and so he had to be retrained. And since the closed-head injury accident, learning was a very difficult undertaking for him.

(<o>).[].(<o>)

And it was a demanding job: shipping and receiving for a major concern. The departmental contraction, Ship-Rec, was an apt one. Workers with years of experience elsewhere had been sunk by the job; transferred away or simply fired.

However, he had a good boss.

Ward Michaels had taken it upon himself to personally see that Remo re-learned his job. The other employees were good too; they had gathered around Remo and supported him, following Ward's lead.

But the relationship was strange. Remo now was like a retarded child who only barely reminded them of the Remo of the past.

The first few weeks had been especially difficult. He was back, but not really – he was still recovering, and struggling with the simplest of things. Remo knew that he wasn't holding up his end. He lost his temper often and fumed at his own mistakes, infuriated and frustrated by his own inabilities. His co-workers tried hard, but the errors created more work for all, and made everybody look bad.

The boss took him out of the usual job rotation and gave him one project to concentrate on, thinking to move Remo to another job when he'd mastered the first one. But Remo never did master that first job, for the work, while not requiring exceptional intelligence, was complex and exacting. The old Remo could have handled it with ease, but the new Remo was out of his depth.

After a while there was pressure from above to fire Remo. The boss refused. He felt strongly that Remo needed his job to regain his old skills and intellect. What Remo needed was work, and practice at lifting and paperwork.

If Remo was going to recover, he required exercise and mental stimulation, his doctor said. It would take time, his brain had swollen badly, but as the swelling went down his capacities might return. His recovery could eventually become complete. The doctor was confident the damage was not guaranteed to be permanent.

So Remo was kept on, the boss working with him, teaching and encouraging. The others were patient at his urging, by word and by example.

After a time, Remo showed some improvement. He began to remember a little of what he formerly knew, but not very much. And, he had the exasperating property of temporary mental lapses, where he could make the most rudimentary mistakes.

As time passed, Remo achieved an elementary level of competence.

At the same time, his co-workers withdrew from him (he just wasn't the same old Remo).

They continued to cover for his mistakes and even defended him to members of other departments. The boss was patient and understanding, teaching him the same things over and over.

Meanwhile, Remo would go to the doctor and return with news that he was getting better and could expect to be fully recovered soon. His work-mates listened and nodded their heads, but privately noted that Remo's performance had hardly increased at all. The work therapy wasn't working, and at the same time Remo was drawing more and more into himself.

Every mistake seemed to scare him just a little more. As time passed Remo began to ask for help more often. The boss always encouraged initiative in his minions, but weary of correcting mistakes and mindful of his unit's efficiency and his company's willingness to fire Remo, he began to aid Remo whenever he requested it.

Eventually, Remo shunned all responsibilities and retreated to the most rote tasks.

The boss didn't like it. He reasoned that doing the same thing again and again was not going to help Remo improve.

Then Remo started to get arthritic.

(<o>)/(6.14)\(<o>)

The first few minutes of a rainfall are the most dangerous on a motorcycle. Oil and grease, sleeping in the cracks and pits of the pavement, is dislodged and briefly floats on the thin sheen of water before getting washed away. And for a minute or two the road is really slick – and it's more than a little possible for a two wheeler to fall down if the rider is careless or trying to hurry.

(<o>).[].(<o>)

I was enjoying an overcast afternoon in the gloom of Doogan's, idly chatting with Fat Henry about the Vikings, who were in training camp down in Mankato, when the phone rang. Cal answered and, as I was trying to catch his eye for another beer, flicked his eyes to mine and wordlessly held the phone up to me.

It was Kendall Koolala, sounding a little jazzed.

"Man, you gotta come get me," he said, "my wheels won't start and if the bossman sees me around he'll make me work overtime. Which I am loath, let me say loath, as in totally loath to do."

Koolala lived a life on the fringe and work was, to him, nothing better than a necessary evil. He was a lazy businessman, constantly working the angles, trying to start the venture that would make him rich, without him actually working above the line, not any more than the absolute minimum.

There was muted desperation in Koolala's voice. I was bored and restless and enthused with beer; a little high-speed back road cruising on a mission to danger run sounded highly enlivening.

"Four minutes," I said, "possibly three."

And I hung up and headed out the door digging for my bike keys.

A single drop of rain splashed on my gas tank as I quickly turned the ignition and climbed on.

"King high, let's fly," I chanted.

I jumped on the kick start. The bike had a history of temperament on rainy days. I'd spent entire afternoons kicking and cursing when the scoot had gotten it into it's hemispherical heads that it was too damp to ride.

It fired and I gave it some gas, executing a neat rubber-burning one-eighty and cutting across Doogan's lot aiming for the narrow space between the tavern and the next building that led into the alley that started the run to Koolala's workplace.

I shot the gap and leaned hard left, the bike spitting gravel.

(<o>)/(6.16)\(<o>)

A one act play in several scenes:

Scene Six –

It is 11:30 a.m. and the lunch crowd has started to assemble. The guys still sit at center stage. There are several beer bottles on the table and empty food plates with crumpled napkins; they have just finished eating. There are several new people leaning at the bar or sitting at the tables. The place is almost crowded.

As the lights come up there is the hubbub of crowd noise, no single voice heard distinctly. Skate is leaning back with his arms crossed, absently listening to the conversation. He's in the center chair, facing straight into the audience.

The lights begin to fade around him and the other characters begin to slowly freeze. As voices drop out a tape of crowd noise is played at increasing volume to compensate. The final effect is of Skate isolated in a broad beam of hazy light amidst frozen patrons apparently oblivious to his surroundings.

A man enters from the front door, audience right, and edges through the frozen people, excusing himself politely but, of course, getting no response from them. He crosses to Skate and stands beside him. He is physically similar to Skate although several years older and they are dressed identically.

The taped crowd noise fades to a barely audible hum.

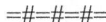

```
     Author
Skate? buddy -- can you hear me?
(no response)
Skate?
```

131

(touches his shoulder)
Talk to me boy

    Skate
(slowly coming aware)
What is it?

    Author
It's me. Let's talk

    Skate
I know you, don't I.
(spoken as a statement, not a question)

    Author
Not as well as I know you.

    Skate
What brings you down?

    Author
(glancing around)
I don't consider this a bring down.

    Skate
Ah, wordsmith punster. You writing me in as your straight man?

    Author
No, no, … well, yes, a little bit.
(shrugs)
I thought we should talk.

    Skate
(glancing around the room)
It looks like I'm at your disposal.

    Author
So to speak.

    Skate
I guess this is one of those moments where time seems to stand
still.

    Author
(laughing)
You got it.

    Skate
I've been having a lot of those lately.

    Author
Yeah, I know.

    Skate
So, to what do I owe the honor of …

    Author
(interrupting)
I wanted to wake you up.

    Skate
I wasn't sleeping.

    Author
Here's what happens. You go through something major, like a
shooting, say …

Skate
(interrupting)
… as a random example …

Author
… or a confrontation with a heavily armed and homicidal
maniac …

Skate
(shaking his head)
It happened again … I just sat there while the actors acted
and the action took place.

Author
Yeah, I know.

Skate
Even Book had something to say, and I just sat there, frozen.

Author
Not scared so much as paralyzed, I know. And now, lost in
thought. And you've got the experience in mind like some kind
of slow motion eyelid movie.
(pauses)
You don't just remember it, you re-live it.
(Skate is nodding)

Author
And that's horrible … to experience it over and over, so you
block it out. This is only natural, and part of the healing
process.

Skate
So what are we talking about?

Author
We're talking about writing. If you want to write, you need to
remember. You need to hold on to the horror, and you need to
heal in a different way. You want to let go, but you need to
hang on.

Skate
The shootings? Don't worry about that. I'll remember them as
long as I live.

Author
Yeah, I know, not that. The stuff that comes before and after,
that's what get's lost … after especially. The circuits shut
down, and the memories don't get recorded. They don't fade,
they're never in there.

Skate
Get off! I don't see it. I witnessed the death of the
Constitution of the United States on Monday. Then I went to
the hospital. Now it's Wednesday, and I remember everything
perfectly.

Author
Yeah? Rexee' just kicked the balls off Delmar an hour ago.
What did Book say right afterwards?

Skate
Um, well, I don't know.

Author
Exactly, and neither do I. It was funny and pointed though,

133

but it's gone.
(pauses, staring into space)
I'll just have to make something up, I guess.

    Skate
Or forget about it.

    Author
Yeah, that's what I'll probably do. Meanwhile, I need you to
stay present, and remain alert.

    Skate
I don't know what you're worried about. I'm sitting here.

    Author
Oh? What were you thinking when I came in?

    Skate
(ponders)
I don't know. Nothing I guess. Meditations on dead air.

    Author
Exactly, and you haven't been writing in your journal either,
have you?

    Skate
So what?

    Author
Okay, look. I'll let you in on it. A few years from now I'm
going to be trying to reconstruct this day. I'm going to be
trying to paint a picture of the web that makes the vision
clear.

    Skate
Yeah, okay, what's the big hairy deal?

    Author
Oh, you SO need to Shut the fuck up and listen more.
(agitated, but pausing)
I can't have you dozing off and missing things. I need to
catch the flavor, the back and forth, the rapport.

    Skate
The witty banter and incisive insights? You're kidding.

    Author
You've been together a long time, and through a lot together.
The bunch of you -- you know each other better than you're
liable to experience again. And your group memory constitutes
your collective roots and the fictions of your biographies.

    Skate
The fictions of our …

    Author
Yeah, the theory behind fiction. Nothing is completely
imagined, fictions inevitably stem from someone's experience.
And, like biography or history, it's a recounted version
filtered through someone's memory.

    Skate
And colored by their perception of it.

    Author
Yes, exactly

Skate
Rexee' said something like that.

Author
But perception is a key element. You can't sleep through
perception.

Skate
You can try.

Author
Oh, you can be so annoying.

Skate
Well, come on, you're asking me to do something against
nature. Forgetting is natural to begin with, and blanking out
trauma is only human. That's why women have that second baby.

Author
I know, and I know, and still I'm telling you this for your
own good.

Skate
I'm not going to do it, I'm sure you know. I'm going to
suppress this violence shit, and pack it down where it can't
hurt me. I'm going to develop a world-class talent for
forgetting.
(pauses)
You know that, and that's why you're here.

Author
Did I mention how annoying you can be. Abrasive is another
word that springs to mind.

Skate
Well, you're all about how remembering will help ME. But I'm
all thinking that forgetting will help us BOTH.

Author
I should slap you.

Skate
You already have.
(Author pulls up a chair in between Skate and "frozen" Rexee')

Author
Let me try it this way. There's nothing cooler than time
travel, right?

Skate
You know it.

Author
But it's a precarious feat. You want to visit the past, you
might even want to "fix" it. But you would, if you could,
change things carefully, for the greater good.

Skate
Couldn't have said it better myself.

Author
Now, how do you play that game? What do you change?

Skate
For me? I dunno. I've been lucky all my life. Maybe a few
things, of course. Some bad moments I'd like a do-over. Two
years ago, and most obviously, I'd have been on my feet, about

135

six feet closer to the door, and lifted Delmar's rifle barrel
before he could waste that poor sodden black dude.

    Author
(nodding)
Yeah, that's a good one -- a real temptation. I've got that
one myself.
(pauses)
Of course, then, he might have turned the deal around and made
you the target.

    Skate
That's not how it plays out in my movies. There's a variety of
endings, but they all come out better.

    Author
Yeah, mine too.
(a long pause)

    Skate
That's a mind-fuck

    Author
Yeah, okay.
(a long pause)

    Author
You stopped journaling.

    Skate
Yeah, so?

    Author
I wouldn't be here if you'd sit down and write a few things
about these days. Enough to help the memory.

    Skate
Can't do it. I've tried. I'm letting go and moving on.

    Author
I'm telling you right now, that's bad. You put it down on
paper or you carry it around even longer. And then you end up
flailing over stuff you can't control.

    Skate
Aw, crap.
(another long pause)

    Skate
Let's back up. How is my remembering going to benefit you?

    Author
Wake up boy. You're my muse. Except, just now, I'm YOUR muse.

    Skate
Yeah, okay, muse me.

    Author
Muse me, that's funny. Muse yourself on a rainy day, your Mom
would say.

    Skate
I've got the body of a lion and the head of straight man.

    Author
It's a big day, looking back. Feature it, Patrick has already
moved out and Carol has a baby due. He won't be around anymore

at all to speak of. Hack's moving into the woods as soon as he
can. You're actually going to accelerate that.

Skate

That still leaves Ace and Book, and, I figure to be back.

Author

You? Your future is extremely tenuous. And Ace moved in with
Annie.

Skate

You're kidding.

Author

Half-way. He'll be telling you himself pretty soon. Anyway,
Book is thinking about graduate school. He probably won't go
to another university, but he could.

Skate

He should. It would do him good.

Author

And where's the Web then?.

Skate

Whaddya mean?

Author

Never mind. It's bad luck to say.
(stands up, as if to go)
You going to ride the old scooter up to Hack's place?

Skate

If I can get it running.

Author

Needs a chain and a sprocket, right?

Skate

Just a chain, I hope.

Author

Don't forget to re-insulate the Zener diode, new grommet, and
get an extra set of points.

Skate

Good idea. Okay.
(pauses)
Is there anything in particular you want me to watch for
today?

Author

No, no, nothing specific. Just be alert for the typical and
characteristic. The day to day stuff that's easy to ignore
over the years.

Skate

Well, alright, I guess.

Author

And watch the liquor.

Skate

Yeah, I know what you mean there. That's why we had the early
lunch -- trying to keep a handle on it.
(pauses)
I haven't felt like eating much, but seeing Delmar laid out
and hauled off. Suddenly I was puckish. I mean, peckish.

Author
Stay alert is all I ask. You've had twelve pretty tight years
together and now comes a transition. There'll always be a web.
I hope. But its bound to change. Just like everything else.
It's the climb of time. Nothing can alter that.

Skate
Except for right here, now.

Author
Well, yes, in a way.
(looks around, uncomfortably)
But I've stayed too long -- I'll have to be going.

Skate
You be stopping back?

Author
I've got something cooked up for the next scene. Otherwise
I'll be staying in the background, pretty much.

Skate
Okay, well, take it easy.

Author
You too -- remember what I said.

Skate
I'll try.

Author
(He touches Skate lightly on the shoulder and turns upstage,
settling into an open spot at the bar, and freezing with the
rest of the patrons).

Skate
(Skate turns out to the audience and resumes his arms-crossed
posture)

(Blackout).

(Skate's voice) See ya! Wouldn't want to be ya!

(Author's voice) Oh, you are such an asshole!

(<o>)/(6.17)\(<o>)

What happened in Doogan's bar that special day in 1976 was, in a sense, a
rerun. Over the years whenever one of us left town and returned we'd make a
point of getting together to catch up. Celebrate the homecoming – "webcoming"
in Ace's parlance – and just get in touch. Ace referred to it as "weave retrieval".

It happened a lot. Some summers, when Hack was working for his uncle in
the woods and Book was afield taking some course and when Pat was on the
road or after he'd moved in with Carol, Ace and I would have the place virtually
to ourselves. Rexee' was capable of disappearing on binges, or what have you,
and being away for days and even weeks at a time in the summer.

Ace was an early riser and he'd shake me out after the coffee was ready so
we could get the day rolling, prepare for work, or whatever the schedule called
for.

Some mornings, awful mornings for me, it would be to get in line at the
pancake joint, Annie's pretty soon, before the doors opened. It might still be
dark out, and he'd be in my room parroting his father, "C'mon boy, it's 5AM –
we're burning daylight!"

Aside from early reveille, I really enjoyed those days, and those gatherings. Sitting around bullshitting or up and out on some hare-brained expedition Ace was dead set on.

It was never dull. One day we'd be sifting through the beloved dump looking for "useful" items, or downtown in some obscure dusty shop scanning for a book on Egyptian jewelry or Eskimo string art, or down at E. Floyds "head shop", perusing the posters and maybe buying a Zig-Zag patch to sew on Ace's bomber jacket. The next day we might be under construction, building shelves in the kitchen, or dressed up in our Goodwill tuxedoes applauding at the opening of a new art gallery, or bopping into some funky club to catch some new band that was making the rounds.

There's a saying, "the streets were alive," in the early 1970s that sort of fits too. You could cut through a park and come upon people around a small fire, passing a joint maybe, and everyone tapping bottles and cans together like cow bells in a funky unrehearsed jam session both rhythmic and remarkable. Or you'd walk by some guy on the sidewalk with a guitar and a hat on the ground, and he's playing some song you knew. So you might stand in with him, nodding and smiling together, and add some harmony to further his busker gig. Then you'd look into his hat and see six coins and three joints in proceeds, so you'd add a coin and he'd give you one of the joints.

Back at the Web it was usually a madhouse with friends and strangers passing through. The music was usually on and loud whenever it was. Book used to get movies through the library, and we'd have our own film festivals from time to time. "Freaks"* and "Fantasia"* were being rediscovered then, and we screened those together once. One Halloween, Book produced a bottle of Amontillado Brandy and a copy of Poe's story,* and we shut down the party for fifteen minutes, passing around a snifter of the sherry brandy and taking turns reading the story aloud.

(<o>)/(6.18)\(<o>)

A pine cone bounced off the tent and woke them.*

Not knowing for sure what it was, Skate poked his head out the tent flap to find a glorious sunny morning.

"You feel like getting up?" he asked, "it's a beautiful day."

"I don't know," Effie answered, "I could lay here a while longer."

They snuggled together for a bit, but the sun on the tiny orange nylon tent soon made it stifling in there.

"Tent's not really made for two, is it?" she observed.

"No, sorry," he said, "it's really just to keep the water off you, and not too good even for that. It makes rough camping."

"I don't mind," she said, "it kept the bugs off us, and promotes early rising, which is well known to be a healthy habit."

"Yeah," Skate smiled, "you should meet Ace's Dad, that's his religion."

"He's not Catholic?" she teased.

"He converted," Skate laughed, and slapped her fanny, "let's get moving, we're burning daylight."

139

(<o>).[].(<o>)

"Look at this," she gasped.

They were packing up the scooter, getting ready to go into town for breakfast. Skate was fastening the gear to the sissy bar with bungee cords.

"What is it," he walked over to her.

She was standing no more than three feet from where the tent had been pitched, pointing to the ground. There was a small pile of moist brown pellets laying there.

"This was not here last night," she said, leaning over to inspect the stuff.

"Don't touch," Skate said, turning back to finish packing, "it's deer shit."

"How'd it get HERE," she asked, cocking an eyebrow toward him.

He laughed.

"Well, either someone crept in here and placed it there for a joke, or a deer came through and felt the need to take a crap."

"HERE!" she yelped, pointing "we were sleeping right THERE!"

"Yep," he said, "when you sleep out in nature, nature is all around you."

"I never would have thought," she shook her head slowly, "we'd have this kind of..."

"Close encounter of the turd kind?" he said.*

She belted out a laugh.

"Okay," she said, "serves me right for stopping in awe to wonder at the glories of the planet."

"Planet, shmanet," Skate grinned, "c'mon, let's eat."

(<o>)/(6.20)\(<o>)

diaria -- 6.0 -- 9/20/76 -- shreveport

another function of the metafictionist, a ploy that's regularly employed, is the use of fable, parable and mythology to get it over. james joyce used it when he patterned ullyses after homer's yarn about the trojan war and borrowed from virgil and dante as he went. and a lot of the modern guys set their stories in bygone eras: coover, barth and barthelme in particular. these guys write about goat-boys and noah's drowned brother and try, as they're about it, to get at the fundamental truths that these old dry fables are into; to COVER THE STORY.

old aesop knew how to tell a story that had a point; and even if simple and a tad obvious, they do get at the meat without a lot of extraneous furtin around. admirable quality and harder to do than ya might think.

so, anyway, two of the things you can expect a fabulist to pull are the inclusion of himself (disguised or otherwise) in the course of the narrative and, somehow, a slice of parable, fable or mythology, (modern or otherwise).

and this is probably a good time to throw in another of the passages that rexee' shared with me:

140

"This is one important dimension of modern fabulation. In a way it is the simplest: the direct plunge back into the tide of story which rolls through all narrative art. Such a return to the story for renewed vigor is a characteristic of the modern fabulators ... writers emphasize the erotic dimension of the form, which, as we shall see, is a fundamental property of the fiction."*

though i'm not sure i can pull all that off.

weel, anyway, i sed i'd be gettin didactic (crammin facts down yer throat) and i didn't lie about it. and hell, like remo sez, if ya gotta endure this crap ya may as well learn sumthin by it.

(<o>)/(Endnotes 6.22)\(<o>)

41. Python, Monty. (1969-1974). Six English comedians, authors of Monty Python's Flying Circus, a British television comedy sketch show from the late 1960s, early 1970s.

42. The boys reformatory in Red Wing, MN where juvenile delinquents were sent "down the river."

43. Dylan, Bob (1965). Highway 61. Highway 61 Revisited. Columbia Records. The title song from Bob Dylan's sixth studio album, released in August 1965 by Columbia Records. Highway 61 runs through Red Wing, MN on the way to New Orleans.

44. Spiro Angnew resigns in disgrace as Vice-president of the United States, October 10, 1973.

45. Combat! A television program that aired Tuesday nights on ABC 1962-1967.

46. Canfora, Luciano. Tucidide continuato. Padova, Antenore, 1970. 260 p. 21 cm. (Thucydides. History of the Peloponnesian War., in Italian). Thucydides (b. 460 BC - d. 395 BC) Greek historian of the Peloponnesian War, 5th century BC between Sparta and Athens

47. Freaks (1932). Metro-Goldwyn-Mayer (MGM). A film about circus and carny folks deemed so 'disturbing' it was banned for many years.

48. Fantasia (1940). Walt Disney Pictures. An animated 'interpretation' of classical compositions, the film was a flop when it was first introduced, but gained an audience in the 1960s for its 'trippy' use of color and movement to accompany the music.

49. Poe, Edgar Allen (1846). The Cask of Amontillado. A famous short story about revenge.

50. Let Amanda be your pine cone. The last line of the Tom Robbins novel, "Another Roadside Attraction" Robbins, Tom. (1971). Another Roadside Attraction. Doubleday, 400 pp.

51. Spielberg, Steven (1977). a famous American director.

52. Robert Scholes, Fabulation and Metafiction (Urbana: U. of Illinois Press, 1979), p. 25.

Chapter 7

I had to testify at Delmar's trial that Fall, 1974.

I found it extremely unnerving.

It turned out he was indeed the kid we remembered from the Cub Scout Jamboree up in Elysium when we were boys. But only some of the rumors were confirmed at trial.

Yes, his family was from up in that part of the state and, yes, his parents were killed before his eyes when a rogue moose attached their car.* But, no, he had not ended up 'down the river'.* He had gone to the Northern Hospital for the Insane* in Oshkosh, Wisconsin. Twice, actually, once for a brief period as a boy, and then for another stint after leaving the Army.

Meanwhile, he was contemptuous of the entire court proceeding, dismissive and arrogant, but seemed ready to jump into the witness box and garrote me when I took the stand.

I tried to tell it as impassively as I could. The defense attorney tried to make an issue of the detachment I perceived in Delmar's actions. They were angling for an insanity plea.

I was the star witness.

Hack had had his back turned, and didn't see the actual shooting. Rexee' had been very drunk and, by trial time, had managed to blot a lot of it out. She had to answer some embarrassing questions from the defense: what had been her relationship with the deceased? (she didn't know his name); where had they met? (in a bar); how long had they known each other? (a few hours); they questioned her about the lustrous unblinking eyeball tattoo on her shoulder; and, from the prosecution, had he indeed raped her (not in any sense of the word – it only turned nasty afterwards).

The only other witness was a young college girl renting a second floor room in the house next to Delmar's. She saw him coming back after the shots were fired. She was very poised on the stand, completely unintimidated (as opposed to me), and made a very strong impression. Her name was Effie Wantow.

We knew each other by that time. We had been there and back.

Through the miracle of the criminal justice system and plea bargaining arrangements, countered by the public interest in the trial by the minority coalition (the guy was from Mississippi on a football scholarship), and veterans groups (though Delmar was not a classic example of post traumatic stress syndrome, dismissed from the military such as he was), the court finally found him guilty on one misdemeanor count of carrying a concealed weapon (a mail order M-16 considered concealed only through astonishing legal logic), and one felony count of involuntary manslaughter (more astonishing yet). He was sentenced to four years in prison – amounting to two years with good behavior and time served.

The sentence appeased the minorities, a little, angered the veterans, a little, and mildly placated me.

I was hoping he'd get life. If the other evidence (things found in a search of his apartment) had not been suppressed he might have.

The entire ordeal had an incredible effect on the Web. It pulled us tighter than we'd ever been – and it made Rexee' one of us.

She was most profoundly affected by it all.

She became more subdued, less flamboyant, and more considerate.

Hack managed to maintain a philosophical attitude throughout. Of the three of us, he was the best able to shrug it off.

I had to learn to live with fear from that day on. Delmar never threatened me, he didn't have to. I saw in his face all I needed to know. My testimony convicted him, it was as simple as that.

He would see I was repaid.

(<o>)/(7.2)\(<o>)

It was one of those summer nights at the Web.

After a hot, sticky, humid Minnesota day with barely a feather of breeze, the evening descended with hardly a whisper of cool relief. It was miserable but, as Hack liked to say, "at least the bugs ain't bad yet."

(<o>).[].(<o>)

The Web house lay in a college neighborhood, which meant a lot of older, run-down, rental properties, some house-like, as the Web, and some multi-unit dwellings, mostly older homes retro-fitted to squeeze in as many tenants as the fire marshal would allow (and then some).

There were also a smattering of fraternities and sororities, largely on the main drag directly across from campus, but also sprinkled around through neighborhoods like ours.

We were off the main drag, but we had a frat nearby.

We always assumed there was a hierarchy and pecking order among fraternities, and we further assumed these guys, being stuck away from the campus like us, were a low caste frat. But we honestly never paid much attention. To us, they were transients. Like college sports teams, it was a new mob of characters every year, and any tradition they might have fostered was only as good as the latest crop of pledges. We were lifers, so to speak – a fixed point in a neighborhood designed for flux on a four year rotation.

The frats were mostly populated by what we viewed as knuckleheads riding around on their Daddy's checkbook (just as the sororities were mostly populated by debutantes flouncing around on their Daddy's checkbook). Besides, the frats were mostly conservative-leaning and tended towards right-handed politics, which we mostly did not, and the frat boys tended to listen to popular Top-40 music, which we rarely did.

We knew about their taste in music because they periodically set speakers into their windows, pointing outward, and blasted their favorite radio stations into the neighborhood when they held a party. We knew about their politics because we often saw the frat boys dressed in Banlon shirts with slacks, or sweaters, or university sports-logo sweatshirts. Then as now, you could often believe you could tell what a person thought by what they wore. And music was a totem – you knew a lot about a person when you learned what kind of music they listened to.

In fairness to them, our attitudes towards the frat boys were little more than ill-informed prejudice and stereotyping. In fairness to us, our prejudices were often borne out. They were full of mindless energy and sheep-like pantomime, embarking on projects like filling all the frat-house windows with curtains made of beer can pull-tops. And they were slaves to campus sporting events, holding loud parties to celebrate a victory by the football team; actually, to celebrate a game, before and after, whether they won or not. We had a particular loathing for this "jock mentality" and jocks in general, going all the way back to high school. And the frat boys were basically that: jocks. Or so it seemed to us at the time.

We had a slightly different attitude towards their sorority sisters, since many of these were highly desirable examples of female femininity: serious babes, some of them. We lusted after them as any red-blooded young American boy would do in a similar situation, but in our case with a resigned sense of futility. The sisters were only there for the frat boys, and not for us. The Web was a little too far outside their norms; we didn't do the normal things, and we didn't present the normal picture. They had little time for us, is the truth. And when on those rare occasions we actually did manage to meet any, they often tended towards the shallow side of the pool.

So the Web lived among the jocks and the frats and the sisters, but there was relatively little interplay. Even Ace, our agent for extroversion, was rarely in their consort.

We would drink their beer however. We were happy to drink their beer.

(<o>).[].(<o>)

The closest frat house to the Web was just around the corner on the street just west of us. We could get there by crossing through our corner intersection, crossing the alley, and walking to the nearest lawn, no more than fifty yards from our front door.

(<o>).[].(<o>)

These guys were beer-drinkers, and in the summer there was hardly a weekend when they didn't have a loud party with their speakers in the windows. Every so often they would throw a "block party", which was no more than buying a keg or two, and putting out some signs. There would be a donation bucket by the keg, and they would hope to get a few dollars back towards the next keg. We usually had something else to do on these summer nights, so seldom went.

But it was one of those summer nights at the Web.

We went.

(<o>).[].(<o>)

The Web didn't do that well with women.

We wanted to, I think, in a desultory way. But we were lint caught in the filter of the tumble dry of the fabric of the time. There were very desirable sorority women in the neighborhood, but they didn't seem to appreciate us. And they were, by and large, dim-witted, which counted against them.

There were other, better suited women around, such as the waifs who worked in the free kitchen on the West Bank, or the counselors who answered

145

phones at the youth emergency services hotline, but they were often politically strident, or carrying a lot of what people were starting to call "baggage" – like hippy boyfriends, or vehement leftist rhetoric, or a serious inner-working me-first habit, or a passel of small children.

There were graduate students at the university – a little older but a little more mature. But they viewed us as largely uneducated in the ways of the academy, which we surely were. Book could hold his own with virtually anybody in intellectual discourse, but we mostly viewed these debates as head-banging, immaterial nonsense – from highly pragmatic and driven women who took more than they gave.

There were rare exceptions, like Rexee' and Effie, but they presented a different set of problems.

There were occasional strangers who wandered through, appearing at our parties sometimes; but they were often on the hustle, living on the street and seeking their next meal – and assessing the street resale value of Book's stereo – more than they were interested in the companionship of us. They usually came in the company of street-wise hustlers anyway, like Fast Eddie.

So there was a central discontinuity. On one hand, we'd been raised and trained to seek the company of clean, well-groomed girls dressed in knee-socks and pleated skirts who were, themselves, trained to seek clean-cut citizens wearing ties and starched shirts. These young ladies were even trained in the art of starching shirts, and ironing, among other things, in order to have the skills a young wife should need.

Our contemporary culture in those days, and on the other hand, aimed us away from that and towards women who had something to say for themselves, and who wore a different uniform, and who made their own way – seeking an empowerment that didn't depend on finding a man to support them (as Rexee' said one time, "not looking for an MRS degree").

The Web, to summarize, had little luck with women.

(<o>)/(7.7)\(<o>)

Fast Eddie, now there was a guy.

Patrick dragged him home one day, and he camped on the porch for weeks. Or, rather, his stuff did. We saw Eddie once in a long while as he checked in from working the streets to work us.

It was one thing after another with Eddie. He hustled everyone without distinction. It was him against the world. But he was calm and smooth about it. He worked everybody, and everybody liked him despite that. Everybody was his friend, to be touched for a favor, but he was nobody's friend, we came to find.

Eddie always seemed to have some deal going, usually verging on illegal and entailing many dubious and interlocking elements. Like, he had a pound of grass to move, but it was sitting in someone's house and needed to be hauled across town to be cut up into bags. But first, there was a problem with a girl, who needed a ride to pick up some other stuff, and she had the key but wouldn't give it over until somebody else returned her stereo, which Eddie thought was in need of repair missing its turntable pad, and at somebody's house waiting for somebody else to pick it up because somebody's dog had chewed theirs and they needed to borrow it for a party.

One thing always led to another, and Eddie was always piecing together the next deal, based on parts of this one. You never got a fully truthful and honest answer from Eddie, but after a while you learned not to expect that.

Meanwhile, Eddie was using the Web house as an address as he went to the county welfare office to get food stamps. Nobody said he could do this, but since he never asked, nobody ever said "no" either. We were a mail drop, which was not so unusual in those days, as plenty of people were roving and at no fixed address. So we held Eddie's mail, and Tiger's too for a while. It was no big thing. We had a house, so people were often hitching through to pick up mail.

Then it turned out that Eddie was collecting addresses, as he was more and more spending his days in circulating through the seven county area, making welfare applications in each.

This turned out to be a lucrative career for him, and soon Eddie was driving an old Cadillac from welfare office to welfare office, pleading poverty and picking up checks at bogus addresses, one of which was ours.

One day Hack walked onto the porch and found Eddie sitting on the couch counting through his driver's licenses. He had seven, and used them to sign up for benefits here, there, and uptown. Another day Skate agreed to drive Eddie around. Eddie was doing his business. Skate was collecting stories. Eddie was as wary as a caged animal, and you could never count on him telling the truth for long stretches.

The thing about Eddie was he wasn't just a street hustler, he also paraded as an artist and a thinker. He actually sometimes made good money selling an oil painting on the street. He had designs on doing an "art opening" at a gallery on the West Bank.

His paintings were primitive, with child-like drawing skills, but depicting street scenes with an uncanny eye, and characterized by deep layers of bright reds. They had an angry feel to them, and a stark quality.

"If I didn't paint," Eddie said, "I'd be tearing it up somehow. I'd be a terrorist like those boys at the Olympics. I'd have that machine pistol, and I'd be burping civilians for fun and Allah. You know it."

"Bertrand Russel, yeah?" Skate had finally learned how to keep Eddie off balance.

"Who's that?" Eddie said suspiciously, "I don't know that dude. What's he got to do?"

"Logical Positivist," Skate grinned, "but he's not from around here."

(<o>)/(7.8)\\(<o>)

Lunch hour was fading fast. They had infiltrated enemy lines and taken the high ground. Now they had to beat a strategic retreat and get back to class with nobody the wiser. Trouble was, Mr. Taranto the janitor usually took a short meal, so they had to get back through before he did. Everyone was afraid of Taranto. He was the one glaring day-to-day male presence in the yard of nuns. We also feared the priests, but that was on a different level – they were an unearthly presence – and we did not see them every day except at Mass in the morning. The nuns were here and now, and so was Mr. Taranto. We could sometimes bullshit the nuns, but never the school janitor.

Hack went first, back down the ladder, followed by the others until just Ace and Skate were left in the steeple.

"You," Ace nodded to the hatch.

"No," Skate said, "last one shuts the door."

Logic won out. Ace was not the person to hang on the ladder with one arm while setting the hatch back in place. He would need all ten white knuckles just to get himself down the ladder.

It was painful and almost funny to watch. Ace on his belly, terrified, inching himself backwards to the hatch opening, letting his legs down through the opening, and easing himself onto the top rungs of the ladder while clawing desperately at the floor to keep himself from sliding out of control through the opening. Skate offered his hand, but Ace just glared at it, balefully, and worried himself into a position where he could begin the climb down.

Once Ace was halfway down the ladder, Skate hoisted himself through the hatch hole and down the top few rungs. Heights didn't bother him, so once he was onto the rungs he was easily able to pull the door back into place over his head. There was no way to re-jimmy the latch and close it, but that was fine. All was back in place.

There was a grey thumbprint near the handle, probably from Hack, and Skate meticulously wiped it clean with his shirtsleeve, while hanging by his crooked elbow on the top rung. There must be no tell-tale signs. It was a mission, and he was tail man.

(<o>).[].(<o>)

Ace was barely off the ladder when Skate got to the ground. Book and Patrick were in the dim ante-room, waiting. Hack had gone ahead down the tunnel. They were lined up, and about to start down the tunnel together, when Hack popped up from below the floor.

"Taranto, he's back."

Everyone looked from Hack to Ace.

"Trapped," Book whispered, "like rats."

"What's he doing?" Ace said softly.

"Something with the boiler," Hack shrugged, "I didn't stick around."

This was bad. If Taranto were in his other room, they could conceive of slipping past him, through the boiler room, and out the side passage leading to the auditorium. But if he was in the boiler room they were, indeed, trapped like rats.

They could creep down the tunnel and wait, hopefully, for Taranto to leave. But they were in a time-crunch. Lunch was over in just a few minutes, and they had to get back to line up in the playground. If they didn't, questions would be asked and trouble would follow.

And, who could guess how long Taranto would take with his boiler room fiddling. They could be huddled, waiting, for half an hour or more: way, way, way too long.

"Maybe," Skate breathed desperately, "we can get down into the choir loft."

148

Without waiting for a reply, Skate clambered up the wall ladder as fast as he could go. That locked door up in the steeple, he knew, let out over the choir loft. They'd seen it plenty of times from church. A short doorway, high on the wall, flush with no landing, and a set of dusty painted wall rungs leading up to it.

No one ever climbed those rungs – not that they'd seen. But they were there, and they were a way out. Maybe.

Halfway up the wall Skate stopped.

"Hack," he whispered, "the wire."

Hack lobbed his coil of hangar wire up to Skate, who caught it smoothly in one hand, clamped it in his teeth, and continued climbing.

Up through the unlocked hatch, and over to the door. Skate hooked an end of the wire into the door jamb behind the lock, and pulled, and, instantly, miraculously, the lock popped open. It happened so immediately he was surprised, and he only caught the door after it swung half-way open. It opened outwards, towards the choir loft. He was high above the back balcony, which was the choir loft with the church organ, and which looked down on the main church floor.

He held the door and peeked around the corner. The church was empty.

Escape. Escape appeared possible.

Skate turned back to the hatchway. Hack was already coming through, offering to help.

"It's open," he whispered to Hack, "we're out."

Hack leaned over the opening and pumped his fist several times, pulling the train whistle: the sign to "peel".

(<o>).[].(<o>)

It was actually pretty impressive. Patrick and then Book came charging up the ladder and into the steeple: quiet and fast. Hack hoisted them into the belfry and aimed them at Skate. Skate had the door open and gave a hand as they went out, back first, down the rungs into the choir loft. Even Ace made good time. The situation clearly called for it.

Hack gently shut the hatch door, remembering to latch it, and scrambled past Skate, backwards out the door and down the ladder.

Skate the tail man had the tricky bit: swinging out the doorway, making sure it was clean, and locked behind him, with little to hold onto once the door was closed. For a moment he was balanced on a ladder rung, leaning forward into the wall, with nothing to hold onto and a twenty foot backward drop if he lost his equilibrium.

They waited for him at the bottom. Sitting around the base of the ladder they were out of sight from anyone in the church below.

Skate, on the ladder above, was in plain view of anyone who might come in to the church. He half climbed, half fell, down to the bottom, slumping in the space they'd left for him on the balcony floor.

"Down to the church," Ace whispered, "up the aisle, then the hallway, and out. Follow me."

But before Ace could move, they heard the sound, their doom – the main door to the church closing behind someone. They froze. They could hear sharp steps on the hard church floor directly below them. They were no longer alone.

Hack was nearest, so he raised his head to look over the choir loft balcony. He saw, he paled. He lowered his head. They could tell by his face. It was a nun.

Each of them slowly rose into a crouch and looked over the balcony; just the tops of their heads showing, as they surveyed the scene. It was Sister Joel, now positioned in the second pew, kneeling with her devout back to them, praying her midday angelus.

Sister Joel! the no-nonsense sixth grade disciplinarian. She was offering her adoration. They were hiding in shame and desecrating her devotion.

Worse yet – they were trapped – like rats.

(<o>)/(7.11)\(<o>)

I did not know Kenny Koolala very well, but we hung out in some of the same circles. He was far more deeply into the weed business than we ever were (Hack was known to parcel out an elbee* from time to time was about our limit).

You probably remember his claim to fame. He invented the famous Koala Bear roach clip, where you could squeeze the metallic buttocks on a cute little metal Koala Bear and clamp your marijuana cigarette in its cute little jaws. Then you could continue smoking your marijuana cigarette down to the super-heated nub, known as a "roach" for some reason, by using your cute little metal Koala Bear as a heat sink.

Calvin was not our social secretary, and would never apply for the position, but he would make desultory attempts at taking messages. He was unreliable in the area of details, and indifferent in the area of precision, and he never really tried to keep track of the comings and goings, but he was inch-by-inch pressed into service as a message center despite all that.

So when Koolala called Doogan's Bar looking for a ride on a rainy day, Calvin surveyed the crowd and handed the phone to me.

(<o>).[].(<o>)

"I don't know," Skate was saying, "it was a tight right-hand curve, and suddenly I was skidding through a curtain of my own sparks."

Skate was talking to Grady the main motorcycle mechanic at the Lake Street Triumph shop.

"What kind of curve?" Grady pressed, "on one of these suck-sack lake country gravel roads, or what?"

"No, here in town," Skate said, "at that intersection up towards Prospect Park, where the road rises to your right a little bit."

"And you laid it down there? Why? Rain slick, grease puddle, flat tire ….what?"

Skate had a double-silver-dollar-sized circular scab up the side of his right knee, and a rip in his jeans displaying his coagulation to the world. His right arm, shoulder to elbow, was black with bruising, and his ribs clicked and squeaked, painfully, when he moved the arm just so.

He was messed up to the point where even the regular motorcycle shop guys took notice. They were downtown cool most of the time, but they gathered around like little girls to hear about motorcycle madness of the mayhem persuasion.

"What to you mean, 'why'", Skate countered, "I was cutting it too short, I guess, and then I was sideways."

Grady was shaking his head slowly side to side, even before Skate finished.

"No, there is always a reason," Grady said, "there is always an explanation."

(<o>).[].(<o>)

Skate pulled up in front of the warehouse where Koolala worked.

Kenny was out front waiting and scuttled down to the curb, anxious to get away.

Skate gave him the usual interrogative, "Have you ridden a bike before?"

When Koolala said 'no', Skate gave him the biker litany.

"Put your left foot here," Skate indicated a foot peg, "and swing your right leg over the seat. Don't touch the tail pipes, they're hot. Then settle in and hold on."

Kenny mounted the bike and leaned forward, stiff-arming Skate's shoulders. Skate did not know it then, but this was a bad sign. A nervous and inexperienced rider will not lean correctly and naturally, into the curve, and in the worst case will do everything backwards, putting a nasty wobble into the ride.

"Do not put your feet down, I will keep the bike upright when we stop. You keep your feet on the foot pegs and lean with me on the turns."

"Okay?" Skate asked.

Koolala nodded yes, and Skate peeled away from the curb, faster than necessary, in the king high of the motorcycle moment.

"Shit Fire!" Skate yelled, "Het up."

Then he canned it north, through the industrial park, along the railroad tracks, and up the hill into Prospect Park. He was hard on the throttle and jamming through the gears, happy to have a hard ride to fly through the graying afternoon. There had been light rain all day, and they passed through a short sprinkle on the way up the grade.

Then they went up a shallow incline and leaned over for a tight right.

(<o>).[].(<o>)

It was one of those don't-know-what-hit-you moments.

Skate was still sitting upright on his bike, but suddenly the road was peeling a layer off his right knee, and driving his right elbow up into his ribs. He looked 'down' past his leg, and saw a rooster-tail of sparks flying 'up' towards him as the right footpeg was being ground down by the pavement.

He came to a halt with his motorcycle facing ass-backwards up the street, and his leg pressed under the motor. It only took a moment before he realized the most pain was from the engine burning through the inside of his leg, so he kicked himself out from under and rolled back and down toward the safety of the ditch.

He laid there for a second, until he saw the gasoline was flowing out of his tank, dripping out from under the fill-cap, and running down the slope towards him.

It was kind of painful, but Skate hopped to his feet. No bones broken. Then he pulled his motorcycle up off the road with a mighty heave, then straddled the seat and backed onto the shoulder of the road, and settled it on the side-stand.

He looked over his shoulder and saw Koolala, sitting cross-legged on the grass margin up from the gravel shoulder. He looked peaceful, rested, and unhurt.

"You okay?" Skate asked.

Koolala just nodded, and Skate started trying to explain.

"I don't know what happened, really. I have never had this before."

Skate looked apologetically at Koolala, shrugging.

"I don't know what happened," he was repeating himself, he realized, "I'm glad you're okay."

Koolala did not appear to have a scratch on him, but he was looking a little shaken and pretty shaky.

"You look a little jumpy," Skate offered.

Koolala smiled despite himself, and hunched his shoulders, sitting on the shoulder.

"Man," he said, "you hit the nail sometimes."

(<o>)/(7.15)\(<o>)

They looked at each other: Skate to Ace to Book to Patrick to Hack.

Ace looked at his watch, and then held his wrist up for them to see. Lunch was almost over. If they didn't get back out to the playground, in order to file in lines through the south-side door, they would be caught beyond caught. If they were discovered in the midst of this mission, they could get "kicked out". It had happened to others, it could be their turn now. That meant disgrace, trouble at home, and "public school".

The squad was in distress.

Skate silently waved a hand until he had their attention. Then he gave the fist sign, to "freeze", then he counted out with his fingers: one, two.

Then, without any further hesitation he rolled to his left and started a walking crouch to the stairs. He could feel the boys behind him, still frozen.

As quietly as a prayer he went down the choir loft steps into the vestibule. He considered bolting out the front of the church and racing around to the playground but knew it was hopeless. Sister Joel would hear the door; and besides, the squad would still be stuck.

He turned instead towards the front of the church where Sister Joel was deep in devotion, her back to him. He stopped at the baptistery and dipped his fingers in the font, touching the oddly greasy holy water. Nobody could explain it, but holy water had a special feel.

He rubbed his moist fingers together. He thought about tasting it, but he did not dare. A Chinese communist had once defiled a church by drinking holy water. It had burned his throat like foaming acid.

152

Skate walked quietly forward, expecting her to whirl and confront him, but she did not hear him. So, when he was almost up to the second pew he let his shoe scuff the floor.

Sister Joel whirled like he'd jabbed her.

"What are you doing here?" she demanded with a feral growl.

"Just looking around," he said.

"Well, that doesn't do," she said, "you're out of bounds."

"The office," she whispered harshly (they were, after all, in church), "NOW!"

(<o>).[].(<o>)

Skate and Sister Joel went to the office.

Nobody asked how he could possibly have gotten into the back of the church. And nobody thought to inquire whether he was there to pray for his sins.

Skate got three whacks with the strap across his tender palms. He was still new in school, and this was his first real crime. They called his mother and sent him home.

Skate would not be delivering milk after this. That was a privilege for top students who did not cause trouble.

(<o>).[].(<o>)

The boys waited two minutes, one, two, and then filed quickly down the choir loft steps and up through the church. They stepped into the hallway near the bottom of the stairs, crossed past the janitor's door, quietly lest Mr. Taranto hear them. Then they slipped out into the playground, through the same door where they'd started, just as the bell was ringing to call them in. They lined up, and went up to class.

A good mission, but not perfect. One casualty.

(<o>)/(7.18)\(<o>)

By 1976 the Revolution was over. It was the year of the big-deal birthday of America, the year of the Dragon, a leap year, and the advent of Skate's 25th year.

The war in Viet Nam was over. We lost. The Radicals were all either in law school, or they were trying to get jobs as professors, or hunkered down back on the farm.

The Vets were mostly all back – some people thought a few were still locked up in camps. America had survived another rash of greed and muddy thinking and, as it always had in the past, was prepared to forget about it and get on with whatever new business was at hand.

But nothing that takes so long, and grinds so hard, is over so easy.

(<o>).[].(<o>)

Patrick came out first, and he came out early.

It was the Spring of 1964, and the guys were still in 6th grade at Our Lady of the Snows when Patrick came to school and announced his belief the Viet Nam war was "morally wrong". We didn't pay too much attention, to be honest. In those days Patrick was just someone we knew, not someone we hung around

153

with much – he didn't start on 'patrol' with us until later. Besides, the war wasn't even a war at that point, it was a "police action", like Korea.

And we were weaned on war movies, and the glories of fighting the Nazis – and the Japs. The Nazis especially, we were given to believe, were just like the Communists – not technically, maybe, but "the effect was the same." So fighting Communists was just like our fathers had done twenty years earlier in Europe.

In those years we didn't know too many people in the active military. Some of the legendary neighborhood tough guys were in the service, but that was always a case of being "sentenced" to serve in the military. After stealing a car or maybe robbing a gas station, the choice would be jail or the Army. The tough guys always chose the Army, and the general feeling was this was a wise choice: the discipline would be "good for them." Nobody considered it a mistake to train embryonic criminals in survival skills and the use of weapons and explosives. And, in truth, the military generally was "good for them." They got out; they developed or continued their drinking habit; and they got dead-end jobs. Some of them took advantage of the GI Bill and took a course in auto mechanics.

That a war against communism could be "wrong" was a proposition that might have appalled us, if we'd considered it seriously. Which we didn't.

(<o>).[].(<o>)

In the Fall of seventh grade, the 1964 election year, Sister Marie organized a mock debate, pitting Skate and a kid named "Salt" Peters, arguing in favor of Goldwater, against Book and Patrick supporting Johnson for President. They each organized their points on note cards, and took turns with debate and rebuttal, all very formal. Book and Patrick prepared a brilliant argument, quoting from the legacy of Kennedy and the vision of the Great Society. Skate and Peters had thrown together a broadside about the communist threat, liberty or death, and the wisdom of nuclear superiority and "bang for the buck."*

The class voted for the debate winner, and Skate and Peters won in a landslide (to the approval of Sister Marie).

(<o>).[].(<o>)

The most profound philosophical question we faced in those days was whether it was alright for spies to do bad things, like tell lies to their friends and family, or steal from foreign governments, or kill enemy agents or soldiers, if it was in the service of democracy in the fight against communism.

For example, suppose you were a spy in Germany during the second world war, and you knocked out a German soldier and tied him up and took his uniform, and then walked up to some other German guards, and shot them point blank without warning from behind so you could get into the German headquarters and transmit false orders that diverted an enemy battalion, so that American lives were saved?

You might think the moral compass for these questions would be Catholic theology, since we were fairly well-educated in that area. But, no. Our moral leaders in these questions were people like Sgt. Saunders, the squad leader on

"Combat", David March, the double agent on "Blue Light", and to a lesser extent, Colonel Hogan from "Hogan's Heroes".

The answer to the moral dilemma?

Are you kidding? NO! Not a problem.

We all knew the rule – wearing an enemy uniform could get you shot without a court martial – but this was cut and dried – what later generations called a no-brainer. Of course it was okay.

So although it might seem strange to say, this ethical climate set the stage for our hi-jinks in grade school. We rifled desks for tests, snuck into the principal's office and read confidential files, searched the nurse's office, stole unblessed sacramental hosts, drank sacramental wine, explored areas of the complex that were off-limits, and abused the trust in every way we could.

Because it was acceptable, at least to us. We were soldiers, in an army of our own, and we were spies: even Patrick.

(<o>)/(7.22)\(<o>)

"Suppose we invented a time machine, when we were thirty years old," Book was saying.

He and Skate were in the back yard, eating peanut butter and jelly sandwiches on white bread. Book's mom cut his crusts off, but that wasn't permitted in Skate's house, so he toughed it out. They were twelve years old.

"And suppose we zoomed back, and landed right here, now."

"Yeah," Skate said.

"And suppose we saw ourselves, and they, us, saw us."

"Maybe we could get on, and go back to the Civil War times," Skate said.

"Or, maybe, we could zoom forward together and meet ourselves when we're forty."

"Maybe we could find out how we made the machine then, and make one now."

"Right, then we could go wherever we wanted" Book said.

"Right, then we wouldn't need to invent a time machine when we're thirty. We'd already have one."

"Then we could go forward, to when we were thirty, and show them, us, our time machine so they could make their own."

"But they'd already have one. Because it's us."

"And we'd grow up knowing what a time machine looked like, and remembering we'd seen one now, for when we built one then."

"I thought you wanted to go and get one for ourselves, now."

"My, yes, of course," Book answered, puzzled.

"Then we wouldn't need to go forward in time to give one to ourselves when we're thirty. We'd already have one, and we could just keep it."

"Yes, sure, I see. That's the same one we'd use to fly back here, like I was saying at first."

"But only if they flew back to today. If we flew back to tomorrow, we'd already have the time machine they gave us."

Book nodded. They continued with their sandwiches.

"Did you see that comic Ace had," Book said, "where they had these time machines that put you in the past, but up on invisible sidewalks. The rule was you couldn't touch anything, cause you might change history."

"Yeah," Skate said, chewing, "he goes back to dinosaur days, and accidentally steps on a butterfly."

"Yup, he goes back to the present, and everything's still in dinosaur times," Book said, "you think that's realistic?"

(<o>)/(7.23)\(<o>)

Terry was the deserter Patrick brought home.

It was the summer of 1971, and the political climate seemed volatile. To Skate, this caused a serious disconnect.

The boys were raised on pledging allegiance and patriotic anthems. They had taken the oath, at age twelve, to be confirmed as Catholic soldiers for Christ.

They had graduated from television glorifying western cowboy heroes, to television glorifying the second world war, to the television era of spies and cat burglars: "Secret Agent", "The Man from U.N.C.L.E.", "T.H.E. Cat", and Al Mundy: "It Takes a Thief".

Meanwhile they lived in streets filled with protest and alive with alternative viewpoints. A lot of people, like Patrick, had turned the corner: they lived a new ethic. A lot of people, like Skate, were not so sure, not so convinced, not so easily swayed (not so easily de-programmed). There was lightning in the air while we rode the night train.

(<o>).[].(<o>)

The boys were assembled on a summer night. Terry was there with a case of beer. Book was manning the platter, switching the discs from Fever Tree to Bach and back to Dylan and The Who.

Terry was living in the shed, which was actually just a storage room adjacent to Rexee's place. Terry was A.W.O.L. from the Army, Absent Without Leave, having taken a weekend pass and extended it through several months of the summer.

Terry was a small-town guy who knew somebody from home that knew somebody that knew Patrick. The web at its finest, a friend of a friend of a friend. Patrick had met him downtown and brought him home.

Terry was technically a fugitive, but the Army was not (probably!) working on tracking him down, and so he was safe enough with us, and we with him – so long as he stayed out of trouble with the law, and didn't make any effort to get back into the system.

We did not want to catch trouble for harboring a fugitive, and if he got caught, or turned himself in, it might come back to us. We worried he might get caught, but turn himself in? There was little chance of that.

Terry was living the good life, hunkered down in his rent-free garage space. He slept the morning away and turned up in the afternoon to hang out. He could make enough panhandling on a daily basis to buy burgers for himself: sometimes near the campus, sometimes downtown. Every so often he would mow a lawn for money, and once he went down to the welfare office and got a handout by giving a false name and presenting himself as destitute. They gave him a small check for food and a voucher for one night in a hotel. Once in a while he'd have enough extra to buy some beer for the boys.

It was dump night.

"So," Ace asked, "who wants to go?"

Hack cracked open a beer, "Me? I'll stick by the brew-ski for awhile."

(<o>).[].(<o>)

The beer was gone. It was still dump night.

"So," Ace asked, "who wants to go?"

"Yeah," Terry said, "let's go."

Utopia to Ace.

(<o>).[].(<o>)

They scrambled up between the footings and came out in the ditch between the tracks. Terry and Hack were leading the way, with Skate and Ace behind.

The easy way in to the dump was to find the drainage pipe and cross under the tracks, then under the cyclone fence with razor wire topping, directly into the dump. There was a harder way, which they had done many times – before Book found the drainage pipe one hilarious night. This was to scale the slope, cross the northbound tracks, and then shimmy under the cyclone fence in a low spot that Ace had dug out.

Terry and Hack were assembled in the trough, waiting for Ace and Skate, when they heard the low rumble of an approaching train. It was a northbound SOO Line freight, creeping along above their heads. The engine had passed by the time Ace made the climb, the tracks were blocked.

"No matter," said Ace, "under we go."

"No!" yelled Terry, enthused with beer, "Von Ryan's Express!"

And then Terry was scrambling up the shallow incline, towards the northbound tracks. The boys followed.

"It's easy," Terry yelled, "just like Frank Sinatra."

It was noisy by the tracks, they shouted to be heard.

"You're not serious!" said Ace.

"Just watch," Terry said.

The train was sliding by, car after car, pretty slowly. The massive steel wheels looked as big as table tops, and the lumbering freight pounded the track. Even though smooth to pass, you could still feel the weight of it – the ground rumbled beneath them – serious weight.

Terry laid down and squirmed his way around to a position parallel with the tracks. His body was half on the rail ties, and the hardware fastened to the cars, the steel ladder rungs and detaching rods, were passing directly over him: slow but forceful.

There were two sets of wheels, last of the first and first of the second, then a gap under each freight car. Then two more sets of wheels. The trick, as Von Ryan had shown, was to wait for a gap, roll over the rails and rest between the tracks, UNDER THE TRAIN, then wait for another gap and roll again to the far side of the tracks.

157

(<o>).[].(<o>)

Ace and Skate were biking. It was a summer Saturday in 1965, they were thirteen. They pedaled over to the library and threw sharp stones at the carp in the pond. They crossed the creek and pedaled up into the woods. Skate had a cigarette, Viceroy, stolen from his mother. They smoked it.

South of them, along the river, they heard a train whistle.

Ace had the cigarette. He loved to smoke.

"Let's go," he said, taking a final drag, "I'll show you something."

Ace launched himself down the woody path, pedaling furiously, high-speed and fearless. Skate followed. They crossed the little bridge and angled along the creek bed. The tracks were just ahead. Ace skidded to a stop, spraying gravel like someone who lived on his bike.

The train was coming.

"Here, this way," Ace said, and scrambled up to the tracks.

They lay together, on the ends of the ties, with the train approaching, maybe 100 yards away by this time. Ace took a penny out of his pocket, showed it to Skate, and then laid it carefully on the track.

"Okay," Ace said, "back up and watch."

They went down the grade to their bikes and waited. The slow-moving freight approached. They stood, down in the right-of-way, their eyes about level with the tracks. The engine came by, they could see the engineer. The front wheel of the engine crossed their vision. The penny fell off the track.

To Skate it looked like the penny had shaken off the rail just before the train crossed it.

When the train, a shorty, had passed, they clambered up to the rail. They found the penny right away, laying on the track bed. It was hot to the touch, and distorted like a piece of well-worked plasticene.

It was the size of quarter, although egg shaped and not round. On one edge it was normal, on the other it was flattened to a knife edge. This penny, this immutable thing, had been distended by the merest touch of the train's first wheel.

"Jeez," Skate said, "Jeez."

"For thine is the kingdom," Ace recited the Protestant version, "the power and the glory. Amen."

(<o>).[].(<o>)

Terry had rolled under the train. He was laying on the ties, flat on his back, his arms crossed over his chest, with tons and tons of freight rolling over him, not many inches from his body.

The boxcars were fairly high off the ground. Skate looked south, hoping not to see a grain car, which was the kind that swept low to the tracks.

Ace was hysterical.

"Move!" he screamed, "Move! you'll be crushed! Oh Jesus! Stay!"

Terry was calm, immobile. He tilted his head back towards the back of the train, and waited for a gap. The train was picking up speed, or so it seemed to Skate, but the progress was still pretty slow.

"Von Ryan's Express!" Terry shouted.

And then he rolled across the next line of track, right between two sets of wheels, just as he should, and flopped onto the ground on the other side, in safety.

Hack was already in position.

"Greeeeen River!" Hack shouted.

Then he rolled across the near-side track, and carried his roll across the tracks, passing under one freight car in one swift double move. Hack was across.

"Screw this," Ace said, backing his way down the slope.

"I'll take the pipe," he went on, "that's enough thrill for me."

Skate considered the options. The train was indeed, although imperceptibly, speeding up. He thought about rolling across after Terry and Hack, felt a twinge in his back, and he followed Ace instead. They went under the tracks through the drain pipe and met the daredevils in the dump.

Ace was practically screaming, the train was still rolling by.

"You two are fucking crazy!"

Skate looked at Hack, "Green River?"

(<o>)/(7.29)\(<o>)

A one act play in several scenes:

Scene Seven –

The opening effects of the last scene slowly begin to reverse themselves. The taped crowd noise comes up to normal levels and then the lights begin to come up around the stage, as the patrons slowly thaw from their freeze, and the sound of crowd noise eventually transfers from the tape to the actors. Finally, the crowd noise lowers to a level where individual voices can be discerned.

=#=#=#=

```
     Hack
(laughing)
… and then Ace comes traipsing downstairs with a wig, makeup,
and dress, looking just as femmy as anything …
     Patrick
(also laughing)
… looked better than Eleanor Roosevelt.
     Ace
And sexier
     Hack
Gawd, and there's Book, doing one of his rarified leaning
drunks. Suckin' suds with a wall for support
(laughs at the memory)
and Ace comes around the corner swishing his hip and Book gets
a look on him like a Panda in heat.
     Patrick
Gorilla his dreams.
     Hack
Haw! and Book gets up some steam and marches right over, full
cup of beer, and says "Madam, you have yet to have the
pleasure of my company."
```

159

        Patrick
(laughing uncontrollably)

        Hack
And Ace says
(laughs) and Ace says
(gruff falsetto)
"I've admired you from afar."

        Ace
No, I said
(believable falsetto)
"I've oft admired you."

        Hack
Yes. Yes
(wiping tears from his eyes)
and Book stands up real tall, getting ready to bow, except he
tilts back too far and falls right on his back, ass over tea
kettle. Beer everywhere. Gawd.

        Patrick
And Ace scoots upstairs and changes.

        Hack
And Book spends two days calling people up asking "Who was
that beautiful blonde in the red dress"
(more laughter)

        Book
(amused but hiding it)
My, that makes rerun number one-thousand-seven-hundred-and-
seventy-some. Why is it that gets retold whenever we're out
together?

        Patrick
Because it's such a good story, of course.

        Ace
Really. Really! Hack, Hack, Hack!
(mock pleading)
Tell it again.

        Hack
(laughing)
Okay. See Book's birthday was coming up and we all started
hinting that some dish had a crush on him. So … wait a minute,
I'm losing my audience.
(he snaps his fingers in front of Skate's reposed face)
Bait to Skate, bite me Skate.

        Skate
(coming abruptly into focus)
What, huh! Oh, sorry men. Guess I took a little doze there.

        Patrick
Long night, eh?

        Skate
Long life, yeah.

        Ace
Meditating on the vacuum between the ears? Becoming one with
the nothingness of space? Achieving the Zen peace of mind?

Skate
Yes, a very small piece
(gesturing),
a tiny piece of mind.

Book
Beatific, was it?

Skate
Oh, wow. I just had a great idea. How about we set a world's
record for the longest, thinnest, American flag?

Patrick
On a roll of toilet paper. Five hundred sheets to the wind?

Rexee'
Oh, please, toilet paper again? Crumpled, folded, what?

Patrick
Hey, that was a perfectly legitimate sociological
investigation.

Rexee'
Mack the Finger said to Louie the King, I've got forty-eight
red, white and blue shoe strings, and a thousand telephones
that do not ring, do you know where I can get rid of these
things?*

Skate
A patriotic happening, portent of the new revolution.

Patrick
Dream on. The symbolic revolution died.

Ace
Ah, but there's been no symbolic end to the symbolic
revolution. Maybe this is the fitting requiem.

Skate
And maybe a fitting requiem for the web too.

Ace
Oh, hell, (annoyed) what does that mean, Skate?

Skate
Oh, hell, nothing I guess. But we've been together a long
time.

Ace
Eons, epochs, geologic periods.

Skate
And things evolve, do they not?

Patrick
Ch-ch-ch-changes.

Skate
Well, a lot of things can happen in a hurry. That's all.

Ace
Oh, doom and gloom.

Rexee'
I see it differently. I see you guys as people I'll know the
rest of my life.
(she pauses)
I'm not the sentimental type, I think you know, but I sat here

161

at this table an hour or two ago, while somebody tried to blow
us up …
    Book
(quietly)
Blow us away, you mean.
    Rexee'
Yeah, and we're still sitting here, and he's hauled off. And I
look at you idiots, and I think I've never loved anyone so
much in my life.
    Ace
Better than Woodstock, yeah?
    Rexee'
Better than sex.
(she looks around the table, embarrassed)
Oh, gawd, all I'm saying is I know you guys now, even if we
haven't all talked that much, and twenty years from now I'll
still feel safe with you.
    Hack
(nodding)
That's something.
(The door opens and Lily of the Alley walks in, a crone
dressed in black. The conversation continues without
interruption. Lily moves slowly to the center of the stage,
behind the table, and sits next to a man at the bar wearing a
brown corduroy jacket.)
    Ace
You know it.
(he surveys the table)
I don't know if this is the right time to say it, but I'm
moving in with Annie.
    Book
And moving out of the house?
    Ace
Yes and no. For the nonce I'm going to keep an address at the
Web. My parents will expire if I live in sin.
    Patrick
You're what? Twenty-four years old?
    Skate
Technically, yes.
    Hack
He can't help it, he was held back a grade.
    Ace
I was not! I was so good at kindergarten they had me do it
twice, is all.
    Skate
That's why you're so mature, compared to the rest of us.
    Ace
Please don't torture me over this. I'll pay my rent.
(Lily leans over, and touches Rexee' on the shoulder. The
other players freeze momentarily, as she whispers into Rexee's
ear).

          Lily
They 'eard you dear, but ney bey acknowledge. Dey 'ave it.

          Rexee'
(startled)
I know you, don't I.
(It's a statement, not a question. She pauses)
It's been a hell of day. And now I'm awash.

          Lily
Mortay came. You'll say. Stoy.
(Lily swivels on her bar stool and turns away, facing the bar.
Rexee' turns to face front.)

          Rexee'
(shouting)
Stick together, that's the thing.
(The table is startled by the outburst)

          Skate
Rex, you okay?

          Rexee'
(embarrassed)
I didn't say anything.
(a man dressed in a brown corduroy jacket swivels off his
barstool and stands behind the table)

          Author
Yes you did, and we all heard it. Right boys?
(Everyone at the table nods their head, as the Author makes
his way out the door. He pauses for a second, and throws a
casual salute).

          Author
Be seeing you.*
(He backs out the door).

          Book
Who was that masked man?

          Skate
Some guy, Secret Agent.

          Ace
Number Six is unmutual

          Patrick
Back to the deal, am I getting this right? Rexee' wants us all
to stick together forever, meanwhile Ace is moving in with
Annie in some kind of Old Testament sense, and Skate's going
up north with Hack to play Davy Crocket.

          Ace
And you're having a Bicentennial bambino -- that won't change
things at all.

          Book
My, yes, that summarizes. And since we're in confession,
forgive me Father, but I'm thinking about applying to graduate
school.

          Ace
What for?

          Patrick
For studies on contemplations of the smart?

163

Hack
For about five years?

Book
Because I'm not inclined to spend the rest of my life in the
library, guarding other people's warehoused knowledge. I'd
like to go forth and make some new for myself.

Ace
Hey, the warehouse is a noble pursuit.

Skate
Oh, puh-leeze.

Book
It may well be, but can you stand it forever? Will it always
be there? Twenty years from now, you want to be driving a
forklift?

Hack
They don't trust him on the forklift yet. Maybe someday.

Ace
Simple pursuits keeping mind and body together. That's what I
want out of my work life. Short hours, long vacations. Like in
France, they get a month every year.

Patrick
It's hard to argue with a "back to basics" philosophy. But you
urban workers are forever the tools of management. You're just
an asset to them, disposable when the next economic downturn
swings through.

Ace
You're any different, wearing a white collar and working the
night shift?

Patrick
Right now, no. I'm no better off than you, and maybe worse. If
you're okay with being poor and having a lot of free time,
then Hack has got the formula.

Hack
Poor, that's the plan alright.

Patrick
He'll be poor, scratching out a living, but on his own terms
and on his own land.

Hack
Until they take it for taxes, you mean.

Ace
Go to ground? That's where the revolution has taken us? Get
out of town and suffer your alienation in the woods. That's
wonderful. What a load.

Patrick
That's where I see it going.

Ace
Back to the wilderness, and scratch the dirt making babies,
and raise a load of simple country hicks with no idea of city
life or what the world is all about? That's a prescription for
disaster!

        Skate
Hey, Hack resembles that remark.

        Ace
Those woods are full of religious nuts and survivalists,
fringe thinkers of every stripe. You want to raise your kids
in the cultural vacuum? Me, I see the city is fucked, but the
woods are worse. Way worse, in my mind. You're just asking to
be simple peasants at the bottom of the food chain.

        Patrick
You're going to change the world, sitting here?

        Ace
Change comes out of the cities, not out of the country. It is
ever thus.

        Book
Except for that simple shepherd, lamb of the flock, and savior
to the world.

        Ace
My turn, I say, Oh Puh-leeze.

        Rexee'
There's never much to hope for, in the country or the city.
Literature tells us that. It's desolation everywhere, and just
hope you're alert when the predators descend. Like this
morning.

        Skate
Are we really that gloomy?

        Patrick
I am.

        Hack
Not me.

        Ace
Neither am I, but I don't see fleeing to the country as an
answer.

        Hack
Who's taking flight?

        Skate
Too easy, too easy an answer, Who is taking flight? The
American Dream, that's all.

        (Blackout).

(<o>)/(7.30)\(<o>)

diaria -- 7.0 -- 11/14/76 -- austin

time frame is always an issue, and it's best if we're
clear on where we're at. This rendering, like a lot of
fictions, is jumping around in time: flashbacks, fast
forwards and all that. There's nothing new about this
and you're all familiar with it in some form or another.

A story doesn't have to be told in linear order,
although that's the way a few people do it. Huckleberry
Finn* being a prime example; the story starts on day one

165

and proceeds, like the river, in single file order to the end: simple, straight forward.

The classics, I'm told, work both ways. Homer, and those guys, often started a story in the middle and then worked forwards and backwards from there -- I've heard the Odyssey* or the Iliad* is like that.

And some people really like to make an issue out of the time thing.

Joseph Conrad wrote the Secret Agent* about anarchists attempting to destroy the greenwich observatory where the master clock was kept. The point being that if time was destroyed then society would fall into chaos.

Interesting premise, a little cracked.

Anyway he took time for a theme and to make some kind of point arranged the chapters all out of order. I'm not clear on his intent, and it's a pretty extreme example, really, but there you are. He was a helluva writer anyway.

Meanwhile we've got our own concerns. The story here opens in the middle, the bicentennial year. At first it was easy -- on a day in June the plane arrives and the guys all go to the bar.

Simple.

The narrative bits were supposed to be from that day -- as with Lily and Annie, or they're supposed to be flashbacks to the 70s, 60s, or even the 50s.

Now, however, it starts to get tricky. Some of the narratives will go back, there's more to say about all that, the play part will have to stay with that day in June (to maintain the classical unities), but other sections will have to go FORWARD now too.

We've got to get up past the bicentennial fourth of July, which I may as well tell you is the climax of the story. Not to give too much away.

(<o>)/(7.31)\(<o>)

Bard by the barges, doing a Siddhartha* thing, listening to the river, and trying to find the place where musings lock. They say there is architecture so pure and perfect that when you walk inside it makes you cry. Can writing do that too? Doubtful. And why no architecture so pure and perfect that it makes you laugh? A better choice anyway. Writing can do that.

Bard stretches out in a shady spot with his back to a slender tree and his journal in his lap. Lunch is working in his belly, and last night's session is working on his brain. The water is lapping and soothing, he closes his eyes. A distant whistle sounds, like a westbound freight or the bells in a steeple, clear and pure. He contemplates the movies on the inside of his eyelids.

53. There are dozens of moose attacks on humans each year, resulting in death once or twice a decade. It is rare, although not unheard of, for an enraged moose to attack a house or a moving car.

54. The Boys Reformatory in Red Wing, MN.

55. Now called the Winnebago Mental Health Institute

56. Elbee (noun, drug slang), phonetic pronunciation of lb. indicating a pound dry weight. Eg. "Hack would occasionally sell an elbee of pot for extra money."

57. "Bang for the Buck" a phrase made popular by Barry Goldwater during the 1964 presidential election.

58. Dylan, Bob (1966). Highway 61 Revisited. ASCAP

59. Prisoner, The (1960s). Television Program. Be seeing you. An ominous salutation implying that you are being watched.

60. Clemens, Samuel Langhorne, Mark Twain's The adventures of Huckleberry Finn. New York, Grosset & Dunlap [1960] 60 p. illus. 29 cm.

61. The Odyssey : The Story of Odysseus by Homer, W. H. D. Rouse (Translator)

62. The Iliad : The Story of Achilles by Homer, W. H. D. Rouse (Translator)

63. Conrad, Joseph, The secret agent, a simple tale. Garden City, N.Y., Doubleday, 1953. 253 p. 19 cm.

64. Hesse, Herman (1877-1962). Siddhartha, a novel about Indian culture and Buddhist philosophy.

Chapter 8: Well Versed

Guy with an earring ain't always a faggot.
Lad who takes welfare is more than a maggot.
Don't look at me, man, you said it first;
It don't hurt to be well-versed.

Trusted and dusted by all sorts of women
Disgusted and burped by some babes on the way
Hammered and stammered, squeezed until burst
It don't hurt to be well-versed.

Dreamy and lovesick and fighting depression
Bruising, forgiving, but learning no lesson
Whining and pining and dying of thirst
All part of getting well-versed.

Raged down some roadways and taken some spills.
Pursued some devils and eaten some hills.
Loved by a legion but ending up cursed;
It don't hurt to be well-versed.

=#=#=#=

"Wait a minute," Rexee' said, "what are you doing here?"

"It's the bare bones of my book, Rex," Skate said, "I'd like your reaction."

He had carefully typed about 30 pages, and pinched them into a slim binder with a clear plastic cover. His hope was to wow her with presentation. It was a fruitless effort with her, and he knew it. But he did it anyway.

"What's the concept?" she countered, "the meter is off on your poem, where does it go from here?"

"I'm not too worried about meter, I'm trying to tell a story."

"You're going to write poetry, but you're not too worried about meter? That's fucked, you know that, right?"

"Alright," he countered, "they're not poems, they're songs."

"Ah," she said, "then where's the music?"

"Don't have it, don't need it, just lyrics. That's what I've got here. Lyrics in wait of music."

She was in a mood, he could tell, and already he wished he'd chosen a better moment. As if such were possible.

"Look," he said, "we can do this another day."

"No, no, no," she said crossly, "we're here, let's do this. What am I holding?"

"Well-Versed," he said, "my novel."

"This is a novel?" she hefted the pages, skeptically, "pretty thin."

"It's the start of a novel," he sighed, "a novel in a novel form."

"THE NOVEL," she retorted, "IS A FORM."

"Well then, that's not what I mean. I mean it's a story, wrapped in the middle of a street poem. The soft chewy center is wrapped in a hard edged street poem."

He paused, weakly, "see?"

168

She checked her watch, "I've got an hour. Are you sure you want to hear what I say?"

"I'm listening. But let me explain the concept."

"Right away, that's bad," she said, "if the manuscript doesn't make itself clear, then there's something wrong."

"I'm just getting started," he moaned, "I just want to know if I was on the right track. It's not done yet, not even close."

"So this is you, pitching a story."

"Right," he said, "it's a what'cha-call, a 'treatment' that I'm pitching. Think of it that way."

"Alright," she nodded grimly, "let's see."

She settled back into her chair and started to read.

Skate started to pace the room, his anxiety verging on panic.

"Get out of here," she said sharply, "I can't read with you prowling."

He disobeyed and sat, and stayed, and waited.

=#=#=#=

I. Summer Dawns: People and Meetings

The Stammer

There's a guy named Stammer. A spidery lean galoot with thread bare cast-off clothing, a wispy beard and amiable disposition. You can see him roaming the streets with a paperboys sack over his shoulder. He carries his belongings in there with a few copies of the daily news.

He gets the papers for nothing because they like him down at the loading dock. He shows up in the morning when it's still dark, drinks a cup of coffee with the guys then scarfs up a few issues and rambles off.

He sells 'em for a quarter apiece to anyone. Spends his days in foot-cruisin' the city, calling on friends and hawking his papers. He doesn't commune with the type of people who subscribe to newspapers. They buy one periodically to patronize Stammer. It's his only source of income. It's his hustle.

Stammer sleeps nowhere, or anywhere, and he doesn't eat much. Eight or ten papers a day, at a quarter apiece, would keep him going. He just won't work, but he'll sharpen your knives for a meal.

The papers aren't necessarily new, either. If one issue is particularly good he'll get hold of extras and deal them for days. Possible souvenirs and landmark editions, don'tcha know.

He performs a public service by giving otherwise apathetic people an opportunity to be informed. He makes a living in return. Wandering hither and yon, peddling papers, honing knives and listening to all kinds of insane raps.

It's not a bad life. He grew into it.

Rocks

I've got a picture taken of Rocks for his high school graduation. He stares out angelically with freshly trimmed hair and long furry sideburns. A pudgy, religious looking character. On the back it says:

UP THE REVOLUTION – SMITE THE OPPRESSORS
PEACE AND LOVE, ROCKS.

…and somehow, that is just what it was like. Rocks would stride into the house with a grin on his face and he'd start rapping. And he'd rap and rap and sometimes say the most outrageous and insane things. Or he'd come in brooding and start talking about the fugging system and making totally inflammatory remarks only half in jest.

We should shoot the fugger, he'd say of Nixon, drag'm out in front of a wall and gun him down. Burp this.

Then his intense frown would ease a little and he'd glance at you and grin.

=#=#=#=

…There are just two kinds of people: Livers and Onions.

=#=#=#=

…The first thing Rocks ever said to me was "You think you're so smart and yet you don't know shid from dirt, boy, not shid from dirt."

=#=#=#=

They called him Junker, he coached boxing. A funny old conservative man, heavily involved with Civil Defense (he taught bomb-shelter management), a retired fire department reservist who worked for the Selective Service. He was quick to point out how valuable a first-aider would be in the event of nuclear holocaust.

He was basically likeable and struck me as fairly well-informed.

=#=#=#=

…Junker said to Rocks…

"Don't let 'em get you down, and don't let 'em get to ya. Just hop on that bike of yours and eat a hill. It'll do it; better'n my old truck here."

Indian Summer and the Law of Sevens

It was the summer of my twentieth year. I'd gone into the public library for some morning reading. I'd woken up with strong dream memories of living in an Iroquois village so my arms were loaded with books as I scanned the room looking for a seat. Saw a female with her back to me sitting alone at a four place table. Didn't want to break stride or appear undecided. Walked past the table and looped back to face her.

- Can I sit here?

…a nod, no more. Sit down, shuffle pages, she's a blond, kind of pretty, aloof. Says nothing. Really kind of pretty. Concentrating on her book, can't quite see the title, smokes low tar cigarettes … trying to quit? Brown bloodshot eyes, needs sleep.

Well, settle down to the books, take notes and make no distractions…work, work, work. Iroquois lived in lodges…religion based on dream interpretation, hmm…marriages often impermanent.

What next? It's hard to remember. I asked

- Interesting?

She shakes her head, attitude screaming leave me alone. I retreat back into the Iroquois. Hit the books, let her go. Light a cigarette, two drags and she lights one, not looking up. More notes.

Then what? Again no memory. She asks me the time. It's one to ten. Then easy talk from nowhere, chatter that feels good like effortless mere moments, she's got an appointment. Comes to the library every morning, reads a lot, can't stay, gotta go.

Every morning, eh? I memorize that detail and delve into more lore. The Iroquois turn out to be real interesting. Time passes, I fidget, the seats are hard, get up and stretch, take off my coat, light a cig and sip some coffee. In she strolls, over she looks. I smile, she smiles and walks right up to sit down.

- How's the reading, says she.
- Better than usual, says I

…and we're off. Rapping for an hour. I like her, she likes me, she speaks well, I listen intently, she returns the favor. I ask her out, she says okay and gives me her phone number.

It's time for me to split. Morning has passed, my factory foreman has been giving me heat, so I collect myself and get up to go. She asks me my name.

- Stammer, says I, and yours?
- I'm Iffie.

=#=#=#=

…Rocks is very funny, he cracks jokes that are supremely hilarious. One of those people; a stranger that you can know for years and never have a conversation. A mellow and together person, he speaks in understatement and has a quick grin. One of those quiet, able, thoughtful, hip organizers. A man you could trust in charge of your defense fund.

=#=#=#=

…you wake up alert, it's a summer day, the sun is shining, the door is open, the air is fresh and cool and soothing. The cup of coffee is hot and delicious, the cigarette tastes pretty good. The radio is on and some band is cutting hot licks, laying down grooves that sweeten the air, and you're cooking right along with them.

Slide guitar, violin and banjo humming through your head, rhythm of livin' and feeling real good. What a day to be alive. Man, I wanna get up and do my dance. Ooee, doin' the dance of life…

=#=#=#=

…I met a woman, said Rocks, who sold tape decks for a living. She had wit, beauty, charm, sparkle, and a boyfriend. FLUTTER AND WOW…

First Neck
Stammer met her at the beach. They snuggled in the sand and then went for a walk in the park after dark. Her name was Iffie.

- We kissed a million times and I felt her breast with my hand. That feel of warm, lush, perky flesh through a thin summer dress lingered with me for months. It was the most thrilling thing I'd ever done, or ever felt. She stopped me when I tried to unzip the front of her green checked summer shift. I was thirteen years old at the time but I can still remember blue-green striped into checkers and warm soft lips...

He walked her to a bus stop and didn't see her again for seven years.

Somewhere Near the Middle

"What is this shit?"

"Like I said, it's a street poem where the middle of the poem is bits and anecdotes jumbled together to make a story."

"Livers and Onions! You think that's clever?"

Skate was in a mood, for once, to stand his ground.

"I," he stressed the 'I', "*I* like it."

Rexee' blinked. She shook her head. She sighed.

"I can tell you like it," she said, "I just can't tell why."

He sagged a bit, but hung in there.

"Okay, let me tell you the structure. There's four parts, which map onto the seasons and the time of day. That's where the chapter titles come from."

He stood and started to pace again.

"It starts on a summer morning, when everything is bright and optimistic. The people you meet are likely to be friends."

She made a face.

"Then," he rushed on, "there's a section of autumn at noon, the best times. Then there's the winter evenings, where things come apart. Then it's Spring nights, where the mysteries descend on you and hope returns."

He stopped and took a breath.

"That's the structure," he halted, lamely, "holding the thing together in the middle."

She looked at him, dumbfounded, and said, "so your theme is that good things start in the morning and bad things happen in the evening, and everything is resolved at night. Is that it?"

He paused, afraid to answer, the critic in her driving him back into a cave of defense.

"It's a structure," he replied, "which is better than no structure at all, I think."

"Structure is good," she said, "but it's got to make sense, or it's nothing more than a constraint to no good purpose."

"C'mon Rex," he pleaded, "give it a chance."

"Look," she said, "you want soft soap or an honest appraisal?"

He was about to say 'soft soap', but he kept his mouth shut out of pride.

"Read on," he gasped, "and tell me what you think. I mean it."

She settled back in her chair.

"Make some coffee, would you?" she ordered, "and quit bugging me."

II. Fall Noons: Birth and Parties

Sampson's Billy

A guy named John, old Johnny Kruch
He had it all then he hit a jam
But it didn't kill him, not too much
He just packed his kit and went on the lam.

When I met him, by the depot
He was picking seed corn off the tracks
And he beat me back with an innuendo
Then disarmed me with a few wisecracks.

He boiled the seed corn in a kettle
And I ate with him and flapped my jaw
While he watched me close to gauge my mettle
Looking back I wonder what it was he saw

He had gray eyes and a keen perception
That time creased bindle stiff old man
And the road was his home and his predilection
He was so damn strong I wondered why he ran

It was quite some time before I heard his story
Bought the rap with some white port wine
And when he'd finished it was all before me
My jaw quit flapping and it feels just fine.

=#=#=#=

Wombman

Wombman, wombman, who do you know
What's up, slow down, where do you go
Take this, what's that, your friend didn't show
Too bad, so sad, it can't always flow
I'm here, you steer, I'll help you go slow
I'm here, it's clear, to lighten the blow.

=#=#=#=

…Ya, I've got a secret ambition, said Junker. To go back to school, finish my history degree, quit my job and buy a farm, twenty acres or so.

Then, he smiles serenely, I'd just sit around and wonder about things…

=#=#=#=

…it sometimes seems that people are like light bulbs; either bright or burnt out.

=#=#=#=

… there's only one way to get a quick doctor's appointment at the University Health Service. Walk in and say…

- I'd like to see my father, please.

173

Stammer told me about a secretary he knew named McGee. She spent her days sorting, shuffling, tearing and stapling. One day he noticed a bandage on the middle finger of her left hand...

- Are you prone to paper cuts in your line of work? He said
- You mean my finger? I hurt it dancing.

He took a breath, how do you injure a finger by dancing?

- I got a blister, she grinned coyly and motioned gingerly, snapping my fingers.

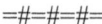

Vet

I remember hitching down to work, said Rocks, when I was in high school. An older guy, late twenties with a moustache, pulled over and picked me up in his Stingray. He had an A.V.M.A. sticker on his windshield. The radio came on with a tune: Soldier Boy, la-la darling Soldier Boy, I'll be true to you...

He shot me a pained glance and turned the radio off saying, "touching goddam song." I don't even know if he was a vet.

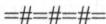

Ocean Sunset

I remember hitching down the coast of northern California, Stammer was saying. Iffie and I were riding in a Pepsi truck with three Buffalo, New York longhairs. Two guys and a girl, they agreed to let us spend the night and ride us farther in the morning. We ate some of their food and walked through a sloping field. Sat on the rocks, picking at moss and watching the sun set over the ocean. A first for both of us.

We zipped our sleeping bags together on that same spot and fell asleep under a brilliant cloudless sky, thousands of stars above us and the sounds of the sea washing over our ears.

Woke up the next day with deer tracks all around us and little piles of fresh spoor glistening in the morning sun. The ocean was clear and blue, all kinds of kelp had been beached overnight. The dew was already drying under the clean sea air and the birds were singing tunes.

Deer tracks! Dozens of 'em, all around us, and fresh too. We'd slept in that idyllic scene and a herd of deer had grazed at our heads. No one disturbed. We'd let them eat in peace, they let us sleep.

=#=#=#=

Round Two
```
We walked by the tracks and through to the park
My newfound charm getting shed like a shroud.
There were stars in her eyes and a moon in the dark
The air was heavy, there was rain in the clouds.
```

174

We knew each other and we knew the moist heat.
There was lightening in the air while we rode the night
train.
And so grounded with the knowledge and a new way to meet
We could break new ground together and that, at least,
was plain.

We'd shared the same street and a pleasant dim
attraction.
Her stride was familiar before I heard her name.
I could glide by her house and wave up with compunction.
Now we've strode that one step further, it can never be
the same.

Autumn noons, people meeting, slumber lightly side by
side.
Lashing rain, lightening heat flash, come together, come
away.
Never knowing where it's going. Chance encounters,
chance decides.
Didn't know before I met her and so not knowing still
can't say.

=#=#=#=

It was like living in a movie. Iffie and I came walking off the beach and find Rocks picking his guitar on a bench, a grin beaming in the sunlight. As I hear a faint "Roll 'em" in the wind.

Right In The Middle

"So, now we're in the middle?" Rexee' said.

"Yeah, the middle. The story is in the middle of a poem, and you're in the middle of the story"

"But at least," she said, "it's half over."

She gathered her robe around her.

"You need to know, this is not making a good impression. It's shot full of cliché and pseudo-clever phrases."

"I like the short stuff," he answered, "the pithy saying, the well-turned phrase. It's for the impatient, short attention span reader."

"Like you," he thought to himself, but dared not say.

"Writing on the wall," she said, "the men's room wall. That's what this is reminding me of.

"Readability, that's what makes literature, isn't it?"

"No, I'm sorry, you're wrong. You might like this sort of thing, but it's not literature – far from it. It's confessional first person postcard stuff."

"It entertains. I saw you laughing."

"The wrong kind of laughing, I'm telling you. As a friend. This is not working."

He thought about stalking out, but he didn't do it.

"Wombman! Gawd!" she went on, "That's just so wrong on so many levels, are you nuts?"

175

"Hey, you know, play it again – with feeling."

"The artist doesn't weep for himself, the artist weeps for others."

"I don't know about weeping, I told you, I'm trying to tell a story in a novel form."

"But, hey, forget the form," he said, as he saw her rising to that battle again, "I'm just trying to tell a story in an interesting way. In short shots and small injections. That's the idea."

"You say too much, and too little at the same time."

"There's supposed to be a rhythm coming across. Like music, where the pauses are as important as the notes."

"If that were true, if that were working,…" she stopped, and sighed.

"You've read Henry James, right?" he countered, "pages and pages of 'internal dialog' that weaves and warps through the psyche of character after character, and nothing happens for a hundred pages."

She nodded.

"That's NOT the idea here," he triumphed, "out with the old, in with the new, we won't get fooled again."

Her smile was a grim slit.

"I would keep that comparison to myself if I was you," she said, "it doesn't have the effect you want."

He was about to say something, but she stopped him.

"Shut up," she said, "I'm reading."

=#=#=#=

III. Winter Evenings: Death and Partings

Ring…ring…ring

-Hello

-Stammer? This is Iffie

-Great Guns! Where have you been?

-I've been thinking

-Oh … to what effect?

-None yet. There's a lot to consider

-Such as?

-Well, I'm pregnant.

-

-Did you hear me?

-I did. Is it by me?

-I'm afraid it might be.

-I was afraid it wasn't. This is fabulous.

-Is it?

-Don't you think so?

-I'm still considering.

-So come on over. We'll talk.

-Not now Stammer. I just found out and I'd like to sleep on it.

-Uh…alright.

-Look, I'll call you in the morning, okay?

-Okay, okay … Iffie?

176

-Yes, Stammer.
-I love you.
-Thank you, Stammer. Good bye.
...click.

=#=#=#=

Vision
- He can't bear to see me out of his sight.
- So, he misses you. I can see that.
- So you see, I can't say I'll see you
- Sure, I see what you mean.

=#=#=#=

Fair to Partly Cloudy
It takes a long time to get your head straight
Look at do's and at don'ts and compare
The value of trying or relying on fate
Should you seize what you want or be fair?

Fare within fare isn't fair at the fair
But somehow it's got to be done
You don't have to go and no one will care
You pay if you want to have fun.

=#=#=#=

Last Call
-I'll sell you a beer if you're gone in ten minutes.
-Give me a beer and I'll be gone in five.

=#=#=#=

It's said that feminism
Is hard on the man
The pressure they feel
Emasculates 'em

=#=#=#=

- who needs to be successful, says the Junker, I can barely drink what I make now...

=#=#=#=

Just Barely
We're barely friends,
But heavy lovers
When we're alone
Conversation suffers
But she wants my time
And I've got it to spare

Folks are just folks
Everywhere.

=#=#=#=

Today
Looking for some rain today
Or mail, good vibes, or pain today
Some time for work, some time for play
It could be worse, that's what I say

=#=#=#=

The One
Staring into space and dwelling on my cosmic blues
The dues and don'ts of living and the language that I
use
You are the one I want
But will I get my chance to say
That I've liked you all the while
And I'm knocked out by your style
If I've got my paste-on good luck grin
With feet on railway tile,
Or mouth to mouth from miles away
With hand poised on the dial;
I want the warm spot next to you
So take it with a smile.

You've had a hard time lately
But I won't take the blame
Sure I've held your hand
And kissed your lips
And called you by your name.
I think I treat you decently
I've told you what I thought
I'd like to take you in my arms
I care for you a lot
You are the one I want.

=#=#=#=

Birthday verse to a former lover
Lives that once were intertwined
Get forgotten when left behind
The time we spent and the life we had --
Sometimes unpleasant, but not all bad
So we're not kin and we're not cousins
Twenty four years is a couple dozen
And you did favors not assigned
So please take this with that in mind

...he gazes dreamily into her eyes while she gazes dreamily out the window...

=#=#=#=

```
I've gotta see ya, man
Can't talk on the phone
I'll tell you in person
When we're alone
Don't write this down
Or chisel it in stone
I've gotta lay low
And I need a loan
It's no one's fault but my own.
```

=#=#=#=

The Bomb

```
If she had the news
That I want to hear
I'd have heard by now.
The poetry's been wasted
Bomb aimed at my forehead
Whistle getting louder
OOOOOooooo-----….. Bam!
```

```
Run for cover, protect your ass
The bombs on the way
You're in for a crash
The bombs gonna drop
There's no where to hide
Allies are useless
No ones at your side
Whispers and whistles
They start out real low
Getting louder and louder
She's going to blow
```

```
The dreams and the visions
Die cold lonely deaths
Alone and afraid
While they gasp the last breaths
If she wanted to help you
To save some respect
What she promised to tell you
One way or another
It's over, exploded
So fergit it, brother.
```

```
He gave his body
She didn't want it
He gave his love
She didn't need it
So he gave her is pride
It was all he had left
And he wanted her to have it.
```

=#=#=#=

```
He waits and he hopes for a call to come
And he sits and stares at the telephone
Silence itself is eloquent, and unwanted
Love leaves you permanently all alone.
```

=#=#=#=

Dear Stammer

Sorry not to call when I promised but found myself incapable. So much on my mind that I'm barely functioning.

I went and had my chart done and then had my palm read. Both confirmed what I already knew. Our signs are in direct conflict. There is no future for us together.

Last night I had a dream, you were in it, everybody was in it. People kept hitting and spitting on me. It's no good for me here.

I'm leaving.

Please try to accept this.

Goodbye,

Iffie.

=#=#=#=

Somewhere After the Middle

"You're kidding, right?"

"Well, yes, there's supposed to be a humorous element."

"I mean, you're not serious!"

"Like a heart attack, I'm serious like a coronary."

"Yes, but what are your themes? This is turning into autobiographical rambling. I know you had a bad thing with that women, but you think this is a novel?"

"Yeah, a novel. You need one-word themes? How about loss and redemption. Read on."

"At best, it's confessional therapy. And that's the sort of stuff that makes people recoil and jump off bridges. At ground level it's painful to read."

"Art is pain."

"No, it's not. It's a celebration of something elemental. You're shitting in your own nest here. This is turning ugly."

He was wordless.

"Pour me a whiskey," she shrugged, pulling her robe more tightly around her, and went on, "I'm afraid I'm going to need it."

=#=#=#=

IV. Spring Nights: Infinity and Movements

Stammer's Statement II

Then there's the story of the rat and the pleasure bar. Someone hooked this rat's brain with electrodes and when he pushed the bar he got a jolt of pleasure. The rat kept pushing that bar until he was dead. At the last he was struggling desperately to push the bar just one more time. Just one more push, and he must have been in dreadful pain, having orgasm after orgasm after orgasm for gawd knows how long.

Just one more push.

=#=#=#=

Gilbert was born without a body. The doctor told his parents to bring him in for a body transplant when he was sixteen. They forgot so the doctor made a house call to remind them. They decided to surprise him with a body for his birthday and rushed out back to tell him. He was playing in the yard.

- Gilbert, said his mother, we've got a surprise birthday present for you.
- Good, said Gilbert looking up, as long as it's not another damn hat.

=#=#=#=

Roses are red
Violets are blue
Some poems rhyme
And some don't

=#=#=#=

Eating a Hill
The breeze is refreshing
The moon is real bright
I'm eating a hill on a starry night

My troubles stay with me
Can't leave them behind
Snaked up or sober they stay on my mind

I've gathered my knowledge
From friends and game shows
I listen and wonder and stay on my toes

I try to make sense
Try to take and to give
Try to make myself happy and learn how to live

181

If I can't probe the corners
And love doesn't rhyme
Still eating a hill is a pleasant pastime.

=#=#=#=

Stolen from somewhere
Sometimes I sit and think
And sometimes I just sit

=#=#=#=

Her name was Sister Louise. She worked a desk at the Youth Emergency Services drop-in center. She wore a bulky University of Minnesota sweatshirt and blue jeans with work boots. Her hair was cut very, very short. She had a tiny gold chain around her neck with a tiny golden crucifix.

Stammer walked in, his hair stringy with grease, his eyes hollow sockets of void. He had not slept, he had not eaten, he was at the end of this tether. He lit a smoke, the millionth one that day. His hand shook slightly while he found the end of the cigarette with his match.

"How can I help you?" Sister Louise said.

"I don't know," Stammer said, "I doubt you can."

He saw her kindly eyes, and only hesitated for a moment, then he sat down.

"I had a girlfriend," he said, "and she's having a baby, and she's leaving me."

"Your baby?" she asked.

"Yeah," he said, "but it wouldn't matter."

"She's doing an abortion?" the sister said.

Stammer sagged.

"I didn't think of that," he said, "I don't know."

"So again," she returned, "how can I help you?"

"It's her who needs help," Stammer said, "she's out there, she's lost, she's brittle and she's fragile. She can't do this, not by herself."

"You think she needs you?"

"She tossed me away. She doesn't think so."

"Where is she now. Do you know?"

"No. Gone. Gone as gone."

"And so," she said, "what can you do?"

"I can't do anything. I can't eat, can't sleep. My stomach feels like there's a fist in there, and I jump like a cat when the phone rings."

Pause.

"I don't know, I don't know what to do. I feel I need to be there, but there's no way to do that now. I let it go too long, and she went away without me. I'm out of it."

"That's what it sounds like, alright. So, why are you doing this to yourself?"

"Why am I doing this to myself?"

Nun nods.

"But the baby. The life. She doesn't want this, she's not ready."

"That," the nun said, "that's her shit to handle."

182

=#=#=#=

How far can you see when you're going it alone
Who wraps the big cuts and sets the small bones
United we stand and divided we fall
There's a whole lot of them, and you are just small

What do you get when you run with a clan
Is it what you want or a grace payment plan
Well what is the sound of one hand clapping?
Does the butterfly dream of manhood when napping?

There's a whole lot of roads and even more forks
You got mantras and voodoos and bottles with corks
You got answers in the wind, you got vultures in the air
And still folks are just folks, everywhere

=#=#=#=

new ain't nothing but a state of mind
keeps a man from missing what he left behind

=#=#=#=

...clouds form and dissolve...brief moments of unity amid turbulent
upheaval...you blow together and blow apart...elemental forces at your back
that drive you into the arms of one and/or out of those same arms...

=#=#=#=

Where does it go, I'd like to know
It has to start slow before it can flow
A plant is a seed 'til it begins to grow.

=#=#=#=

You can't run and you can't hide
You can't put it off
You've got to decide

Is there life after death
Is there life here at all
Can you face what you're doing
Get up when you fall

You run across things
Like sobbing on paper
Your heart balls up tight
You just want to help her
But nothing you can say
Will make it go smoother
Just live with the pain, see
It can go no further

He's got those cosmic blues again
No reason to be feeling low
No one's hurting, he's got dough
Might just need somewhere to go
With those cosmic blues again

=#=#=#=

A married couple, said Stammer, were out in the woods parking for old times sake. The windshield wipers turned themselves on and wouldn't turn off. Then the radio. The car started itself and the engine raced. Then the car caught fire and was destroyed.

You wanna buy a newspaper?

Just About at the End

She closed the manuscript, so carefully stapled into a plastic binder showpiece; and she sighed. She shook her head. She riffled the pages. She closed her eyes.

He knew what was coming, and his stomach clenched to a fist. He waited. Finally, she looked at him.

"I'm sorry," she said, "I know this means a lot to you."

He looked at her with pitiful moist eyes.

Suddenly, she was angry. She hated grading papers.

"The very best thing I can say, and this is reaching, is that this is uneven. You've got a few nice lines, a few nice lyrics, and otherwise it's a big mess."

"It's not done yet," Skate offered, softly, "I've got to fill it out quite a bit."

"Shit," she said sharply, "this is shit. It's not totally shit, but it's basically shit ... you should seriously plan to burn this and start over."

=#=#=#=

Smashing and crashing and eyes filled with hate
Glaring and staring and staying up late
Reading, re-reading and snapping back terse
It don't hurt to be well-versed

Said hello and goodbye to lovers and friends
Came up real fast with emotional bends
Reeling with feeling but sounding rehearsed
It don't hurt to be well-versed

Hooked on a book and blown to the brows
Backed in a corner repeating the vows
Looking for answers when feelings are hurt
All part of getting well-versed

Paid some bad debts in taverns and bars
Laid down some scooters and busted some cars
It could have been better, it might have been worse
It don't hurt to be well-versed

Chapter 9

It was the Fall of 1972. Terry was freaking out.

"I saw the same guy again today," he said, "watching me from the opposite corner. I think he's got me staked out."

"Be reasonable," Ace soothed, "if they had manpower to track down a deserter, we'd be hearing about it – it would be in the news. You guys don't get made unless you're arrested for something else. They're not looking for you guys, they're looking for bombers."

The radical arm of the anti-war movement had taken the serious step of planting bombs in department stores. Mostly they were just loud and scary, but innocent people had been hurt, and there had been deaths. The country was edgy. Terry was too.

"Well, maybe he's made me as a bomber, I don't know," Terry was sweating, "but it takes me two hours to get back here every day, just making sure I'm not tailed."

"Besides," Book chimed in helpfully, "if he gets busted as a bomber by mistake, he's still just as busted."

They were starting to get tired of Terry (Terry the Tramp,* as Rexee' was starting to call him), who had now been 'hiding out' in their garage shed for over a year. He was an okay guy, or so he seemed at first, but he was becoming more a shirker and wastrel. He supported himself by groveling handouts, and by taking out small loans from the guys. He was, by this point, 'into them' for several months of free rent, which nobody stood to collect, and had an individual tab with each of them for at least a few dozen dollars. Plus, he drank their beer, he ate their food, and as time went on he provided beer and food at increasingly infrequent intervals.

He was getting a little bit crazy too, and lately had taken to bringing more of his street pals around to crash in his space and hang out.

With everything else that was going on, Book didn't like the taint of unsavory element that was beginning to develop around the house. Rexee' didn't like strange men outside her door at all hours of the night. And everyone was just a little tired of having him hanging around all the time. Patrick, who knew him longest and had brought him by in the first place, counseled patience: partly as a political statement and anti-war protest. But nobody missed the point that Patrick wasn't even living there at the time – and they were. Ace was most tolerant, but when he grumbled, as he often did, about being the only one to ever mow the lawn, he included Terry in his vituperations.

Now Terry was seeing shadows, and it was time for him to go. Strangely, it was Hack who provided the ticket.

"When you're ready," Hack said, "I can get you out of the country."

(<o>).[].(<o>)

There is a long tradition in the United States of America of what's called the "Underground Railway". The boys had studied about it at Our Lady of the Snows.

It's not what it sounds like, tunnels and subway stations, which was a big disappointment to Skate when he was twelve. It's a sequence of "safe houses" where refugees can hide out during the day, and then travel at night on their way to a new life.

The famous instance was operating on the eastern seaboard before the end of the 18th century, transporting escaped slaves from "down south" up through New England and into Canada. This went on from Revolutionary times before the 1790s through to the Civil War in the 1860s. Sympathetic farmers up through the east would provide a bed and a meal (often just a place to hide in the barn and crust of bread), so people of color could move through the night towards something other than slavery.

The risks were high. The law-abiding public could not be trusted, and people caught in the act might be beaten, tried, shot or hung. The law of the land was against it. And the government of the people was against it. It was an act of civil disobedience: and a dangerous one. There was lightning in the air while they rode the night train.

But there were people willing to take the risk, for whatever reason. And there was a constant, albeit small, but steady trickle of people, underground, so to speak, and moving on the railroad.

It was against the law. It was dangerous. But you ask yourself, and it's not too hard to answer. If you were in the same situation, what would you do?

(<o>).[].(<o>)

"It's actually pretty easy," Hack was saying, "but there's no turning back."

And it WAS pretty easy.

Terry packed up his meager belongings into a duffel, and Hack drove him to Unkafrank Lake. Skate tagged along, as it was a weekend. They arrived late Friday night.

They camped on Hack's family land, near the burnt out ruins of the 'home farm', and in the morning Hack paddled across to the nun's island. He insisted on going alone. When Hack got back the deal was done.

That moonless Saturday night they paddled across together. The nuns lit a small fire on their stony beach to guide them through the darkness.

(<o>).[].(<o>)

Unkafrank Lake is a relatively small, football shaped lake that spans the American/Canadian border. The "laces" of the football are on Canadian soil, the Hackney property is slightly right of center on the bottom of the football. The island is very near the northern shore, close to the laces. Depending on the season and the level of the lake, which varies from year to year, the shallow channel from the island to the Canadian shore might be fifty yards, and it might be twenty.

The precise border between the two countries has never been settled. Various surveys have provided different conclusions. Some maps draw the border as a straight line from point to point of the football, placing the island on the Canadian side. Other surveys draw the border along the northern shore, making the island part of the U.S. Another survey puts the border on a bulge that includes a line that runs through the island, making it half and half. The dispute first arose in the 1870s as Civil War veterans, including Hack's great-

great grandfather, were venturing into the area to homestead. The issue went to court, where it stalled, and then got forgotten about.

The land is not rich in any agricultural or mineral sense. There is no apparent underground treasure; and so there is no great pressure to settle the question. The case is technically under the purview of the US Department of the Interior in negotiation with the Canadian Ministry of the Interior. Half the case file is in some basement warehouse in Washington, DC; the other half is in a similar warehouse in Ottawa. Nobody has actively worked to settle the question since about 1912. It is still not resolved. And nobody cares.

(<o>).[].(<o>)

Unkafrank Lake is relatively small, but if there's even a hint of north wind against you, it still takes nearly half an hour to paddle from the south shore to the northerly island. They beached the canoe away from the fire and got out. They were still clambering ashore when a figure emerged from the shadow of the tree line. It was a woman wearing, incongruously, a hooded sweatshirt and cut-off denim shorts. Her legs were chubby, she wore red baldies on her feet.

"Terry," she said.

"Yeah, I'm Terry," he answered.

"Grab your stuff and follow me," she said, and then she turned and walked off into the gloom.

Terry looked at Hack and Skate. He had a hangdog expression.

"I guess I'll be seeing you," Terry said.

Hack nodded.

"Go, Terry," said Skate, "a brave new world awaits ye."

"Yeah, yeah," Terry said, "you know THAT's a bunch of crap."

Then he turned and hoisted his duffel and followed the shadow into the dark trees.

Hack and Skate waited until he was out of sight in the gloaming, and then got into their canoe and paddled away.

(<o>).[].(<o>)

They paddled in silence. Skate in front, pulling their momentum, Hack in back, J-stroking to steer. There was no fire on the beach to guide them back, but Hack knew the way. There were stars, but a new moon. It was a radiant night sky, but with little illumination.

"If I get a low enough number, I might be back this way," whispered Skate.

"If you get a low enough number," said Hack, "I'll take you across myself."

(<o>)/(9.7)\(<o>)

diaria -- 9.0 -- 12/5/76 -- austin

anyway, one of the devices that is sometimes talked about is the plot curve. ...

this is where they get the phrase, "story arc" most likely. It's the idea that a story grows through events and increases in dramatic tension as the story moves towards it's climax.

187

Surprisingly, many people will try to draw this as a graph, like, y'know, a bell curve in a X-Y coordinate system. They'll label the X-axis as the progression of the story, through time or through pages, and they'll plot the Y-axis as dramatic tension.

Then they'll draw a line describing what's called a "normal" distribution -- a bell curve if you're a statistician, or , if you're not, a line that looks like the hump on a single humped camel -- y'know, a whatchacall, dromedary.

How you can usefully think about story telling in this way is frankly beyond me. But maybe it's true. I think about King Arthur's tales, where the whole story turns on the moment when Guinevere forsakes Arthur. There's a lot of drama after that point, but that's the critical moment, I guess.

It's like the point, they'd tell you, when everything starts to go downhill.

Me, I see stories having a sequence of turning points, and turning back points, and the plot curve thing is more for discussion afterward, it seems to me. It's always looking back. There's hardly ever a time you know for sure that you've turned a real corner, life keeps coming at you linearly. Once in a while, sure, there's a birth, a marriage, a death. Nothing's the same again.

But the plot curve is a story construct, not a life construct. It might help you understand what's past, but it doesn't help much while you're in the middle of it.

You never know when you've turned the corner.

(<o>)/(9.8)\(<o>)

A one act play in several scenes:

Scene Nine –

It is afternoon, and the lunch rush has passed.

At center stage the six are sitting at one table and are arranged as before: Patrick, Ace, Skate, Rexee', Hack, and Book. Fat Henry and Old Man Sutter still occupy their booths to audience right. Calvin is behind the bar, to the audience left, opposite Remo sitting at the bar with his back to the audience.

=#=#=#=

  Hack

You should eat something Rex.

  Rexee'

Food is rarely the solution for me.

  Skate

Me too, the stress and the excitement go straight to my gut. Even when it's good news I feel a fist in my stomach. Food? No room for it.

188

          Book
Never had that problem …
(he is licking his fingers after his meal)
… and I don't understand it. When everything else is crashing
into chaos, food is sometimes the best and only comfort.

          Ace
(laughing)
Not the only comfort.

          Book
My, yes, okay, not the only one, but the least messy, in many
ways.

          Patrick
I don't even like to eat in public. I don't know why.

          Book
Certain very high caste Hindu will not eat in public. They
view it as vile to witness the cause of the later effect.

          Ace
The excrement, you mean?

          Book
Yes, the effect.

          Ace
Well, not too surprising, they wipe their butts with their
bare hands. Right hand to eat, left hand to wipe.

          Patrick
Carol says if you're healthy, you don't need to wipe.

          Rexee'
Is there just possibly a more elevating topic we could switch
to?

          Ace
Let's argue about music …

          Hack
Groan.

          Ace
… or politics

          Book, Hack, Skate, Rexee'
(in unison)
Groan.

          Patrick
Hey, I like to talk politics.

          Ace
No! Really?

          Book
My, it's sure been an interesting morning so far. Whatever
could the rest of the day bring?
(Fat Henry gets out of his booth and lumbers over to their
table)

          Fat Henry
That was the guy, right?

          Ace
Yep, Delmar, that was him.

189

        Fat Henry
I heard about him, but never saw him before.

        Skate
Let's hope he's gone for a while more.

        Fat Henry
Yeah, I saw that gun come out, and I'm stuck in that booth,
and I'm thinking there's nowhere to hide.
(Old Man Sutter gets out of his booth and walks past, hearing
this)

        Old Man Sutter
In a well played ambush, you've got no chance at all. You go
down to the toughest bar on the strip downtown…

        Ace
Moby Dicks?

        Old Man Sutter
… and three trained men with the right ordinance can clean the
whole place in two minutes.

        Rexee'
Very reassuring.

        Old Man Sutter
We were all damned lucky.
(offers his hand to Hack)
Young fella, we'd likely all be lying in puddles of our own
blood if it wasn't for you.

        Hack
(shakes his hand)
Calvin is who cooled it out.

        Old Man Sutter
Oh, yes, Calvin cooled it out. But the young lady put the
issue at rest.

        Rexee'
You want to know the truth, I barely remember it even now.

        Skate
I'll never forget it as long as I live.

        Old Man Sutter
Let's hope that's a long time, for all of us.
(turns to go)
Calvin, I'm leaving. Tab me up.

        Fat Henry
Me too, Calvin.
(to Rexee')
I'll never forget it either. You jammed that guy's balls up
into his lungs. It was beautiful.

        Rexee'
Aw shucks.
(Old Man Sutter and Fat Henry pay up and file out)

        Ace
I suppose we should adjourn this meeting too.

        Patrick
Yeah, we can argue about music any time.

                    Ace
What's everybody doing?

          Hack
Sleep, sleep…

          Book
…to knit the raveled sleeve and so forth.

          Hack
(smiles)
Yeah, that's it.

          Rexee'
That's your other unmessy comfort, Book old boy, and it's
sounding pretty good to me right now too.

          Hack
(smiles)
It don't hurt to be well-versed.

          Rexee'
Ge-roan.

          Ace
Patrick?

          Patrick
Yes, I guess, it's past time to hit the sack.

          Ace
And the good bard?

          Skate
(shrugs)
I'm going up north, today, right now. Hack, the key to your
little trailer in the usual hiding place?

          Hack
You got it.

          Skate
Okay, that's it then. I'm on the road. I'm a trail before your
eyes,* even as I speak. I'm a vapor. I am gone.

          Ace
Now?

          Skate
Yes, oh yes. There's still plenty of daylight, and the scooter
is minutes away from making the trip. I'm going.
(he looks around the bar and at this friends, and pauses for
just a moment).

          Skate
So long, suckers.

          (Blackout).

          (the house lights stay off, the entire theatre remains
black)

          Rexee'
(a voice in the darkness)
Bull fucking shit!
(pause)
You heard me.
(the stage lights come up, they are sitting as before, the
house lights stay off)

     Rexee'
It's 12:30 in the afternoon. You've been sitting here since
before dawn pounding beero. And now you want to ride up to the
northwoods? On your motorcycle?

     Book
The lady makes a valid point.

     Rexee'
Calvin, give me that baseball bat would you. I'll just bash
his brains out here at the table, and save time.

     Patrick
She's right. That would save time.

     Skate
Hey, I'm movin', I'm groovin' I'm well-paced and good to go.
I've got a fine, high, do something buzz.

     Ace
Gentlemen, …

     Rexee'
I mean it Calvin, gimme that damn bat.

     Ace
… I think it's decided.

     Hack
Yeah, Skate, we're pacifists, so don't make us use Rex to use
force.
(Calvin gets the baseball bat out from behind the bar, and
hands it in Rexee's direction. She leans over backward and
reaches for it.)

     (Blackout).

(<o>)/(9.11)\(<o>)
Skate leaned over and extended his arms, then pulled the drawknife towards
himself, skinning a plate of bark off the trunk he straddled.

(<o>).[].(<o>)
Imagine a heavy, sharp, steel sword blade about two feet long. Imagine it
with handles on each end, bent towards you like the handlebars on a tricycle.
Imagine a tree trunk laying on the ground, as big around as a power pole – not
so big as a barrel, but way bigger than a bucket. Imagine you're sitting on this
log, riding it like a horse and you need to strip the bark off it, like peeling the
skin of an apple. That's where your drawknife comes in. You sit on the log, lean
over and extend your arms. Then you pull the blade toward yourself and peel
the tree bark off, in big sheets if you're doing it right, like shaving a stump.
Simple, labor-intensive, effective, time-consuming, and tiring.
    Skate and Hack are toiling on the shores of Unkafrank Lake in the great
northwoods of northern Minnesota. It is the third in a row of sunny, warm, late-
June days, and they are making hay. To their north is a line of trees and the
shore of the lake, small enough to see across to Canada. To their east is a pile of
felled trees, branches stripped, each about 30 feet long – close to 100 of them:
in a big, big pile. To their west is a rectangle of logs laying on a foundation of
rough concrete blocks: 15 feet on the short side, 30 feet on the long side. To the
south is the rest of the property: rough, hilly, rocky, wooded, wild. About 50

yards uphill to the south is the foundation of the old family cabin, burnt to the ground years past, and a small camper trailer, parked near the ruins.

(<o>).[].(<o>)

Skate reached out and shaved a strip off the log and stopped for a second, looking up. Hack was on the same log, at about the midway point with his back to Skate, just finishing his swath.

Here's how you do it. One man starts at the end of the log, moving backwards as he strips bark. The other man start about the middle of the log and moves backwards towards the far end. If the tree has been seasoned (by lying around for a year or so), and the bark cooperates, and there aren't too many branch knobs in your way, and if you've been at it for a couple of days, then the bark comes off in big plates and it only takes three or four draws to clean the spot in front of you. Then you move back a giant step, sit back down, and do it again.

When the first man reaches the middle, and the second man reaches the end, they stop and roll the log a quarter turn. Then they turn the opposite direction and move back the other way. After four or five passes the log is round and bare and smooth.

Okay, not round like a power pole, because a log is full of knots and bumps where branches once stood out, and not bare, because there is always some stray bark, and not smooth, because nature is like that – bumpy and rough. You just need to deal with it.

A log cabin is built in layers. First the two long side logs, thirty feet each, are laid on the concrete blocks, which have been set in a straight, level, shallow trench. The start of the cabin is these two 30 foot logs lying in parallel, resting on the blocks. The next run of the cabin is the shorter 15 foot pieces, forming the top and bottom, the short end, of the rectangle. Each log is one to two feet in diameter, so it takes five to seven runs to build a cabin with eight to ten foot walls.

You move logs by attaching a "come-along", which is a pole, like an axe handle, with a large pinching hook dangling from the middle. You drop the two pincer sides of the hook over one end of the log, and then when you lift, one man on each end of the axe handle, the hook closes like a carnival game. Then all you have to do is lift, the two of you in unison, side-by-side, raising one end of the log. Then you drag it, maybe five hundred pounds, across to the building site. Easy, if you're a donkey.

Once the third log is stripped of bark it gets cut in half, into fifteen foot pieces. Each of these shorter pieces gets dragged into position and lifted so it rests across the ends of the two longer logs. Then the shorter logs need to be fitted to the longer ones.

(<o>).[].(<o>)

Here's the problem. You've got two big side logs laying near the ground on concrete blocks, parallel to each other, nearly fifteen feet apart. They're each maybe 18 inches through the middle. If you lay a short end log across these two, the short log will be about 18 inches off the ground, more than enough room for a skunk or a wolverine to crawl under.

Picture it this way. If you interleave your fingers at the first knuckle, they form a corner like the logs of a cabin. Notice, there is a finger width of space between each of the fingers on one hand. If your fingers were the wall of a log cabin, you would want to plug these gaps to keep the wind and the animals out.

Part of the solution is to cut a big gouge in one of the logs, called a notch, so there will be less gap between each one. If you did this to your fingers, it would REALLY hurt. Now, suppose you cut such a notch so that it's almost half the width of the log. Then you will have logs laying pretty close to each other in parallel. Close enough that you can stuff the cracks with mud, or clay, or sphagnum moss, or whatever is at hand on the land.

That's the basic idea. If you had "Lincoln Logs" as a kid, you know immediately what is needed – notches in the logs so they lay close to each other.

The other consideration is whether to cut the notch in the top of the lower log, which is easier, or into the bottom of the upper log. This is one of the major debates in the log cabin community.

The argument for notching the lower log, called a saddle notch – because that is what it looks like – is that it's much easier to do, and much faster to get a nice fit. However, these notches are like bowls, and will collect water when it rains. And water in the notches will lead to rot in the corners of the building, and rot is bad. Rot leads to mold and decay and sagging walls, among other things.

Anyone in the construction business will tell you, water is the enemy. Water might be the elixir of life, and the human body might be 98 percent water, and so on and so forth, but water is the root of all evil in the building trades. Water is bad.

The argument for notching the upper log, called a top notch, is that it sheds the water. Water being bad, this is good. Besides, it sounds better: top notch.

The response from the saddle notchers is a pragmatic one. Cabins rarely die of water and rot. They usually burn down before that. It seldom fails, so why bother? And top-notching takes longer. It holds you back.

Still, hope springs eternal, water is bad, nobody believes they will be the ones to burn down their own cabin by mistake (a lot of times it's lightening or a forest fire, beyond your control, but never mind that), and Hack was raised in the top notch tradition by his family. So that is what they do.

(<o>).[].(<o>)

Hack worked the chain saw, cutting the latest log in two. Every log has a fat end and a skinny one. Every cut piece has the same configuration. One of the regimens in log walls is to alternate the logs, fat end with skinny end, so the fat end of one is laid over the skinny end of the previous. The other regimen is to gauge the size of the logs so that higher ones are smaller than lower ones (so you're not lifting the biggest logs over your head to put them in place). Ideally they're all the same size, but that never happens.

They were cutting a thirty-foot log into two fifteen-foot pieces. The trick is to cut the log, laying on the ground, without it sagging and pinching the saw blade. This is easy when you've done it a few times.

Skate stood at the log's end while Hack worked the chain saw, cutting about halfway through from the top, and then stopping just before the saw blade starts to get pinched, and rolling it over with his foot to cut the rest. Skate's job was to steady the log from the end, so it didn't roll while Hack was cutting it.

They'd been at it for two solid days, and this was the morning of the third. The first day was mostly Hack showing Skate what to do and explaining why. Not a very productive day, but an educational one. The second day was a lot of Skate practicing what he'd learned the day before. There were mistakes and disruptions, but Skate was loving it, and Hack was good about it. By the end of the second day, Skate was a pretty good hand. Skate was capable of the physical.

By this, the third day, they'd reached a voiceless communion. They both knew what to do, and they were making serious hay. Skate couldn't keep up with Hack, nobody could, but Skate could hold his own, and that was more than good enough.

Sore? Oh yeah, Skate was sore. He'd gone to sleep each of the last two nights with his muscles feeling like rags, and he'd woken up each morning feeling like a stiff, achy, impaired old man. But Hack had the coffee ready when he rolled out of his sleeping bag, and like every working man knows, the best medicine for sore muscles is more work. After scrabbling around like a geriatric for a bit, the muscles warm up, and what doesn't kill you, after all, makes you limber.

The hands are the thing. Skate's hands already looked like hamburger. His forearms, shins, and even his ribcage, looked about the same: covered with welts and gouges. They wore work gloves to protect their hands, but half the time you needed them off in order to do the delicate work. And every time you rolled a log, or hoisted a tool, or nudged a log into place, it took another tiny hunk of skin off you someplace, usually your knuckles. That's the working life: minor abrasions, lacerations, contusions, and skin torn off and scabbing.

(<o>).[].(<o>)

Skate never felt better.

There had been hard work in the past, and contact sports, and so there were little wounds and sore limbs – and he knew the score, the manly score, that you didn't cry about the slings and arrows and gouges and nicks – it was part of the deal.

But this was different, and better – this was in the service of building a building.

Shelter – it did not get much more basic than that.

He was sore and creaky, achy and painy, and a walking scab.

Skate never felt better.

(<o>).[].(<o>)

They had two short logs, cut in half from a big one. They used the 'come-along' to drag the first one of them into place, at the short end of the cabin.

Then they got on each end and lifted it.

The wall was nearly five feet tall at this point, so they were hoisting to about shoulder level.

Like this. Down into a squat, grip the log, eyes meet, Hack nods, they lift together. Up to waist level and then, because the log is short and relatively light, up past the chest and onto the wall. Smooth, easy, done it a dozen times.

They inch the log around, finding the flat side – there's always a flat side somehow, then Skate holds it in place while Hack fishes for his chalk.

This is where the top-notch art comes in. Hack eyeballs the log as it rests on the wall, and draws a semi-circle on the new log, trying to imagine how much notch is needed to make the top log rest close to the next log down. Too little notch and there's an unwanted gap between the logs, too much notch and there is unwanted gap to fill in the notch, which will need to be stuffed later. In general, too much notch is slightly better, but if so much material is taken from the log there is danger of it being flimsy. This, too, is bad.

When the chalk lines are drawn, the boys get on each end and take the log down again, off the five-foot wall, dropping and rolling it on the ground until the chalk circle underside is showing. Then Skate sits on the log while Hack gets the chainsaw and starts to remove wood, cutting the notch according to the chalk line – working towards a tight fit.

(<o>).[].(<o>)

Hack works the chainsaw like a sculptor – like their friend Abel, or Michelangelo himself – removing the material from the log to reveal the notch within. This is mostly done with a series of vertical cuts, so the notch looks like it holds the teeth of a comb. Then you knock out the teeth, and sculpt the notch with the chainsaw until it's smooth. When Skate gets to practice, maybe once every third log in the morning, he knocks the teeth out with a maul. Hack knocks them out with his fist. By the afternoon, when they're tired and trying to get things done, Hack does them all. He's much, much faster at it, and besides he's got the eye. He can see what needs to be cut better than Skate ever will.

First one end, and then the other.

Hack cuts the notches, Skate takes a position crouching on the log at the opposite end and steadies it to keep it from rolling. When it looks pretty good they hoist it into position again: squat, grip, eyes, nod, lift. Now the log is married to its neighbors, and they look for nubs causing gaps.

If Hack is working the saw, there's nothing to do but fine tuning. So rather than hoist it off, they'll just roll it in place, five feet off the ground, saw a little more material out of a notch, and then roll it back over to check the fit. No need for chalk at this stage.

It usually takes two tries to get a tight fit: sometimes three, and sometimes four – when Skate is doing it. But that's the process, trial and error, until the logs are snug enough.

Once it's right they do the same with the other short fifteen-foot piece, on the far end of the cabin. Then it's time to auger.

(<o>).[].(<o>)

The boys don't actually auger. This would be a process where they drill down, with a brace-and-bit, through each end of the top log, down through the top-notch, into the log below, and then drive a wooden peg into the auger hole. This pegs the logs in place and keeps them from shifting.

Augury is the traditional method, which would require them to actually stop and consult the humors, and then drill the holes by hand, and also whittle the wooden pegs.

That's just not part of the plan.

In the old days, nails were expensive and you built your cabin out of found materials: the stuff you had on your land. You made pegs, they were cheaper. Nowadays, nails are cheap, and Hack has a crate of spikes to work with (one of the many, many treasures Ace brought home from the dump over the years).

They hammer the problem instead.

They settle each short-side log into place, top-notched to keep out the evil water, and then they bang the spikes through the top with a five-pound maul; just like the Romans crucified Christ.

These spikes, they are nails alright, but about as big around and as long as a #2 pencil: heavy hardware for heavy going.

It feels good to wale the tar out of a nine-inch nail with a heavy hammer. After a little practice you can drive it through a log with three or four heavy strokes. Sacred Blood of Jesus.

(<o>).[].(<o>)

The walls were up, the roof remained. They had done a heck of a job on day three.

Hack said, "Town tonight, I think."

Skate could hardly argue. They had raised the walls of the cabin in three short days. Hack, by himself, would have needed two full weeks.

A night on the town seemed about right.

(<o>)/(9.19)\(<o>)

Truth is, they went to town every night. But most nights it was just to stop into the diner for supper, and then buy some beer to take back to camp.

Hack could whip up eggs and coffee for breakfast. And they could live on sandwiches for lunch. But neither of them was enough of a cook for supper, unless they did sandwiches again: which they had done, but only once. Dinner in town at the end of a long day; that's what they did.

Tonight, though, was a night out. Tonight, the diner again, and then the bar, and probably Maid-Up for pizza afterwards. They both felt they had it coming.

(<o>)/(9.20)\(<o>)

Once the walls are up, you need a roof. That was next.

In the great northwoods you want a steep roof so that the snow will slide off. Too much snow collecting on your roof is like an anvil. Snow is heavy, and many cabins collapse from the weight. The trick is the ridge pole.

The ridge pole forms the peak of the roof and runs the length of the cabin. The roofing material is anchored by the ridge pole. It must be stable.

Many cabins simply rest the ridge pole on the short end logs as they taper towards the roof peak. This is another one of those controversies in the log cabin community. The taper can buckle, and often does. Hack and Skate elected to take the Swiss A-frame approach.

This meant two logs on each end of the cabin, anchored against the concrete block base, raised up and meeting in a tee-pee-like manner. At the apex of the tee-pee would be a 30 foot long log, the ridge pole, the best and straightest one you could find. You might have fifty logs in your cabin – you use the best one for your ridge pole. The roofing material would then angle from the peak, formed by the ridge pole, down to the top of their log walls.

Many in the log cabin community view this as over-building. Most of these cabins burnt down, the rest eventually collapsed under the snow, and none of them lasted more than 30-40 years. Why go to the trouble of super-fying the construction?

Again, hope springs eternal, and the boys wanted to have a monument to roofing over their heads. This meant doing a little geometry.

They had a fairly spacious 30X15 foot cabin (many are built 15X10), they wanted the roof pitch to be 45 degrees or more, and they wanted the roof to be covered with as few 4X8 sheets of plywood as possible.

By this time they were in the bar. Skate grabbed a couple of napkins and took to ciphering.

(<o>).[].(<o>)

Consider a triangle with a sixteen foot base (the short end of the cabin, built with fifteen foot logs, with half a foot extending beyond the long sides on each end, which gives a sixteen foot span between the walls). Imagine the sides of the triangle at a 45 degree angle. Easy, an equilateral triangle, sixteen feet on each side. Plywood is four feet by eight feet, so two pieces end to end cover sixteen feet, four feet wide, which is perfect as it gives a two foot overhang on the eaves. Just right.

Now, the cabin is thirty feet on the long side, so that means eight sheets, covering the thirty feet, with a two foot overhang on each end. Again, perfect.

So, let's see, that's two times eight, times two for the other side. Thirty-two sheets of plywood for the roof; or one thousand twenty four square feet of plywood.

(<o>).[].(<o>)

"Thirty-two sheets," Hack said, "that'll run into a coupla hundred dollars."

"Yep," Skate said, "about what we thought."

Skate went on, "It's up to you. I'll figure the alternative, which is to get hold of that portable saw mill from your uncle."

They could make their own roof cover, from their own logs, if they sawed them out themselves, using a portable saw-mill that Hack's uncle would loan them.

"Yeah, okay" said Hack.

(<o>).[].(<o>)

The math is a little harder on this. Imagine each log as a thirty foot long cylinder, sixteen inches in diameter at the slender end. To cut boards out of a log, you need to imagine the rectangle that's bounded by that sixteen inch circle. Figure the rectangle as two right-angle triangles, each with a sixteen inch hypotenuse. Then we're looking at Pythagoras and the square of sixteen, which is two hundred fifty six, being the sum of the squares of the other two sides.

That means sides of eleven inches and a bit. Figure the saw blade removing material, and fudge factor, and we're looking at ten one-inch boards each thirty feet long, or twenty boards of fifteen foot length, which is what we want.

Each log then gives us twenty fifteen foot one-by-tens, which covers about a quarter of the roof, meaning we need to saw four logs, which will give us about seventy two boards to cover the roof, with about eight left over.

(<o>).[].(<o>)

"These will be green boards though," said Hack, "which will season on the roof, meaning they'll warp, twist, and split over the next couple of years."

"That's right," said Skate, "it's that, which will take us a few days to do, given we need to borrow the portable saw mill and do the cutting. Or it's that coupla hundred dollars to buy the plywood."

"Or," Skate added, "we make the call."

Hack pondered.

They had to raise the ridge pole, which would take another day or two, and then they'd be ready to cover the roof with, well, whatever they covered it with.

(<o>)/(9.25)\(<o>)

The noise level in Maid-Up Pizza slowly rose, drawing with it the activity quotient of the bored waitresses who, languorously inactive an hour before, were now laboriously and resentfully performing their roles as the last organized functionaries in the tragi-comedy of the Vernal Equinox. Vestal Virgins in the Spring Rites, they poured coffee and listened to mumbling drunks for clues as to what they wanted to eat. True democrats, they ignored the lewd or rude comments of the booze-ridden locals with the same disinterest that they ignored the lewd or complimentary remarks of the tourists – wan, blissful masters of ignorance, with accents on the ignore.

The winter had closed much like the bars had, with typical Northern Minnesota reluctance, grumblings and dragging of feet, as the Confederate States of America, beaten but not whipped, over but not done, refusing to believe that the war, or the season, or the party was over. Memorial Day, the end of May, had arrived barely a week after the final stubborn shade-protected snow had departed. And so the party had begun, with locals so relieved at the arrival of Spring and tourists intoxicated to start with by the freshness of the air, the sunshine and greenness that leaves Minneapolis or Chicago so pale in comparison. The bars had been crowded to bursting, people popping out the doors to look at the night sky as though squeezed or forced out by something beyond that sky, or behind their backs. The liquor flowed like liquor always does on a holiday, freely, sloppily, and to good effect.

The only thing was, in Elysium the Memorial Day party lasts until the 4th of July, at which point a new celebration begins. These were the latter days of June, on the cusp between the bacchanals. In other words, a normal night in town at closing time.

They were all together, hardened mine-working, or resort tending, or services rendering locals with soft fish-catching business men or lean nature loving students, altogether first in the Iron Range bars and then together again on the street and then in Maid-Up Pizza, the only after hours eating place in town, together to drink coffee and order pizzas from the still bored, but now rapidly moving waitresses.

A loud, garrulous and intoxicated crowd was on the street, everyone at least a little loose, laughing, talking, and telling. It felt like a rare interplay between locals and tourist, thrown together unusually closely by the day, the night, the place, and the celebration. The Sacred Rites of Spring, the Saturnalia where tourist becomes yokel and local becomes fool.

(<o>).[].(<o>)

Except for Lon.

Lon sat at a table in the corner, his back to the wall facing the crowd. Lon was quiet and subdued, not subdued in the submissive sense but subdued like a man who is out of place, and knows he is out of place. Coming into town and getting as drunk as he had was asking for trouble. Coming into town at all was like asking for trouble.

"I've got as much right to be here as anyone."

He kept repeating that to himself as he leered drunkenly around the room.

"I was born in this town and have as much right as anyone else to be here."

No one had talked to him all night. Lon, like most quiet people didn't talk much anyway. Tonight he'd decided to come into town to say something, not in words (because he knew no one would talk to him), but just by being there. To tell the town that he had a right to be there; and to tell himself too.

No one had expected Lon to come into town, not even for the Vernal Equinox. His situation was too precarious, his status too uncertain.

So Lon sat in his corner, with his back to the wall, alternately gazing unto this coffee cup and leering, almost defiantly, around the room. The waitress (a true democrat), had brought him some coffee right away, the first person to talk with him all night. He sat there, feeling the disturbing lump in his stomach being counter-acted by the reassuring lump in his armpit. Lon was there to tell his fellow townspeople something, and to tell himself something. Because he had a right to be there; and because of the carefully concealed automatic pistol under his jacket.

Lon was surrounded by life-long acquaintances in the town he grew up in; packing a load on his back and a gun under his arm.

(<o>).[].(<o>)

Elysium is a typical Minnesota Iron Range town in a lot of ways. A former iron and lumber boom town in the 20s and 30s (vast quantities of low grade iron ore wrenched and scooped from the red earth leaving cavernous open pits or lumber cut down with wild and exploitive abandon), as though there was enough to supply the whole world and never run out (but it did run out). The mines have mostly shut down, and the area has now become a National Forest and not timbered enough to be worth the logging. Virtually all the buildings in town date back to the boom days, a third of those are simply foundations or empty holes in the ground.

Many of the locals drive the twenty miles to Bittum to work in one of the few surviving mines, but most exist on the tourist trade during the summer and collect unemployment in the winter – seven months a year the population hovers below four thousand, but from May to September the influx of sportsmen and campers more than quadruples that number.

The surrounding area is dotted with lakes and lined with rivers; a virtual wilderness now protected by federal law and federal agents. An expanse of virgin timber still does exist because of this. A place with no roads, except the portage trails between the lakes, where disposable cans are not allowed, bottles and packages are counted on the way in – by the Forest Service – and again on the way out. Motors above a certain horsepower are not allowed, and littering is absolutely forbidden.

People come to Elysium from all over the Midwest (indeed, the world), city people who need to get away, fishermen of varying degrees of eptitude, or nature lovers.

To accommodate the people, a unique form of business, known as the outfitter, has been invented. Outfitters provide tourists with rented equipment, maps, food, canoes, and even guides, for a price. The price is often high but the crowds get bigger every year (outfitters, once small businessmen, now employ roughly one quarter of the town on a seasonal basis and can carry a lot of economic and political clout), so the town thrives on a resource, depletable but in a different way, much like it thrived during the boom days.

(<o>).[].(<o>)

A matronly waitress bustled up to his table, a Vestal Virgin, untouchable, pen poised above pad waiting to translate his whim into script then labor then service and reality. She looked at him, not knowing who he was, or caring very much either.

"Yah ready to order?" she cracked her gum.

He was ready, ready to tell the town his rights, to tell himself his rights, to proclaim.

"A small pepperoni and some more coffee, ok?"

He smiled.

"No sense being hostile," he thought to himself.

His being there was hostility enough. She waddled off to place his order, he slumped back in his booth. Jeez, he was jumpy. The pistol did little to reassure him really. Lately his nerves had gone up as the sun had gone down, and it bothered him to carry a pistol just for a night in town as much as it bothered him that he might have to use the pistol.

Lon didn't like to shoot at people; the Marines had taught him that, by making him shoot people. He resented the Marines ever after for making him find that out, and he was starting to resent the town, most of the town, because he feared he might have to find it out all over again.

(<o>)/(9.29)\(<o>)

Abner Hackney was starting to worry. The corpse in front of him shuddered a post-mortem nerve clutch, but that didn't worry Abner.

Dewey was dead.

Abner had snapped his neck like a pencil, which was pretty good for a guy with his shoulder torn off by shotgun pellets.

No, Dewey had it coming. Abner wasn't worried about that.

It was almost dark and getting cold. Cold like northern Minnesota does in January: a biting, stinging, painful cold. Cold that pulls heat right through your coat. At least he was out of the wind. That made it better. But Abner wasn't worried about the cold and the wind and the dark. He didn't care about that.

He wasn't too worried about his shoulder either. Sure, his arm was gone for good, he could see that. But it didn't seem to be bleeding too bad, and it didn't hurt that much either, which was probably a good sign, or a sign of the cold. Either way, Abner wasn't too worried about it.

Abner wasn't too worried about his breathing, which was labored and painful. It had gotten a little better, a little easier, once he'd pulled himself up on the liquor crates. Half-standing, half-leaning and propped up from behind he was able to get the air he needed.

And he wasn't too worried about being alone, wounded, in the middle of nowhere in the Minnesota woods. There was no help on the way, he knew that, but it didn't worry him. Nobody heard the shotgun blast, he was sure of that.

First, he and Dewey chose this spot precisely because it was way remote.

Second, they were in a narrow, steep-sided cutbank with high walls on three sides.

Third, they were both in the back of a big stolen liquor truck when Dewey fired the shot. And it was a thick-walled insulated truck, at that.

It had been deafening inside the truck. A shotgun fired from two or three feet into the back of your left shoulder. Aiming for his heart, likely, and missing. The blast was still ringing as Abner swung right and snapped Dewey's neck with one sharp backhand fist behind Dewey's jaw. Dewey looked stunned for just a tick, then dropped like a slaughtered steer; dead when he hit the floor.

No, Abner figured to drive back out, just like he got here. Out through an incredible passage of logging cuts and dry creeks. An incredible feat of driving, even for a healthy man. But Abner could do it – he had no doubt. He just needed a little more time to set himself, rest up, get ready. Pretty soon now.

Maybe just haul ass back to the cabin until morning – a short half mile. Maybe that was quicker and simpler. Either way, he wasn't worried. Not even Abner could drive to the cabin from here. He'd have to walk practically straight uphill and down again. But he could do it. Probably. When he felt just a little better.

Abner didn't worry about Zelda much as a rule, and wasn't about to start now. She could take care of herself, even if Abner didn't make it home from this. She still had her looks and her circus skills; bareback riding, trick shooting, the aerial acts. Zelda could do it all and would never hurt for work if she wanted it. Abner didn't worry about his wife.

What worried Abner was the gravel.

(<o>).[].(<o>)

Stealing the truck had been easy and according to plan. He and Dewey took the train from Minneapolis to Winnipeg and then the bus east to the little town of Mentieth, Manitoba. They waited at the truck stop there. Every Sunday a Royal Liquor truck stopped in the Mentieth truck stop on the way to Winnipeg.

They couldn't know what the shipment was, but it didn't matter. They knew the truck was full. And it was there for the taking.

In January, on a cold night, truckers leave their motors running. Abner and Dewey just waited for the driver to go in for his coffee break. When he was gone, they hopped in and drove off.

They went towards Winnipeg, but only for four miles. At that point, Abner pulled off the highway and crossed the ditch, slipping the truck into a slim gap between two pines at the forest edge, and headed through the sloping clearing. Abner stopped the truck and ran back to the road. He pulled brush into the opening and shoveled over their tire tracks. Then, in the cleverest ploy of the heist, he strapped on a pair of deer hoof stilts and trampled back and forth over the obliterated tire tracks. Then Abner inched that truck, driving through the night, across southern Manitoba and into northern Minnesota.

It was a drive through thickets and over logging trails, across frozen portages on long forgotten fur trails. It was a masterful drive of courage and skill. Not five people in the world could have made that drive, but Abner could.

By daylight they were so far back in the woods, no one would see. They drove until evening and made it onto the shores of Unkafrank Lake. The last few miles were across frozen water, four feet thick and as strong as steel. They drove and made it to the Hackney property, which Abner's granddad had homesteaded after the Civil War. They drove across their lakeshore and inland until they reached the steep sided cutbank of an ancient stream. Then they pulled the truck in, nose-first, as far as it would go.

They were 160 tortured miles from where they stole the truck. They were 800 yards from the cabin, where Abner had been born. A stiff climb.

They were pals and partners in crime until Dewey fished his sawed-off from under his coat and emptied both barrels into Abner's shoulder back.

Abner never suspected a thing and never saw it coming. He never knew that Dewey had taken an obsessive notion about Zelda. Abner never knew that Dewey figured to fill his spot with Zelda and needed him to have an "accident". Zelda never knew it either. Dewey never knew he never had a chance with Zelda.

But none of this worried Abner at the moment. He was feeling just slightly better and thinking about tackling the hilly climb back to his cabin, a half mile away. But the gravel bothered him. He was starting to worry about the gravel.

(<o>).[].(<o>)

Normally, in January, in Minnesota, the ground is frozen rock hard. Usually, the ground will have frozen to a depth of three feet or more. But when Abner had stepped out of the truck, right after pulling into the cut-bank but before getting shot, he had heard the unmistakable hissing noise that rolling gravel makes. And as he hoisted himself to breathe better, he realized he could still hear it.

Gravel was rolling down the steep cutbank and was starting to fall and bounce off the top of the truck.

Abner didn't believe he'd bumped the sides of the cutbank while driving in, but maybe he had. Maybe the weight on the bottom of the banks was causing stress above. Abner didn't know. But it was starting to worry him a little. If the gravel and rock above him on the banks started downward, nothing could stop it. And if he was here then, he'd be digging his way out with one arm, which could take a while.

Abner really started to worry when the two vertical walls gave way at the base and started to converge under the truck. The gravel spilled down and around the truck on all four sides. Then Abner really worried when the force of the gravel closed the insulated door of the liquor truck and left him in total black.

But Abner stopped worrying when he realized the back of his coat was snagged on a nail from the crate he was on – and he was too weak to free himself. Then when Abner's heart finished pumping his abdomen full of blood, he went beyond light-headed, and then he went beyond life. Abner stopped worrying then.

Abner never knew that his carefully chosen cut-bank hiding place had collapsed finally of it's own weight. And he never knew that gravel and earth continued to fall in mute isolation until the truck was completely buried and covered by the earth.

And so Abner, who had covered his tracks so well, was entombed in an insulated liquor truck under several feet of soil and gravel, without any hope of ever being found.

And so he stayed for a very long time, without worry.

(<o>)/(9.32)\(<o>)

The nuns. They lived in a sort of compound on the island on the far side of Unkafrank Lake. They were multi-denominational on the island: travelers from all corners of the Church. They wore jeans and sweatshirts, work boots and work gloves, and a variety of hats and headpieces, mostly baseball caps or knitted toques.

We wondered about them, and we ignored them, and we were mystified by them.

Most were young with pink healthy sincere faces. A few were older with wizened laugh creased faces. Some were pretty in their civilian clothes, which they wore with casual indifference. You could see them moving around their campsite sometimes. They hooted and guffawed while they worked.

They kept to themselves, pretty much. They were seldom seen in town. We could only guess at their politics.

They were a wilderness convent in the middle of nowhere, doing who knows what all day for Jesus.

We saw them. We wondered about them. We tended to avoid them.

(<o>)/(9.33)\(<o>)

Hack was from around there.

It wasn't for sure how long there had been Hackneys in the area, but the property on Unkafrank Lake was homesteaded by his great-great grandfather, sometime around the time of the Civil War. Or so the story went.

As a family they were known locally as "colorful" which is Minnesota nice for saying they were largely shiftless, half-criminal, and virtually unemployable. The Hackneys normally didn't come to town much, or hold much truck with city living. But as the years and the generations passed, Hackney men found themselves involved in a variety of local pursuits, not all of them illegal. While the family may have started out as hunters and trappers and scratch farmers, some moved into logging, some moved into the guiding business, and some went into iron mining.

The family homestead was both cursed and blessed by proximity to wilderness that eventually became National Park, and by the fact that tiny Unkafrank Lake formed a teeny part of the Canadian/American international border. The national park land provided opportunities for hunting and guiding and poaching, so Hackney children seldom went hungry. The border also provided almost irresistible opportunities and temptations for smuggling, so few Hackney men made it through to retirement without some sort of criminal record. And a fair number of Hackney men never made it through to retirement.

The first generations had built on the land. A simple log cabin, much like they were building now, was constructed and then added onto, again and again. The land and the "home farm" as they called it, had passed through generations of improvements and expansions – until it burnt down, sometime after Hack's grandfather had disappeared.

The family story was that Zelda, Hack's grandmother, had used the place to entertain St. Paul mobster friends of Abner's until one winter night a dispute over a card game had progressed to gunfire and eventually to conflagration.

The burnt outline of that old homestead was still visible from where Skate and Hack were building. It was Hack's plan to finish their cabin, move into it, and then start building a new "home farm", on the site of the old one.

Hack's father had been among the first to move 'down to the Cities' as a young man – making a life for himself in factory work and raising a family out by the suburbs near the river, where Hack grew up. Dad Hackney had led a citified and largely low-key life as a working stiff, with only the unfortunate margarine smuggling fiasco on his record.

Hack knew the river area near our school, and felt at home there. Meanwhile, there had been plenty of trips to the old hometown through the years for family gatherings and such. We'd all been along on these trips from time to time, sometimes several of us at once. Packed in the car like Boy Scouts to spend a weekend in the woods. It was not a surprise to us, who knew him growing up, that he would contemplate moving back at some point.

There were several shirt-tail relations still living in the area, and his uncle was a local figure who lived in town, delivered propane by day, and worked any number of side jobs to make ends meet. He was who could produce a portable saw mill, if the need arose.

In Hack's generation there were several cousins of roughly our age. Some were solid citizens working on living down the Hackney legacy. But most were stoners and boozers who lived in trailers or their Mom's basement and eked along, working scratch jobs and getting high every day.

For the most part, Hackney men were large, loud and boisterous, and tended to marry women who produced a large number of unwashed and unruly male children.

Hack was the quietest of his family; not educated so much as thoughtful, and an extraordinary physical specimen, even in the context of his extraordinarily physical family.

(<o>)/(9.34)\(<o>)

Bard bouncing.

This won't work, but he tries it anyway. If you get on the bus in the neighborhood, and make sure to get a transfer – then you can ride to the end of the line and back for low cash. If you get on the right line, you can ride for hours in a heated bus, and nobody will bother you. People rarely talk to each other on the bus – like a men's room, or an elevator.

It's a warm winter day after a cold spell. The snow is melting but the bus is toasty to a turn. The driver cranks up the heat.

He has his journal on his lap, and his pen in his hand, and he divides his time between jotting notes and gazing at the scenery. But it's warm in there, and it's making him sleepy.

He jots.

The bard's chin drops onto his chest. He dozes in the heat.

"End of the line," the driver says, "everybody out."

Bard dozes. Driver leaves him. Drivers have been known to fish into a sleepers pants to get the next quarter. This driver just wants to drive. That's enough. Small town boy, in the cities to make his fortune. He's close. He's driving a bus, and that's steady work. A good thing.

Home. There's nothing quite like it. If you go there, they have to let you in.*

(<o>)/(Endnotes 9.35)\(<o>)

65. Wolfe, Tom, The Electric Koolaid Acid Test. New York: Bantam Books, 1968.

66. Vonnegut, Kurt (1969). Slaughterhouse Five. Dell Books.

67. Frost, Robert. Poetry of Robert Frost : The Collected Poems, Complete and Unabridged, Edward Connery Lathem (Editor). Paperback - 607 pages (May 1979) Henry Holt (Paper); ISBN: 0805005013 ; Dimensions (in inches): 1.40 x 8.35 x 5.49

Chapter 10

It was the morning of the fourth day. Another sunny masterpiece – the air fresh and clean. Towards the lake they could see sunlight on tiny ripples. In the distance, they could hear a faint purr, like a baby growling. It was the sound of a chainsaw, but across the water, and miles away.

"Darn those nuns," Hack smiled, "just listen to that racket."

Skate and Hack made their way down to the building site.

"Walls up," said Hack, "roof soon."

They sat down on a stripped log and sipped through their coffee. It was a glorious morning, and haste, well, it makes anxiety. Today, especially after last night, was no day for anxiety.

The cabin site was away from the lake, behind a stand of trees. Skate had thought a lakeside cabin would be better. And there was plenty of room by the water to build.

It would be cool, he argued, to wake up with a lake out the window. Besides, why not?

Hack had filled him in. There were, indeed, many lakes up in the great northwoods where the landowners built right down by the water. In fact, that was the usual case. But not Unkafrank Lake.

"We've got neighbors here," Hack said, "all along the lakefront. But you don't see cabins from the water. It's the way Abner wanted, and everyone went along. We don't build on the water here, that's it."

They built behind the line of trees, hidden from the lake. That's it.

(<o>).[].(<o>)

"Thirty two sheets," Skate said.

"Okay," Ace said, "what day is it today?"

"Thursday."

"Right. Turn up around noon on Sunday. We'll do it then."

"Talk more later. Long distance."

"Yeah, later."

It was the night of the fourth day. Skate had a pile of napkins in from of him with geometrical calculations. It figured.

Skate hung up the phone at the end of the bar and swiveled his barstool towards Hack.

"We're on," Skate said, "noon Sunday."

(<o>).[].(<o>)

Ace hung up the receiver in the "felony phone booth" and walked out to the car.

"Sunday, midday," he said, "we must prepare."

"No trouble with the call?" Book asked.

"Zero," Ace answered, "your reign of crime continues."

It was Book who had noticed that long distance operators had no way of knowing who was receiving their connections. If you used an operator to make a "collect" long distance call, where the charges were accepted by the recipient, the operator just arranged the call and billed the charges to the number. They couldn't tell if the recipient was in a house, or an apartment, or, as they had just done, in a phone booth on the edge of a college campus.

It took a little planning, and they were always careful to keep the calls short, lest there was a response team, and they were always careful not to use names, especially real names, lest someone was listening or worse recording. And they used different phones from time to time.

So, it worked like this. Somebody, say Skate, would place a call from a pay phone, asking the operator to 'reverse the charges' – a 'collect' call. Somebody else, say Ace, would be waiting in a phone booth at the appointed time. When the phone rings, Ace answers and the operator asks if he will 'accept the charges'. Ace says 'yes' and the call is put through. The charges for the call are assigned to the phone number that accepted the charges. Which, if that number is a phone booth, means nobody is billed and the call is free.

It was stealing, pure and simple; but it was the 70s, and it was stealing from the phone company, which wasn't so bad. Ma Bell, big brother, the CIA, these were all the same to most people. Stealing a phone call was both beating the system and striking a blow for the revolution. Right on.

(<o>).[].(<o>)

They had been to the diner – they were now in the bar. They each had a shell of beer in front of them.

A woman came in wearing a University of Minnesota sweatshirt, with hood, jeans, and work boots. Her hair was very short. She nodded at Skate.

"You men done with the phone?" she asked.

Skate got up from his stool, at the end of the bar by the phone, and moved around her, to sit on the stool beyond Hack. On the way around he smiled at her. She was older, probably in her thirties, but she had a fresh pixie face: kinda cute. Her legs were chubby, but she was definitely cute. Especially to a hard working log cabin worker.

Skate settled onto his new stool as she dialed a number.

Hack looked at Skate, locking eyes.

"Nun," Hack mouthed.

"Hello," she said into the phone, "it's me, Louise."

Then the jukebox came up, and she turned in toward the wall, plugging her ear and mouthing directly into the receiver, so they could hear no more of what she said.

(<o>).[].(<o>)

"Do I know you?" Skate said.

She was off the phone.

"It's possible," she answered, "I make calls from here."

"No," Skate said, "not from here."

"Maybe," she said, "but I'm on the run now, my ride's waiting."

She smiled and hopped down from the stool.

"Another time, maybe," she said, and headed out the door.

(<o>)/(10.6)\(<o>)

A one act play in several scenes:

Scene Ten –

The lights come up on the interior of Powder's Tap; a dimly lit, crummy little dive like so many others. Center stage is dominated by a pitted Prohibition era bar; a scuffed brass rail along the bottom and a featureless spittoon at each end. There are some dusty "top shelf" liquor bottles behind the bar and a cloudy mirror on the upstage wall in back of it.

On a level two steps down from the bar is a line of four or five small, cheap, Formica tables with a few chairs around each. At the far right are a beat-up, coin operated pool table and an equally beat up jukebox.

Standing at the audience-left end of the bar is Larry, an older man with a greasy apron and a slight limp. Larry was a logger until he got hurt on the job, now he tends bar for a living.

The bar is almost deserted. A lone figure sits at a table on the far audience left side with back turned. Hack is sitting at the far right end of the bar, nearest the door, where it curves towards the wall. Skate is sitting on the last stool where the bar meets the wall, and talking on the payphone hung on the wall.

It is Thursday, June 24th, 1976, just after supper in the Central Time Zone, in Powder's Tap, Elysium, Minnesota.

=#=#=#=

    Skate
Thirty two sheets.
(he listens)
Thursday.
(listens)
Talk more later. Long distance.
(hangs up and swivels on his stool)
We're on. Sunday noon.
(A short haired woman walks in wearing a hooded sweatshirt, jeans and work boots)

    Woman
(to Skate)
You men done with the phone?
(Skate gets off the stool and sits next to Hack where his drink is. The woman sits where Skate was, next to the phone against the wall, and dials a number. The stage lights go black, except for a spotlight on Hack and Skate and another on the woman)

    Hack
(to Skate)
Nun.

    Woman
Hello, it's me, Louise.
(Skate turns to look at the woman, her back is to him. She hangs up the phone and turns to get off the stool.)

    Skate
(to the woman)
Do I know you?

    Woman
It's possible. I make calls from here.

        Skate
No, not from here.

        Woman
Maybe, but I'm on the run now, my ride's waiting.
(she gets off the stool)
Another time, maybe.
(she walks out the door)

        Skate
(watching her leave)
I could swear …

        Hack
She's on the island, been there off and on quite a few years I
think.

        Skate
Was that her, that night with Terry?

        Hack
Yeah, that was her.

        Skate
Hmm. That's not it.
(turns to Hack)
So, on another topic, what's up with this range war?

        Hack
We should talk about this while we're working.

        Skate
And nobody can hear, I get it. I don't want your fulminating
political rhetoric and inflammatory opinions.
(he stresses his diction)
It's AN historical question

        Hack
(sighs)
Okay, there's four points of view, two national and two local.

        Skate
Only four?

        Hack
(grins, nodding)
Nationally, there's the DNR and the conservationists, who want
to preserve the wilderness.

        Skate
Department of Natural Resources.

        Hack
We whisper around here when we say DNR. Then there's the rest
of the nation, who don't give a shit.

        Skate
The silent majority.

        Hack
Yeah them, then locally there's the regular folks, and the fat
cat outfitters who figure to profit from the wilderness.

        Skate
Ah, capitalism in the forest.

        Hack
Yeah that, and a fair number of folks, big and small, with a

lot at stake.
(a group of husky men come into the bar and sit near center
stage)

    Skate
And thus, I'm guessing, ends the lesson.

    Hack
You could say that.
(Larry brings them two more glasses of beer)

    Larry
You boys hungry?

    Hack
Naw, we ate.

    Larry
You know I care deeply about your well-being, and that you not
leave here too drunk to drive.
(from his tone you know he does not especially care)

    Hack
Keep 'em coming, Larry, we'll let you know.

    Larry
It's my sensitivity training, coming through.

    Skate
You took a course?

    Larry
Oh, yeah, you bet, I got my degree in bar-ology.

    Skate
(catching on)
Yeah, I studied for the bar exam too, but I flunked.

    Larry
(rapping his knuckles on the bar)
Keep practicing.
(turns to serve the newcomers)

    Hack
How's your back holding up under all this construction?

    Skate
Not a wibble, not a wobble.

    Hack
You never did tell what the doctors said.

    Skate
I hate to.

    Hack
Bad news?

    Skate
No, no news. After all the pain, and all the fear … at one
point they thought I had cancer in my spine … and then after
all the grief, and a trip to the Mayo Clinic for the final
word, it turned out to be nothing.

    Hack
You're kidding, that's great.

Skate

I had "the fear" deep in my bones, and it turned out to be a smudged x-ray and a pinched nerve

Hack

Oh, no.

Skate

Yep, they brought in a chiropractor.

Hack

Fuck a red duck, Rex would say.

Skate

Yeah, quack, quack, quack. But I tell you, the guy cleaned me up in about ten minutes. Not a twinge since.

Hack

(raising his glass)

Well, here's to modern medicine.

Skate

(clinking his glass with Hack's)

Here's to modern medical insurance. If it wasn't for the job that Book hooked me up with, I'd be sweeping floors for spare change.

Hack

Here's to Book, then.

(they don't bother clinking glasses this time)

Skate

I mean, I'm broke. Hardly a dime except for my cash stash at camp. But at least I'm not in crushing debt.

Hack

Here's to cash stash, then.

(again, no clinking)

(the lone figure at the audience left of the bar gets up and walks out the door at audience right)

Hack

(nods as the man walks by)

Hey Lon.

Lon

(nods, but does not pause, and speaks flatly)

Hackney.

Skate

(after a short pause, as the man leaves)

Once the cabin's sea-worthy, I'm going to have to give up this high life.

(gesturing around the bar)

I'll be on a sandwich diet to make the cash stash last.

Hack

Got it, me too. I'm glad to hear about the medical picture, though.

Skate

I'm embarrassed to tell it. After all that, fear and doubt about my spine, it turns out to be a red heron.

Hack

Might have got you out of the draft, though.

        Skate
Yes, well, there is that.

    Hack
Should we plan some chow?

    Skate
We just ate. Didn't we. You mean here?

    Hack
Definitely not. Maid-Up.

    Skate
So, not now, but later, or what are you saying?

    Hack
Nothing necessarily, just talking food. Should we get more
beer? A pitcher?

    Skate
Yes, plus we've got to draw the ridge pole plan. Grab me a
couple napkins.

    Hack
(reaches over the bar for napkins)
More geometry? Better you than me.

    Skate
Yes, but not too hard. We should have more beer, though.
(drains his glass and puts dollar bills on the bar)
But where, I return to the question …
(he looks towards the door)
… where do I know that nun from?

    (Blackout).

(<o>)/(10.7)\(<o>)

The Swiss approach to ridge pole construction is probably the most stable
method, although it takes space and requires a little more geometry.

The idea is to provide independent support for the ridgepole by putting it on
the apex of a triangle formed by two slanted logs independent of the walls.

To imagine this, draw the "house" you learned to draw in kindergarten: a
square with a triangle on top. Then, draw two new lines from the lower corners
of the square to the tip of the triangle. These are the slanted sides of the Swiss
'A'.

(<o>).[].(<o>)

The geometry wasn't too hard in this case, but it required a construction.
The walls were ten feet tall, fourteen feet apart. The roof was supposed to have
a steepish forty-five degree angle, meaning the point of the roof was destined to
be 12.1 feet above the walls, or 22.1 feet above the ground. This meant a right-
angle triangle of seven feet on the base, and 22.1 feet on the long side, and
solving for the hypotenuse. After a couple of napkins, Skate had the figuring
done. Each A-frame piece needed to be a little over twenty-three feet. Say
twenty three and a half. This would give the roof a nice sharp pitch.

(<o>).[].(<o>)

By this point, with all the building experience they had together, this was
easily done. They cut four logs to twenty-three and half feet, and hauled them

213

into the cabin with the come-along. The geometry worked out so they could lay the first two logs on the dirt floor and shape them together. Hack cut a nice angle into each, leaving a notch for the ridge pole to rest in, then they wired them together and just stood the A up against the first short side wall.

(<o>).[].(<o>)

"Man!" Skate said, "that looks tall. Did I figure this right?"

"Yep," Hack squinted up at the A, "you want a steep pitch, otherwise you're out there in the winter shoveling your roof."

"Shoveling your roof. I've done it, when we were kids at home – some fun."

"Yeah, moving snow to keep the weight down. This way it slides off. Much better."

"The trade-off? The downside?" Skate asked, "there's got to be one."

"Yeah," Hack allowed, "your heat rises into the pitch point. High ceilings make for lost energy. That's the rub."

"No fix for that?"

"Not really," Hack answered, "unless you've got ceiling fans to push the heat around."

"Ceiling fans! Dream on. Why not wish for maid service?"

"I do, but I also cut an extra cord of wood to make up for getting out of roof shoveling. That's how it works in the great northwoods. That's the deal."

(<o>).[].(<o>)

They fixed their A-poles to each end of the cabin with metal strapping and Ace's heavy spikes. Then there was a tricky moment as they lifted the ridge pole up onto the top of the A. This required hoisting the ridge pole up onto the wall tops, and then standing on the wall tops and then sliding the pole up the sides of the A, until it rested in the notch they'd cut in the apex of the A. Of course, this meant raising a 30-foot pole to a height of 12 feet, so they did one end at a time, with Hack shinnied up above, pulling with rope, while Skate shoved and steadied from below.

Once the ridge pole was secured in place, the rest was (relatively) easy. They tapered the end pieces on the short wall to meet the ridge pole, and then notched the rafter logs into the ever shorter end pieces. It took just seven more runs to finish the frame, and then they were ready for roofing.

(<o>)/(10.12)\(<o>)

The bar was full, the music was loud, the crowd was close.

Skate and Hack had worked like trojans and the cabin was shaping up nicely. They were out for the night. Dinner at the diner, then beers at the bar. It was close to closing time, Maid-Up Pizza for after hours chow was next. They were still sitting at the bar near the pay phone.

"So, what's the deal with this Range war?" Skate asked.

Hack looked over his shoulder before he answered.

"It's a long story," Hack sighed, "and I keep telling you, it's not one to get into in the bar late at night."

"Just asking," Skate said.

Hack sighed again, "You've read the papers, you know the outlines. There are people who live here that think the land is theirs, and the decisions about the land ought to be made locally. Then, there are government officials and environmentalists who think these decisions ought to be made by them."

"At the national level."

"The Federal level, yeah."

"So, what's the real beef," Skate countered, "everyone presumably agrees that nature is good. What's the beef?"

Hack gave Skate an unusually sharp look.

"This is not the time or the place," he said, "just talking about it, we could be fighting our way out of this bar. Short story: a lot of people's jobs are hanging on how it plays out. To a lot of the folks in this room, it's a question of food on the table."

"Okay," Skate said, "I'm getting it. Ix-nay on the alk-tay."

"Yeah," Hack nodded emphatically, "later."

(<o>).[].(<o>)

The bar was closing, they were in Maid-Up Pizza for some after bar chow. The place was crowded to capacity, full to the gunnels, bulging with humanity. They got a small table as somebody cleared out, and they sat down.

"Hi, Lon," Hack said, "how's it goin'?"

Lon had his back to the wall, and his posture verged on rigid.

"So happy, I could shit," he said.

"Yeah, I can see that," Hack said, "you met Skate?"

"Pleased to know you, " Lon said, "you from around here?"

"No, no, but maybe now," Skate said, "I'm sort of homesteading."

"Well," Lon said, "maybe in a hundred years your kids will be treated like locals. Probably not, though."

There was a clatter of dishes, and a glass fell and exploded into a thousand pieces on the floor. Lon flinched and reached toward the inside of his jacket. Nothing further happened, and Lon relaxed. Skate saw the butt of Lon's pistol from where he sat, Hack didn't need to see it, he knew it was there.

There was a long awkward silence. Nobody wanted to talk about Lon's gun, and nobody could think of anything else to talk about.

Skate was feeling good and loose and invulnerable.

"I'm not from around here, and I'm not any part of anything" he said, "so I'm going to ask. Are you the one who had the fire I heard about?"

Hack sagged a little, then turned his chair to face the room. He knew the answer.

"Yup," Lon said, "that's me. One of my sheds burned down, mysteriously."

"You know why?" Skate asked.

"Yeah, well, everybody knows why." Lon said.

He repeated himself, loud and drunkenly, so everyone could hear, "EVERYBODY KNOWS WHY!"

Hack turned his chair a little more, he was now able to see the entire Maid-Up clientele. Skate could see he was coiled, despite how relaxed he seemed.

"I work for myself, on my own land," Lon said directly to Skate, "but I contract with an outfitter which some people think means I worked for and helped the Feds, so now I'm a target. These bastards are burning down my sheds."

"What could you have possibly done?" Skate asked.

"I made my stuff, and helped out," Lon answered, "because I think they're basically right. Now I'm basically an armed camp, with sentries and soldiers."

Hack turned to look, "How so?"

"I'm forming a survivalist camp on my property," Lon said, "so the posse types can live off my land and train for the end-times."

"Maneuvers, and rations, and booby traps, and target practice," Lon added, "an armed camp of soldiers learning to fight for freedom."

"No, really, Lon" Hack was casual, "is that a good plan?"

"Yes it is," Lon answered, loudly, "and besides, it's done. The perimeter has already been secured."

Lon was lit up, and liking it.

"TRY ME NOW," Lon shouted to the room and nobody in particular, "I'VE GOT AN ARMY AND I'M WAITING!"

"Jeez, Lon," Hack said, "that's kinda radical."

"Yeah, well," Lon replied, "burning down sheds is radical, too."

Then the pizza came, so they ate.

(<o>)/(10.14)\(<o>)

The guys were raised in a mostly working class neighborhood, roughly divided between Scandinavian Lutherans and European Catholics. By the time they were coming up, in the 1950s, a lot of the older religious enmities were evaporating. It was rare that anything hostile would develop solely on the basis of religion, as opposed to the generation before them, where old-style gangs might meet for a "rumble" on the basis of church leanings.

Not that a rumble would be used to settle religious questions.

More likely was a young catholic boy pestering a pretty Lutheran girl, and getting cuffed by her older Lutheran brother, which would lead the boy's older Catholic brother to enlist a Catholic pal to gang up and get into a shoving match with the Lutheran brother, escalating into meeting under a bridge with fists and sometimes baseball bats.

Nothing too serious.

The guys lived, by the same token, in neighborhoods that were 'mighty white'. They were out on the far north side, and the 'colored' neighborhoods were south of them, on the near north side. There were absolutely no black children at Our Lady of the Snows, and the closest thing to a Native American was Book, who was one-thirty-second Chippewa. Hispanics? None, not one.

As obsessed as they were with cowboys and Indians, Book's heritage rarely came up. He was one of them – his father worked in a printing shop and was a Boy Scout leader. And while Book was fat and slow and bad at games like basketball, he was smart, a little bit lazy, and willing to put up with more-or-less perpetual hazing, which endeared him to us.

Book was actually the first kid that Skate met when his family moved in. They lived near enough, and encountered each other in the Bookmobile one summer Monday, standing in front of the cowboy fiction. Young boys who didn't know each other would not usually speak to strangers in the Bookmobile,

216

but Skate was a little interested in making new friends, and there was something about Book that made him approachable.

Skate took a mustard colored volume from the shelf.

"Kit Carson," Skate said, "I've been reading about him."

"Yes, he's good," said Book.

"You read this one?" Skate asked.

"My," Book answered, "I've read all these I think. I come here because they let you return books you checked out of the branch library. It's closer."

"This any good?"

"Yes, I liked it because there's a part about Three-fingered Mordecai, who was a real mountain man."

"I've heard of him, and Jim Bridger, but I mostly like the older eastern times. Like Simon Kenton in Kentucky."

"The dark and bloody ground," Book whispered.

"What do you like most, history or fiction?" Skate asked.

"I like history and fiction, but I like history a little more."

"Me too," Skate said, "but I like fiction the most."

(<o>)/(10.15)\(<o>)

The squad was assembled.

Ace and Book were in Patrick's beater, a grayish-white '66 Chrysler Newport with push-button transmission, parked on the side of 9th Street downtown: the engine running. Skate and Hack had just pulled in behind them in Hack's dilapidated sky blue 1956 Dodge pickup truck. Ace got out of the car and walked back to the truck. It was Sunday morning, about 11 AM. Hack and Skate had driven down from the woods that morning, a five-hour trek. When they got to the corner, the boys were waiting.

"The sign has been up all morning," Ace said, "we came out at dawn to set it up."

"Check." Skate said.

"Cops have been by about four times, once an hour roughly," Ace went on, "we don't have any way of predicting their movements, but none of them batted an eye on the way by."

Skate started laughing, "This is going to be great."

"Let's hope," said Ace, "you two pull around the corner, it's on the left, clearly marked. You'll know it when you see it. We'll leave the car here and walk over."

Hack nodded.

"Remember," Ace said, "plausible deniability."

Skate was still laughing when Hack dropped the truck into gear and pulled around the corner.

(<o>).[].(<o>)

It was a construction site.

There was a downtown building in the middle of being erected, with bare steel girders reaching several stories overhead. The chain link fence around the site was high and locked. The signs said, "Hardhat Area", and "Restricted Area".

217

On the curb, though, outside the fence, was a big jumbled pile of cast-off construction supplies. Some junky two-by-fours with cement stuck on them, some bent metal poles, a length of folded and useless chain link, scraps of lumber cut at odd angles with nails sticking out, some big chunks of torn insulation – a pile of junk – and nestled amidst the detritus, a couple of pallets of fresh plywood.

It looked like the pallets had been laid there, then the construction junk had been thrown in the same vicinity, and the plywood had been forgotten about. Patrick, who worked nearby, noticed the mistake, and checked every day all week. Opportunity knocked.

Hanging on the fence above this jumble, a sign, nicely lettered on a white background, identical in color and style to the other signs on the fence:

"Free Materials – take what you want."

In full view of the street, bold as brass.

This sign however, had only been hanging here since just before dawn that day. Ace had hung it there, right after breakfast at Annie's. The paint was still damp.

Skate said to Hack, laughing "You s'pose this is what we're looking for?"

Hack pulled over and they started to load. The rest of the squad sauntered up and pitched in.

(<o>).[].(<o>)

"Beat cheeks, boys," Ace said, "we don't want to be here too long."

"Nice sign, Patrick" Skate said, "very convincing."

"Thanks."

(<o>).[].(<o>)

They worked like coolies, loading plywood onto Hack's truck. The sheets stacked nicely into the bed, and thirty two sheets of plywood forms a stack that's heavy but not too tall. They hauled them in stacks, and loaded like banshees. It only took a few minutes.

"Thirty two, right?" Ace asked.

"Yep."

"I'd like a couple," said Book, "for a shelf."

"You got it," Hack said, and hoisted two more.

There was another three pallets still sitting there. There was plenty of room in the truck.

"You know, Hack," Skate said, "we didn't figure on the flooring, or the loft."

"Yah," Hack said, "you're right, I forgot."

Skate stared at the sky, figuring.

"Another twenty should do, easily."

They went back to work.

"Ooh!" Book said, "look at this."

He had uncovered some big rolls of fresh tarpaper.

"Golden," Hack said, "absolutely goddam golden."

They threw a few rolls in the truck.

"Let's move," Ace said, "this is broad daylight, after all."

Loaded with contraband, they fled the scene.

They left the sign.

(<o>).[].(<o>)

They went to the Web house and dumped Book's boards. Then they stopped for a minute and talked.

Skate looked for Rexee', but she wasn't around. He glanced up at Effie's window, but it was black. She wasn't looking down any more.

Skate said, "What are you guys doing now?"

Ace said, "I say over to the Stockholm Bar on 8th street downtown, they do those free snacks on Sunday afternoon."

"My, yes," Book agreed, "cardboard plates full of beans and little wieners. All you can eat, free. A lovely concept."

"You guys want to come?" Ace asked.

"I don't think so," Hack said, "we got a lot of ground to cover."

It was time to go; they needed to complete the crime and make their getaway. Which meant a long drive back to the great northwoods. Still, they hung around and chatted like old pals.

"How's it up there, fellows?" Book asked.

"Fresh air, sunshine, brutal work," Skate said, "and my hands feel like dogmeat."

He held his hands out for Book to see, "and I've never felt better."

"Cabin'll be closed in within the week," Hack added, "you all should think about a trip. Plenty of fresh air, plenty of room, plenty of finish work yet to do."

Hack started up the truck, sagging on its springs.. It was five hours to Unkafrank Lake.

"It'll happen," Ace said, "maybe for the Bicentennial."

(<o>)/(10.20)\(<o>)

Delmar was out, he was on the street.

He'd seen his chance, he'd taken his shot, he'd shot his wad. He'd found himself on the ground without a thought in his head. He'd foraged for food, he'd stopped for a drink. And one thing had led to another.

He'd had his nuts crushed.

Then, still sucking for air, he'd been scooped up and landed in stir.

Again.

This time it was a petty beef, an ice cream sandwich ripoff, but it had a violation component that could get tough. He was a convicted felon, out on parole, unable to exercise his voting rights, unable to bear arms, unable to consort with other felons. It was an atrocity. He, a loyal son of the American Revolution, unable, by law, to defend himself against the unlawful.

It was a travesty. All he'd done was execute a rapist in the commission of his crime. And here he was, himself convicted of manslaughter.

Manslaughter! That implied a man was slaughtered. Far from it, it seemed. A rapist, and there it was.

But there he was. On the street with a record and a parole officer, and a bail payment just to get himself out of the slam. With all kinds of administrative and legalistic machinery about to spring into action against him on Monday.

Yes, the ice cream heist had busted him. Yes, they had accepted his driver's license as identification, which still had his old address. Yes, they had let him go. But they would surely find out he didn't really live there any more. That he had simply paid a little every year to keep a storage locker there. They would soon find that he had no real address, and no source of income, and that he'd been using his key to sleep in the storage locker during the day, while he scouted the terrain at night, and waited the chance to fire his ill-fated shot.

Time to go.

He knew a guy – time to fly.

(<o>).[].(<o>)

It takes about thirty minutes to walk from the downtown lockup to the Web house neighborhood. You head towards the river, and then downstream to the bridge. Then you cross and work your way across a few blocks. Then you're home.

It's Sunday, near noon, and the streets are mostly deserted. There's a couple of cars, and a few pedestrians. The bars don't open until 1PM in Minnesota on a Sunday. Many are at church. Many are holed up until after church. It's a sunny Sunday summer morning in Minneapolis. Nothing much going on.

(<o>).[].(<o>)

Delmar has been walking for nearly thirty minutes, and is passing the House of Rip-off, closed at this hour. The source of his demise, in a small way. Then around the corner and onto his block.

He turns right up his back alley to save a few steps, now walking away from the surf frat, and goes to the basement side door leading down to the storage area.

Across the street, he sees a knot of people in the yard of that damned Web house.

(<o>).[].(<o>)

They pissed him off, those guys, for so many reasons it was hard to list, and for so long it seemed like he'd always hated them. He'd wanted that woman, and they had blocked him. He had whacked that rapist and they'd testified against him. They talked to him, sometimes, and then he thought he heard them whisper against him afterwards. They seemed to flaunt American principles. That whole damned bird thing, the "Constitution of the United States", made a mockery of righteousness, and besides, he simply did not like them.

Now, there they were, assembled, the old pickup stacked with plywood and materials, and the clubbish nature of it all. They were an insular fraternity, an exclusive klatch, and he loathed them for it. A bunch of local boy hale fellows, and a pain in his side.

Delmar thought briefly about trying another shot. They were lined up like ducks. But the impulse quickly passed. It was full daylight, and he didn't have a plan – no exit strategy. He was half on the run, and their time would come, he was sure of it. They would crash into dust, and he would be the instrument, he was sure of that too, and that was enough for now.

Delmar slipped into his storage locker, and packed his kit. It was a small military pack of clothing and trinkets with a bedroll, and a duffel of weapons, each wrapped in cloth with ammunition.

At one point, he looked out a basement window and saw the truck pull away, with the big guy and that other one, Skeet or whatever, heading toward the freeway. The others got in a car and went the other way.

Delmar didn't care. He had his own travel to plan. He hoisted his bags and headed out the door, stopping for a moment to look back at the life he'd made there, for what it was: a cot, a few magazines, the White Album, a telescope.

Nothing to him now.

(<o>).[].(<o>)

Three in the morning on a Sunday night (actually Monday morning), and Delmar is on the street. He's been hitch-hiking all day, walking a lot of it, and it's been a long grind. He finds the one pay phone and calls the one number he knows. The phone rings.

"Yeah," it's a groggy but suspicious voice.

"Is this Lon?" Delmar says.

"Who's asking?" is the reply.

"It's me, Delmar. I heard you're looking for men," Delmar says, "and I'm here, locked and loaded. Come and get me, Uncle Lon."

(<o>)/(10.25)\(<o>)

```
diaria -- 10.0 -- 3/26/77 -- las cruces
```

Another guy who fools with time (there's a lot of them, by the by, Pynchon, Heller sometimes, Borges I guess) is Kurt Vonnegut. In Slaughterhouse Five* he tells of beings with four dimensional perception who can see a persons past and future connected to them.

It's a nifty little bit of writing and I recommend it to anyone. Anyway Vonnegut's of interest here because he's also a metafictionist in that he includes a writer, Kilgore Trout, who is presumably an alias for Kurt himself.

He's interesting for another thing too, and that's the construction of his books. One of the things Rexee' had me read sed, "He has written short sentences, small paragraphs, tiny chapters, and little books in an attempt to reach busy, unliterary folk with his criticism of life and his help in making it bearable."*

and I personally like that sort of thing, as you might guess by the construction of this little number. it seems to me to be more engaging.

when you're paging through the sports section what's the first thing to catch yer eye? For me it's the quotable quotes, the short little bits of trivia or wit that can be digested in a gulp. One of my favorites is from Yogi

221

Berra, "you can observe a lot, just by watching"* which
is sort of thematic with what is going on here.

be that as it may, we've got to press along with this
deal.

(<o>)/(10.26)\(<o>)

Like much of the lakeshore property in Northern Minnesota, the Hackney
land was more-or-less pie-shaped. At the lakeshore there was several hundred
feet against the water, forming the blunted northern edge of the wedge. Then the
property boundaries extended in jagged lines like the hands of a clock at four
o'clock towards the southeast, ending at the borders of the National Park, and at
seven o'clock towards the south-southwest, a considerably longer side, bordered
by an old logging trail that met a gravel township road.

The entire homestead was a series of rocky ridges and gulleys, whorling
through the property like a fingerprint. The basic ridge pattern was uphill
parallel lines arising from the lake, but there were plenty of dead ends and
cutovers. From fourteen thousand feet, it looked like a child had dug his fingers
into a lump of soft green clay.

Very little of the land was flat, and very little of the thin soil would support
even a garden. Much of the property had been logged over at one point or
another, and most of the remaining timber was jack pine of some variety. There
were a few stands of old growth forest too, including a gigantic elm that stood
near the site of the "home farm". But mainly the land was covered with dense
undergrowth lined by a few narrow deer trails.

The lakeshore with their cabin site and the burnt-out ruins of the home farm
house was in a wide thumb-shaped valley. To get to town entailed a precarious
traversal up a looping rutted driveway that started near the lake and went
steeply up over the first line of ridge, then back over the other side and through
a twisting progression of gulleys that finally emerged on the old logging trail.

Most of this "driveway" was two tire tracks, pocked with rocks, and barely
wide enough for a single vehicle. On a breezy day, tree branches would slap the
windshield on the drive out. From there it was a relatively straight shot down to
the township road.

The township road was gravel and itself barely maintained, although
slightly wider. It contoured through a sequence of valleys until it met a paved
county road, far to the south and west of them, which ran more or less straight
to town.

(<o>)/(10.27)\(<o>)

Monday, and they were on the final leg.

Sunday they spent on the road, down to 'the cities' and back, picking up
supplies, so to speak. They drove up, slept like logs and hit it early. The end was
in sight, so to see.

(<o>).[].(<o>)

The ridgepole and rafters were in place, ready for the plywood to be laid.
They had decided to put a loft into the western end of the cabin, so log joists
were in place for that too. They spent Friday and Saturday putting in all the

finish work they could. This included hanging a beat up door that Hack had pulled off a wrecked shack, and installing the window units into the holes they'd left on the east and south side walls. They didn't have any more window casements, so they'd have to board up the west and north side windows when they got around to it. It was summer, so they were left open for now.

They debated putting a window on the north wall since, on one hand it faced the lake, providing a nice view in the summer, and on the other hand it faced north, making for a heat sink in the winter. They decided to leave room for a smallish pane, and resolved to build shutters to keep in the heat in the winter when there would be almost no light from that direction anyway. For now they left it open, since they didn't have any glass for it.

They also started packing the west wall with clay, squeezing it between the logs by the shovel-full.

This is a dirty, tiring, and aggravating job, as the clay was too stiff at first, and mostly fell out of the cracks, and then when they had watered it down, became too runny, and made a sloppy mess of their walls. This would take time, but it was still summer, and the clay caulking could wait.

The next big job was to install the truckload of plywood that was backed up to the site.

Once they began, it didn't even take the whole day.

They used twelve sheets for flooring after laying horizontal timbers to support them, and carefully shaving them so the floor would be flat.

Then another six sheets covered the loft area.

This was done by lunch time.

Then they started on the roof, piecing the plywood together as tightly as possible. They used Book's found tarpaper to cover the whole thing, tacking it down with short nails. By mid evening, long before dark, they had it all closed in. At long last.

(<o>).[].(<o>)

"Town tonight?" Hack asked.

"Oh, no, I don't think so," Skate said, "I just want to sit around and admire this baby."

Skate and Hack were standing in the yard near their campfire, facing the cabin. It was straight and tall and black on top. The most beautiful thing Skate had ever seen.

"You know, I've never done anything remotely like this. The closest thing was building an oak nightstand in ninth grade wood shop."

"I remember that nightstand," Hack said, "it was good."

"Yeah, I was mighty pleased with it. But nothing like this. I can see why guys go into the building trades. This is satisfying, really rewarding."

"Yeah," Hack said, "it's a damn fine cabin."

"A work of art, you mean."

"Yeah, like that," Hack smiled, "it's got anthropology and linguistics too."

"Oh, definitely," Skate laughed, "it's got anthropology with linguistics on top."

"Speaking of which," Hack said, "let's eat. You want cheese and baloney, or baloney and cheese?"

223

(<o>)/(10.30)\(<o>)

The blizzard had been threatening and it finally broke, and Dewane and Shorty were damned glad to be indoors. Little Margie, whom they'd only recently met, drew another round of beer.

"It sounds like a bad one."

Margie had a gift for understatement.

Beyond the icy window of the Silver Spur Tap the wind howled with a lupine cadence. Skate's Batmobile, parked in the front lot, was only half visible through the thickening drapery of snow that ran, right to left, past the little window on an almost horizontal plane.

Shorty and Dewane were railroad men, heading south and west at the end of their working week. They had planned to take their line truck to their outfit car, park it, then change into civilian clothes and drive home to their families for the weekend. The roads were getting bad, though, and the visibility worse, so they pulled into Silver Spur to take a break and see how the weather developed.

That had been around noon.

They were both old hands, in their fifties with thirty years on the job. They'd been snowed in before, and neither had a young bride to rush home to – just wives and kids and dogs and cats that were used to them being away. Once in awhile it was okay to stay over. Didn't hurt a bit.

Now it was well past dark, and bunking in the outfit car looked like a real possibility – they had done it before – and they were not too anxious about it.

Skate on the other hand was heading north and east, towards Elysium and a weekend in Hack's trailer. Hack spent many weekends up there, hunting, fishing, and hanging out. Skate normally went up for one or two weekends every winter. He liked tramping the quiet snowy woods, he liked splitting firewood, he liked sitting with a cup of coffee and a cigarette and scribbling in his journal, and there was something about the town that drew him. He liked just hanging out and getting to know the place.

He too had pulled over to escape the weather and get in off the icy roads.

Outside the storm was intensifying and the railroad line truck, painted white with red lettering, was almost lost to view. Only the running lights, winking in and out of sight, and the occasionally audible purring of the of the idling engine came through between gusts.

Shorty and Dewane had been there since lunch and were well into their beer by now, and as the weather got worse, they were looking less like getting home.

Shorty was the driver, and he was adamant about keeping the truck warm, so he went out every two hours religiously to start the engine, coming back inside and waiting for 15 minutes to let it get nicely warmed up, and then going back out to shut it off. It was one thing to be stranded – it was altogether another thing to be stranded in a bar with a truck that wouldn't start. Shorty and Dewane were far too canny in the ways of the north to let that happen. You kept your gas tank full, and you kept your engine warm – that was the deal – that was the way you did it, if you were smart.

Meanwhile, a sloping, sculpted snowdrift was forming around Skate's car, and he was reminded of a Huskie mother and pup, burrowing into the Arctic waste, tails to the wind, huddling for warmth beneath insulating snow. Skate, with his crappy car and non-functional heater, was double-damned glad to be indoors.

(<o>).[].(<o>)

Elizabeth Vera Alberts was gripping her steering wheel with white-knuckled concentration. As usual in emergency situations she was reviewing her life and trying to discover how she'd gotten herself into this mess.

Raised by her aunt in rural Minnesota, she had met, and married, a US Marine on an impulse. Transplanted to Baltimore, a city she detested, she was an expatriate. After leaving her husband, on another impulse, she had moved back to Minnesota and "gone to the U". She'd gotten mixed up in several unpleasant things while there, and dropped out, pregnant, the very day her divorce became final. Now, after eleven months in Florida, and down to her last few dollars, she'd decided to surprise Margie, her second cousin and childhood chum with a Christmas visit.

Romance at short notice seemed to be her specialty. And once again, she deduced, it was the root of the mess she was in. Because now, in a Florida Volkswagen without a heater, on a road she could barely see anymore, with her windshield coating over with ice, a nine month old child wrapped in blankets beside her, no one expecting her or even suspecting she was enroute, with sheets of ice forming beneath her balding Florida tires, on a night where no sane mid-westerner would even consider venturing outdoors, she was four miles out of Silver Spur, Minnesota, driving into the very teeth of a killer blizzard.

(<o>).[].(<o>)

The snow was nearly an impenetrable veil. It hit the windshield so thickly she had a difficult time seeing the road. The painted lines of the highway were long since covered and not even a tire track guided her passage. Only the ditches that paralleled the road provided a faint point of reference – and they were filling with snow.

Beside her, the child mewled sleepily

The low beams barely left the headlight lenses before they hit thick swirling snow and bounced back into her eyes. She tried the high beams. They were worse. The wind drove snow into her windshield faster than the wipers could wipe. She'd never encountered a situation of this sort, and not knowing any better she tried what seemed like a reasonable ploy. She shut the headlights off.

(<o>).[].(<o>)

Skate was several beers into it. He tried his Scottish accent on Margie.

"It's nae fet naight far main nar beastie."

Margie smiled, "another beer?"

"Okee," the brogue wasn't thick enough – he'd try again later. He was stuck in a blizzard, but he was stuck in a bar with a pretty girl and two fairly congenial railroad guys. It could be a lot worse.

(<o>).[].(<o>)

Instant vertigo – disorientation – confusion. She was, by this time, only traveling 20 miles-per-hour along the crusted slippery road, which was lucky because just as she was reaching for the headlight switch she felt a sickening tilting drop as the bug left the road and unceremoniously plopped into the left-hand ditch.

It was a low-speed impact, into a snow-filled ditch, and not even enough to bounce her forehead off the steering wheel – a non-event in the history of car crashes, and a soft landing compared to most.

It was a moment before she realized what had happened and where she was. After another moment the gravity of the situation began to creep over her. The grim reality started to needle her consciousness.

She was, after all, from this part of the country, and she knew the stories. Motorists stranded in a blizzard had a fair chance of dying from exposure. The odds were better if someone was looking for you, but that was not the case. Frostbite and exposure were real possibilities, she knew second-hand. Things could get real serious, real fast.

She was from this part of the country, but she had never been in a situation like this. The stories she had heard, growing up, were alarming. Now she was faced with living one of those stories. This, she suddenly realized, could get suddenly serious.

Cursing, she tried to back out of the ditch, her bald Florida tires spinning hopelessly in the frozen waste. The engine killed. Furiously she tried to restart it, pumping the gas, and flooding the warm engine instead.

Snowbound.

The lips of panic nibbled on her brain. She tried to think. She knew it was less than four miles to Silver Spur. She'd passed the sign what seemed like hours before. There was nothing for it. She would have to walk. Four miles, on a good day, would take less than an hour. She had walked for miles to ban the bomb, a little stroll through pastoral Minnesota should be a snap.

(<o>)/(10.35)\(<o>)

Ace stopped into Doogan's on his way to work that Bicentennial Monday morning. It was happy hour, the usual crowd was there. He worked the room.

Remo was playing solitaire at the bar.

"Bicentennial is coming up," he said to Remo, "you got plans?"

"Naw, that means nothing to me," Remo said, "you having a party?"

"Yeah, sort of," Ace said, "Skate'n'Hack are having us up to Elysium. They built a cabin."

"Elysium!" Remo said, "that's the end of the earth."

"Almost," Ace agreed, "you can see it from there."

"I don't know," Remo quailed, "I don't think so. That's a long goddam haul. I've got no way to get there."

"We're organizing rides," Ace said, "maybe a bus, maybe cars. Don't worry, we'll get you there and back."

"I don't know," Remo said warily, "I don't do that sort of thing anymore."

"Yes, well," Ace said, "it's the bicentennial."

Remo looked uncertain. Skate moved along.

"Think it over," Ace said, "one group will leave sometime Friday, another on Saturday, probably."

"Yeah, okay, we'll see."

"We'll come back on Sunday or Monday, so pack for two or three nights, and bring a sleeping bag if you've got one."

"Oh, yeah, I've got the gear alright," Remo hesitated, "I'll let you know."

Ace could tell – no sale. He turned to the room.

"Henry, my man, what are you doing this weekend?"

"I dunno," Henry said, "working, probably."

"Take the weekend off," Ace said, "we're heading into the woods for the Fourth. You're invited."

"The woods?" Henry said, "what woods?"

"Up north, you know, the Iron Range." Ace said, "We're going to descend on Hack and Skate and all those bears and mosquitoes, and celebrate the birth of our nation."

Henry gulped. He didn't usually let on, but he was an inner city boy. He'd been born in the University hospital, had lived in the neighborhood all his life, went to Marshall High, and got his job at the "U". In between he'd ventured as far as Como Park on a field trip in eighth grade, and up to the north side for bowling tournaments when he'd "played league". Otherwise, Henry had never been more than twenty blocks from where he was born. He'd never been in the army, he'd never been to the suburbs, and he'd never seen the need to do either. He was in his thirties, and he'd never actually left the confines of the Twin Cities metropolitan area.

Henry was a home-body, pure and simple, raised in a family of home-bodies. He'd never been anywhere, and he'd never wanted to go. The woods? No way!

"Bears?" Henry swallowed again, "in the woods?"

"Don't worry Henry," it was Old Man Sutter, "those bears are all smaller than you. You'd be the king of the forest."

"What about you?" Ace asked Sutter, "up for a road trip?"

"Can't see it," Sutter said, spreading his hands, "I'd miss all this."

Calvin came in from the back room just then.

"Cal, my man," Ace said, "you need to shut this joint for the Bicentennial. Then come up to Elysium with us."

"You crazy, honky, Doogan's never closes."

"Sure, sure it does, Cal," Ace explained, "every two hundred years for a Bicentennial."

Ace looked around the room.

"That way," Ace added, "this bunch of misfits will be locked groatless on the street out front, and they'll have nothing better to do than come up with us too."

"You're talking Hack's land up north?" Cal asked.

"Yes, exactly," Ace said, "you could come up with the second wave, Saturday morning, and back with the first wave Sunday night. Perfect, see."

Cal mused, "I've been wanting to see that place. We'll see"

"Yes," Ace said, " oh yes, we will definitely see."

(<o>)/(10.36)\(<o>)

Tuesday, and Hack had gone to town for supplies. Skate was enjoying some sunny solitude in front of his shiny new cabin, and scribbling in his neglected journal. Sucking his teeth, he put down his pen and laced up his boots. He headed out along the driveway for a walk. After crossing the first ridge he stepped off onto a little trail he'd noticed from the truck.

"Where's that go?" he'd asked Hack.

"Nowhere special," Hack said, "we've been up there as kids. It loops around and about. It's just a deer trail, I think, comes out with an old cut probably for a logging trail."

Skate had spent all these days on the property, but mostly within eyeshot of the confines of the building site. When they were boys they had played in these woods, but not for many years now. It was time to take a little look see.

The trail took him down into a low spot, where the moss on the rocks was damp. It veered left, and upwards to the top of a ridge and then followed this high ground in a long slow rightward curve until is stopped abruptly at a bald gravel downsloping face. It was sunny spot, and a little bit of a scenic overlook, so he sat down on a warm rock and pulled out his little 38-cent wonder: a notepad he kept in his pocket at all times.

Skate pondered and jotted, mostly staring at a point just a foot from his face. It was quiet, and he stopped to listen to the silence. There was a dim hum from behind him, those darn nuns running their infernal chainsaw. There was an occasional bird call. And there was, if you listened, what sounded like a faint hissing noise, something like air leaking from a tire, but not quite.

Skate got to his feet and scrambled slowly down the gravel face into the low area formed by the confluence of what looked like three gulleys. The one to his right was mostly filled in, the other gullies both behind him, mostly choked with brush and sizeable trees. But he realized the one to his left was flatter, full of brush but free of trees, almost like an old long-forgotten logging trail.

"Huh!" he thought out loud, "a road to nowhere."

Just then he heard the truck, far distant behind him. Hack was heading home, up the driveway far to his left, hauling supplies from his trip to town.

From where he stood, Skate calculated, the shortest distance back to camp was not back the way he came, but to his right, and up the filled in gulley. From there, if he was correct, there would be a steep climb over the next ridge, and then a long slope back to camp. It might be a strenuous traversal, but probably no more than half a mile as the heron flies.

(<o>).[].(<o>)

Skate was only a few feet up the filled-in gully, clambering over loose gravel, spraying left and right, slip-sliding back and forth, when his left hand struck a hard metal point. It nicked a small gouge into the meat of his already brutalized southpaw.

"Yie," he yelped, and stopped to see what cut him.

It appeared to be the corner of a metal box, maybe a footlocker.

"Treasure," he thought, instantly, "far out."

A man could buy a triumph if he found a buried trove.

(<o>).[].(<o>)

Skate paused.

He was halfway up a gravel incline, in the middle of nowhere, and there was a box jutting out of the earth at his feet. This could be cool. It would not be normal, but it might be pedestrian – a dumbass nothing dropped from nowhere. It happened all the time, and nothing would usually come of it.

Still, this was weird and different, and worth looking into.

(<o>).[].(<o>)

He started to scoop away gravel with his hands, trying to find the dimensions of the box, to dig it out. But every handful exposed a little more of the container, and brought down a little more gravel from the up-slope. Whatever it was, he determined, it was big – possibly bigger than a footlocker. But it was hard to tell; every time he scooped some gravel away, almost as much flowed back down into place. He gave up the digging and clambered past the box corner, up the ridge towards the lake. This would require a shovel. And Hack would want to hear about this – and Hack would help him dig.

(<o>)/(Endnotes 10.40)\(<o>)

68. Vonnegut, Kurt, Slaughterhouse-Five : Or the Children's Crusade : A Duty-Dance With Death Hardcover - 205 Delacorte Pr; ISBN: 0385312083 ; Dimensions (in inches): 1.03 x 8.04 x 5.34

69. Quote about Vonnegut, "He has written short sentences, small paragraphs, tiny chapters, and little books in an attempt to reach busy, unliterary folk with his criticism of life and his help in making it bearable" is a hole in the scholarship. The author is not able to accurately attribute these words to a source. Sorry.

70. Berra, Yogi. Commonly accepted folk-lore.

Chapter 11

"What the hell," Hack said, "is this?"

They were standing at the base of the filled-in gully, looking up the gravel incline. Everything appeared as normal, as it did everywhere else on the property. Except there was the corner of a metal box sticking out of the gravel, about twenty feet ahead of them and maybe ten feet above their heads, where Skate had scooped away enough material to show it.

"Who knows," said Skate, sardonically, "maybe it's buried treasure."

"Maybe it's a box of military ordinance, too," Hack said, "dropped in a training mission."

"You mean unexploded bombs?"

"Could be, or who knows, a regimental supply of toilet paper."

"Let's find out," Skate said, "carefully."

(<o>).[].(<o>)

It didn't take too long, even as cautious as they were, to determine they were not digging out a footlocker or an ordinance crate.

They dug into packed gravel with sharp-tipped five foot shovels. They worked along the topside edge, back into the hill, and along the leading edge, expecting to find the corners to their box.

They commenced carefully scooping gravel away from the exposed corner, and it just went on and on.

The earth moved. They dug and dug. No second corner surfaced.

They dug down from the corner.

Pretty soon they'd exposed a seam and a hinge. This was no crate. It was a painted box, perhaps a railroad car abandoned in some bygone age?

They continued to move earth, until as the hours passed it became clear. There was a truck buried here.

(<o>).[].(<o>)

"What the hell," Hack said.

"Beats me," Skate said, "but a couple of things are clear."

It was getting dark. Hack sat on a stump, Skate crouched on the gravel.

"We're pretty clearly looking at the back end of a truck," Skate said, "and it's buried pretty deep. If we come back tomorrow and work on the down side of this slope, I'll bet we can clear enough to get the doors open."

Hack surveyed the scene.

"Screw that," Hack said, "I say we excavate this devil tonight."

(<o>).[].(<o>)

Hack worked at the gravel, which was a tapioca proposition. Every shovel-full removed caused another to slide into its place.

They had gone back to camp and brought all the shovels and the ancient Hackney wheelbarrow, as Hack had started to recognize the scope of the project.

"There's a lot of dirt to move," he said, "and we'll need to get it away from the site."

So, for a while, as the sun went down, they filled the wheelbarrow with gravel and hauled it off downhill and off to the side. Then, as the sun

230

disappeared, Skate had worked on gathering material for a bonfire to light the work as Hack continued scooping. Once the fire was lit, they worked together, filling the wheelbarrow with gravel and hauling it away, slowly removing the material.

Pretty soon, they could read the door.

(<o>)/(11.5)\(<o>)

Uncle Lon had a nice property, Delmar thought to himself. Acres of forest near the Canadian border, fresh water in abundance, a single road in and out, and a wilderness escape route if things went bad. Remote and defensible, everything you'd want when the revolution came and the cities collapsed under the weight of their own pollution. That was it, a nice phrase – a pollution of race and waste, stupidity and bureaucracy.

Yes, Lon had a nice thing going.

Crappy accommodations, though, with Lon staying in his little frame house and the rest of them in sheds or tents. It wasn't much of a way to run a bivouac, and the food was bad too. The Army had been far better, even insofar as Delmar had been around to enjoy it.

Worse still, Lon didn't seem to have a PLAN. All he seemed to want was sentries. So here they were, three bedraggled guys, ostensive mercenaries, sitting around cleaning their weapons and eating bologna sandwiches three times a day. Sure, they had enough manpower and enough firepower that Lon could sleep at night, but what was the MISSION – where were they taking it?

Headquarters was a picnic table by a campfire on a flat spot near Lon's creekside. The three of them, Delmar, Jack, and Hank, were each assigned to a 12-on-and-12-off schedule. This meant that Delmar, as low man, was on duty from 8PM to 8 AM. Jack and Hank worked opposite each other: Jack noon to midnight, Hank midnight to noon. The job was mostly to monitor the road in, and stop anyone who wasn't authorized to enter the property. When there were two of them on duty, one man would watch the road, and the other would patrol the property line, guarding against intrusion. That was Delmar's job.

Jack and Hank were basically lazy locals, and so the patrolling fell to Delmar. From eight at night, as the sun was setting, until the next morning, he moved through the woods with a flashlight taped to his carbine. Delmar loved his carbine. He had stolen it during his all-too-brief stint in the Army, and had lovingly reworked the action until it had a hair trigger. This is my rifle, this is my gun.

He occasionally stopped at the roadside checkpoint to give Jack, and later Hank, a break from their guard duty. But mostly he was in the woods.

Delmar tried to move quietly through the forest, but it was rough country, and he had little experience in the wilderness. He had been a boy once, and up in these very woods, but that seemed like decades ago.

Besides, it was dark almost the whole time he was out there. He wanted to see the enemy coming and lay in ambush, but for the most part he was crashing through the brush frightening the animals and broadcasting his position to anyone who might have been slipping through.

(<o>).[].(<o>)

Delmar, and the brothers, Jack and Frank, had a few things in common. They were all familiar with weapons and viewed themselves as paramilitary.

They all had good reasons for being out of circulation.

Delmar was a convicted felon and a parole violator. He needed to stay away from the law for a while.

Jack and Hank were brothers in crime, both cunning simpletons. They had broken into the Silver Spur Tap after closing time one night, and then sat around the walk-in cooler drinking beers. In the wee hours of the morning they staggered drunkenly to their car and, after arguing about who would drive, and then wrestling over it (Jack won) they made their escape – sort of.

Jack mis-handled the gear shift and drove their car, full speed in reverse, through the back wall of the bar. Then, with their rear-end stuck hopelessly into the building, and the motor still running, they fled to Lon's for a place to hide.

They were Minnesota northwoods dumb-asses, pure and simple: jackpine savages.

This was Lon's army. He fed them, but he paid them nothing. In exchange, he hoped to forestall another assault on his property and secure his perimeter, such as it was.

One shed was burned to the ground. He did not want another.

(<o>)/(11.7)\(<o>)

Friday, and Lon was in town again, tempting fate by drinking beer and making himself a quiet target. It wasn't much of a plan, he had to admit, but he still didn't know who crept out to his place and burnt that shed – and he wanted to find that out – he needed to know that.

Now that his rag-tag security force was in place, the perimeter secured, Lon wanted to make a retaliatory strike. He wanted to creep onto someone's property and burn down one of THEIR sheds. He wanted someone else to feel the jumpy pain of lying awake listening for footsteps in the dark. He wanted to know they were feeling the same fear that he walked around with. He wanted to get even, dammit.

But first, he had to know who it was.

He had a few suspects in mind, of course. After all, he had lived there all his life – and he knew who was who – and what was what.

It was likely Simonson, who had the most to lose if the wilderness area was re-regulated. He would lose much of his business, or maybe all of it. It was probably Simonson, he reasoned, or his flaky son Marty, who would burn down a shed for fun, and wouldn't need much urging from his father to strike the match.

Lon was looking for Marty, in fact, in order to get into an argument and see if he'd give himself away. Marty wasn't too smart. They called Marty "shit fer brains" back in high school, after all. Lon had known him since before that. Lon could get Marty to talk, he was sure.

Hackney was also a suspect, Lon figured. He was, for one thing, not really from around there. Yes, his family was from town, but Hack was a city boy. Besides, the property was close by his, downstream towards the lake, so it would be pretty easy, if he'd done it, to pull it off.

Lon didn't really think so, honestly. Hack seemed okay, and being not really local made him less likely to get involved enough to follow through and actually burn a shed. Still, he was a Hackney, and gawd knew that family was capable of near enough to anything.

So, yes, Hackney was a suspect too, although they'd sat together in Maid-Up Pizza just a couple days before, and nothing had come out in conversation except his pal, Scratch or whatever, was pretty darn good at playing dumb.

Friday, and Lon was in town again, night after night, making himself a target of abuse – in order to sleuth out a culprit. It wasn't much of a plan, he had to admit, but that was all he had.

(<o>).[].(<o>)

Delmar could see Jack through the trees, silhouetted by his dim bulb. They spent the first days of their bivouac building a telephone booth sized shack a few feet from the end of Lon's driveway, and running a thick heavy logging chain between two thick posts. It was a guardhouse of sorts, Checkpoint Charlie, and the idea was that either Jack or Hank would man the post at all times. If someone should come out to burn down another shed, and foolishly chose to drive up the driveway to do it, there would be a sentry to deter them.

Meanwhile, Delmar was supposed to patrol the perimeter to prevent overland sneak attacks. He mostly stumbled around the woods in the dark, but he was getting the lay of the land, and after several nights of no action, and no prospects of any, he had started working on approaches to sneaking up on Jack and Hank.

It was painfully easy.

Once he'd beaten down a path through the woods, he could walk along with little or no sound. Jack and Hank were not very alert to begin with, so it was already no challenge to get the drop on them. He'd done it several times.

"Freeze!" Delmar would shout, and step out of the shadows, "your position is compromised."

Jack, up until midnight, and Hank through the rest of the night, would raise their arms and sigh.

"You got me Delmar, I surrender."

Then Delmar, having the upper hand, would step into the pale light and take a break, sitting with whomever he'd bested, and trying to strike up a conversation, or acting superior while they tried to talk with him.

(<o>).[].(<o>)

Friday, and Lon was in town again. The cat was away, the mice fraternized.

"Jack," Delmar sat down, "we've been at this all week. Nothing happens. Don't you think it's time we took a little R&R?"

Jack looked at Delmar with cunning suspicion. He didn't trust Delmar, and he didn't really like him either, but he knew what R&R meant, and he liked the sound of it.

"You mean, what?" Jack said hopefully, "grab a bottle and sit around the guard post here?"

"No," Delmar said, "I was thinking about a trip into town."

"Lon would fry if he found out," Jack said, doubtfully, "I dunno."

"It's Friday night," Delmar said, "and you know he's going to close down the bars and then go eat. What time has he been rolling in these last few nights?"

"Oh, two, two thirty, usually."

"Yes, I know, so all we've got to do is come back here when the bars close, and we'll beat him by an hour."

"True, true enough," Jack said, "but what about Hank?"

"Hank can come along," Delmar replied, "unless you figure he'll come down here and cover for us."

"Naw," Jack laughed, "I don't see that."

"Me neither," Delmar agreed.

"What if Lon sees us, though?"

"First thing, we find out where he is," Delmar answered, "then we go somewhere else and keep a lookout for him. He'll never see us."

Jack looked at his watch, it was barely 9:30.

"Okay," Jack said, "you stay here, and I'll go get Hank. We'll be back down here with the truck to pick you up in a jiffy."

"Good plan," Delmar said, "I'll stay here, and man the gate."

"Bring your money," Delmar added, "I'm a little light."

(<o>)/(11.10)\(<o>)

Back at the Silver Spur Tap, Skate was telling Margie why he had a Batman insignia on the side of his worn black 1968 Ford Fairlane 500. He was working on his seventh shell of Foxe Deluxe. He had a good start on the makings of a skunky Foxe Deluxe buzz.

The little oil-burner in the corner radiated benevolently, it's cap plate glowing orangely.* Outside, the temperature was approaching thirty below and the wind came from the northwest at fifty miles an hour. In the morning, sparrows would be found perched frozen to death on the telephone lines. Skate pitied anything caught out on a night like this.

Less than a mile south of them, a woman was dying. The fierce wind was stripping the heat from her body faster than she could produce it. Bent nearly double, head down into the wind, a thin cotton coat, a flimsy blouse, a wool skirt, nylons and high heels; she had a wool sailors cap and no gloves, her fists were jammed into her coat pockets.

Her nose, ears, and toes were already frostbitten. Her legs would hardly function, her knees bloody from stumbling on broken pavement. She'd once fallen onto the point of her jaw and had bitten her tongue quite deeply. Then she had gotten up, and slogged on.

She no longer heard the wind. She utterly refused to look into the storm because it froze her eye-lashes together and she had to use her brittle fingers to thaw them so she could see her feet again. She navigated by the still visible depression of the roadside ditch. It was clutch and stagger, barely moving, and dying with every step.

At first she'd been shocked by the cold and later she'd thought of 'To build a Fire' by Jack London.* Soon she was dreaming of toasty fireplaces and thick feather quilts and once she'd fallen and considered staying down in the soft feathery snow and curling up for a quick, blissful nap.

It had been a close thing but she'd gouged her nails into her frozen palms, thinking of her daughter and forcing herself to go on. Now she just watched her feet (though they hardly seemed like hers anymore), and numbly plodded on, beyond thought and beyond pain. She just … kept … walking.

(<o>).[].(<o>)

Skate was looking out the window, admiring the might of the elements, and the awesome surge of a king-hell winter storm, happy to be safe and warm, when she staggered into view, out beyond the parking lot, on the road going north. He'd been watching the storm, wondering at the power and cruel majesty of it all. He was, by this time, several beers into it and quite well lit. At first he did not comprehend what he was seeing. Then he thought, well hell, people walk around in storms all the time, just for the fun of it – don't they? Or, he paused, do they?

Outside, she was totally oblivious and concentrating on putting one foot in front of the other. She did not see the lights of the Silver Spur Tap, and she could easily have walked right past – and on out into the country again, where her doom was waiting.

(<o>).[].(<o>)

It was the usual tavern situation. The men chatted a bit at first, but Skate was mostly keeping to himself while Shorty and Dewane worked through their beers and their bar talk, also keeping mostly between themselves.

"Boys," Skate decided to speak up, pointing loudly, "is that a pedestrian?"

Shorty and Dewane looked at him, startled at the outburst, and then followed his gaze out the window.

Shorty looked out the window, then turned back and said, "Fuckin A, Rover."

Dewane the foreman was the first to think clearly.

He hopped off his stool, went to the door, and hollered out to her –barely audible over the force of the wind.

She heard him, though.

She stopped walking and stood still on the road – frozen, so to speak.

But she didn't look around or otherwise react, remaining bent over at the waist, stuck stiff.

Then she began to crumple; and slowly collapsed to her knees into a heap on the pavement.

Shorty and then Skate rushed out the door at that point, staggering across the snow-drifted parking lot, then up onto the road, and picked her up off the ground, one on each side.

She was so light and rigid, she felt like a frozen, hollow-boned bird.

Dewane followed them for a few footsteps into the storm. Then, seeing they had her in tow, turned and beat them to the door, holding it open. They hustled back inside with her.

They pulled her across to the far corner of the bar, and gently set her down on a chair in front of the oil-burner.

"She looks half dead," Margie said, "poor thing,"

235

The men stood back, and Margie started pulling her clothes off – first the stiff frozen coat.

"She is," Skate said, noting the white nose and cheekbones, "half frozen, for sure."

Since Margie was busy, Shorty hustled behind the bar and poured a tumbler of blackberry brandy, the northwoods cure-all. Margie stopped what she was doing and poured a little of the potion into the frozen bird-woman's mouth.

Some of it trickled down her throat, but it gagged her and she began choking and coughing. She was wracked for a second, but it seemed to perk her up a bit, because she greedily grabbed the glass and drained it in two gulps.

Then she suddenly looked frantically around, as though she'd just woken up from a nightmare. She looked at Skate wild-eyed and tried to speak. Only grunts and vowel sounds came out. They could see her mouth working but couldn't catch any of it.

"Take it easy," Margie said, with a cup of coffee miraculously in her hand.

They could see that her tongue was swollen in her mouth where she had fallen on her chin and bitten herself, and frozen blood was beginning to thaw around her mouth and her palms and her knees.

Margie carefully took her shoes off.

"High heels," she said, "on a night like this."

The woman's toes were grayish-blue. She'd be lucky to keep them.

Finally, she was able to croak out a few barely distinguishable words.

Shorty looked at Dewane, Dewane looked at Skate. Her message scared them sober.

"Effie," Skate said, "stay here, we're on it."

Margie looked at Skate.

"Effie?" she said.

"Effie," she said again, looking back to the woman, "is that you?"

(<o>)/(11.13)\(<o>)
diaria -- 11.0 -- 4/28/77 -- phoenix

There's a wrinkle in that point of view controversy and it bears on the whole metafictional idea.

When you read, hear, or makeup a story you're in this performer -- perceiver situation. Someone is telling a tale and the rest are receiving. Your contemporary fabulist will say "why hide it? if that's what yer doin' then make it obvious. put it out front." Traditional fiction has always hidden that, you see. Conventional wisdom dictated a story that granted the WILLING SUSPENSION OF DISBELIEF.*

As an audience, we're supposed to conveniently "forget" that we're getting a production number and believe what we're seeing is "really" happening.

Now, we can get into an entire dialogue about what "really" means. I'd just as soon not. All you viewing THIS production know what "really" is, without a lot of mental gymnastics and dictionary massaging. Old Sam

236

Johnson kicked a rock and said, "this is how I know I exist", or something to that effect.*

When we sit around a campfire, or in front of the tube, we're prepared for a story and let ourselves get into it. The narrative unfolds and if it's done at all well, we participate. Long ago, someone, Aristotle maybe, broke the story telling art into three distinct sections. (he was big on that by the way, making everything into a system to be reduced into smaller and smaller segments). He sed there was a teller, the tale, and the hearer (tellee, if you will).

What has happened over the centuries is the teller has receded into the background, putting the tale forward. This is opposed to the origins of the form when the children of the village would gather at the knees of the resident wise man for their regular dose of oral history.

They recognized the man for what he was, the transmitter of cultural knowledge and the passer of tales. The fact his position was acknowledged didn't detract from his effectiveness or I miss my bet.

And so, in a fine sense, what the Gonzo journalists and the metafictionists are doing is not so much breaking new ground as re-writing ancient traditions -- covering the story, from within the story, for good or ill.

(<o>)/(11.14)\(<o>)

Elysium is the last town before the wilderness. The woods are filled with ghosts and wind and spirits of the past. You clamber over ancient rock and drink from crystal streams. The water is so clear and cold it hurts your teeth. The locals don't drink from the streams, though, something about parasites – they pump it up from wells, or haul it out from town in jugs because they fear their own pollution dregs.

To city folks that's laughable, they don't care about parasites. "If you just saw the stuff we had to drink or saw the river where our stuff comes from you would not drink at all down there." They laugh and think, "what would these mortals do in Mexico?" The locals mostly never go to Mexico. It don't come up.

As boys we'd go for hours in those woods. With moccasins we'd learned to make in Scouts, and compasses and matches on our belts. We learned to move through brush without a sound, and learned the tracker's trick from Hack's old man.

"The trackers in the movies aren't for real," he said, "a tracker is a man who knows his ground."

"He knows the land in his back yard, he sees it every day. He doesn't look for sign so much, he looks for change."

"He knows that rock was over there the day before, and so he sees a man must have come through from here to kick it over there."

"It takes a little luck, experience as well. But mostly it's a man who knows his ground."

We grew up in those woods.

(<o>)/(11.15)\(<o>)

Elysium is the last town on the road to wilderness.

As such, it's an outpost of commerce and a jumping off point for thousands of tourists every year who come to camp in the woods and fish, and in certain seasons to hunt. Things slow down considerably in the winter, but there is commerce all year round. They come to Elysium in droves to buy supplies and rent equipment, and some hire guides.

There was a time when the timber industry was a major employer in the region, but that has mostly ended. There was a time when iron mining supported a large percentage of the families, and at the time of the Bicentennial there were still a few low-grade mines operating. But it's tourism that mainly supports the town now.

Elysium sits in a fortunate notch of geography. It is surrounded by lakes and streams, rich with fish. It is near to Canada and sits within the confines of Superior National Park that extends for 150 miles along the Canadian border. It is the last point of civilization before the Boundary Waters Canoe Area Wilderness.

The Wilderness Area is part of the National Park – over a million acres of water and wood, with 200 lakes and hundreds of miles of canoe paths and portages (paths through the woods to the next lake). It is now an area protected by Federal statute as a "wilderness" with no roads or buildings – no signs either. But it has not always been that way. Motorized craft are not allowed, not land vehicles, not motorboats, not snowmobiles – but it has not always been that way either. It is a "canoe only" area, and you need a permit just to get in. You may not bring cans or bottles, just food packed in plastic or foil, and you are required to bring all your garbage back out with you.

But it has not always been that way, and that is a big part of the problem.

(<o>).[].(<o>)

Before it was an officially designated "wilderness area", it was just a wilderness, and people owned property up there, and lived there. Families had homes, and some lived there year round.

But at some point in the 1940s Congress, at the prompting of the National Park Service, declared it to be "a wilderness area", and started moving the people out.

Most had their property bought out at fairly reasonable, albeit low, prices. Some recalcitrants were forced out by the principle of 'Eminent Domain', which means the federal government, if it 'needs' your property, can "condemn" the land and move you off it – whether you like it or not.

A few old-timers were 'grandfathered in' and allowed to stay as long as they lived, on the promise that, at that point, the property reverted to the government and not their kin. Some of these people were of long-lived stock, and were still hanging on when the Bicentennial rolled around – some for many years after.

This "federal" approach to natural resource management and conservation of wilderness was viewed by many locals as highly high-handed, which fostered the first resentments.

It was believed by many that the federal government already had too much power over the lives of everyday citizens, and that massive acquisitions of private land back into federal hands was an inappropriate abuse of governmental power.

In the first years, however, the reaction was mollified by the gradual imposition of "wilderness" rules. For example, gasoline motors were not banned in the first decades, and a substantial number of people made their living by bringing supplies in to campers, leading fishing expeditions, and ferrying people and supplies into the lodges that continued to dot the landscape in the "wilderness", sometimes by air with seaplanes. In addition, snowmobiles were allowed into the wilderness area during the winter.

Eventually, and gradually, the new rules came into effect. And one by one, as new rules came into force, the locals came to believe the restrictions were excessive.

Eventually, nearly everyone in Elysium believed the whole thing had gone too far. But the power was with the federal government, and the changes occurred.

At the national level, the country was becoming more ecologically aware, and environmentalists argued that pristine wilderness areas represented the greatest good for the greatest number. In general, the country sided with the environmentalists and the local complaints were viewed as short-sighted and against the 'national interest'.

The locals countered that it was easy for people, not from around here, to support wilderness areas in somebody else's backyard – but they would not like it so much in THEIR backyards. Nobody would.

But the locals were vastly outnumbered and their complaints, often poorly presented, fell on deaf ears. The deal got done – the pristine wilderness would stay that way, whether they liked it or not.

Meanwhile, the house divided against itself, as the larger outfitters foresaw the inevitable and began to side with the government. The bigger outfitters were run by businessmen who could see there was no percentage in protesting the foregone. They re-tooled their business to comply with the new rules, and continued to make money. Never mind they were viewed by the locals as the worst kind of hypocrites. One year the outfitters were selling snowmobiles, the next year they were siding with the "motor free" regulations.

(<o>).[].(<o>)

This set up the incendiary situation that Lon found himself in.

By the Bicentennial, nerves were frayed and tempers were short. Lon's principal business was the manufacture of custom curved canoe paddles, which he made on his property, in his own workshop, and sold in most of the outfitter's showrooms.

Then, one ugly night, somebody crept onto his property and set his shed on fire.

This shed, sitting right next to his workshop, contained all the seasoned woods he used in his production process. The shed had gone up like a roman candle, and had threatened to spread to his workshop, and the forest beyond.

It was only through an hour of frantic fire-fighting that he had saved the critical wood-working machinery; but he lost his materials so he was out of business, just the same.

So he assembled his trusty mercenary force to see that he never suffered the same kind of loss again.

(<o>)/(11.18)\(<o>)

Against all predictions, Cal decided to close the bar for the Bicentennial. There would be little business, he reasoned, with everyone out of town for the holiday weekend. Besides, he had long wanted to see Hack's place in the woods, and now that Skate was up there, "homesteading" as he called it, there was another reason: to see how white city boys made out in the forested hinterlands.

(<o>).[].(<o>)

It wasn't like Cal was exactly part of the group. He was altogether too wary and shrewd to become lifelong friends with bar patrons. The cash came first.

But over the years he'd become chums with the guys, and there was a little bit of friendly banter and such. They were a pretty good group, and never caused trouble, although it sometimes found them.

For the most part they, this Web group, were better to talk to, and more interesting, than the college crowd. And, truth be told, all the regulars put together.

Then, too, they'd come through for him on a couple of occasions. Once, when his water main broke in January on a Sunday, they had waded into his freezing basement and helped him shut it off and pump it out when he couldn't get a plumber for beer nor money.

Even Book had pitched in – useless at mechanical tasks – he kept the bar open while the rest of them labored and cursed below.

You are in a pretty low ring of hell when a water main bursts in your basement in Minnesota in January, and Cal had really appreciated the guys that day.

(<o>).[].(<o>)

The Bicentennial Fourth of July was on Sunday, so Calvin first thought about working the Friday night, and then leaving with the second group on Saturday morning. But then he thought, "what the hell."

There would be pitiful Friday evening business, and it was a long ride to make two days running: Saturday up and then Sunday back. So he elected to catch the first ride, leaving Friday.

This worked nicely with Ace's planning, since he had counted on Calvin's Volkswagen mini-bus to form part of the fleet. As soon as Cal let on he'd be willing to leave on Friday, it became Cal's job to decide what time to leave, and how to swing through and pick everybody up.

And against additional predictions, the barflys succumbed in the end.

Cal posted signs the bar would be closed at noon on Friday, and the bus was leaving shortly thereafter. Remo, and Fat Henry, who worked the night shift, and even Old Man Sutter agreed to be there before noon. Ace was riding along to act as guide. Rexee had needed a little persuading, but Ace wore her down.

They were all on the bus.*

Book and Patrick simply could not get the day off work, so they were the Saturday morning wave, riding up in Book's parent's station wagon.

Carol, pregnant and all, was not feeling like the trip, and then there was the problem of finding someone to watch the two kids, so Patrick was going to stay behind with her. But she ordered him to go along.

It was shaping up to be 'an event', and she didn't want to be the cause of his missing it. Carol was basically okay.

Annie was also making the Saturday timetable, closing the diner to make it work.

Then, at the last minute Carol's Mom volunteered to take the kids for the weekend, and Carol decided to come along too – much to Patrick's relief.

(<o>).[].(<o>)

Friday mid-morning. Ace tapped on Rexee's door.

After tapping gave way to pounding, he heard some rustling within. She appeared at the door, opening it a crack. He could see she was hung-over and just out of bed.

"Rex," he handed her a cup of coffee, "you've got about an hour."

She reached out to take the cup, letting the door swing open and her robe swing apart. She was wearing panties but no bra. Ace kept his eyes fixed firmly on her eyes.

"I'm going to walk over to Doogan's and see how things are looking."

She wasn't registering what he was saying, he could tell.

"You'll need clothes for two nights, and any other camping gear you've got."

She sipped a bit, grateful for the coffee.

"Thanks," she said, "what the hell are you talking about?"

"Bicentennial, Rex, we leave for the great northwoods in an hour."

Rex groaned, she had forgotten.

"You have a sleeping bag?" Ace asked.

"Yeah, yeah, I got all that," she moaned, "this is happening today?"

"Friday, today, around noon," Ace said mildly, "in about two hours, we are on the road, like we agreed."

"Fuck a red duck," Rexee' said, "I just want to soak in a tub."

"I'll get things organized at Doogan's," Ace went on, oblivious to her quailing, "we're loading around noon, and then back here to get you and go."

He looked at his watch.

"Figure ninety minutes from now."

"Shit!" she slammed the door.

Fat Henry was afraid of bears, and regular bears were afraid of she-bears with cubs, and they, she-bears with cubs, were afraid of Rexee' in the morning.

Ace knew she was already climbing back into bed. He'd call in an hour and get her moving again.

Nobody could control Rexee', but you could manage her a bit, if you did it just right.

(<o>).[].(<o>)

There was an impressive pile of gear stacked just inside the door at Doogan's. Remo had two duffel bags, one full of clothing, the second full of camping gear, a small tent, C-rations, all of it army issue. Down under his clothes he had secreted an Army issue M-16 rifle with two full clips, and his clasp knife. He'd almost brought his hand grenades too, but decided against it, and then changed his mind and packed them. Remo hadn't been in real remote country since the Nam, and he was surprised how nervous the whole idea made him. He didn't figure to do much shooting, but he didn't want to be the only dick out there without protection.

Fat Henry had packed two hard-sided suitcases. One was full of clothes and food, since he didn't plan to starve in the woods. The other was full of blankets and bedding. Henry didn't own a sleeping bag. Henry had never been camping. Henry had never been anywhere, and he couldn't figure out why he was doing this. But he shrugged away his concerns. Like Ace said, once every two hundred years, maybe it was time to try something different.

Old Man Sutter had brought a tightly packed old-fashioned backpack and bedroll. He hadn't been out in the fens since he'd been in-country and on foot. But he knew how to do it, and how to prepare for it. He was another case of someone who hadn't been on a mission for a mighty long time, but he knew if he had to, he could make his way across any terrain and get back to base. It would take him a lot longer maybe, but he could do it. Training, it stayed with you. Still, the whole idea of this trip made him uneasy. He hadn't been out of his chosen element for a very long time. But he knew he'd be okay. He'd survive. He'd also brought a small footlocker of booze. He didn't like to be unprepared.

Calvin also had a footlocker, but no booze. He was damned if he'd spend the weekend being bartender. He had gone out special and bought himself a brand new pair of hiking boots. Cal planned to walk the land. He'd also bought himself his first fishing pole, a nice spin caster. He came from a long line of fishermen, and he intended to try his hand if he could. His grandpa used to take him down to the pier on the Indiana shores of Lake Michigan, and they caught cats and suckers. It had been years, but he knew he could still do it. And he'd also brought about a dozen paperback novels. People didn't suspect it of him, but Cal was a reader, even when he wasn't behind the bar, where he often had a book for slow times. Detective fiction was his thing. He read it all. He was a relentless reader. Cal didn't even own a television.

(<o>).[].(<o>)

Ace walked into Doogan's that Friday. There was a mountain of gear by the door. The usual crowd was there. He worked the room.

"You ready to roll," he asked Remo.

"Locked and loaded," Remo said, "hurried up to wait."

Remo was dressed in Army fatigues, playing cards with himself with his arthritic claws. There was a set to his jaw that Ace couldn't interpret.

242

Old Man Sutter looked like a weekend sportsman. He wore canvas pants and a khaki shirt with four loops over each shirt pocket that looked big enough to hold shotgun shells. He wore an old-time Aussie-looking bush hat, camouflage color, with one side of the brim pinned up.

Poking up from behind Sutter's neck, barely visible, Ace could see the butt of a hunting knife. The old guy was strapped with a knife sheath, like they used to see in the old movies. Sutter looked serious, their eyes met, Ace did not comment. He nodded, Sutter was ready.

Fat Henry had a shell of beer in front of him, per usual.

"Henry," Ace said, "it's a long drive. You might want to hit the head before we go."

"Don't worry about me, " Henry slurped another mouthful of beer, "I can hold it with the best of them."

Ace turned to the bar.

"How's it shaping up, Cal? We on schedule?"

"Yeah, you betcha," Cal put on a Norwegian accent, which always sounded absurd coming from the slender black man, and always made Ace laugh.

"Yumpin Yiminy," Ace laughed, "gimme dem keys den. I'll get da truck ready."

Calvin was already pouring him a beer.

"Oh, okay den, maybe yust one."

(<o>).[].(<o>)

Considering how unusual the situation was, it went pretty smoothly. Calvin called "last call" at about 11:30 AM and the place started to clear out. The few people who came in for an early lunch were turned away with apologies. The signs had been posted all week, so the regulars knew the bar was closing, and nobody complained too much.

By and large it was a cheerful closing. The momentousness of the bicentennial made it an auspicious occasion. At the last minute, Traci, an attractive young working girl in a gaudy, revealing dress, implored to go along. Nobody knew her, nobody objected, but they told her, in no uncertain terms, the bus was leaving right after noon and, if she wanted to go along, she needed to pack for two days, and bring something to sleep in.

Traci ran out the door at 11:30, saying "I'll be right back."

Nobody expected to see her again that day.

Ace pulled the van around out front and started packing gear into the back. He stopped to call Rexee. The phone rang about fifteen times, and she finally answered.

"About twenty minutes, babe," he said.

"Crap," she said, and hung up.

(<o>).[].(<o>)

The luggage was heavy and awkward, but Ace had everything loaded and packed just as the noon whistle was sounding at the depot.

The barflys lingered as the place emptied, and tried to get just one last drink out of Calvin. He obliged, but with his eye on the clock, and cut people off as time ran out.

243

It was only a little past noon on Friday, then, when the bar was emptied and the van was (mostly) packed. Calvin was behind the wheel, with the engine running, and Henry and Ace were putting the last packs and sacks onto the luggage pile.

For four people, they had a LOT of gear. The entire back of Cal's VW mini-bus was jammed with stuff. And they still had to get Rexee', and her stuff, and pick up Ace's gear too.

It was looking like an extremely tight fit.

They had just managed to squeeze the back doors shut, and Cal was exhorting them to get in, and get going.

Then a cab pulled up, beside and in front of them, blocking the way, and Traci stepped out.

"Thanks for waiting," Traci shouted as she jumped out waving her arms, "I'm so glad you're still here."

Then the cabbie got out, a wizened old man with a limp, and started emptying the trunk. Traci had nice Tourister hard-sided luggage, and a lot of it.

Calvin shut off the engine.

"There's no way that all fits!" he declared, "we're not going on a damn cruise!"

"I packed as fast as I could," Traci wailed, "I didn't know what to bring."

Ace was picking up bags.

"We can fit it in," he said, somewhat grimly, "let's just get going."

Traci looked at him gratefully and handed him her makeup box.

"Thanks," she said to Ace, and then she turned to the cab driver, "pack it up Dad, you heard the man."

(<o>).[].(<o>)

Friday just after noon. Ace tapped on Rexee's door.

After tapping gave way to pounding, he heard some rustling within. She appeared at the door, opening it a crack. He could see she was hung-over and just out of bed.

"Yeah, I got it," she said, "pack that stuff and give me a minute."

Ace was relieved to see she was ready, and she didn't have too much stuff – just a full gear hikers backpack with a sleeping bag.

Remo helped haul her stuff into place on the van, while Ace ran to the house and grabbed his gear, stacked and ready to pack, just inside the door, earlier that morning.

(<o>).[].(<o>)

They sat in the van and waited. The motor was running for a while, but eventually Calvin shut it off.

"What's keeping her?" he asked.

Nobody answered.

They sat and waited, Cal, Remo, Henry, Sutter, Ace, and now Traci.

Seconds ticked into minutes.

Finally, Ace jumped out of the van and knocked on the door again.

"Ex-Ray!" he knocked and shouted, "what's the hold up?"

"One last thing," she said, and bustled past Ace, "pull that door shut, would ya?"

Rexee' clambered onto the bus, and started the churn of people and bundles that ended up with her laying on the van floor, Traci draped across Sutter's lap, Remo and Henry jammed into a seat barely able to accommodate Henry by himself, Calvin driving and Ace sitting shotgun up front.

"Are we ready?" Calvin said, somewhat sharply, "to get this honky freak show on the road?"

"Ground control to Captain Cal," Ace said, "you are cleared for take-off."

Calvin nodded, wordless and trying not to smile, and eased his mini-bus out onto the street. He chose a good angle and a good slow speed, and still there was a lurch as he went down the minor incline from Rexee's parking lot onto the street. The van did not scrape bottom, but it came close.

They were seven people with way too much luggage, packed in like soup cans in a crate, traveling north in an underpowered Volkswagen mini-bus on a hot summer day with 243 miles in front of them.

The Bicentennial beckoned.

(<o>)/(11.28)\(<o>)

A one act play in several scenes:

Scene Eleven –

The stage is split. On the audience left there is a Volkswagen Mini-bus cut in half with its innards exposed. Its nose points towards the right half of the stage, the direction it is heading. Calvin and Ace are in the front seats. Fat Henry and Remo are in the seat behind them. Old Man Sutter and Traci are in the back seat. The space is jammed with various pieces of bulky luggage. Rexee' is laying on luggage and duffel bags, on the floor towards the back of the van.

On the audience right side of the stage are Hack and Skate, sitting at a table in their new cabin. They have a spare existence: a table, two chairs, a shelf with canned goods. Behind them is a ladder leading up to a loft with a bedroll, a crate with a lantern, and a small stack of books and papers.

Focus is held by spotlights which switch back and forth. When one half is in darkness, the players freeze.

It is Friday, July 2nd, 1976, at Two P.M. in the Central Time Zone, in Elysium, Minnesota.

=#=#=#=

    (There is a moment while the whole stage is illuminated,
then the cabin is lit, and the van goes black)
    Hack
(laughing)
… all we need now is a maid service.
    Skate
(also laughing)
I was thinking wine cellar. Which we could double as a bomb
shelter. That and the lace curtains would set this place up to
a turn.

245

Hack

All the comforts of home, you bet. We should see about getting
milk delivered in the morning.
(he picks up a coffee pot from the table and swishes it)
Last of the joe?

Skate

No, governor, I insist you have it. The servants will make
fresh soon, I'm sure.

Hack

You're still liking it, I can tell.

Skate

Seriously, seriously, liking it. I wake up in the morning and
open my eyes, and the first thing I think is "I built this
place." I climb down and feel how solid it is, and I think,
"who'd believe something like this, so hefty, so substantial,
could come from the hands of a guy like me."

Hack

Me too, I'll confess.

Skate

I build castles in the air, and I think this, this might be my
culminating contribution. This will stand for ten thousand
years.

Hack

(smiling)
Oh, definitely, at least that.
(the cabin goes black, the van gets lit)

Fat Henry

There, I think that's it.

Remo

What?

Fat Henry

Coon Rapids. I think this might be the farthest I've ever been
from home.

Remo

The furthest with the mostest?

Fat Henry

I used to take the bus up Nordeast for bowling, but this is
farther, I think.

Remo

(turning back to Old Man Sutter)
Are you hearing this?

Old Man Sutter

I was practically born on the road. A military family. But
there's plenty of people like Henry around. Never been on a
trip, and never felt the need.

Traci

I'm pretty much the same. I've been to Chicago once, on
"vacation" with a client, but that's the only time. Otherwise,
I've been around the city and into the suburbs. That's it.

Remo

I've been around the world. Boot camp in Georgia. Stationed in
Germany. Shipped out to Southeast Asia. Medivac'ed to Japan.

Held over in Hawaii. Processed out of the Corps in San
Francisco. Sent home from there on a bus.

    Old Man Sutter
One circumnavigation. Like Drake.

    Remo
Yep, a one-timer, like Frank, that's me. One and Done. Never
again.
(the cabin gets lit, the van goes black)

    Skate
You thought any more about the treasure trove?

    Hack
I think about it all the time. I was going to go back over
there this morning, but I went fishing instead.

    Skate
That help get your mind off it?

    Hack
For a bit, but there was no action, and pretty soon I was
turning it over again. How do I tell my dad?

    Skate
I'm not saying, but are you sure you need to?

    Hack
I wish I knew, but I think yes, I've got to.

    Skate
I'm glad I'm not you.

    Hack
You'd want to know, right?

    Skate
I wish I could say. He lived his whole life believing his
father up and left. He became the man he became. Who, I should
say, I've never been able to read very well.

    Hack
He's not that complex, but he's closed in, in a lot of ways.
Like most dads are.

    Skate
I'm thinking about adoptees, for some reason. They get raised
in a family, and they sometimes know, but sometimes they're
never told. And maybe they're never told, but they know
anyway.

    Hack
Yeah, so?

    Skate
I don't know the statistics, but many DO NOT try to find out
who their real parents are. Their birth parents, I mean. The
biological ones.

    Hack
Really? You'd think you'd want to know.

    Skate
Book is adopted, you know. And he doesn't seem to care at all
about finding out about that.

    Hack
You're kidding. Book?

Skate
Yeah, it's weird. He'll tell you if you ask, and without much
emotion. But he'll never volunteer it.

Hack
I've known him for 20 years and he never said so. How'd you
know that?

Skate
One rainy day, when we were kids, we were looking through his
family photo album. There was a picture of his Mom, dated with
Germanic precision. And I did some quick mental arithmetic and
said, "your Mom must have been pregnant when this was taken."
(shrugs)
And he tells that's how he found out. He did the same math,
and asked about it, and that's when they told him he was
adopted. His sister too.

Hack
(stunned)
I always thought he LOOKED LIKE his sister.

Skate
Me too. But not like his parents, right?

Hack
Well, actually, kinda.

Skate
So, one other time, the only other time we talked about it, I
asked him if he was ever curious about his "real" parents. And
he was very low key, and said, first, if someone adopts you
and raises you, they ARE your real parents. You belong to
them. And second, no, they didn't want me, for whatever
reason, and he just didn't see looking for them.

Hack
(whistles, softly)
Wow, I had no idea. What a thing.

Skate
Not to Book, not really. It's not much of a thing to him. I
don't think.

Hack
And what's this got to do …

Skate
Not much, or maybe a lot. You ever talk to your dad about his
dad?

Hack
Not really, no. It wasn't a topic.

Skate
Exactly. There's half a chance he doesn't want to know. Book
doesn't want to know, or so he says, and I believe him. If you
knew something, and told him, I don't know if he'd thank you.

Hack
But is this the same thing?

Skate
Beats me.
(the cabin goes black, the van gets lit)

Calvin
(to Ace)
So, you're clear on the directions, right?

Ace
Oh yeah, I've made this trip several dozen times, starting
when I was a little kid.

Calvin
No chance of getting lost, then?

Ace
In my sleep. No problem. In fact, I've done this in my sleep,
more than once.

Remo
(leans forward)
Good places to camp?

Ace
Infinite places, don't worry. I'm just hoping they've got
their roof up, otherwise we'll all be staring at the stars.

Calvin
What's wrong with that.

Ace
Nothing, unless it rains, or …
(he adds for Henry's benefit)
… unless the bears come a' roaming.

Fat Henry
You know, that's really not very funny.

Old Man Sutter
Don't listen to them Henry. I told you. You'll be the biggest
bear in the forest.

Ace
That's right. You'll be the king of the bears. They'll band
around you looking for leadership.

Fat Henry
For some reason, you all seem to think bears are funny. I
really hope I don't end up laughing over your mauled corpses.
I really hope that.

Remo
I got to go along with you there, Henry.
(to Ace)
So, you figure there's a cabin plus plenty of places to camp?

Ace
We'll find out about the cabin. They might have been loafing
up there. I don't know.

Calvin
You haven't heard from them?

Ace
Not lately, no.

Fat Henry
They don't know we're coming, do they?

Ace
(suddenly sheepish)
Well, no, not exactly. No.

(pauses)
They probably suspect, though. They're not idiots.
(cabin gets lit, the van goes black)

    Hack
Town tonight?

    Skate
I s'pose. It's Friday, right, on the Bicentennial weekend.

    Hack
Pretty much, yep.

    Skate
You expect company?

    Hack
Ace and them? I don't see it. We'd have heard, wouldn't we?

    Skate
Would we?

    Hack
Good point.

    Skate
Okay, what are we doing this afternoon?

    Hack
Nothin' much, it's Friday after all. Just help me get that
door to hang right and swing smooth, and then we'll loaf.

    Skate
Sounds about right. I've got more writing I want to tackle
today.
(picks up a wood plane and laughs)
Let's shave that bitch.
(the cabin goes black, the van gets lit)

    Rexee'
(sits bolt upright, awake for the first time)
Fuck a red duck, where are we? I've got to piss like a Russian
race horse.

    Traci
Ohmygawd, so do I.

    Ace
We're through Coon Rapids, maybe 40 miles from home.

    Rexee'
Forty miles! I was hoping to wake up and this would all be
over. I need a smoke.
(she lights one)

    Ace
Forest Lake coming up.

    Old Man Sutter
Air, I need air.

    Rexee'
We have got to stop, my water is about to burst.

    Ace
Calvin, you'd better take this exit.

    Calvin
Do we ever get there? That's what I'm starting to wonder.

Ace

Maybe, once we're back on the road, we should figure out the windows and see about ventilation.

Traci

But we're stopping, right. I've really got to pee.
(cabin gets lit, the van goes black)
(the door is hung, they are sitting at their table)

Skate

Do you vote?

Hack

Every chance I get.

Skate

You're serious about it?

Hack

Yeah, pretty much. Why?

Skate

I hate voting. I never feel like I know enough.

Hack

I'd like to say I was an informed voter, but I'm not, not really.

Skate

Yet still you pull the lever.

Hack

Yep, it's a duty, I figure. I've got little enough to say about what goes on. It's my one time to get my voice heard.

Skate

But you're guessing half the time, am I right?

Hack

At least.

Skate

See, that bothers me. Not about you, about myself. I vote for people on no basis whatsoever. I stand there, and even though I've had Patrick give me the lowdown, I still don't recognize most of the names. So I vote by party, which I hate.

Hack

I skip it if I don't know the people.

Skate

I feel compelled, even when I don't know the people. Maybe that's wrong.

Hack

I don't know. You vote, that puts you in with about half the people, the rest of which don't even bother.

Skate

Yeah, democracy.
(cabin goes black, the van gets lit)

Ace

No more liquid for Traci, we've got to skip at least one potty stop, or we'll never get there.
(Henry waits until Ace isn't looking, and then hands Traci a can of beer from his lap)

        Calvin
We're never going to get there, are we.
(cabin gets lit, the van goes black)

        Skate
Besides this voting thing is too all about winning and losing.
I think if two guys want the same office, they should both get
it, and argue between themselves the whole time about what to
do.

        Hack
Yeah, that'll work.

        (Blackout).

(<o>)/(Endnotes 11.29)\(<o>)

71. Orangely -- not a word, I know.

72. London, Jack The Call of the Wild, White Fang, & to
Build a Fire : White Fang ; & to Build a Fire Paperback
- 288 pages (October 1998) Modern Library; ISBN:
037575251X ; Dimensions (in inches): 0.67 x 7.98 x 5.21

73. "Willing suspension of disbelief" is an concept
attributed to Samuel Taylor Coleridge (the guy who wrote
"The Rime of the Ancient Mariner" and "Kubla Khan" (the
"Xanadu" poem), but not "Confessions of an English
Opium-Eater" (1821) which is actually by Thomas De
Quincey).

74. Johnson, Samuel, (b. 1709 - d. 1784) an English
literary figure, whose death in 1784 marks the end of
the 'classical' period in literature, and leads to the
'romantic' period.

75. Wolfe, Tom, The Electric Koolaid Acid Test. New
York: Bantam Books, 1968. The Merry Pranksters had a bus
named "Furthur" and according to the stories, you were
either 'on the bus' or you were 'off the bus'.

Chapter 12

"Holy shit," Hack said.

"Christ on an aluminum crutch," Skate answered, dryly.

It was well past midnight, and they were both goofy with fatigue. They'd been digging for hours, and moving mountains by firelight, and all they had to show for it was the top third of an exposed set of doors on the back end of a mystery truck.

They were sitting by their campfire, exhausted and hardly able to lift another shovelful, but intrigued by the mystery and unwilling to call it a day.

They had moved tons of gravel, and they could see a small portion of their goal. They could see what it said, they could read it – but they couldn't get in, not without another full day of bull labor, or so it looked.

But they could see white letters against a brown background, spelled out across the doors of the truck. They could see what it said.

"Royal Distribution."

(<o>).[].(<o>)

They were too tired to work, and it was too dark to work, but their fire hadn't gone completely out yet. So they sat in the flickering gloom and they pondered.

(<o>).[].(<o>)

"What the hell?" Hack inquired.

"Beats me," Skate shrugged.

Their fire was going out, and they were done for the day. They went back to the cabin, and turned in.

(<o>).[].(<o>)

Hack was shaking Skate to wake him. It was first light, and they'd barely been asleep.

"Lets go man," Hack said, "we gotta get to the bottom of this."

Skate woke up quickly. Normally slow to start moving, he was rolling out of his sleeping bag before Hack finished speaking.

"Yeah," Skate said, "yeah, you betcha. Let's go get it. We're burning daylight."

(<o>).[].(<o>)

Noon.

They had moved miles and piles of frustrating gravel, yard by yard, and watched it fall from above to fill in what they cleared. It was maddening and soul destroying. And yet, they were closer to the goal.

They just needed to clear enough material away so those damn doors would swing open. They learned, about halfway down, the doors were not even locked.

Once the handles were exposed they had hopelessly tugged to open them. The doors were willing, but the flesh was weak. It was impossible to move them more than a micron with the bottom half of each door still covered and blocked by gravel.

There was no short-cut, no end around, no half measures, no faking it, no choice but full commitment or, as Ace sometimes said, 'Do it, to it'. The doors must be cleared before they would open, and nothing but bullwork would clear them.

So they labored.

But now, high noon, the doors were mostly clear. Hack threw a final shovel full of gravel, and then he dropped the shovel like it was a turd in his hands. He was going to burst that seal, and nothing could stop him. He moved to yank on the door handles.

"Wait!" Skate yelled.

Hack paused.

"God knows what sort of Christmas we're going to find in there," Skate said, "I think we should hold on for a minute. Savor the moment. Besides, I think this warrants a picture."

Skate had brought his camera over from the cabin. He'd taken a photo when they'd started that morning, with just a third of the back end of the truck exposed. He took another shot now.

"Okay," Skate nodded, "now, let's do it to it."

(<o>).[].(<o>)

There was still a half-foot of gravel blocking the bottom of the door, but Hack was on the muscle and turned the handle with total conviction and pulled with even more.

And then, saints be praised, there was a sliver of an opening – a real opportunity. Skate reached in to push, throwing his weight into it.

The doors were inches thick, like a bank vault, insulated, he realized, for refrigeration. Skate crouched and hunched his shoulder against the truck, and then pushed like hell while Hack pulled.

So Skate was there, nose to the opening. when the first waft of air steamed out of the truck

"God! That stinks!" Skate said.

The stench billowed over him.

"Aggh! That really reeks."

He stood and staggered back a step, away from the opening, then tangled his footing and stumbled over onto his back, sliding down their gravel slope. He was ticked off at falling, but awkwardly relieved to be away from the stank. It was rank, it was bad, it was nasty to the nose. It was offal.

(<o>).[].(<o>)

Skate was laying on the ground down the slope, on his back looking up, but Hack kept pulling, and so Skate had a first-look-front-row-seat when the truck door finally opened.

(<o>).[].(<o>)

The interior of the truck was HUGE. Skate had been expecting a small container, maybe the size of a storage shed or an ice cream truck.

No. It was more like the interior of a city bus. It was close to a full-sized semi-trailer.

As he laid there, with unspeakable stink rolling over him like little cats feet,* Skate tried to make out the contents of the interior. All he could see was crates back into the gloom. Lots and lots of crates.

Hack let go of the door and staggered back a couple of steps. The gates of the castle were open. He paused and looked down at Skate.

"You okay?" he asked.

"Don't inhale," Skate said, "you'll puke."

(<o>).[].(<o>)

It was a hallway of wooden crates, stacked three deep on each side and strapped in place. The crates had labels like "Windsor Canadian" and "Bosch Beer".

The truck appeared to be completely packed.

Down the end of the 'hallway', between the stacks of crates, there seemed to be an open area. It was a bright midday in the woods, but the truck was so big and deep it was difficult to see anything very far back in the gloom.

Hack went over to the cold campfire and lit the propane lantern they used the night before. Then he clambered back up the inclined gravel to the back of the truck.

"You ready to do this?" he asked

Skate was on his feet and ready to go. He nodded.

He was not really 'ready to go' in any solid sense, and he was suddenly realizing his back was hurting like hell, and he had fleeting visions of wild bears leaping out of the musty darkness, but he was ready enough, despite all that. It was like H-Hour on D-Day, hunkered on a LCT* approaching Omaha Beach on the Longest Day.*

Or so it seemed.

It was spooky. Skate was scared shitless.

Hack hopped in, Skate right behind.

It was like stepping into an ancient Egyptian crypt.

The smell was almost overpowering, but they were starting to get used to it. It was like rotten meat with battery acid corroding it – a sharp, nasty, sickening smell.

Every small movement kicked up a little cloud of dust from the floor. Hack went ahead, lantern held high, one tiny step at a time. Skate followed. At one point he reached up overhead to shift a topmost crate. It was full, and tinkled slightly of glass. They were all full. It was a truck full of glass.

The passageway between the crates was narrow, barely wide enough for Hack's shoulders. It went on and on like this – for perhaps fifty feet. Ahead, at the front of the trailer, Hack could see the crates were stacked to form a wider opening, like a small room at the end of a tunnel. He moved forward.

Then Hack could see what looked like a pile of clothing spread on the floor and, finally, he could make out the profile of Dewey – what was left of him.

"Hoo boy," Hack said over his shoulder, "we've got a stiff on our hands."

(<o>).[].(<o>)

Hack and Skate stood in the opening, deep into the truck, surrounded by glass and mystery, neither moving. It was a funereal scene of death and decay.

Hack was holding the lantern high. At their feet was a skeleton, fully clothed, hands and skull exposed. Sticking out from under the corpse, the tip of the butt of an old-time shotgun.

They were already reeling, so it was only a small additional shock when they saw the rest of it. There was the body on the floor, AND at the far end of the little room, there was a more macabre sight.

Hack hoisted his lantern a bit and they saw another fully dressed skeleton against the wall, sitting upright on a short stack of crates. This one appeared to be leaning back waiting for them. The eye-sockets of the skull looked into their souls. It was creepy.

Skate felt pain in his spine, but stood his ground.

Hack was frozen, overwhelmed by the input.

"Don't touch anything," Skate said, "I've got the camera, let me take a shot."

(<o>).[].(<o>)

"What the hell?" Hack said.

"Beats me," Skate shrugged.

They had retreated from the far end of the truck in orderly fashion. It was freaky, but it didn't freak them out – they had seen weird scenes before. They were on the ground now, by the fire pit, beyond the gravel, outside the truck, trying to take stock.

"Boy, oh boyo, I just don't know," Skate said, "how long has this been here? This stuff looks brand new, but old fashioned."

They had pulled a couple crates out with them from the near end of the truck. Hack used a shovel tip to pry open the top of one. It held 12 bottles of Canadian whiskey, each with a Canadian government seal, looking dusty but brand new.

"And bodies, freaking skeletons. This could be a crime scene, seriously."

While Skate talked, sitting by the cold campfire, Hack was scooping a little more gravel away from the truck, in the center below where the two doors met. It only took a minute.

"1936," Hack said, "holy hell, 1936."

"Where do you get that?" Skate countered.

"License plate," Hack said pointing, "Ontario, 1936. That's how long it's been here – forty years.

"1936!", Skate said, "that's the Berlin Olympics, Jesse Owens and Adolph Hitler. That's Prohibition and Al Capone. That's Roosevelt's first term, the New Deal."

"I mean, holy crap," Skate continued, "that's before the Second World War, that's a long time ago. Holy crap."

"My dad would have been …", Hack said.

Hack paused. He turned to look back at the truck. He turned slowly back to face Skate. It almost looked like he was about to cry – something Skate had never seen, after all these years. Hack didn't cry, not ever.

"My dad," he choked, "my dad would have been six years old."

Hack went on, "My dad was six when my grandfather left."

"His father, you mean?" Skate asked

"Yeah," Hack nodded, "Abner Hackney, the lost grandfather. I saw my dad misty-eyed exactly once, and not when my mom died."

"He was six when his father went away," Hack added, "which affected him for the rest of his life, and still does, I'll bet."

"Holy crap," was all Skate could think to say.

(<o>).[].(<o>)

They were sitting, simply staring, hours later as the sun went down.

Each was sitting on a case of hooch with their makeshift campfire between them, unlit.

Skate looked at Hack, "Man! I'm tired."

"Me too," Hack said, "and I stink worse than I've ever stunk."

"Smell of death," Skate said, "I suppose is what you'd call that."

In the distance they heard a pop, then a pause, then two more pops.

"What's that?" Skate asked.

Hack cocked his head.

"Gunfire," he said, "heavy pistol probably. Up towards Lon's place."

(<o>)/(12.13)\(<o>)

"That's not funny!" Jack shouted.

He was laying on his belly as the sky darkened.

Delmar laughed from the woods. He had come on duty and crept through the brush, using his new-beaten trail up from the campsite. Then he'd lain prone in the bushes and waited for Jack to step out of his guard shack. But Jack was lazy, and simply sat on his little chair in the shack, not moving. So Delmar had crept back and found a fair sized stone, and tossed it into the bushes from across the road.

Jack heard it, and stood up to investigate. His head and the bare bulb were in alignment for that moment. Then Jack stepped out of the shack, and Delmar squeezed a round from his .357 Magnum, blowing the light bulb to dust.

Jack hit the dirt, yelling. So Delmar squeezed off two quick shots into the air. It was funny, it really was.

"Soldier Franke, reporting for duty," he paused for effect, "Sir!"

"Very funny!" Jack howled, "very, very, fucking funny."

He got to his feet.

"Now I've got to go get another light bulb," he was still shouting, "you stay here until I get back."

Jack stomped off.

"Sir! Yes Sir!" Delmar laughed, "don't fall down in the dark."

(<o>)/(12.14)\(<o>)

Shorty had been outside to get her. He still had his coat on.

"Let's go," he said, and went out the door. He was jacked up.

Skate paused while Dewane pulled on his coat to follow Shorty out into the storm.

"Effie," he said, "how far?"

She gulped out the words, "Four miles."

She was struggling to say more, but still frozen and incapable, so he waited.

"Less than four," she finally added, "this side of the road sign."

Skate turned and bolted out to the parking lot.

257

Shorty had the truck running, and Dewane had finished brushing snow off the headlights – he was sitting inside the truck beside Shorty. They were already pulling out of the parking lot when Skate ran across the snowy pavement and jumped onto the running board. Shorty kept the truck creeping through the snow drifts up towards the road and Dewane moved over so Skate could climb in.

"Less than four miles, she said, this side of the road sign."

"Good," Dewane nodded, "that's good to know."

Shorty looked grim, "what road sign?" he barked.

"I think she meant the mile sign," Skate answered, "four miles to Silver Spur, forty-five to Elysium, that one."

Shorty pulled the truck onto the road, heading south. The wind howled the snow horizontally past them from behind. Visibility was really poor, but better because the wind was at their back, and the cab sat high off the road. Shorty went as fast as he could, which was no more than ten or fifteen miles an hour. He was watching the road which was covered in white, keeping an eye on the odometer.

When the wind is high and the snow is flying, there is little to fix on while you drive. The road and the ditch look pretty much the same, and there are no reference points. When it gets bad, really bad, like it was now, you creep along blindly and hope for the best. Nobody smart drives on a night like this. It's called 'asking for trouble'.

Shorty was a seasoned driver, in the Abner class, as good as they get. But he could hardly see a thing, and he was crapping his pants. That's how bad it was out there – as bad as it gets, which is holy-hell goddam bad.

Dewane fiddled with the heater.

Skate hawkeyed the road ahead, concentrating on the ditch to their left.

"That's three miles," Shorty growled.

They were almost past the car when Skate saw it, not on the opposite side of the road, but on their side. She had crossed the center line in the dark and gone into the farside ditch.

Skate barely caught it in the corner of his eye – he was looking to the left, and it was on his right – a cream-colored VW bug, deep into the ditch, and almost completely mounded with drifting snow.

"Stop!", he shrieked like a goat, keyed up and edgy, "we just passed it, on my side!"

They had gone four miles at fifteen miles an hour, about fifteen minutes of total terrifying focused attention. Enough to make anybody a little bit jumpy. It was only by a miracle they found it. Even up close and looking at it, knowing it was there, you could hardly see it.

Skate bailed out while the truck was still moving, hit the road on all fours, and scrambled back to the ditch, afraid he was wrong and scared he was right.

Shorty brought the truck to a careful halt, keeping it on the road, before thinking about backing up. The kid, Shorty saw, Sketch or whatever his name was, was already out in the weather plowing back up the road.

The bug was there, alright, wedged in the ditch and covered with snow.

Now, they had to deal with it.

Shorty and Dewane had equipment, shovels and such, plus a winch if they really needed it. They were seasoned, and took the time it needed, while working as fast as they could. Neither Shorty nor Dewane was ever known to panic. But they could kick it into gear when it was needed. This situation seemed to call for it.

Dewane grabbed a flashlight waited for the truck to stop, then jumped out right after Skate. He ran back up the road to where Skate was thrashing around in the ditch. He used the flashlight, and guided Shorty who backed the truck up to the spot.

Then Shorty parked the truck and raced around to the ditch, grabbing shovels in hand. It looked like digging would do it, so they dug.

Furiously.

They had to dig quite a bit to get the door open – the bug was laying on its side and really buried in the ditch – under mud and dirt and snow.

Skate was virtually certain they would be too late.

He was mistaken however.

Before she'd left on her march up the road, Effie had opened her suitcase and piled clothing all over and around the child, leaving only a space over it's face for breathing. Effie was 'from around there', and she understood the concept of insulation.

They descended on the car and dug snow like madmen. The aim was to clear enough stuff, and yank the door open.

It took them several agonizing minutes. There was a LOT of snow packed around the car. They were in almost total white-out, and the wind was strong enough to fight against.

When Shorty finally yanked the car door open, falling backward with his effort, Skate reached past him and scooped up the babe and as much swaddling as he could gather in his two arms.

"I've got her," Skate shouted against the growling wind, "let's get the hell out of here."

They scrambled then, out of the ditch and into the truck.

Shorty was wet to the waist from falling into ditch water, he needed to get into the truck. Skate had a baby cradled against his chest. Dewane ushered everyone into place.

Then they were in the truck, and the heater was running full blast.

Skate looked to his chest, and saw the baby was alive, not thrashing, but breathing, which was enough for now.

"She's alive," he said, "how are you boys doing?"

It was warm there, the baby was alive, and they all succumbed to a minute of relief. Warmth in the winter – it's a thing. They were in the nice warm truck cabin, and now they just needed to find shelter from the storm.

They took a few seconds. Shorty came to action first.

"Time to peel", he said, and put the big line truck into gear. They were on a narrow road in the teeth of a killer storm facing the wrong way, but nobody doubted he was up to it.

Shorty executed a nifty turn-around job on the icy highway, and they crept back to the Silver Spur, this time into the teeth of the wind – blinded by the storm. But Shorty knew the road, and he was a seasoned driver. If Shorty couldn't do it, it could not be done.

It took a good long while, crawling into the weather, but they got back. It took so long, they were warm and getting dry before Shorty steered them back into the parking lot and dropped them off at the door to the Silver Spur Tap.

A railroad line-truck limousine service in a winter storm emergency. Skate stepped from a warm truck, baby in his chest, to a warm diner in one smooth move. Shorty dropped them off, then took care of his truck, a work horse and a life saver, both of them.

By this time, Margie had her cousin bundled up in blankets by the stove with her frozen feet in a pail of warm water.

When they walked in smiling, the poor blizzard-scarred mother broke completely, sobbing in relief and pain.

The decision, to leave the babe and go on alone, was the sort of thing you could look back on proudly, if it worked out right. And if it didn't, you were damned for life. Do you take your baby with you into the teeth of a killer storm, or leave it behind and go for help? Such are the choices offered by the savage northwoods – it's not life and death every day, but sometimes that's what it comes down to.

She was starting to thaw by then, her feet and hands, and there is no pain quite like it.

Margie poured the men a round of drinks.

Dewane went to the pay phone to call home, collect.

They were snowed in for sure, and riding out the blizzard in the warm embrace of the Silver Spur Tap.

Truth was, nobody was going anywhere, even if they could. They would see this through, this thing with the mother and child – this was a blizzard they would weather together.

(<o>)/(12.15)\(<o>)

In the neighborhood when the guys were growing up, it was possible to find yourself in a fight just for looking at someone the wrong way. There was a question, "what are you looking at?" which generally signaled trouble. There was another expression, coined by some unknown philosopher, "don't try to be tough, unless you're tough." Despite the Zen overtones of this koan, it represented the basic tenet of the north side warrior culture.

Not everyone was tough. But for those who were, there was a hierarchy and an order that was rarely disturbed. In other words, there were tough guys and there were tough guys – another Zen-like principle.

The city parks were pretty much the center of social life in the 1950s and the early 1960s – when the guys were young. That's where you'd go to play softball or baseball or football, or hockey in the long winter. That's where you'd go hoping to see a girl you liked, or get back that quarter you'd loaned somebody.

You might go down to the park with your baseball glove and play ball, or you might end up trading cards. You might go down with your bathing suit and swim, or you might end up working on baby drops from the monkey bars. You might light firecrackers, or break them open to collect their gunpowder into a tin can, or you might hide out in the stand of brush and trees by the warming house and puff away on stolen cigarettes.

It was rich and unfettered and good – filled with promise and choice.

In those days, kids went to the park without adults. Parents would 'send the kids out to play' – and they would go to the park. And within the confines of the occasional bruising fall, or a fat lip from a big kid, it all seemed perfectly safe.

When the guys were eight or nine, they could walk to the park with their mitts and start a game of baseball, or find a game of baseball to join. Sometimes if you got there early, there would only be enough for 'work ups'. If you were lucky and got there early enough, you got the nice diamond with the backstop made of two-by-fours and chicken wire.

If the big kids were already there, you were relegated to the other diamond across the park. If you had the good diamond and the big kids turned up, you went off to the smaller one without a word of complaint. That's the way it worked.

In those days, too, adults had moral authority. Suppose you took a glass pop bottle out into the street, full of water, and flipped it high in the air to see it explode on the pavement. If a 'grown-up' saw you, and ordered you to clean up the broken glass – you did it. You cleaned it up. Otherwise you might get into even more trouble.

The big kids were only in eighth or ninth grade, but they wore black pants or tight jeans with sharp-pointed black leather shoes. They horsed around, roughly, shoving and kicking at each other's head with their pointy boots, and playing at out-toughing each other. An eighth or ninth grader might have money from a paper route, and they probably had a way to get cigarettes (illegally).

And they were in most senses more powerful and frightening than adults.

These were tough guys, and you didn't want to get mixed up with them in the wrong way. If you were smart, you didn't even want to be noticed by them.

To an eight or nine year old, the eighth and ninth graders were like street lords. They were tough, and they ruled the park – they had all the power.

There were rarely occasions when any part of this power was challenged, as the raw energy was frightful to behold. Everybody knew who was tough, and who was tougher. There was a pecking order in the park that everyone understood.

(<o>).[].(<o>)

Sometimes the tough guys would fight, and sometimes they had a knuckle busting.

This was a simple game.

You hold your fist out in front of you, and I hit the back of your hand, as hard as I can – with the first knuckle on my middle finger – rapping on the back of your hand, one time, like it was a heavy wooden door.

Then I hold my fist out in front of me and you do the same to me – and then I whack the crap out of you in turn.

Back and forth we go, whaling on each other, until somebody backs out.

The boys had gathered in awe, and watched Tony Taranto (the janitors son) knuckle bust with 'Crazy Legs' Kellailly one day (so named for his foot speed, perhaps the fastest runner in the area – certainly the fastest tough guy – Kellailly was a 'specimen', fast, strong, and tough).

The two of them went back and forth, Tony with his powerful shoulders and his withered polio leg, and Crazy Legs with his lean whipcord frame. They abused each other in turn, hacking harder and harder at each other, like hatcheting on oaken limbs. Neither giving an inch. Crazy Legs would sometimes fake a strike to make Tony flinch, but Tony never did. And after Tony hit his knuckle, with a sickening crunching sound, Crazy Legs would shake his hand and laugh. These guys were tough – truly tough

And they kept at it, just taking their punishment and handing it back. A magnificent, epic battle that went on until a policeman, a rare sight in the park, saw the crowd and moved in and broke it up. .

Afterwards, Skate happened to be standing by Crazy Legs and his tough guy friends as he was showing them his hand. It was purple and appeared to be twice it's normal size, and most hideously, the middle knuckle looked to have been split. As Crazy Legs opened and closed his fist, the knuckle bone stretched the skin like a cloven hoof.

Crazy Legs went 'down the river' to reform school in Red Wing later that summer for breaking car windows with his fist. He had it in a hard cast by that time. He did it for a goof, because he could.

His family moved away and he never came back to the neighborhood. We never heard another word about him, or whether he regained full use of his hand. There was a story later that he got arrested for car theft and went into the army instead of serving a jail sentence. But that was likely just a story. Tony Taranto came out the best on the game, and went on to a janitor's job with the public school district.

(<o>).[].(<o>)

After eighth or ninth grade the tough guys would go into high school and get cars and jobs. Then they didn't come around the park so much, except after dark. These guys were more likely to get arrested for racing their cars, or would get in trouble for getting their girlfriends in trouble.

Like Ricky Pawlowski's oldest brother Gordy, who did both.

Gordy was almost a mythic figure to us. The Pawlowski family lived on our block, and Gordy was the oldest.

When you're eight or nine years old you don't go to the park after dark very much. So we rarely saw Gordy – he left the house in the morning and came back after we were in bed. Gordy, in his late teens, was a lean figure with pointed leather boots and a real motorcycle jacket, his hair carefully greased back.

Gordy was beyond the pecking order of the park. He was older and truly tough.

The rest of the run-of-the-mill tough guys existed in a fairly inflexible caste system. Some were jokers, some were smarter, some had younger brothers and sisters, and some didn't. But they were all tough, and they were all fairly clear on their place in the toughness scale. They settled the scale by fighting, although they didn't actually fight that often. The scale was set over the course of years, through a sequence of occasional fights.

Gordie aside, who was above it, everybody knew Crazy Legs Kellailly and Dan Kelsey (before Gus Garrison, who was our age, grew into the role) were the toughest guys in the neighborhood. They were so tough they never had to fight anymore. Tony Taranto was somewhat out of the system, with his withered leg. He might have been the toughest of them all, but he was mostly a gentle soul and never really found the need to fight. Lou Granifaldi was crazy and flew into a fury in a fight. One time he'd ripped the ear half off a younger kid. He never fought Kellailly or Kelsey in his prime, although many would have loved to see it. So Granifaldi was figured to be next toughest. After him was Paul Janosich who worked out with weights. Janosich was powerful, but slow. Both Granifaldi and Janosich's little brother would play a part in cementing the Garrison legend at different points in time. The elder Janosich actually found the need to fight fairly often, as did everyone below him in the pecking order.

Some in the tough crowd were jokers, who would just punch a little kid in the shoulder for a laugh. If tears of pain welled up in their eyes, they'd laugh loudly and call them sissy or girl or queer. Funny stuff. Some in the tough crowd, low in the order, would bully and swagger amongst the smaller kids and throw their weight around. "Sneaker" Peters was one of those.

(<o>).[].(<o>)

Skate was playing workups with a few kids. This was the game you played when there weren't enough to make a real baseball game. Somebody pitched, somebody batted, somebody fielded, and every new kid would take a fielding position: first base, then third. The batter swings away until they get a hit. Then the batter takes the outfield, the pitcher plays catcher, the catcher bats, first base pitches, third goes to first, and so on: they work through the order – workups. When another kid showed up they would play in the outfield, and everyone would move over a position. And then finally there would be enough to choose sides and play a game.

They had a game going this one day, and Skate was playing outfield when somebody found the sweet spot and the ball flew over his head. He chased it back towards the warming house. He didn't run too hard, it was going to be a home run no matter what he did.

"Hey kid," he heard a voice, "let me see that ball."

"We're playing," Skate said without looking, and threw it back into home.

Then, running to the diamond, he looked back over his shoulder, and his stomach dropped. It was Sneaker, scowling at him. He looked mad.

This violated the principle. Skate had been 'noticed' by an older, tougher kid. This was bad.

(<o>).[].(<o>)

To get home, Skate had to walk the park from the far diamond and cross the street at the corner. It was lunchtime, so the game broke up. Skate was looking over his shoulder all the way across the park. He was on the sidewalk when he was surprised to see Sneaker step in front of him.

"You think you're tough, kid?"

"No."

"You think you're tougher than me?"

Sneaker was 15, big and fat, with bad skin and stringy, limp, greasy, unwashed hair. He wasn't tough by the standards of his tough crowd, but he was in the tough crowd just the same. Skate, meanwhile, was nine years old and scrawny. It was no contest.

"Let me see that ball, kid," Sneaker said.

"We were in the middle of a game," Skate tried not to wail.

"I said gimme that ball."

Skate was carrying his baseball in his glove. He tossed it underhand to Sneaker, who caught the ball walking forward.

"I told you that before," Sneaker said, then he swung his fist, with the ball in it. Skate was terrified, and stepping back when the fist hit his jaw. He saw it coming and turned his head. Still, the punch knocked him off his feet, and he fell on his back.

Sneaker moved in, about to kick Skate on the ground, the beginning of a beating.

They both heard the voice. It was Tony Taranto.

"That's enough," he said, and that was enough to freeze Sneaker in place and enough to make Skate grateful forever.

Skate jumped to his feet and ran home. He left his ball with Sneaker and never saw it again.

Later he reflected on it. It was strange, but a punch in the jaw was just like the movies – it knocked you down, but it hardly hurt at all.

(<o>)/(12.20)\(<o>)

When Skate was learning how to shave he hid in the small bathroom down the stairs. The mirror had two hinges and he set his face at points in space to get a perfect view: triangulation of reflection. For fun he set the mirrors to see infinite halls of reflected Skate on down a pipe of ever smaller faces.

(<o>)/(12.21)\(<o>)

Three years had passed and Terry was miserable. He had expected Canada to be like Minneapolis, but it wasn't. In the Cities he had scraped by on handouts and street favors. He had enough charm and enough easy conversation that he was able to slide along without too much notice. He could work the street, or fade into the background, as the situation unfolded. He knew how to 'work it' – easy-peasy, loosy-goosy. He was in his element.

In Canada he was out of place, and people picked him out as American after four words. He did NOT know how to 'work it' in this strangely familiar but oddly foreign place. He was a goose out of water – a heron with no rookery.

The nuns had been good enough to begin with. They took him in and, after a couple days, arranged a ride to Winnipeg. He was provided a room to sleep in, with a nice Catholic family. They fed him, but kept away from him too. He was a boarder, not a guest, and they needed him to move, to make room in case there was another.

There was considerable anti-war and anti-American sentiment in the land, so he was quietly welcomed. There was something like 25,000 others like him, deserters and draft dodgers, hiding out up there at the time. But Canada in the

1970s was a country of vast expanse and only 20 million people. So it wasn't like he could join a Wednesday evening support group. When you high-tailed it up to Canada you were safe, but you were not coddled or nurtured. You were on your own.

It was clear to Terry – he needed to get onto his own feet as soon as possible. He felt compelled to find a job and move along. The nuns had provided a few hundred dollars and, miraculously, a Manitoba drivers license.

But that was it.

Within a week he was living in a seedy room just off Portage Avenue, and washing dishes in a low-scale Chinese restaurant.

From there it was more of the same.

Washing dishes, washing cars, sweeping floors, even shoveling snow – until finally landing a waiter's job in a slightly better restaurant in St. James, just west of downtown.

The restaurant job was alright, the best gig so far, but nerve wracking. The place was frequented by city police and federal Mounties – the RCMP – the Royal Canadian Mounted Police. It gave him the willies to wait on law enforcement, the Mounties especially, who were soft-spoken but sharp-eyed. They always got their man.

Terry did his best to acclimate. He had adopted Canadian lingo and phrasing, working "eh" into his speech and developing a passion for hockey. He tried to melt into the Canadian melting pot, and he did okay for years and years.

(<o>).[].(<o>)

Then the war ended.

Terry was sweeping the floor in a lousy railroad bar, supplementing his restaurant income, when he saw the story on television. The images from the evacuation of Saigon in 1975, even on the crackling black and white set, transfixed him. He stopped sweeping and sat at the bar, and had a beer to celebrate.

But it didn't mean he could go home. Oh, no. He was still a deserter in time of war – treason punishable by death. Going back to face the music, even now, would be a very discordant symphony. He was still stuck.

(<o>).[].(<o>)

At one point Terry met a pretty college student, studying Commerce at the University of Manitoba, and they spent considerable time together. But she was of mostly Indian extraction, and from Yellow Knife, an outpost in the Northwest Territories. It was expected she should finish her degree program and move back to her homeland. Which is what she did.

Their parting was sweet sorrow, but she was tied to her heritage, and he was not willing to jump into a northern outpost. First, he just did not want that life. Second, he could be anonymous in a big city like Winnipeg – that would evaporate in a place like Yellow Knife. He hated to see her go, but he could not go along – no way.

(<o>).[].(<o>)

When he wasn't working, Terry spent most of his time in the bars, drinking, and nothing like a relationship ever came from that.

He got a guitar and taught himself to play a bit – three chords and energy. Soon he was in with a liquored up thrash band that played in the low-rent bars on Saturday nights. Then the band switched lead singers, and started to get a little local notoriety. Then they'd played on the radio, and there was talk of a record contract. Soon they were playing Fridays too, and drawing small but loud crowds.

It was not long before Terry could see there were police in the crowd looking for drug abusers and other petty criminals. Terry hated to do it, but he had to quit the band – too much heat in the air.

He was a fugitive, and an illegal alien, and he never really felt at ease. He lost touch with the people who had helped him, and who knew his story, and he could never tell a stranger his real story. Terry was only on the verge of deeply paranoid, and he knew that much about himself. Through the months he spent with the Yellow Knife woman, he never told her the truth about his life.

When he thought about it, which was becoming more frequent, he longed for American soil. It was not a sentimental thing, as Terry was not a sentimental person, but as the years went on, he felt the need to feel at home.

(<o>).[].(<o>)

By this time Terry had his own car, and a little money in the bank.

After a year or so he had taken the chance and written to his father. His Dad had been deeply shamed when Terry deserted the army, and it was a big obstacle between them. Dad was no big writer, and the correspondence was mostly Christmas cards, but it was clear that, as the years passed, and with the war now long over, his Dad would take him back in – if he turned up at the door one day.

As the Bicentennial drew near, Terry was more and more taken with the idea of making a trip back to his old stomping grounds, with a swing through his home town.

Maybe it would be okay. Nixon was out as president, and Ford was filling in. Perhaps a sojourn could be arranged. Perhaps he could take the chance.

Green River!

(<o>)/(12.26)\(<o>)

Friday. They were sitting by the lake.

Wednesday had been wrenching. They dug gravel all day, until the afternoon, when they finally found the contents of the box. Then, they had searched it, and they had savored it, and they had pondered it.

Then they just sat by it, finally beyond thought.

At last they left.

Hack shut the doors. Skate picked up the tools. Hack stamped out the fire, which was already out. Skate went up the trail to the driveway and loaded the tools and the wheelbarrow onto the truck. Hack started the truck. Then they drove back to the campsite with hardly another word.

Hack said, "I'll see you in the morning," and went into the trailer to sleep, although it was just barely dark.

Skate went into the cabin and lit a lantern, and then spent the next several hours writing in his journal. Then he crawled into his sleeping bag and dreamed of gravel.

Thursday they nailed stolen tarpaper on the roof and didn't talk about it. Skate sort of wanted to, but Hack clearly did not. So they didn't.

(<o>)/(12.27)\(<o>)

Friday. They were sitting by the lake.

"I don't know what to do," Hack was saying, "but I know what I don't want to do, and that's run into town and report to the law."

Skate nodded.

"Until I know what happened here, this is Hackney family business. I hope you can respect that."

"Yeah, yeah, I see that," Skate said, "I don't know what to do either, but I don't see a rush. Whatever went down was forty years ago."

Hack nodded.

"Whatever you want to do," Skate continued, "that's cool with me. And if that's nothing, that's cool too."

Skate raised his eyes to look at Hack and, instead of locking eyes, he realized Hack was looking past him – Skate turned to look over his shoulder towards the lake. There was a canoe heading towards them.

"Nun," Hack said quietly.

"Good grief," Skate said, "what now?"

(<o>).[].(<o>)

Sister Louise beached her canoe and stepped out. She wore a U. of M. tee-shirt, and cut-off jean shorts. Her legs were brown and shapely, and just slightly chubby, and her hair was cropped short, although not mannishly. She sat without irony on a case of whiskey.

"Hack," she said, "can I talk to you for a minute in private?"

"This is Skate," Hack said, pointing with his chin, "I think you two know each other."

"Hi Skate," she said, a little doubtfully, and shook his hand with a firm grip. Then she looked back at Hack and went on, "this is important."

Hack just stared, distracted.

"Whatever it is, let's hear it. Skate's okay."

Louise nodded.

"I think I remember you," she said to Skate, "I think you and I have history. And you were there for the front end of this, paddling in the dark."

Skate shrugged, he sort of knew what she meant, but it was sort of beyond him too.

Louise launched into it.

"Terry is back," she said, "and he wants to come back over."

"Terry?" Skate said, "you mean Terry the tramp, our deserter?"

"Yeah," Hack shrugged, "that's it. Terry wants to come back across. What's the problem?"

"Terry!" Skate said, "gawd, it's been years, hasn't it?"

Louise settled into a hunch.

"The railroad only goes one way," she said, a little too fiercely, "we don't want to be, and we CANNOT be a smugglers port."

Louise took a breath. The boys were a little surprised at the vehemence.

"We sent young boys to safety, but we are not a pipeline back and forth. This will not do. This is out of bounds. This can not work, and can not be tolerated. You know what I mean, right?"

The boys were nodding their heads. You always agreed with a nun, if you wanted your immortal soul to rise unto heaven, that is.

They sat in silence for a moment.

"Where's Terry now?" Skate finally asked.

"He's parked on our lakeshore, and he will not leave," said Louise, "and we need him to leave."

"Okay," Hack said, rising, "I understand. We'll come and get him tonight, after dark. But he understands, it's a one-way trip. The railroad is closed to him after this."

Louise looked relieved.

"Bless you, boys," she said.

"The old signal?" Hack asked.

"Yes," Louise answered, "we'll be waiting on the beach."

"Nuns at night," Skate said, "it's been a long time."

"Not long enough," Louise said.

Then she got up, and got back in her canoe – and she paddled away.

"She's kind of cute," Skate said, "for a nun."

"Down boy," Hack smiled, "you've been in the woods too long."

(<o>)/(12.29)\(<o>)

Friday. The van ploughed northward, heavily laden.

Onto Como, then 18th, then Stinson, then the freeway. They were on the road.

At Roseville, Traci needed to pee. They stopped. Henry saw a liquor store and bought two six-packs.

They were on the road again.

The next stop was in Coon Rapids. Remo needed to get out and stretch. His arthritis was bothering him.

Then, right after Rexee' woke up and lit her first Camel, Sutter needed to get some air. They stopped in Forest Lake.

They passed the Wyoming exit, even though Traci thought it would be fun to see.

And they almost made it past North Branch, but Traci had to pee again.

"No more liquid for Traci," Ace commanded, "we've got to skip at least one potty stop, or we'll never get there."

When Ace wasn't looking, Henry slipped Traci a beer. She was still dehydrated from her night's exertions.

They drove and drove and drove. Finally Pine City came into sight.

"We've got to stop," Rexee' said, "my water is about to burst."

They had covered 65 miles on their way to Elysium, still nearly 200 miles away.

They had started just after noon, it was now 3PM. They stopped.

268

(<o>).[].(<o>)

The van ploughed northward, heavily laden.

They stopped at Hinckley, Remo was starving.

The site of "The Great Hinckley Fire". They read the plaque. They stopped to eat. They had covered a total of 79 miles.

They continued north, they ploughed. Henry wanted to stop at the Finlayson/Askov exit, to stretch his legs, but Ace vetoed the idea: both towns were miles from the road.

The van ploughed north past Sturgeon Lake.

"We should stop," Rexee' said.

"Forget it," Ace growled, "we're on the road."

They stopped in Barnum. They looked for Bailey. No sign of him. They went on.

They skipped the Otter Creek exit, although Traci needed to pee again. They shouted her down.

In Cloquet, Calvin said, "we're at a half tank, should we buy gas?"

Ace nodded.

"In the great northwoods," he said, "we never, ever, want to run out of gas – never, not ever, not once, ever."

They pulled into the Lindholm Oil Company Service Station in Cloquet, and everyone piled out.

"Look at this," Rexee' said, "this is outrageous."

She had never been there before.

"Yeah," Ace said, "this is the Frank Lloyd Wright memorial gas station, renowned the world over. Japanese tourists cover continents and skip a side trip to New York City in order to take pictures of this, instead."

Remo read from a sign, "Constructed of concrete block, cypress wood, glass and steel, the Lindholm service station features a cantilevered copper canopy, radiant heat, glassed-in observation lounge and four service bays. Fire codes thwarted Wright's plan to supply gas from overhead pumps, which would have left the ground level open for vehicle movement. Although Wright's hopes for his gas station of the future were never fully realized, elements of the design were later incorporated into many Phillips 66 stations."*

(<o>).[].(<o>)

They were back on the road, all bladders empty, all gas tanks full.

"Cloquet is just about the halfway point," Ace announced over his shoulder, "we're into the woods from here. The deep woods, I mean."

Henry stiffened. Rexee' saw him do it.

"Relax," she said, "at some point there's no going back. Just go with it."

"Go with the flow, Henry," Remo said.

"Yeah, yeah, sure, right," Henry said, staying as calm as he could.

Henry had gone with many flows, he considered, most of which he did not like. And he certainly did not like this one. He was flinching at every new thing. He did not like to be crowded into this van. He did not like new scenery.

That gas station was fun for the rest of them, but not for Henry. He was so far out of his element, it took all his courage just to sit there. He wanted to go home. He sat as quietly as he could, and ignored as much as he could, and wished for something familiar.

He cracked a beer and nursed it. That was his version of coping with change. It would have to do.

The van ploughed northward, heavily laden.

They went up highway 33, past Grand Lake, Silver Spur, and Canyon.

(<o>).[].(<o>)

The tire blew just outside of Cotton.

It was the right front tire, and it blew loudly, like a rifle shot. Remo clutched his chest.

Calvin fought for control. The van was sliding sideways down the road, and he was automatically steering against it, and suddenly it was lurching straight again as he slowed down – tapping the brakes like a veteran, not slamming them, which saved them.

He carefully aimed for the shoulder which was gravel and very narrow. Calvin rode them to the shoulder as best he could.

Calvin was a thin black man, but his knuckles were white.

Finally he got the van stopped, in good order, off the road, but out of the ditch, a huge success. This was the sort of blow-out accident that could take lives – in the worst case – but not in this case.

Ace let go of the dashboard, which he had been clutching, and looked back from the front seat to survey the damage.

The lurching and caroming had tossed everyone and everything. Luggage had bounced around, and then fallen on Rexee' as she laid on the van's floor. Remo, in the back, had taken a crack to his temple where Sutter's crate had smacked him. People and luggage were strewn all over the van, tossed by the chaos.

"Everybody okay?" Ace shouted.

"Fuck a red duck," Rexee' yelled back, buried under luggage, "get this shit off me."

(<o>).[].(<o>)

They piled out, freeing Rexee in the process.

Then they apprehended the tire needed to be changed.

The spare tire being safely tucked in a compartment under the passenger area, they then unloaded all the luggage to get at the spare tire.

That's right, relish this – they had to unload ALL the luggage to get at the spare tire. They moved a mountain of baggage before repairs could begin. To their credit, they moved it as a group, setting up a fireman's brigade, passing hand to hand and stacking the luggage on the side of road – a huge stack, a monument to packing and stacking.

Then, after all that, the spare was soft.

But it had some air – enough to drive.

But then, the burst tire, a total loss and cut to ribbons, did NOT want to come off.

Calvin and Ace labored over the rusty lugnuts, cursing in unison, while the rest of them milled around on the side of the road.

A county mountie stopped, and parked behind them with his gumballs flashing.

He got out and walked up to do his duty.

The van reeked of liquor, since one of Sutters whiskey bottles had broken open and splashed onto one of Remo's duffel bags – the one with his clothes.

The cop stuck around long enough to see the tire change was proceeding apace, albeit slowly, and to determine that Calvin was the driver, and not one of the drinkers.

Then he went back to his car and waited. This was a service, since his flashing lights would tend to slow the traffic as it passed. Which made repairs easier.

(<o>).[].(<o>)

The cop appeared to be filling out forms, like a good public servant, and they all stayed away, out of respect and fear. Except for Rexee' who walked back and saw he was just doing a crossword puzzle in a big book of puzzles.

Rexee' had a can of beer in hand, which might look like 'public consumption of alcohol', a crime, to some.

But Rexee' had the liberty that every pretty woman enjoys, and the casual manner that made her easy to like.

She just sauntered back, beer in hand, cool as a cuke, and pulled open the door to the cop car and sat down in his vehicle.

Then she chatted with the cop, like it was nothing, drinking her beer in his car.

Public consumption of alcohol, at this juncture, was not an issue. She just hunkered down and chatted with the man.

When the tire was changed, and the luggage reloaded, Rexee' got out and hopped into the van. The cop said goodbye, and she did too.

(<o>).[].(<o>)

Another mutiny erupted in Eveleth.

"Pull this damn vehicle over!" Sutter demanded.

Calvin wanted to resist, but it was futile.*

They piled out.

Remo wanted to go see the Hockey Hall of Fame. The motion did not carry.

They skirted Virginia.

"Hey," Henry said, "is this the 169 that runs through town?"

"Oh yes," Ace said, "it's the west river road – extended, insanely."

(<o>).[].(<o>)

"Tower and Soudan," Ace said, "we're so close, you can taste it."

"I need to pee," Traci pleaded.

"Okay, okay," Ace said, "but this is the last stop. I'm serious."

They stop.

They go and go and go.

"Eagles Nest," Rexee' said, "sounds interesting."

"Nein!" Ace responded, "Cal, keep moving."

Go, go, go, they do.

"McComber?" Traci asked.

"Nay, lassie" Ace said, "we're almost there."

(<o>)/(12.37)\(<o>)

A one act play in several scenes:
Scene Twelve –
The stage is still split. On the audience left is the Volkswagen Mini-bus cut in half with its innards exposed. The passengers are arranged as before. On the audience right of the stage is Hack and Skate, still sitting at the table in their new cabin. They have fallen into quiet time. Skate is bent over his journal notebook, writing furiously. Hack has an old fashioned door latch on the table in front of him – he is taking old paint off it with a dental pick: refurbishing it for the cabin.

As before, focus is held by spotlights which switch back and forth. When one half is in darkness, the players freeze.

It is Friday, July 2nd, 1976, at Eight P.M. in the Central Time Zone, in Elysium, Minnesota.

=#=#=#=

(There is a moment while the whole stage is illuminated, then the cabin is lit, and the van goes black)

Skate
(sighs and puts his pen down)
How's that coming?

Hack
Pretty good. This was one of the door latches on the old home site. I picked it out of the ashes -- thought I'd try to fix it up so we can lock this place if we want.

Skate
I like it. Preserve the old stuff. It's better made half the time.

Hack
That's true. This has been through a fire, though. So it's pretty rough to work with.

Skate
But not beyond redemption?

Hack
No soul is beyond redemption …

Skate
… through the bless-ed sacrament of Confession. Yes. I think I remember …

Hack
How's it going on that side of the table?

Skate
Hot and cold, good and evil, up and down, and, uh, yin and y'know, yang. The usual.

Hack
Same over here. Do you save the old piece of junk, which takes hours, or buy new, which takes less hours, and isn't as good, plus costs money.

272

        Skate
Oh yeah, redemption. It only sounds easy.
(nods to the door latch in Hack's hand)
Take it to confess, bless me lord for I have sinned.
(the cabin goes black, the van gets lit)

        Ace
Tower and Soudan, we're so close, you can taste it.

        Traci
I need to pee.

        Ace
Okay, okay, but this is the last stop. I'm serious.
(the cabin gets lit, the van goes black)

        Skate
Hack, I may as well tell you. I'm trying to write a story
about the underground railroad, and that human drive for
freedom. So I'm writing a thing based on Terry and his flight
across the border. I'm going to weave this in with a Civil War
element, because the slaves up the pipe are similar enough to
draw parallels.

        Hack
Okay, I suppose. You'll have to do some digging to get the
slave part right, I guess.

        Skate
Yes, well that's a problem actually. Anyway, I'm thinking of
folding in a lighter parallel smuggling type element. Maybe
you can fill me in.

        Hack
No, oh, no, no.

        Skate
Yeah, oh yeah, yeah, you got it. Tell me what you remember
about the margarine smuggling fiasco. That fateful night.

        Hack
Gawd, that was funny. But, look, names changed to protect the
guilty, right?

        Skate
Yes, but of course. It was the night that shall not be spoken
of -- whose name shall not be named.
(he stops to laugh).
Man! For something not to speak of, that's the most talked
about thing in history.
(they both laugh).
Okay, yeah, sure, I'll mash the whole thing around. Nobody
knows what the nose knows. I've heard the story many times
myself, but I can't remember how it all started.

        Hack
It all started,
(meaningful dramatic pause)
on the fourth of July.
(the cabin goes black, the van gets lit)

        Ace
It was right along here, just outside Tower-Soudan, that I got
busted for the first time.

Calvin

Yeah, busted?

Ace

Yep, rounded up like a criminal and hauled into the pokey.

Remo

Moving bricks for the cause?

Ace

Oh, yeah. The cause was noble. We were fighting the MAN. We were a liberation army. It was like the Revolution. We were minutemen in the battle against tyranny.

Fat Henry

This sounds good. You don't usually hear pot dealing stories in terms of patriotism and the American Way.

Remo

He didn't say pot. You're assuming. It might have been hash.

Old Man Sutter

(calling from the back)

It might have been gun running. Now that's in the patriotic pantheon. I did it myself in the Lafayette tradition. Arm the peasants, this is good.

Rexee'

(calling up from the floor)

You smuggled guns! I believe that. I'm selling a bridge down here.

Traci

He might have. He was young, and adventurous. Right? You can tell us.

Ace

I was young all right. I was young and foolish.

Calvin

(driving and looking straight ahead)

And strong and brave and stalwart and patriotic and … all that stuff. So tell it. It was right about here, when you struck a blow for liberty and got busted for the first time.

Fat Henry

And it was pot? Right? I've got a dollar on pot.

Remo

Or hash? Was it hash? Or opium?

Old Man Sutter

(snorts)

Opium. Like it was opium.

Rexee'

Well?

Traci

Yes, how old were you?

Ace

I was eight years old. But I remember it like yesterday. I was a victim …

Traci

Eight years old!

Ace
… I was a victim of margarine. I was a casualty in the
margarine wars.
(the cabin gets lit, the van goes black)

   Hack
There were those family get-togethers on the Fourth of July,
when we were kids, you remember. But it was mostly barbecues
at your house, or Ace's or Book's. I would be there, hanging
around, but my folks would never come. Just because WE were
all friends, it didn't mean the folks were too.

   Skate
Most summers, it seems to me, you were up here in the woods
with your family. Not down in the city with us.

   Hack
Yep, mostly, except when we were about eight. Summer of 1960,
I think.

   Skate
Sounds about right, or maybe 1961.

   Hack
In there somewhere, I guess.

   Skate
So …

   Hack
So, my Dad came to one of the barbecues, one year it was at
Ace's house. In those days …
(the cabin goes black, the van gets lit)

   Ace
… in those days, margarine was a new product, made from corn,
from the corn states, and in competition with butter … the
dairy farmers were up in arms against it.

   Old Man Sutter
They feared for their livelihood, I remember. Butter was a big
part of a dairyman's living.

   Ace
Right. So there were LAWS against margarine. Here, in
Minnesota, and in Wisconsin. It was verboten.

   Old Man Sutter
Yes, I remember. I was in Cuba, this about 1960, but we
heard about it. News from back home.

   Ace
Right, 1960 is about it. So, in those days you could NOT buy
margarine up here. It wasn't in the stores. It was illegal.
But you could get it in corn country, down in Iowa.

   Remo
Oh, yeah, I remember this too.

   Fat Henry
Me too. You could get these bags of white goo, with a little
red pellet in the bag. And my job was to massage the bags my
mom brought home, so the color would spread through the bag.

   Remo
I'd forgotten all about that! Oleo! You squeezed the bags like

for an hour, and the red pellet would turn all the white goo into yellow goo. Just like butter.

          Ace
Yes, that was the technology. But that was a little later. At first you could only get those bags in Iowa. They were not for sale in this state.

          Traci
But why? Why eat yellow colored goo?

          Ace
Good question. It was cheaper, I think. And it was illegal, and hence …

          Calvin
… Desirable.

          Ace
… yes, I think that's it.
(the cabin gets lit, the van goes black)

          Hack
So my dad, and Ace's dad, who hardly knew each other, ended up talking at the fourth of july barbecue that year. And they're half lit up, I suppose, and they get into hatching this money-making plot.

          Skate
And we're what, eight?

          Hack
Yeah, 1960, so we're about eight. And Ace's dad has a brother-in-law who travels for some reason.

          Skate
(nodding)
Yeah, Ace's Uncle Moe. He was a salesman -- and a piece of work in general.

          Hack
Right, and this guy has got a trunkful of margarine bags. You remember those?

          Skate
Yep, sure, it was my job to squeeze them into yellow.

          Hack
Right. Except that was later. This was before you could get them in Minnesota. They were illegal at this point.

          Skate
Contraband.

          Hack
Contraband, exactly. So they struck a drunken deal, I guess, around the barbecue that day.

          Skate
(dramatically) That fateful Fourth of July.

          Hack
(laughs)
Right. They struck a deal. Ace's dad would produce a bunch of margarine bags, from his salesman relation, and my Dad would sell them up in Elysium.

Skate
This was Ace's dad's idea, I suspect.

Hack
I dunno. This is one of the stories my dad doesn't ever like
to tell.

Skate
And then …

Hack
Well, there was so much of it, they decided to drive up in two
fully loaded cars. Hundreds of dollars worth of the stuff.

Skate
And they decided to drive up that night, right.

Hack
Enthused by liquor, is all I can think. My dad wouldn't
normally do that.

Skate
Ace's dad either.

Hack
But away they went. Two cars, heavy with margarine, Ace with
his dad, and me with mine.
(the cabin goes black, the van gets lit)

Ace
And that's the story. We were driving along this stretch of
road, and it was getting towards dawn, and maybe somebody
crossed the center line, or something, and we got pulled over
by the state patrol. Both cars.

Remo
And they searched?

Ace
I honestly don't know what happened. Why we were pulled over,
or what happened next. Except I was asleep in the car, in the
early morning, and I wake up to see my dad opening the trunk
for the MAN to see. And there it was, a treasure trove of
margarine.

Remo
And then?

Ace
And then we were busted.
(the cabin gets lit, the van goes black)

Skate
And then?

Hack
I really don't know. We followed the cops to the hoosegow, and
they took all the margarine.

Skate
Did you serve hard time? Prison tattoos and such?

Hack
Confiscation. That's the smugglers fear, and that's what
happened. I think. I was pretty little, and we never talked
about it again.

277

         Skate
With your Dad?

         Hack
With anybody. I do know, my dad never forgave Ace's dad for
opening that trunk. He should have refused, on constitutional
grounds, but he didn't. Every smuggler knows about that. Make
them get a search warrant.

         Skate
And that was the end of it.

         Hack
More than the end. I don't think they've spoken since that
day. Which is what? Sixteen years ago?
(the cabin goes black, the van gets lit)

         Remo
And that was the end of it?

         Ace
Pretty much, except my dad hasn't talked to Hack's dad since.
He blames him for getting him involved.

         Rexee'
And your criminal past? The blot on all your records?

         Ace
Yeah, for that too.
(the cabin gets lit, the van goes black)

         Skate
And then?

         Hack
I don't really know. They let us go. Ace and his dad drove
home, and we stayed up here. I do know my dad was pissed at
himself, too.

         Skate
Yeah?

         Hack
Yeah, I think he was happy to be out of the Hackney family
shadow, all those years working the job in Minneapolis. Living
the straight life. Then he finally, for once, except for the
poaching, he gets caught in the middle of something. And it's
up here, right in the old home town.

         Skate
Yeah? Herons home to roost?

         Hack
Just another Hackney, following form. He hated that.

         Skate
The Hackneys aren't so bad are they?

         Hack
In Minneapolis we're almost respectable. We were the poor
family that lived near the river and down by the tracks, but
we were still respectable. Up here, we're, uh, notorious, or
let's say colorful.

         Skate
Ah, I see, of the colored persuasion.

                            278

Hack
Little bit, yeah.

Skate
Huh! I had no idea. You Hackneys always seemed like regular
white folks to me.

Hack
Yeah, that's how my dad wanted it, I think. To fit in with the
white folks down south.
(the cabin goes black, the van gets lit)

Ace
And thus ends the tragic tale.
(he looks ahead, out the windshield)
We'll be there soon, Calvin, within half an hour.

Calvin
I'll believe that when I see it.

Remo
(perversely)
Let's turn around. Let's go back. This is close enough. Let's
head home.

Calvin
Momma, tell them kids to be quiet. Don't make me stop this
van.

Ace
Keep going, man. The end is in sight.

Rexee'
Miracles! Will they never cease? We are transmogrified. What's
the word?

Traci
I have to pee.
(the cabin gets lit, the van goes black)

Hack
Well, I s'pose.

Skate
Yep, it's gloaming in the glen, and time to pick up the
'package' like you smugglers say.

Hack
Yeah, let's do that. Lets pick up the package, and then head
to town.

Skate
Terry the Tramp. What a trip. I wonder what he's been up to
all these years. Underground, on the run, probably dealing
illicit margarine to make a living.

Hack
Could be, who knows, let's go.

Skate
One more run for the underground railway.

Hack
This'll go in your story, I suppose.

Skate
Yes, oh my, as Book would say, yes. Let's do it.

(sarcastic pause)
Let's go get 'THE PACKAGE'

    Hack
Maybe you need a little camouflage face paint, to get you in
the mood. Or some night black. That's what us smugglers do, ya
know.

    Skate
Right, face black, after you.
(Pausing to light a cigarette)
Just so I'm sure I've got this, the man doesn't open the trunk
without a search warrant. Right?

    Hack
We should quick put a trunk in the canoe, then.

    Skate
Assemble the squad -- Moose, Kirby, Doc, Cage* -- we're on a
mission, let's rock.

    (Blackout).

(<o>)/(12.38)\(<o>)

Elysium at last. Their five hour drive has taken over eleven hours. It was way past dark, and in Elysium, in July, nightfall was late and gradual. But they were finally there, alive and in good order – no deaths or disasters, suicides, homicides, or margarinecides. Calvin pulled over in front of the first tavern he found. It was Powder's Tap, a crumby little joint like any other.

They piled out of the van like they'd been on a death march across the Sahara.

There was much stretching and groaning. You'd have thought they had just gotten off the Orient Express at the Siberia end of it.

They were standing on the sidewalk, still getting acclimated, and not even Rexee' had plunged into the bar yet.

Hack and Skate walk up, Terry lagging behind.

Ace saw them first.

"Hi guys."

"Hi yourself," Skate deadpanned, "you looking for us?"

"Yeah," Ace answered, "we just thought to drop in."

Rexee' looked at Hack, accusingly.

"You knew we were coming, right?"

"Well, no," Hack said, "no, not specifically."

"Not at all," Skate added, "not in the least."

Rexee' wheeled around to Ace, her eyes blazing.

"Surprise," Ace said, flat, and without blinking.

Skate laughed. Finally, he thought, Rexee' at a disadvantage.

Rexee' jabbed Ace in the chest with her forefinger, hard.

"You're buying, Timothy" she snarled.

They piled into the bar.

(<o>)/(12.39)\(<o>)

They parked on Washington Street, near the tracks. This way they could scout the town and, if they saw Lon, they could retreat to the truck without being seen.

Delmar led them along the tracks to the west end of town, thinking to work their way up the street until they found Lon, and then backing down the street to safety. They cut the corner of Camp Street, and then over to the main drag.

They stood in the darkness for a bit. Delmar issued his orders.

"You stay here," he said, "and I'll look in the window. If he's in there, we move to the other end of town, if he's not, we reconnoiter up the street until we find him. Until then we stay in the alleys, in the dark."

Jack and Hank nodded in unison. This was Delmar's deal, they just wanted to get drinking, and the sooner the better.

"Wait here," Delmar said, and then he sauntered casually over to the bar and looked in the window.

(<o>)/(Endnotes 12.40)\(<o>)

76. Sandburg, Carl (1919). The Fog. Louis Untermeyer, ed. Modern American Poetry.

77. LCT, Landing Craft Tank, a vehicle used to storm the Normandy beaches on D-Day, June 6, 1944.

78. Day, The Longest (1962). Twentieth Century-Fox Film Corporation. An epic war movie.

79. Frank Lloyd Wright memorial gas station, National Register of Historic Places, Minnesota Historical Society.

80. Borg (Star Trek), a fictional race of cyborgs in the Star Trek universe.

81. Moose, Kirby, Doc, Cage -- the squad on Combat! (1962-1967)

Chapter 13

Morning in the Silver Spur Tap.

The storm had raged long into the night, and they weathered it indoors. Shorty continued to go out every three hours to start the truck, beating a path through the drifts each time. He wisely parked near the building, so there was little chance of getting snowblind and lost on the way. Nevertheless, Dewane watched him out the window until he was safely in the cab with the motor running. They had discussed running a rope from the building to the truck, a pure northern Minnesota blizzard emergency measure.

In the old days a farmer would run a rope from the house to the barn, so they could follow it in the worst of conditions. However, you strung such a rope in preparation for blizzard. Trying to run such a rope in the teeth of it would be folly. They decided it wasn't needed – even at the worst of the gale they could still make out the shape of the truck, just outside the bar.

Margie fussed over Effie and over the child. Margie saw that Effie always had a warm drink at hand. The baby was still nursing, so when it could no longer be consoled, Effie would feed her – tits up. The men kept their backs discreetly turned. Mostly the baby slept.

(<o>).[].(<o>)

The men reviewed their exploit.

Shorty had been so worked up when they found the car that he'd stopped the truck and jumped out without setting the brakes. Skate was already on the ground by then. But Dewane was halfway out when the truck started to roll.

Dewane tried to pull himself back into the truck, but his momentum and truck moving unexpectedly had caused him to pitch out onto the running board, hollering at Shorty the whole while.

Shorty saw his mistake as soon as he hit the ground, and clambered back up into the cab right away, stopping the truck. But this caught Dewane as he was straightening himself, and lurched him into the open cab door, knocking his glasses off.

"Goddam it, Shorty," Dewane cursed.

"I got, I got," Shorty said, stopping the truck and then jumping back onto the road, leaving Dewane to fend for himself.

Dewane could have been killed, but he wasn't – just bruised on his forehead and knocked goofy for a minute.

By this time Skate, who was skittering into the shallow ditch at full speed, lost his footing and went sliding into the side of the car, careening down the ditch on his back.

He jumped to his feet and started feverishly scooping snow away from the passenger side door, which was nearest to the road. There was only an inch or two of the window showing – the car was almost completely buried in snow.

Shorty had a shovel.

"Stand away," he said.

Skate obeyed, and jumped onto the car's hood and swiped snow off the windshield and the roof with his arms.

Shorty started scooping snow, furiously, like he was really pissed off. Dewane turned up, his glasses back in place, with another shovel, and the two of them went at it, hammer and tongs, working their asses off.

It only took a couple of minutes to clear the snow from the upside door, by which time Skate had climbed over the top of the Bug, knocking snow off, and had landed on his feet, thigh deep in snow but in position to reach in when the door came free.

Dewane threw his shovel away when he saw it was clear enough, and yanked on the door handle with one foot planted on the car – exerting considerable force. Shorty was still shoveling. The door swung open, just as Shorty was lifting his shovel. The effect was the door swung wildly open and drove Shorty's shovel handle into his ribs.

Shorty exhaled a huge 'oof', dropped the shovel and then leaned over to pick it up. Meanwhile, Dewane lost his footing and stumbled as he swung the door open. The two of them collided and grappled each other but did not fall over.

Meanwhile, Skate dived into the car and after some frantic searching found the baby, covered with mounds of clothing. He was nearly hysterical with fear, but pressed his lips against the baby's face and found it was warm and responsive – the baby was cold and asleep, but alive.

He scooped up as much as his arms would hold, baby and clothing in an armload of swaddle, and backed out of the car, just in time to see Shorty and Dewane's clumsy embrace.

"Quit screwing around you guys," Skate said, joking, "let's get this kid out of here."

Dewane picked up his shovel. Shorty forgot about his, leaving it in the ditch forever.

They scrambled back into the truck, Skate now sitting in the middle with the baby cradled in his arms.

"Oh, man," Skate said, as Shorty started to turn the truck, "Crank up the heat. I hope this kid is okay."

"Rover," Shorty said, grim-faced and working it like a madman, "let's peel like a carrot."

He turned his truck on that dark icy road, no small trick, and took them home.

(<o>).[].(<o>)

They brought the baby into the warmth of the bar, and into the arms of it's mother. They felt like Green Beret's, and they had a right to. They had pulled off a king-hell rescue, and the day was saved.

They talked it over at length, like you do when you're still a little drunk and highly jazzed with energy, adrenaline, and success.

At midnight the power went out, as the storm howled and brought power poles to kindling. But Margie had lanterns for just this emergency, and the oil stove in the corner beamed heat without interruption.

Sometime around two in the morning, Skate laid down in a booth and caught a nap. Soon Shorty and Dewane followed his example, and Shorty set up a steady wheezing snore. The baby slept on the pool table nearest the stove, with barriers of cushions and clothing to keep it safe and warm. Margie and Effie stayed up and chatted like cousins do. Effie wrapped in blankets, with her feet in a washtub of water.

It had been agreed that someone would stay up with Effie, and at about 4AM, Margie shook Skate awake with a cup of coffee before she went to lay down herself.

(<o>).[].(<o>)

Skate sat beside Effie, facing the stove.

"You need anything?" he asked.

She was sitting on a straight-backed chair, bundled in blankets with her feet in a tub of warm water.

"No," she said, "Margie warmed the water. I'm just sitting here feeling my toes. They hurt like hell."

"Yeah, I'll bet," Skate said, thinking how bad they looked at first.

Frostbite was a funny thing. You could have a finger looking practically black that was saved. You could have an entire foot looking gray then pink, and lose the whole thing up to the ankle.

This was northwoods lore. Skate kept all this to himself.

They sat silently. Effie gave a little shiver from time to time.

"Keep pumping fluids," Skate said, "it's the best thing."

"Margie already made me drink a quart of water. Funny I don't feel a need to pee yet."

"Yeah," Skate countered, lamely, "that's how it works, sometimes. Freezing dehydrates you."

Skate got up and went behind the bar. He topped up her water pitcher and poured himself another cup of coffee and sat back down.

"I guess you know I've got to ask," he said, finally.

"Of course," she answered.

"I mean, the last time we spoke it was implied your baby was also mine." She nodded.

"It was more than implied. And when you left, I had no way to track you, and no information – just guilt.

He paused,

"And yet I can't help but notice," he smiled, "this beautiful little girl, a cute kid, by the way, is decidedly of the colored persuasion."

She hunched her shoulders.

"Effie," Skate went on, "the baby is black."

"Yes," she said tartly, "I know."

"And therefore not mine, yes?"

"Yes, yes, yes," she looked at him, somewhat fiercely, "she's half black and half mine."

"Yeah," Skate said softly, "I got that. You care to elaborate?"

"She was born March 14th."

"The eve of Ides," he noted.

She was silent.

"I mean," he said, still soft, "I just saved her life, after all."

284

He went on, "And you could drop the chip for a second, and tell me the story, for old time's sake."

(<o>).[].(<o>)

"He was a football player, " she nodded, "you knew him very briefly."

Skate puzzled over this, he didn't know any football players.

"You don't mean …"

"Yes, yes, Perry Rotbart," she sighed, "the late lamented."

Skate reeled. He relived the scene. The black man on the floor, Delmar in the doorway, the sound, the smell, the death.

"Wait a minute," he said, "you KNEW him?"

"Obviously, yes. I met him, the night before," she said, "I laid with him, he left."

"But whoa, that never came out at trial."

"No," she shrugged, "it never came up."

"So you were there…"

"Yes," she allowed, "I was watching."

She sagged.

"I was there watching because I'd been waiting for him the night before, to, uh, take things up again … and he came to the same bar, and immediately zeroed in on her, what's her name, without even seeing me. Like I wasn't there."

"Rexee'," Skate breathed, "her name is Rexee'."

"Yes, her."

"And Rexee'?"

"She scooped up the man," Effie said, "that I was waiting for. He did me the night before, and did not even see me that night. I waved 'hi', and he didn't know me."

"So you sat and watched them," Skate went on, "and you followed them home, and surprise…"

"Yes, surprise, they closed the bar and went out for more drinking, and finally stumbled back to our street."

"About five."

"Yes."

"And when the screaming started … later"

"Yes, yes," she said, "I heard it, and I saw Delmar go over, just as I testified."

"Just like that?"

"Well, no," she paused again, "not exactly. I saw him come out with his rifle, and he looked at me."

She sobbed.

"And I pointed," she said.

"Pointed?"

"Yes, I pointed across the street, so he knew where the sound was from."

They sat together. Skate put his arm around her.

"I've thought about this a thousand times," she said, "if I hadn't pointed, he might not have known where to go. But I think he did, anyway."

She stopped.

"I was mad at him, and really mad at her," she said piteously, "but I didn't want him to die. I just wanted to get them both in trouble – to embarrass them."

She shivered.

"I was mad at them," she repeated.

They sat together. Skate was at a loss, but there was more to know.

"So," he said, "when we started seeing each other – during the trial…"

"Yes," she replied, "I was already pregnant. I was stupid and young, and I didn't know at first, but yes, pretty soon I knew."

"And you didn't tell me?"

"No," she turned away, unable to look at him, "I didn't."

Skate reeled.

"And you let me believe …"

"Wait," she said, "at first I didn't know. I was stupid and young, and my period was always irregular."

She went on.

"At first, I really didn't know. Then you made me go to the doctor, and I was already more than five months along."

She stopped.

"But I wasn't showing, and I just couldn't tell you at that point," she looked him in the eyes again, "you were too nice, and the truth was too horrible, and it hardly showed."

They sat in silence.

"So I left."

They sat in silence some more.

It was getting close to morning, the sun was coming up, but Skate could barely see.

(<o>)/(13.6)\(<o>)

Delmar sauntered over from Washington Street, keeping a low profile. He didn't see Lon's truck, but that didn't mean much. In a town as small as Elysium you would park someplace and walk from joint to joint. If you were planning a lot of drinking you would park on the edge of town nearest home. That way you could sober up on the way to your car, and drive away from there, without driving through town where the police might be watching.

They looked for Lon's vehicle on the way into town, and had not seen it, either on the road or parked. But, again, that didn't mean much.

There was a car and van parked out front of Powder's Tap, but Lon's truck was not.

Powder's Tap was like most gin joints in the northwoods: two fairly large but largely unwashed windows facing the street, with a neon beer sign in each, and a recessed door in the corner of the building.

Delmar sidled up to the nearest window to peek in without being seen, not a big challenge.

There was knot of people sitting at the bar, and a few others at tables. He didn't really look at them, through the dirty window – just long enough to tell they were NOT Lon. He went back across the street to find Jack and Hank.

"Go on in," Delmar said, "he's not there. I'll keep looking up the street."

They walked together over to the bar, all three. Just as Jack and Hank were about to go in, Delmar stopped them.

"Go in and write down the phone number," he said, "if he's heading your way I'll call."

Jack and Hank went in, and Jack came right back out with a napkin.

"Stay here," Delmar said, "and rendezvous at the truck if I call."

Jack was already turning back towards the bar, where Hank was buying him a drink.

Delmar headed up the street, hunting for Lon, his stalking senses sharply honed by a week on patrol in the woods.

(<o>)/(13.7)\(<o>)

A one act play in several scenes:

Scene Thirteen –

The lights come up on the interior of Powder's Tap; a dimly lit, crummy little dive like so many others. It hasn't changed in thirty years, and certainly not since scene ten. Larry is still here, at the audience left end of the bar. He hasn't changed either.

Near Larry is a knot of people, standing with beer glasses. Hack and Skate are wearing jeans and work shirts. Rexee' is wearing painfully short cut off jeans and a diaphanous men's undershirt. Ace is wearing jeans and a t-shirt, as is Terry.

Two of the audience-right tables are occupied: the farthest right has Old man Sutter, who is slumped in his chair as though he had just come in from a 20 mile hike. He drinks brandy from a tall tumbler; he is sitting with Fat Henry, an enormous man dressed in blue overalls and a loose-fitting cotton shirt. Henry has a pink face and pours small shells of beer for himself from a pitcher. Near them, at the next table is Remo, wearing Army fatigue pants and shirt. Traci is wearing pink hotpants and a blouse tied at the waist, revealing her ample breasts, standing with her back to them, feeding quarters into the jukebox.

At the center of the bar a whipcord thin black man sits slumped over a fresh Bloody Mary; he is the picture of exhaustion.

It is Friday, July 2nd, 1976, just after Eleven P.M. in the Central Time Zone, in Powder's Tap, Elysium, Minnesota.

=#=#=#=

```
    Hack
(laughing)
… that was funny, that was good, "Hi Guys," like it was
nothing.
    Skate
(also laughing)
Hi yourself, you looking for us?
    Ace
Yeah, we practice deadpan on each other.
    Rexee'
(imperious)
We were led to believe this was all arranged.
```

287

Skate

You lookin' for us? You lookin' for us? Well, who the hell are you looking for? We're the only ones here.*

Rexee'
(turning away and gesturing to Larry the bartender)
You, who are you?

Larry
I'm Larry ma'am, I make the rules around here.

Rexee'
Larry, we're going to be friends, I can tell. You just need to be clear on one thing
(she jabs Ace in the chest).
This piece of crap is buying.

Ace
Larry, my man, any chance of starting up a bar tab here?
(Larry looks at Hack, Hack nods. It's settled.)

Terry
Hi Rex, you remember me?

Rexee'
(she regards him coolly)
It's been a long while since a wino vomited on my sidewalk. But not long enough. You paid your debts to society yet?

Terry
(looks around, shifty eyed, his head hunched into his shoulders)
I'll talk to you later.
(Terry walks over and sits with Remo at the table next to Henry and Old Man Sutter)

Skate
(glancing at Larry and whispering to Rexee')
Ix-nay,* seriously.

Rexee'
(shrugs and sits on a stool)
Yeah, Yeah, okay.
(The audience right door opens and two men enter: Hank and Jack. They are hulking brutes, cut from the same mold. The first goes to the bar. The second goes to the phone hanging at the audience right end of the bar, writes onto a napkin, and then goes back offstage through the same door.)

Hank
(sitting on a stool near the phone)
Two whiskey-waters, Larry.
(Jack comes back in and sits by Hank).

Jack
Beer back, Larry.

Terry
(sitting by Remo at the table next to Henry and Sutter)
Okay I sit here?

Remo
Sure, you know these guys?

Terry
A long time now, but I've been gone a long while, just about
five years.

Remo
Prison?

Terry
Sort of, yeah.

Remo
(producing a deck of cards)
You play gin?
(strains of Elvis fill the bar, Traci turns away from the
jukebox and sits at the nearest table, with Remo and Terry)

Traci
I'd like to play. Who are you (to Terry), you're cute.

Terry
Just a traveler, ma'am. Pleased to know you.
(he reaches out and they shake hands)
(the lights go down as the bar breaks off into clumps of
conversation. A spotlight jumps from clump to clump, the bulk
of the bar recedes into shadow)

Skate
(to Ace)
Ace, man, We've got some shit to deal with, I'm glad you're
here. This is not your ordinary shit, it is special shit, like
highly active full bore shit. The real stinky deal.

Hack
(Hack looks at Skate, and Ace)
That might be an overstatement, but Yeah, we've uncovered a
mystery. It beats me what to do.

Ace
Heavy, Sounds heavy. Fill me in?

Skate
Better to show you, we are thinking, right Hack? The less said
here, the better.

Hack
Yeah, more Ix-nay.

Rexee'
(swiveling on her stool)
More Ix-nay! What the hell? More secrets?

Ace
Yes, Ex-Ray, I think "shut the fuck up" is the expression
we're looking for at this special bicentennial moment.

Rexee'
No, I think "screw you" is closer.

Hack
More later, count on it. C'mon Rex.
(Rexee' slides off her stool, her feelings are hurt, and she
moves down the bar, sitting by Jack and Hank. The spotlight
follows her)

Rexee'
What are you two beefcakes up to?

Jack

Sittin'. Drinkin' The usual for a Friday.

Rexee'

You boyos seem like healthy stock. Are you brothers, or cousins, or what?

Hank

Yup, we're kin.

Rexee'

And doing what? Doing what to get by?

Jack

(Jack leers at Rexee')
We're soldiers on leave, home from the war. Looking for a good time.

Rexee'

And females, right? Looking for nooky, hippy nooky. That's what a soldier boy does. Admit it.

Jack

Yeah, that'd be good.

Rexee'

Yes, I bet it would.
(The spotlight goes to Henry and Sutter)

Henry

You been here before?

Sutter

Never.

Henry

You been this far from home before?

Sutter

I've been to Cuba, Henry, this is nothing to me.

Henry

This is it for me. The farthest I've ever been.

Sutter

Enjoy it, this could be just the beginning.
(The spotlight goes back to Ace, Skate, and Hack. Larry the bartender has his back turned.)

Ace

Okay, Ix-nay for now.
(looking at Larry's back).
How did the plywood work out?

Hack

Finest kind.

Skate

Finest, yeah. We've built ourselves a first-class cabin in the finest bicentennial tradition, and we've gone across the lake to fetch Terry, in the finest anti-war tradition. And we've dug up a deep-dyed mystery. A full-bore holy fuck what is this, are you kidding, who-done-it crap bag.
(pauses to sip his beer)
Pretty much the usual web routine.

Hack

(deadpan) Same old, same old.
(The spotlight goes back to Terry, Remo, and Traci).

Traci

I just wanted to get away, you know. Get away from the stuff I was stuck with. I haven't been out of my usual routine for a long time. I just wanted to get away for a few days. Find a little bit of peace.

Terry

In a way it's the opposite for me. I've been away, and away too long, and I just wanted to get back. I've been stuck in a place, and had about enough, you know, I was sick of where I was and wanted to get back to where I was before. That's all.

Traci

We're sort of the same, it looks to me. The regular life is not SO bad, but a newer life might be better. Once you get stuck, you can get really stuck.

Terry

Oh, yeah, I hear that. I know what you mean. Any too much of any one thing is too much for sure, you know what I mean?

Traci

(dreamily) I'd like to be a new person. I'd like to get into a new place. I think so. I really think so.

Terry

I know so.

Remo

Are we playing or not? Terry, draw, would'ya?
(The spotlight goes to Rexee', Jack and Hank)

Rexee'

So, there's more to Elysium than I've seen so far.

Hank

Yeah, we're just at the edge of town. There's a lot of bars up the road.

Rexee'

Well maybe you should show me these places. Maybe there's more to life than just sitting here. You boys ought to show me around, don't you think?

Jack

(hunching his shoulders)
I'd like to, I would. I'd like to take you out, and, and,

Rexee'

And make a night of it.

Jack

Yeah, make a night of it. But, we can't.
(The phone rings, and Hank lunges for it, but Larry is there first)

Larry

Powders.
(Larry listens for a moment, then hands the phone to Jack)
It's for you.

Jack

(speaking into the phone)

Yeah. Yeah. Okay.
(Jack hangs up the phone, and speaks to Hank)
We've got to go. Drink up.
(the spotlight goes to Calvin, sitting center stage. He sits
upright and swivels on his stool)

    Calvin
Let's move people. It's been too long. We need to finish this
trip, once and for all. Let's go, the bus is leaving.

   (Blackout).

(<o>)/(13.8)\(<o>)

diaria -- 13.0 -- 6/25/77 -- Big Sur

Cover the story, that's the gig.

This is the story of the guys in all their different
guises, and blah blah like that. But one can hardly tell
their story without telling about their times. And
hardly tell about the times without telling about the
war. And the scene on the street. It was the "late-
sixties-early-seventies" which was an era and a label
for the times used at the time, although you won't find
it as such in most contemporary histories. It was a
category of music, too. As in,

"What music do you listen to?"

"Jazz and Blues, mostly -- you?"

"Late sixties, early seventies."

And as much as I resist it, you can't really cover the
story unless you cover "illegal substances".

"I saw the best minds of my generation destroyed by
madness, starving hysterical naked, dragging themselves
through the negro streets at dawn looking for an angry
fix."*

I don't really want to, because the time I tell this and
the time you read this is nothing like the time this all
happened. Just as I was raised to be appalled at the
lunch-counter, back-of-the-bus racism in the post-war
south, you, reading this, might have been raised to be
appalled at the irresponsible social climate of the
late-sixties-early-seventies (which was the tail end of
the sixties, at least in the Midwest, where this story
takes place). Or maybe the pendulum has swung, as it
will often do, and you've been raised to applaud these
times as a monument to freedom and humanist ideals.

Because I'm here to tell you both these impressions are
right and wrong at the same time. And so there's no easy
way to say what was there, they were there all the time,
and they were everything but they were nothing.

Like art, they were in there, they were out there, and
they were nowhere.

As my good friend Ken sed "Psychedelic Sixties. God knows that whatever that means it certainly meant far more than drugs, though drugs still work as a handle to the phenomena. I grabbed that handle."*

How can I tell you that it was just a prohibition era thing, like booze to my grandparents. Or margarine to my parents. It was all illegal.

But it was openly done, and it screwed some people up pretty bad, especially after there was real money in it. But it was casual too, and a dirty underground thrill at the same time.

Cover the story, my good friend Hunter sez, for good or ill.

Okay, reportage, here goes.

There was pot around in high school, which was the late sixties, and many got into it, each to their own degree. Meanwhile, the war was on and their age group was keenly aware of the irony that they could vote, and they could go to war, and drive cars, and pay taxes, but they were not supposed to drink.

The logic behind this, to them, then, was laughably dismissible, so there was never a time when "prohibition" was taken seriously as a moral or legal precept.

I mean, come on, I can get snatched out of my life by the draft, I can go to a foreign country and kill or be killed, but I'm not mature enough to have alcohol pass my lips?

Again, you might be reading this in a time where that reasoning makes sense somehow -- but to the guys it was absurd, and never treated as serious.

And once you've made that small leap, the idea of prohibition in general lacks much authority.

Yes, yes, it was the rule of law. But we'd just been through a time, raised you might say, on the rightness of civil disobedience where the law was wrong.

This is a reference back to the back-of-the-bus racism thing. If the laws were wrong, in that case the voting laws, in this case the prohibition laws, then you were right to break them. There was a joke on the streets at the time that went, delivered in a black ghetto voice, "if loving jesus is wrong, then I don't want to be right." Then too, there was the draft to resist.

Anyway, there was pot around, and booze too, but in some ways, pot was easier to get. In the summer after high school, when the guys were just assembling into the web house, there were also downers on the scene -- reds and yellow jackets -- seconal and demerol, technically speaking. The guys didn't indulge in these, much, as they were hard to get relative to pot unless you were connected, which they weren't and didn't feel the need to be.

The next summer, 1971, was "acid summer" and all sorts of exotics started to appear, orange barrels, primarily. The purple haze of stage and song were gone from the scene by then. Also brown "pharmaceutical" psilocybin and psilocybin mushrooms (pronounced sill'-o-sy-bin) and peyote buttons (pronounced pay-oh'-tay).

The orange barrels were Tiger's downfall. He started tripping, seeing shapes and colors and gawd-knows-what, then went to that Who concert in 1971 with the guys, and never came down. This was a phenomena of the times -- some people "never came down" and wandered off through their next years as head cases. A few people were casualties that way, with an etiology something like addiction.

They were up and they didn't want to come down, or they couldn't get down, and the drugs were in them for freaking ever. I don't know if there's a medical explanation for this. I tend to think these were people destined to jump off some building at some point.

There was some cocaine around in those years, but it was expensive and also hard to obtain.

These are not the late seventies or the eighties, when the war was long over and excess was its own reward. These are a different time, when the spectre of the war and, in some measure the atomic bomb, cast a shadow over everything.

On the other hand, I can't kid you, this wasn't debauch with a political agenda, not really. It was debauch for the sake of it, but under the pall of politics.

If you were there, you maybe remember and know what I mean. If you weren't there, then there's only so much that anyone can tell you. Wherever you're coming from, or wherever you are, you're going to read this through the filter of your time, whatever century or era you happen to be in.

I can't explain it any better than that. So it goes.*

Cover the story, that's the gig.

(<o>)/(13.9)\(<o>)

The things he felt through out his life were doubt and hesitation's oily fear. When it came time to act, or simply make a choice, it gave him pause. What if he made a choice that could not ever be undone?

You're raised on guns and war and heroes in the fight against the evils of the world. You learn what you are told, and take it in to where you live your life. But then you're told to go and fight –and you're not fighting tyranny, your fighting for the tyrant side. How can that work? But then, of course, you ask, what can you do? What else?

You can't say no, or can you, now?

Resist, your friends will say to you. But how? You took the Queen's hard shilling when you came into the world. You got to play in parks and learn to swim. You lolled around through summer days and ate fast food. You joined the scouts, and went to prom, and drifted through your youth.

Then comes the time to pay the piper and you do not want to go.

It's wrong.

But there's a membrane on your brain, and it won't go away. You're raised to serve, and if you don't, it's just as wrong. Or close.

Equivocation reigns, and there's the rub. He sobs, he wails, he hurts this throat, his kingdom, for he's hoarse.

(<o>)/(13.10)\(<o>)

Delmar worked his way up the street, crossing from joint to joint. There were about fifteen bars in town, not all of them on the main drag, so he had to criss-cross in order to make sure he was covering the terrain without letting the prey slip behind him. There were times, when he was north of the main road, he worried that Lon might get past him while his back was turned. So he had to move quickly, but without drawing attention to himself. It was a complex mission.

After thirty minutes Delmar had traversed the main drag, and never found Lon. This meant one of two things. Either Lon was somewhere off the main drag, visiting a friend or tending to other business, or Lon had left town. If Lon had left town, Lon might be headed for home – FUBAR.*

There was no choice. The mission must be aborted. Since he couldn't locate Lon, the worst must be assumed. They had better get their asses back to base, or they would be found derelict in their duty.

Delmar dropped the dime.

Then he moved swiftly and quietly back to their vehicle, which they had parked near the tracks, and which took him back past Powder's Tap on the far end of town.

(<o>)/(13.11)\(<o>)

They boiled out of the bar.

Calvin led the way, followed by Henry, who did not dare to be left behind, with a cold 12-pack of package beer under his arm, and then Sutter who was closest to the door. Then Terry, Remo, and Traci. Then Jack and Hank and Rexee'. And finally, Hack and Skate and Ace, after paying the tab.

Twelve souls on the sidewalk, it was a churning chaos.

"Get in the van," Calvin ordered anyone listening, "the bus is leaving."

"I'll ride with you," Traci said to Terry.

"No, there'd be no room in the pickup. I'll ride with you."

"Can you find the place?" Hack asked Ace.

"Yeah, easy, but we'll follow you anyway," Ace answered.

"Skate," Hack said, unconvinced, "you better ride with them, I'll take Ace, and we'll meet you there."

"Gotcha," Skate said, "I'll see you back at the ranch."

"Where you boys off to," Rexee' said to Jack.

"Back to Lon's, I think," Jack answered, "we're still on duty."

Jack and Hank headed north, towards the rendezvous.

Rexee' started to walk with them, but Hack tugged softly at her arm.

"Stay with the group," he told her, "at least for tonight."

Rexee' didn't like it, she didn't like rules. But she would listen, if it made sense. Hack usually made sense. She waited.

The gang was scattering in every direction.

Rexee' turned towards the van just in time to see it lurch to starboard with Henry's weight as he clambered aboard. Sutter hoisted himself in behind. Everyone else seemed willing to wait. After a day in the van, it was no joy to jump back on..

"Remo," Ace said, "why don't you ride with us?"

Remo nodded and shuffled behind them.

Calvin was getting strident.

"Get on the bus!" he shouted since nobody was listening, "we NEED to go. The bus is LEAVING."

The crowd mostly obeyed, even Rexee', piling on in good order.

Terry sat on the luggage with Traci. Skate jumped into the front seat, where Ace had been. Rexee' moved forward to see out the front.

"Everybody set?" Skate hollered, "here we go."

Calvin got the gang in gear. The van lurched away from the curb just as Hack's pickup turned in front of them from the side street, now with Ace and Remo on board. They convoyed slowly north and east towards the other end of town – the wilderness end.

They were sloshy and jolly, moving out into the night towards the woods and the lakes, as happy as could be.

(<o>).[].(<o>)

Delmar stood across the way, with rising bile.

He had scoured the town, looking for Lon, and found him not. Now he was back to collect his troops, and his brain could not believe his eyes. There they were, the instruments of his destruction, plus those damnable barflys, all standing in a group on the pavement, laughing and hollering, and milling around like they were normal or something.

Delmar seethed.

That Hack, and the cripple, walked away east with that other guy, the one who talked to him sometimes. The rest of them piled into their van, including the bastard who fried him in court, that curse, whatsisname, who had been the cause of all his trouble. And that witch was with them too, talking to Jack and Hank!

Delmar simmered.

Jack and Hank stood with the enemy for a moment, and then crossed the street towards their truck, parked on Washington.

Delmar angled to meet them. His anger was both new and old, hot and cold.

"Boys," he shouted, "made some friends, did you?"

Jack and Hank stopped short, harkening to his voice.

"Yeah, I guess," Jack said, wary of Delmar's hard tone, "where's Lon?"

"I don't know, and that's the problem," Delmar answered fiercely, "let's go. Let's just fucking go. Now. Move!"

(<o>).[].(<o>)

The van pulled away from the curb, steered by Calvin and guided by Skate, heading east by north.

Rexee' screamed, "Did you see that!"

"What, Rex?" Calvin muttered, riven and intent on his driving, "what is it?"

"That bastard, that turd!" she screamed.

She was swiveled on her knees, trying to look out the back windows through the jumble of people and luggage in the van.

"Stop! stop the van!"

"Hell no," Calvin said, "we're moving, finally."

Calvin was concentrated and determined.

"If we get lost now, we're cooked," Calvin hissed, "and that is not going to happen."

After eleven hours of driving, and the end in sight, Calvin had his eyes locked on the pickup in front of him, and after this long, long day of driving, Calvin just wanted to follow it home. He was drop-dead tired of driving, and locked on a target. Nah, negatory, he could not improvise at this point. He was an ass-bandit, just going with the ass-end of that pickup, wherever it went.

Wherever it went, he would follow – focused, locked in, and staring into the darkness like a bare-knuckle boxer on a white-knuckle mission, trying to finish the round, to go and go and go. When you need to keep punching, you keep punching, when you need to keep moving, you keep moving.

They kept moving, slowly eastward down the main drag.

"Shit!" Rexee' said, turning to face front, "I swear I just saw that murdering turd. I swear it was him."

"Delmar?" Skate said, his flight/fright meter rising.

Startled into craning his neck, trying to see, but seeing nothing, he was happy to believe she was wrong.

"Not too likely, Rex, not much chance."

"Yeah, well, whaddayou know?"

Skate had no answer except, "C'mon, Rex."

She had been tracking Hank and Jack, and thought she saw Delmar. This was so weird, even Rexee' had to dismiss it.

She turned back to look at the passengers behind her, shortening her focus, "Henry, my love, how about one of those beers?"

(<o>)/(13.14)\(<o>)

Lon was sitting in the Portage Bar, about the middle of town, next to the grocery store, when he saw Hack's truck go by. It was after 11 PM and he was getting tired of sitting by himself. He was thinking of calling it a night. The 'being a target' plan was no plan at all, and it was starting to wear thin.

He also noticed the van following closely behind Hack. It was unknown to him, and Lon was vigilant to new and unknown vehicles. Like many American males, he had a good memory for trucks and cars, and being from a small town, was able to easily pick out which were local and which were not. In this case, the pickup was local, and the van was not.

The van appeared to be full of berry pickers and was following very closely. He concluded they were city friends of Hack's. He was turning back to his drink when he saw Jack, Hank, and Delmar drive by in his truck.

"What the hell," he thought, "are those idiots doing in town?"

They were supposed to patrolling the property while he was away.

Lon slammed a dollar onto the bar and ran out into the street in time to see his truck stopped at the red light a block down the road. By this time, the van was disappearing behind Hack out the far end of town.

Lon started to run towards the truckful of his so-called employees. But the light changed just then, and his truck took off before he got close.

Lon continued at a jog on to his brother's house, over one street. He parked in his brother's garage for his nights in town, not trusting to leave his vehicle out where shed-burning vandals might do him even more harm.

(<o>).[].(<o>)

"This is good," Delmar said as they waited at the light, "let them get ahead."

The light turned green, and Jack pulled slowly through the intersection. Like most northwoods drivers, he rarely looked in his rear-view mirror, so he did not see Lon sprinting after them, a block behind.

"What's the deal, Delmar?"

"I need to know where they're going. We will need to pay them a visit later."

They trailed the van, a discrete distance in town, and then letting the gap increase once they were on the wooded country roads. Jack didn't complain, the van was leading them towards home anyway.

"No sign of Lon?" Hank asked after a while.

"None."

"Well, then, we need to get back in case he beats us to camp."

"We'll be okay," Delmar gritted his teeth, without explanation.

They proceeded along the hilly east-climbing paved county road, following the twin pair of taillights This was the main east-west route, and they met a few cars along the way, coming into town from various campsites.

After six miles of twists and turns on the paved county road, the convoy turned right onto the gravel township road that itself looped left and paralleled the county road for a time. They were essentially still heading east, although it was difficult to keep direction sense in the dark. They were still on their road home.

"Are they heading to Lon's place?" Jack asked.

"Let's hope not," Hank answered, "we're supposed to be on duty."

The gravel township road contoured through a sequence of valleys.

They were the only vehicles out there.

"Stop the truck," Delmar said, "and turn off the headlights."

Jack pulled over and did as he was told. The van, already around a bend and out of sight, continued on behind Hack's truck. They could still see glimpses of lights through the woods, off in the distance.

"Close your eyes," Delmar ordered, "we need to get used to the dark."

They sat by the side of the road, engine idling, for twenty long seconds.

"Okay," Delmar said, "get after them. But no headlights."

Jack looked across Hank at Delmar.

"You heard me," Delmar said, "there's the moon, and you know the road. Look ahead, you can see well enough. And this way, they won't see us behind them. Get going."

It was true. On a moonlit night, with a clear country sky, and knowledge of the road, you can drive without headlights. Once your eyes are adjusted to the gloaming, it's actually pretty easy.

Jack took off, slowly at first, but gradually faster. It's exhilarating to drive at night without lights. He took to it right away. They gained ground quickly.

Soon they saw the taillights of the van, creeping along the gravel in front of them. Hack was taking it easy so that Calvin could keep up. It didn't take long to catch them.

"Get up behind them," Delmar ordered, "but don't tailgate. Twenty or thirty yards is close enough."

Jack obeyed.

"They'll never see us – they'll never think to look back, and they wouldn't see us, even if they looked."

Jack nodded, intent on his mission.

"Stay off the brakes, though," Delmar cautioned, "they might see taillights."

(<o>).[].(<o>)

The road to Unkafrank Lake is a twisting gravel python laid over the landscape to avoid engineering and construction costs. Back in the woods, a road will often go around a hill rather than over or through it. A steep grade is treacherous and hard to clear in the winter. A road that avoids hills is longer, but cheaper in the long run. As a consequence, the 'east bound lane' of a township road is often heading westward.

The convoy, now three, continued up the winding gravel for another fifteen minutes. They knew where Jackson and his buddies were going, but they did not know where Lon was.

"Lon's place is coming up," Hank said, "what if he's there?"

"We'll find out," Delmar said grimly.

When they came to Lon's driveway, Delmar had them stop. He pulled a flashlight out of the glove compartment, and played it over the chain.

"He's not here yet," Delmar announced, "I left a twig in the chain, and it's still there. We're okay."

"Hank," Delmar went on, "Jump out and take your position. Me and Jack are going to keep on with this."

Hank jumped out, and they went on. Jack, by now, was confident with driving without lights. He barreled down the road, and they were in time to see the van pull off onto Hack's logging trail slash driveway, turning left towards the lake.

"I thought so," Delmar said, "they're just up the creek from us."

"Turn around, go back," he went on, "this is going to be easy."

(<o>).[].(<o>)

Lon was in his own driveway, fuming at Hank, when they pulled up.

"What are you guys doing in town!" he was shouting, for the third time, when they coasted up.

Delmar stepped out.

"We were tracking a lead, Lon," he said evenly, "there was activity on the property and we followed them out. Maybe we should have stayed, but we left Hank at the gate and took out after them."

Delmar opened his palms to Lon, "I know you've been trying to find out who was behind it all, I thought we had a suspect. Maybe we were wrong."

"He's lying," Lon thought to himself, "I just saw the whole bunch drive through downtown. All three of them – Hank too."

Lon cooled.

"What did you find out?" he asked.

"They're just up the road, Lon, two driveways."

"Jackson!" Lon said, "I don't believe it."

"Sorry, Lon," Delmar said, "that's the story. What do we do now, that's the question."

(<o>).[].(<o>)

Friday, July 2nd, 1976, near midnight.

The two-car convoy pitched over the last rise and glided down to the shores of Unkafrank Lake. Hack stopped his truck near the campfire, and Calvin stopped the van next to him. Their lights shone over the construction site and onto the black waters of the lake. The new cabin stood to their left, the old burned-out home cabin was behind them.

Everybody got out into the darkness.

"First thing, I suppose, is a really big fire," Hack said, "some of you grab an armload of wood from the pile over there, and I'll get something started."

(<o>).[].(<o>)

The fire was roaring, the night was warm, and they soon broke into two groups. Hack, Skate, Ace, Remo, and Rexee' sat outside around the campfire. Henry, Sutter, Terry, Traci, and Calvin settled into the cabin which Skate illuminated with lanterns.

"I've got my little trailer, which can take one or two," Hack announced.

There was plenty of floor space in the cabin for everyone.

"Does anybody have a tent they want to pitch?"

"Yeah," Remo said, "show me a good spot, and I'll throw down my tent."

"This way, Remo," Skate said, pointing up the rise, "C'mon, I'll give you a hand."

Henry soon saw there were no private accommodations, so he unpacked in the back corner of the cabin, laying his blankets and pillows out under the loft.

Considering the group, it was a quiet night. They were mostly exhausted from their day, which involved many miles and many visits to Sutter's liquor cabinet, and it was late and dark.

Hack and Ace used the come-along to drag a couple of big logs over by the fire, to provide extra seating, and for a while they all sat around the flames, facing the fire with their butts planted on unstripped logs.

Stories were told, jokes emerged, commentary was exchanged.

"Did you see the pile of luggage Traci brought?" Remo asked, "I've seen battalions move out with less gear."

"I looked at the van," Ace said, "bursting at the seams, and I said to myself 'I can do this – and if I can't do it, then fuck it, it can't be done."

"And," Sutter added, dryly, "at that point, we still needed to get Rexee's and your stuff, too."

"This was all part of the executive calculation," Ace nodded sagely, "and my faith that anything can be packed into anything, if you shove hard enough."

"Hey," Traci said, "nobody told me what to bring, and a girl needs to be ready for anything, doesn't she?"

"There is no doubt," Sutter acknowledged, raising his glass, "that everybody needs to be ready for everything."

"Fuckin-A," Remo answered, raising his glass.

"I'm ready for another jolt," Rexee' said, raising her glass too, "who's got some hooch of the liquid persuasion?"

Sutter poured whiskey, but they had forgotten to pick up any ice. Henry had cold beer, but that quickly disappeared.

One by one, they faded from the campfire scene. Calvin was first, exhausted from driving all day, and still thinking he might get up early and go fishing – he crept into the cabin and found sleep. Remo went up to his tent. Henry and Sutter followed Calvin down to the cabin and curled up.

Terry prevailed on Hack to let him and Traci have the trailer, so, later, Hack ended up spending his one and only night in the cabin.

Rexee' and Ace and Skate and Hack ended up around the campfire, long after midnight, when everyone else had gone to lay down.

"It's quiet here," Rexee' said, "way too quiet."

(<o>)/(13.20)\(<o>)

"Lily," Annie said, "I'm closing after breakfast, and taking off for the weekend."

"That man," crooned Lily of the Alley, "e's good an yu."

Annie blushes. This crone sees through her, and seems to know things, and mysteries described are secrets revealed. Morning after morning, they chat, or sometimes they just sit, and Annie feels a calm sometimes that can't be handled or predicted. It's just two women, thousands of generations apart, who see eye to eye.

"So you understand, right? Breakfast somewhere else tomorrow, I won't be here."

Lily stoops, which is her way to nod.

"Unless, you know, you want to take a trip," Annie ventures, "you could come along and see the forest."

The toothless crone smiles at that.

"Nae for me," she waves her hand, "there's nae for me up there."

Lily cackles.

301

"But yu," she adds, "will nae be beck the same."

"It's dark and let thet way," Lily adds, "bleck and wet, god and aevil. Ye'll see it both, but ye'll be beck. Not temorrow, may, but soon efter."

"I'm coming back on Sunday, Lily, and I'll be here Monday morning. Don't worry. I'll see you then."

"Wurried? Nae. I see fane. Be fretful, thet's m'advace."

"Like usual," Annie said, "I don't' quite get you. All I worry is that you'll eat tomorrow morning. Promise me you will, okay?"

Lily stooped, which is her way to nod.

(<o>).[].(<o>)

Book had the keys to the war wagon, as Ace called it, and the engine was purring. His parents kept this 1969 Chevrolet Chevelle Station Wagon just for him to borrow. He was not much of a driver, and rarely needed a car, but when he did, the war wagon was there for him, and he appreciated the availability.

Here, for once, he was taking a trip out of town, which his parents endorsed as "good for him", and he was scripted to make it happen. The script, as follows.

First, Patrick and Carol, then Annie as she was closing the diner. By 8 AM they would be on the road, and by 1 PM they would be in Elysium. Then it was just a matter of Book remembering the way from town to Hack's place, which he had done several times as a boy, but which could be a problem with the diminishing memory of passing time. Still, he could see it, and Ace had sketched out a map, so nothing was likely to go amiss.

The war wagon was strong and tuned, and little could go wrong.

Except Carol. Carol could go wrong, if that was the right word, in that she was about two million months pregnant and could deliver up a little Patrick at any moment. Still, what were the odds of a baby coming to term at exactly the moment they were driving to Elysium? Astronomical, probably.

That was an expression Book liked, "astronomical odds." People used it from time to time, but usually without knowing what it meant. Book knew what it meant, in precise mathematical terms.

Book loaded his gear onto the war wagon: clothes, equipment, and books – lots of books. Not least of which was a birthing manual. Book was a librarian, and he didn't actually DO much of anything, but he liked to be prepared, prepared, prepared, for anything.

Book threw his last gunny sack into the back of the wagon, and shut the tailgate. Then he got behind the wheel and eased out onto the street. He chose a good angle and a good slow speed, and still there was a lurch as he went down the minor incline from Rexee's parking lot. The war wagon did not scrape bottom, it had a good smooth suspension – not even close. He was on the road.

It was Saturday, July 3rd, 1976, in the early morning. The Bicentennial beckoned.

(<o>).[].(<o>)

Carol was not huge, she was normal. Book had not seen her lately, and with the pregnancy announcement, expected her to be really, really huge. She wore a smock with a loose t-shirt and moved with a sort of duck walk

"My," Book said to her, "you don't look very pregnant."

Carol smiled peacefully. She didn't actually know Book that well, but enough to get that he was harmless and without a stitch of malice or rancor.

"Looks deceive, Book," she laughed softly, "right now I'm technically pregnant, and visibly pregnant. Except in the morning, occasionally still, when I feel miserable, which is the only time I'm mechanically pregnant."

"Reverse peristalsis," Patrick walked out with two backpacks.

"Yeah," Carol said, "medical retching."

Book and Carol stood back while Patrick hauled gear.

"Any weird dreams?" Book asked.

"Oh, lord," Carol gasped, looking at him, a little startled.

"I read about it," Book shrugged, "it's the hormones. Most women report weird dreams during pregnancy."

"Oh, thank you for telling me that," Carol blushed, "I've had such bizarre dreams I thought I was losing it. So weird I've been working on NOT thinking about them."

"Normal," Book replied, "not weird – or so it says in the reading I've seen."

Carol nodded, gratefully and wordlessly.

Patrick shut the tailgate.

"All set, I think. You ready hon?"

Carol nodded again, and moved to climb into the back seat.

"Alright, Book," Patrick said, "it's time to put your foot down, and go and go and go."

They both laughed, and climbed in, and went.

(<o>)/(13.23)\(<o>)

In the fifties and sixties it was more common than subsequently for families to pack up in the summer and take 'family trips'. Sometimes this entailed real camping with tents and such, and this being Minnesota often involved 'going up to the lake'.

Patrick's family did this most frequently. More often, at least with the guys, this amounted to Mom and Dad renting a trailer or a camper, and picking a destination, and packing everyone in the car for a week or two of long distance driving. Along the way, depending on equipment and family tradition, there would be small roadside motels or campgrounds or trailer parks.

Yellowstone, the Grand Canyon, Yosemite were common destinations in one direction.

Washington, DC, Montreal for the World's Fair in 1967, or even New York City, were common in the other direction.

DisneyLand, or later DisneyWorld, or simply Florida, were common otherwise.

Hack was the exception.

His family never 'took a trip' – however it was fairly usual for him to be away with his family 'up north'. As a consequence, there were periods every summer when somebody from the group was absent because their family was gone.

In a way this was good, as it unsettled the social dynamic a bit, and might lead to two guys hanging around together a little more than they might have normally.

This was particularly true when Ace and his family were away, since we all gravitated to his house for the most part, where he always seemed to have ideas about what to do that day. In his absence the rest of us got together in a slightly different format, and while the differences were not necessarily profound, they were not without significance.

Ace was out of town, for example, when we found the raft.

(<o>).[].(<o>)

Go and go and go – this was an old Web laugher.

Patrick and his family had taken a trip out east, and stayed an extra night in Baltimore. So they were pressed to get back in time for his father to be at work on Monday.

They made it to Cleveland by Friday evening, and started from there early Saturday morning. The idea was to make the drive in two jumps, stopping somewhere in the middle, and arriving back home by Sunday afternoon. But by mid-afternoon on Saturday they had made such good progress they decided to keep going.

So they drove from Cleveland to Minneapolis in one shot, a stretch of over 700 miles in the family car, in the days before the Interstate system was completed. That is, on a lot of two lane country highways, where the speed limit was just 60 miles per hour, and you had to stop at the sign in the middle of every little burg and one horse town along the way.

When they finally got home, it was nearly midnight, but still Saturday. The parents decided to leave the car packed in the driveway, and unload in the morning. Everybody just crawled out of the car, exhausted by the trip, stumbled into the house, and went to bed.

The next morning, they were unpacking the car when Book's father drove by with Book in the car. Book's dad stopped the car and rolled down the window, calling out, "Long trip?"

Patrick's dad stopped to talk, and said, "Yeah, a long day yesterday."

"That's what we do too," Book's dad said, "we get in the car, and I just put my foot down, and we just go and go and go."

Patrick's dad nodded.

"Like yesterday," Book's dad went on, "we had a real marathon. We came down from the cabin in Detroit Lakes in one shot, hardly stopped at all. That's over 200 miles."

Book's dad put the car in gear.

"We just go and go and go," he said as he pulled away.

(<o>)/(13.25)\(<o>)

"What the hell," Hack said.

Book looked back over his shoulder at Patrick.

"A raft," Skate said, "this could be fun."

They were on the shores of the Mississippi, just north of Camden Bridge in the "wilderness" along the river that existed in the 1960s.

It wasn't much to look at, just a few rough boards nailed onto three thick, short poles. A rope was nailed to one corner of one pole. The other end was tied to a slender tree by the riverbank. The whole thing was no bigger than a sheet of plywood. But it appeared willing to float. When Hack stepped onto it, there was a little settling, but not too much.

"What you guys think?" Hack said.

Book looked pale. Patrick was silent.

Skate said, "you know, I've always wondered about that island."

Ace was away with his family on a trip.

If he'd been there, Ace might have led the charge. Or, he might have advised against. For one thing, this was a raft made by others, more industrious than them – kids that were probably older and tougher.

It was a fair sized wooded area they roamed, and they seldom saw anybody else, but when they did, they invariably looked aggressive and tough. The guys tended to avoid contact with these groups. It was safer that way. Indeed, many of their woodcraft skills were developed and honed in their efforts to avoid other kids and avoid being seen. They were Scouts, but they were also spies, and they played 'guns' as children – all training for moments such as these.

Meanwhile, without doubt, some bigger and older kids had built a raft, and left it there. The guys were thinking about stealing it for a joy ride. The implications were manifold. They could find themselves adrift in the river and possibly drown. Or they could get themselves in REAL trouble if the bigger, older kids found out they had stolen the raft.

This was a perilous adventure that could carry severe ramifications.

Book and Patrick were shrinking with intent to shirk. Hack and Skate were a little bolder, at that sunny moment, and intent on taking the plunge.

Skate stepped aboard, joining Hack. There were loose boards laying on the raft for paddles.

"I say safety first," Skate looked back at Book and Patrick, "we're good swimmers. You guys hang here for the first trip."

He thought for a second. What would Ace do?

"You guys stay put and keep an eye out. If somebody comes, run for Hack's house and we'll meet you there. If we make it okay, we'll come back and get you."

Skate looked at Hack, "Okay?"

Hack nodded, then said to Patrick, "Untie us."

(<o>).[].(<o>)

The guys lived on the north side of Minneapolis in the eastern neighborhoods towards the Mississippi River. Considering how close they lived, and the storied history of old man ribber, there was little about the river injected into their lives. In a smaller town there might have been more activity on the riverside, picnics and band concerts and public events. But in north Minneapolis there was little or nothing. The area along the river was controlled by public entities: the city and the state. But it in those days it was not viewed as 'a resource'.

In that stretch of the river there are no less than a dozen small uninhabited islands. To the guys these were tantalizingly close, and yet implausibly far away. For although they were river people of a sort, they were not boating people. And while their parents made them take swimming lessons in the public

305

pool, they were instructed to never swim in the Mississippi – the river being relatively swift and dangerous.

Mostly it was wild acres of public land, untended by anyone and largely uncontrolled, but with trails and hiding spots and massive trees, and equally massive storm sewer pipes. It was a micro-wilderness with a criss-cross of trails and hiding places.

It is hard to describe the freedom the guys felt down there. They knew the whole area.

They could tell when a stone was overturned, or when a hobo was wandering the river banks, because they were there all the time. They learned about wilderness survival and knot tying from the Scouts. They learned about tracking and moving silently through the woods on their own, after school every day and all summer long.

(<o>).[].(<o>)

Their domain was bordered on the east by the sequence of small forested islands in that part of the river, just out of reach. The west border was the river road, dotted with light industry, junkyards, a couple of gas stations, a 'greasy spoon' diner, and a few warehouses. In those days it was called Highway 169, renumbered through deviant logic but still known by the locals as west river road. At the south end of this strip, at an ancient intersection near the Camden bridge, there were houses, stores, a movie theater, and the branch library. However, the river road was straight, running mostly true north and south, while the river meandered. So there was, in some stretches, wide areas of forested bramble between the street and the river, sometimes acres of impenetrable yards across.

In a smaller town, the river would have been more of a center of activity, perhaps. But in the neighborhood it was largely ignored. Strangely, in a smaller town, the river would have been better known, better regarded, and more feared. There would have been signs about dangerous swimming areas, for example, and the parents might have restricted their kids from going down there without supervision.

There was little of that in the neighborhood. The teachers did not often warn against visiting the riverbank, and they never took a field trip down that way. The parents didn't really know what was there either.

In a smaller town the kids might have skated on the river, and the parents might have been alert to the danger of falling through the ice. But nobody skated on the Mississippi. It just wasn't done. For skating you went to the park, where they had a rink and a warming shed. The tough guys rarely visited the river either – it was enough to be lords of the public park.

They spent a lot of time by the river. Hack lived very nearby in a lower income slough bottom neighborhood, and Ace liked it down there, and so did Skate. You could wander through the untamed woods for hours and never see anyone, so you could practice your stealth and your woodsmanship. Sometimes they would run across a wino camped under the bridge. Once they found a hole in the fence behind the jam factory, and wandered in there seeking mischief. Mostly they just hung around, maybe smoking a stolen cigarette or setting off firecrackers under a coffee can. Ace was nutty about firecrackers and seemed to always have some when the occasion arose.

(<o>).[].(<o>)

They paddled with boards, making faint progress across as the current carried them downriver. However, while the current was steady the angles worked for them, and they landed on the island they were aiming for, albeit many dozens of yards downriver from where they planned.

Hack jumped ashore with the rope in his hand and tied the raft to a slender tree. Then Skate got off and they pulled the raft up, halfway out of the water.

They turned and saw Patrick and Book still watching. They could have shouted, as it was under a hundred yards, and sound carries over water, but they didn't. Skate just gave the high-sign, hand high overhead, fist pulled down to chin level, "everything okay", and then they turned inland, and climbed out of sight.

It was an amoeba of land, with several trees and a lot of brush, no bigger than half a football field, but elongated. Skate was thrilled to be there, but disappointed to see there was a trail leading from their landing point up into the trees. He'd been secretly hoping to be the first people ever to land there.

No such luck. The trail led up through a few trees to a flat spot halfway up the hill with a campfire and a litter of beer cans and other trash: food wrappers, paper bags with empty liquor bottles, and amongst the detritus, a small white plastic capsule, the size of shooter marble, with a heavy white balloon inside.

"What's this, Hack," Skate said, handing it to him.

"I dunno," Hack shrugged, "maybe it's a rubber."

"Really," Skate said.

"Maybe."

Skate pocketed the capsule. He was old enough to know having a rubber could be a good thing, but not old enough to know he had a carnival prize, a balloon in a plastic capsule and not a condom.

Hack was moving up the trail, and Skate followed, not wanting to miss anything.

(<o>).[].(<o>)

There was another campfire spot in a clearing on the peak of the island. It was a good camp spot, with the fire ashes embedded in a shallow pit, and logs in a rough circle to sit on. They could see the whole island from there.

Just below them on the other slope, nestled in a small weedy hollow, there was a carpet roll, wrapped with tape. The carpet was brown and faded red. The tape was black. The bundle was the size and shape of a human body.

They were sitting on the logs around the campfire site when Skate spotted it. His fifteen year old imagination was inflamed.

"Man," he said to Hack, "that could be a stiff."

"What, there?"

"Yeah, could be," Skate said, "we should see."

"I don't think so," Hack said.

Skate was already three steps in that direction.

"Why not?"

307

"Poison Ivy," Hack smiled, "would be the single biggest reason."

Skate stopped. Then he looked ahead of him, closely.

"Yeah, I see it."

"Besides," Hack went on, "if it is a stiff, then what to we do? Call the cops? Tell our folks?"

"Look around," Hack gestured expansively, "They'll crap if they find out we're here."

"I wonder what Ace would do?" Skate said.

"Ace," Hack snorted, "Ace would rupture if he thought that was a dead body."

"Ace," Skate laughed, "would expire with the vapors."

"Ace would fall to his knees weeping."

"Ace would," Skate paused, "Ace would get the hell out of here."

"Yeah," Hack said, rising, "let's hit the road."

"The high seas," Skate corrected him, "the briny main."

(<o>).[].(<o>)

Getting back took them even further downstream, so they beached the raft at least two hundred yards from where they found it.

"Anything to see?" Patrick said, catching the rope from Hack.

"Not really," Skate said, "there's quite a bit of junk laying around, and a couple of places for a campfire."

"Skate almost walked into a poison ivy patch," Hack added.

"Poison ivy," Book recoiled.

Book had had a very unpleasant encounter with poison ivy as a Cub Scout. While everyone else was out canoeing and frolicking, Book was back at camp covered with salve, taking the derision of the assistant cub scout leader who was saddled with watching him. Book knew you could 'get poison ivy' from touching the plant, or another person, or touching tools, or touching blankets. Book stayed away from poison ivy, religiously. He did not even like to talk about it.

"You two want to take a trip over?" Hack asked, "we pull this back upstream and you're set to go."

"I don't know," Patrick said – he wasn't the strongest swimmer, and tended to avoid the water as a rule.

"Not for me," Book added, "I can see the island just fine from here."

"Good on you," Hack said, "let's just leave it here and move along."

(<o>).[].(<o>)

They were in the same spot a week later, this time with Ace who was back in town. The raft was no longer there.

Perhaps a month after, there was a story in the paper about a dead body found on the island. A couple of men had been over there drinking, Stu and Pete. A drunken argument had escalated to drunken violence. Stu stabbed Pete to death.

Stu rowed across the river in his boat, bringing back a scrap of carpet, along with some tape and a shovel. Then Stu wrapped body, leaving his fingerprints in perfect relief on every piece of black tape he touched.

Then he tried to dig a grave, but his drunken energy left him, and the sun was coming up by this time. So he simply dragged the body into the brush and left it.

The police solved the case without much trouble. Relatives of the dead man identified Stu from the last time Pete was seen alive. Plus, they had his fingerprints on the tape.

When police went to pick him up, Stu was still covered in itchy blistering welts, all over his body, from an extreme case of poison ivy.

(<o>)/(13.32)\(<o>)

He has taken the canoe and paddled into a shady spot downshore from the cabin. It's perfectly calm, and he drops anchor in just a few feet of water. He baits a hook on a line with a bobber, tosses it in, and ignores it. Instead, he slumps onto the floor of the canoe, his back against a cross piece, and opens his journal. He looks around nervously, all that water and his writing so dry. The last thing he wants is a wet fish flopping on his pages.

Bard boating. The sun is warm, he listens to the lap of the water against the boat. The mind floats, like a bobber on a short line.

The three musty queers, three stewpots, all for one, one for all, all for her, her foregone. What ever happened to her. Makes you wonder.

Rover.

A two pound Crappie nibbles at his bait, tugging the bobber. The bard is oblivious. The fish takes the bait, leaving the hook. Free meal.

Ix-nay on the ystery-may. Now we're into bowery boys, another fine group of reporters, covering the story. Anupholsteraphobia:* fear you won't cover everything. I've got that, doctor, what's the prescription.

Mission, unlikely, for the Lon ranger.

Convoy, this here's the Rubber Duck. Ten-Four.

Driving in the dark, on a moonlit night.

The second wave.

A ripple slaps the side of the canoe. He rises up to check the bobber. No action. Good, a fish in the boat would just complicate things.

But it's getting late. Time to go. And go and go and go. Bard smiles, and puts his writing safely away. He pulls in the fish line. Nothing, bait gone. Skunked.

He looks across the lake at the Nun's island, but sees no movement. He pulls up his anchor and settles in to paddle back. Island. It rolls off the tongue. He lost a nickel to Book when they were seven or eight, Book betting that "island" was spelled "island." Skate was sure Book was tricking him – "ISLAND" he reasoned, would be pronounced "IS-LAND" not "EYE-LAND." It didn't make any sense. The first of many bets he lost to Book. Until he got sense and stopped trying. Book didn't make book unless he had it cold.

The lake and the island. Maybe that was his story. The river and the island, that was another story. Twain had done the river to death – the river as a sequence of events, flowing through time and space: picaresque.* He could do the lake and the island – let's see, the lake as a circle of events, around the shore, leading from beginning to end, and back to beginning.

Hmmm.

82. Famous line from Taxi Driver (1976). Columbia Pictures Corporation. Starring Robert De Niro and Jodie Foster.

83. Pig Latin euphemism used by the Boys, Bowery (1946-1958). Monogram Pictures. About a bunch of guys: Slip Mahoney, Sach Jones, Whitey, Chuck, and Butch.

84. Ginsberg, Allen, "Howl and Other Poems", 1956, Pocket Poets Series from City Lights Books

85. Kesey, Ken (2002). Introduction. One Flew Over the Cuckoo's Nest. Fortieth Anniversary Edition. Viking Press (The last thing Kesey wrote before he died at 66 in November, 2001).

86. Slaughterhouse-Five : Or the Children's Crusade : A Duty-Dance With Death Hardcover - 205 Delacorte Pr; ISBN: 0385312083 ; Dimensions (in inches): 1.03 x 8.04 x 5.34. Also known as the "so it goes" book.

87. FUBAR, a military term, later borrowed by the Lisp community.

88. Anupholsteraphobia, a term coined by Bass, Randy (2001). PBS broadcast.

89. A literary structure where the hero undertakes a sequence of adventures. The principal example in American literature is Mark Twain's Huckleberry Finn.

Chapter 14

"It's quiet here," said Rexee', "way, way, way too quiet. And way too dark."

She tossed another log onto the fire, and it roared some more.

(<o>).[].(<o>)

Delmar loaded up. He had his rifle and his binoculars. He ordered Hank to take his position at the gate, as it was midnight and his turn to pull guard duty.

He advised Lon to wait in the cabin, and took Jack with him on patrol.

"Walk behind me," Delmar said, "and keep quiet."

They headed off overland, following Lon's stream as it ran down through the forest towards Unkafrank Lake. Delmar kept low and picked his way along his path beside the stream. He had patrolled this area at least twice each night for a week, so he knew his footing fairly well. Jack struggled to keep up. The moon was out, but it seemed to help Delmar more than it did Jack.

Delmar stopped at the property line, marked by an ancient post and wire fence sunk into the forest floor and tumbling down to left and right. Lon brought him this far his first day, and then walked him along the property line each way. The fence only extended a few yards into the woods in each direction, but there were enough poles and markers to delineate the border. Remote properties in the northwoods are not normally fenced, mostly just marked. There is little to dispute over property, so the boundaries are only casually kept, within a few yards either way.

"You're making too much noise," Delmar whispered, "stop a minute and close your eyes – get used to the dark."

Jack was moved to protest, but he didn't. It's a strange fact in the woods that your sound carries behind you. To Jack, it felt as though he'd been mostly quiet, while he heard every twig that Delmar snapped. Delmar, meanwhile, was in a hyper-vigilant state, and could even hear Jack's breathing behind him.

They stopped.

Jack moved to light a cigarette. Delmar hissed to stop him. Jack put the smoke away.

"No smells, no sounds, no lights, " Delmar hoarsed, "we're on patrol. You watch my back, and when I signal you to wait, you wait. And if I come back in a hurry, you cover my retreat. Got it?"

Jack just nodded. He didn't mind the military crap, but he didn't recall exactly when Delmar was appointed god. He'd follow along for a while, but right now he was more interested in getting a 12-pack and laying down with that little coozy he'd met in the bar back in town.

(<o>).[].(<o>)

"Let's go," Delmar said, "we follow this stream to the lake, and then come at them from the west."

Just then, they were bathed in a blinding white light. Their eyes, now adjusted to the dark, were overwhelmed.

"Hold it," a voice commanded.

It was Lon, holding them in the beam of his giant industrial-sized flashlight.

"Get back to camp," Lon commanded, "tomorrow I'll go talk to them. Then we'll decide what to do."

Lon paused.

"Report back to camp. Now!"

(<o>)/(14.4)\(<o>)

Saturday morning, July 3rd, 1976.

They crawled out, one by one, to greet the Unkafrank morning. Hack had the jumbo coffee pot in the campfire, and a smaller one too, so coffee was ready to each as each appeared. A cup for each. They sat around the fire, the rough circle filling as they stumbled out, one after another.

Hack and Skate were first, still on their internal work clock. They sat and sipped and discussed who should be told. Ace came out next, and they told him right away, of course.

"I don't know, boys, I'd have to see it. Where is it?"

"Not far," Hack said, "about a half mile is all."

"We could try to go now, I suppose, but this army needs breakfast. What are we going to do about that – first things first."

"Town, I guess," said Hack, "we didn't lay in enough grub for the Clampet family surprise hoe-down. Eggs at the diner, and then a grocery run for lunch. Play it by ear after that, I guess."

Just then Remo crawled out of his tent, on a flat spot just up the slope from them. It was painful to watch. He dragged himself out with his arms, and then slowly tried to stand. His fingers were curled, and when he pushed himself up on his knuckles, his legs wouldn't straighten. Skate walked over.

"Can I help you, Remo"

Remo lay on his side, flexing his legs into his chest.

"It takes a long while to warm up in the morning, that's all. Get me a belt, and I'll loosen up."

Hack appeared beside them.

"There'll be plenty of belts after coffee," Hack said, "come on."

Then the blonde giant hoisted Remo to his feet and half-carried/half-dragged him to a log stool by the campfire.

"Belts after breakfast," Hack said firmly, "coffee now."

Skate poured a steaming cup of joe.

Remo accepted the cup with his clawed hands, and sat quietly sipping.

Sutter wheezed out and sat next to Remo, pouring himself a cup from the smaller pot.

"I didn't sleep a wink," Sutter said, "until about thirty seconds after I lay down, until now. But for thirty seconds there, I was tossing and turning."

Sutter looked out at the glistening lake, "what a beautiful morning."

"Come see, come saw," answered Skate, "we get this every day."

(<o>).[].(<o>)

There were ten of them, and they came awake in sequence as people will do. They had three vehicles, and it was a twenty minute ride to town. So there were people on the way into breakfast, and heading back again, while others slept.

312

Hack, Skate, Ace, Remo, Sutter, and soon Calvin, were early risers, trained by the sunrise. Rexee' and Henry were prepared to sleep the morning away, but Calvin and Ace went into the cabin to get them moving, and they both appeared before long. Rexee' was alert and refreshed looking – she accepted a cup of coffee and lit a cigarette, and surveyed the lakeside scene. Henry dragged himself to the fire, wearing bib overalls with no shirt, and slumped on a log – a heaving mass of humanity. Sutter handed him a cup of coffee, and it was only a few moments before Calvin was herding people into the van so they could drive to town for breakfast. Henry poured himself onto the van and tried to will himself back to sleep.

Nobody wanted to disturb Terry and Traci in the little trailer, so they went to town without them.

Hack and Ace led the way in the pickup truck. The van followed, with Skate in the front seat to navigate.

"It's back there," Hack said, as they passed the point in the driveway, "we'll slip out there on the way back from town."

Ace peered through the trees, seeing nothing.

"Yeah," he said, "later."

(<o>).[].(<o>)

Annie was waiting when they pulled up. She had opened the diner, fed the usual morning crowd, which was sparse on a Saturday, had her goodbye with Lily, and closed the place down. It was the first time since she acquired the place without her keeping normal hours.

The grill was clean, the salt shakers were full, the napkin dispensers fully loaded, and Annie was ready to try something new, for the first time in a long time. Ace was in her life now, and things were changing.

Yes, change was basically bad. But even Lily could see Annie was ready. Or maybe Lily was the first to see it.

Annie was locking up the diner when the station wagon pulled around the corner. She was both glad to see it and frightened at its aspect – the war wagon on a roll.

As it was, she didn't have too long to stand on the curb and worry about it, and there was no time to change her mind. Book pulled up, Patrick tossed her bag in the wagon, and she climbed into the back seat with Carol – end of story.

The station wagon had an 8-track tape player, and when Annie was settled in her seat, Book pushed in the tape he had chosen for the moment.

Canned Heat, "On the Road Again." – doo-doo do-do-do, dah-do-do-do-do.

"Patrick," Book said, it was another Web-laugher, "are the kids in back?"

Patrick surveyed the back seat, where Annie and Carol were sitting.

"Yes, dear," he said to Book, imitating Book's mother, "the kids are in back."

"Well, then," Book said, "let's go."

Patrick smiled back at the ladies.

Book went on, "Let's go and go and go."

313

They ate breakfast in town at the diner, and Skate took up a collection for grocery money. They sat around the tables and made a shopping list. Then it was decided that Skate would ride in the pickup with Hack and Ace, to borrow a canoe from Hack's uncle, and the rest of them would go grocery shopping with the money, using the van. They would meet up back at Hack's place. They drew a map on a napkin for Calvin, but he swore he didn't need it. He'd been from town to Hack's in the dark, and then from Hack's to town in daylight. He could find it again, he was sure. Both Sutter and Remo were pretty sure they had the directions down too, so they resolved to split up. Hack gave them the phone number of his uncle in town. If anything should go wrong, they could call for help or directions or guidance – whatever was needed.

They sauntered out into the street after breakfast. Calvin and the van were headed farther west, another two blocks, to the grocery store. Hack in the pickup, with Ace and Skate were headed back east, with Skate riding in the bed to hold the canoe steady once they had it.

At the last moment, Rexee' backed away from the van and jumped into the pickup bed with Skate.

"I'll do the canoe thing," she said, "those boys can handle the groceries without me. Which is more than I can say about you bozos."

That left Sutter, Henry, Remo, and Calvin in the van.

The last thing they heard, before the van door slid shut was Remo saying, "time for a belt, right boys?"

The van went further into town towards the IGA, and the truck went back towards the edge of town, the canoe, and then the woods from whence they came.

The Portage Bar was right next to the grocery store.

"I guess we'll know where to look if the groceries get lost," Hack said.

Hack's uncle lived near the east edge of town, just off the main road. It only took them a few minutes to load up the canoe and paddles and tie it down in the back of the pickup.

Skate looked at Rexee' and then looked at Hack. Hack looked at Skate, and then looked at Rexee'. Ace looked at Hack and Skate looking at Rexee'. Ace looked at Rexee'. Ace looked at Hack and raised his eyebrows. Hack looked at Skate, and then back at Ace. Ace looked at Skate and raised his eyebrows. Skate looked at Rexee' for a second and then looked at Hack. Hack shrugged. Skate nodded. Ace shrugged.

It was decided, Rexee' could come along.

They headed back towards Unkafrank Lake.

"Try not to touch anything," Skate said as they walked down the trail, "we kept it as clean as we could."

"Yeah," Hack said, "we walked in, we backed out, we buttoned it back up. It's pretty much as we found it, except we hauled out some cases."

"For evidence," Skate interjected.

They walked into the clearing, and there it was.

"What the fuck is this? Rexee' said.

"Rex," Hack said, "this is me trusting you. This is me saying this is nothing to talk about. If you don't like that, then you need to go wait in the pickup."

Rexee' was quiet for a moment, looking at the back end of the truck as it poked through the gravel. She looked at Hack. Then she looked at Skate.

"What's the deal?" she asked Skate.

"Like he said," Skate answered calmly, "it's family business and a shut up about it type deal."

"The pickup is back there, if you don't like it here," Skate added, nodding back towards the road, "but you can stay, so long as you get it."

"Ya, ya, ya," she said, "any idiot get's it. I get it. You bozos growing pot in there?"

Ace was transfixed.

"1936 you said?"

"Yeah, that's the license plate."

"Forty years. Damn. Hitler was just barely in power. The Berlin Olympics and all that. The depression was full on. and the second world war hadn't even started. This is Elliot Ness times. The Dust Bowl."

"Yup," Skate deadpanned, "that's about it."

Ace looked at Rexee' and then at Hack.

"And you think this might be your grandfather's doing?"

"Yeah," Hack said, "that's the prospect, that's the fear."

Ace hardly hesitated.

"Okay, let's take a look."

Hack opened the back of the truck and swung the door open. The smell had dissipated considerably, but it was still evident. The footprints from their first exploration were clearly visible on the floor, even in the dim light. Hack produced a flashlight.

"I'll go first," Hack said, "try to walk in my footsteps."

They all lined up behind him, Rexee' too.

(<o>).[].(<o>)

"Far, far, far freaking out," Ace exclaimed, "let me hold that flashlight for a second."

Rexee' shivered.

"My dad drinks Bosch beer," she groaned, "and this looks like about a thousand years worth of booze."

(<o>).[].(<o>)

They were back outside. Hack was shutting the doors. Ace, Skate, and Rexee' were sitting on the level ground behind the truck, around the cold campfire they had used to dig through the night.

"So," Skate stated flatly, "you see the problem."

Ace just nodded and shrugged.

"We need to know what happened here, before we do anything," Skate said, "So we've just been sitting on this, thinking it over."

"Murder," Rexee' said, "it looks like murder to me."

"Yeah, me too," Hack walked up, "that's how it looks. But I need to know, and then I need to think about it, and then I need to decide what to do."

"And maybe," Ace paused, "maybe nothing is the right thing to do."

It was then they heard a vehicle stopping on the driveway, back where they left the truck.

"That's not the van, is it Hack?" Skate said.

"No," Hack said, "it's not."

(<o>).[].(<o>)

Lon was waiting for them when they walked out to the driveway. He had pulled his pickup over to the side behind Hack's. He was sitting in the cab, his engine still running. Lon looked nervous. It was a warm day, but Lon was wearing a light jacket. They couldn't see it, but Lon had his pistol under his arm.

"Need to talk to you Jackson," Lon said gruffly.

"Sure Lon," Hack said, walking over, "what's up?"

"Hi, Lon," Skate said, walking up behind Hack.

Lon eased his hand under his jacket, resting his palm on his gun butt.

Hack saw him do it, and tensed. Skate saw Hack tense, and stopped walking.

"Easy, Lon," Hack said, "what is it?"

"Ask your friends to stand over there," Lon nodded ahead, "where I can see them. This is private."

Hack spoke over his shoulder without turning around.

"You guys wait by the truck, okay."

He locked onto Lon's eyes, "Okay, Lon, let's get to it."

"But," Hack added, "let me see your hands while we're talking."

Lon looked sharply at Hack. Hack shrugged and showed his hands were empty. Lon wrapped his fingers around his steering wheel, and started to talk.

"My shed burned down, you know, and it figures to be any of a lot of people."

Lon looked Hack in the face.

"I had you on my list for a while, but it made no sense. We talked that night, and it just didn't figure. I guess I knew all along, and realized finally – you're not the type."

Hack shrugged agreement.

"But I needed to protect myself, and called a few army buddies, and spread the word a little. And now I've got this bunch of idiots on my land, camped out and walking sentry. Looking, I don't know, looking for enemies."

"How many?" Hack asked.

"Three," Lon answered, "three stooges."

Lon sighed. Then he started talking, fast.

"Thing is, only two of them are local idiots, Jack and Hank Bauer, you might know them. The third is a strange creep, and not stupid like the others. He's cunning and slippery. A shirt-tail relation to me. I haven't seen him in twenty years, since he was up here that time. And somehow, I don't know how, I think he maybe has a crank on for you."

Hack tilted his head, skeptical.

Lon went on, still racing, "He said you were on the property last night with your friends, and they followed you out. But the story didn't make sense. By the time I got there, they were grabbing rifles and headed this way. I think he meant to shoot up your place and maybe everyone up there. I don't know."

Lon looked at Hack, "I stopped them…"

"Who is this guy?" Hack said.

But Lon went on, "…but if ever there was murder in a man's eye, it was then. I thought he was going to shoot ME for second. The guy scares me, I don't mind saying."

"Jeez, Lon, you've got more problems than you need."

"Yeah, well, I can take care of myself," Lon offered roughly, "I thought you'd better know, though."

Lon dropped his truck into reverse and shot gravel backing up.

"Wait, Lon," Hack yelled, "who is this guy?"

Lon was looking over his shoulder, backing up, and deftly pulled onto a wide flat spot to turn around. He stopped, and shouted to Hack over his engine.

"I told you," Lon shifted into drive, "his name is Delmar. He's been in trouble with the government. He's not from around here."

Lon peeled away, up the driveway towards his land.

Hack turned back to his own truck.

Ace was in the pickup, fiddling with the radio, oblivious. But Skate and Rexee' were waiting in the pickup bed, sitting on opposite sides of the canoe, facing back toward Lon's retreating pickup. Skate was stunned, but Rexee' was furious.

"I knew it!" she screamed, "I saw that piece of shit in town last night. I knew it! That whore-bait is back. I knew it, I fucking knew it!"

She started thrashing in the back of the pickup truck, pumping her arms and legs, convulsing with rage.

Ace popped his head out of the cab window.

"Hey, keep it down would'ya," he said, "I've got 'Ride Captain Ride'* on the radio here!"

(<o>).[].(<o>)

They stood by Hack's truck, talking things over.

Hack told them what Lon said, word for word.

Then they went back to the liquor van and sat around the cold campfire, talking some more.

"He didn't come up here after us," Skate was saying, "right Hack? He came up here to work for Lon. It's just bad luck he found us."

"That's how it looks," Hack said.

"But he knows we're here now," Ace said, "with murder in his eye."

"Yeah, that's how Lon made it sound."

"Let's think it through," Skate said.

"Think it through!" Rexee' shrilled, "let's pack up and get the hell out of here!"

"There's a certain logic to that," Ace admitted.

"No," Hack said, "we're safer here right now."

317

"That's right," Skate said, "he could be watching camp at this very moment.. Our only advantage is he doesn't know where we are right now – he wouldn't know to look for us here."

Rexee' looked around the clearing, nervously.

"Says you," she whispered, "he could be out there right now."

"And," Skate went on, "he doesn't know Lon talked to us. Right Hack? Lon wasn't about to tell him. So Delmar doesn't know that we know he's here."

Hack nodded.

"Lon said he's afraid of the guy. He's at home arming himself, or he took off to stay away. That's my guess. Either way, no, he won't tell Delmar anything. Not after coming out here to warn us."

"You trust this guy, then?" Ace said.

"Lon's okay."

"Shit," Rexee' said, "what now?"

(<o>).[].(<o>)

They were sitting together around the cold campfire, just yards from the back of the buried truck. All they needed was a plan.

"First, the perimeter," Ace said.

Hack nodded.

"Skate, you and me walk back up to the driveway, casual, and then we work a circle from there."

"Yep," Skate said.

"Ace, you and Rex, casual like, get your backs against the liquor truck. Cozy down by the tailgate and you'll be protected on three sides."

Hack looked at Skate, "anything else?"

"Yeah," Skate said to Ace, "listen for the van. If you hear them coming, run out and flag them down."

Skate looked at Hack, and shrugged, "Then bring them all back here, I guess."

Hack nodded.

"Yeah," Hack said, "I guess so."

"Sorry, man," Skate said to Hack, "the circle just keeps getting bigger."

Hack smiled, "try to keep Remo out of the booze, at least for a while."

They stood briefly in a knot.

"One more thing," Hack said, looking at Ace and Rexee', "if you hear the shit fly, lock yourself in the liquor truck. You're safe in there, like a bomb shelter."

They stood together for a moment until Skate broke the silence.

"Okay," Skate said, "let's go, low and slow."

Hack and Skate sauntered, casually, back up the path towards the driveway where the pickup was parked.

Ace and Rexee' sauntered casually to the shadow of the liquor truck and sat with their backs to the doors. Hack and Skate removed some crates from the truck that first day, and they were on the ground, tucked away behind the exposed back end of the truck.

They sat together on crates. With the slope of the gravel excavation, and the straight wall of the truck, they were indeed protected on three sides. It wasn't Fort Knox, but it was a cozy cove.*

"If you think," Rexee' said when they were out of earshot, "that I'm locking myself in a pitch dark truck with two dead bodies, then you're not thinking straight."

Ace attempted a smile. He had the flashlight.

"I'd rather run down to the lake and drown myself," she went on.

Ace just kept nodding. He felt the same way.

"I've got Skate's torch, Ex-Ray, but if it comes to it," he held the flashlight up for her to see, "and the batteries die, we can run down and drown each other."

"You got it," she said, grimly.

(<o>).[].(<o>)

Hack and Skate stopped just short of the driveway under cover of a cluster of brush.

"This is good," Hack whispered.

"Yeah," Skate said, "keep low, move slow, and meet up in the gully directly above the truck – a half circle each."

"If you see him," Hack said, "backtrack and catch me from behind. Agreed?"

"Oh, for yeah," Skate said, "he's armed, we're not. Locate him, and leave, that's the plan."

"Okay, I'll see you in the gully," Hack said, and pushed off the path into the brush, "stay low, move slow."

(<o>).[].(<o>)

Skate crouched and listened. Already, he could barely hear Hack to his north. Hack was good, quiet. Skate looked into the brush towards the south and sighted a small opening. Then he looked around, in all directions, took a breath, and stepped off the path. He was in the woods.

He chose the hard ground, watched his step, and angled his way around the liquor truck, far to his right. He'd played this game before, and he picked his steps carefully. Keeping to the higher ground, there were rough spots to traverse. Every few yards he stopped and listened, surveying the ground.

It was slow, and it was laborious, but he never made an untoward sound, and he never exposed himself for more than a second, as he worked his half-circle of the campsite. He kept under cover, with one eye on the clearing below. He stayed out of sight of the truck-site, but within the line of fire they were scouting. All he had to do was verify the vantage points, and he inspected them one by one, all the way around.

It took nearly half an hour, but when he arrived at the gully above the truck he had his answer. Nobody was up there, sighting down on the liquor truck campsite, and nobody had been there – not for a long, long time. The perimeter was secure on his side of the clearing. He stopped at a point just above the gully and hunkered down. If Hack came up from his side, Skate would see him. If Hack was already there, he would have seen Skate.

319

Just then, he saw slight movement across the gully, and once he determined it was Hack, he stepped into the open and gave the high sign. Hack saw his movement, and gave the high sign too. All clear. They scrambled carefully into the gully, and met in the middle, on the gravel slope high above the truck. From there they could see the exposed top of the truck and the whole clearing.

"Nothing, right?" Skate said.

"Nada por nootin, we're good."

"Okay," Skate said, "let's break the glad news."

Just then, they heard Calvin's van straining to climb the driveway, and saw Ace bolt out from cover and race up the path. Ace ran low, and zig-zagged as he went: classic combat stuff. Hack looked at Skate and smiled.

"Should we shout down the all clear?"

"Nah," Skate said, "he's into it. Look at him go."

(<o>)/(14.17)\(<o>)

diaria -- 14.0-- 8/7/77 -- Kansas City

Lots of writers write about writing, why should I be any different?

I like Stephen King's account, about how you do it for yourself, and anyone who doesn't is a monkey.*

Critics use words like "self indulgent" to describe a novel, sometimes.

And I don't see their point.

Of course a novel is self-indulgent.

The writer writes, I've come to believe, the book that he or she would like to read.

In composition class we were told to consider our audience, and write for them.

But a novel isn't like that, is it? A novel is both more personal and more public than that.

In the end, after only a little reflection, I decided to write the book that would interest me.

A book that I would be amused by and would find fun to read.

I do, any author will confess, I'm sure, sort of hope there are others out there who enjoy the same sort of things as me. And I'm sure most authors hope there are MANY others out there in that category. But I've found I can't write that way.

If you ponder a lot on who's going to like this or that, you end up paralyzed from the writing itself. It's not true for most forms, but for the novel, I think, you write for yourself. You tell the tale you want to tell. You Cover the Story, as my good friend Hunter sez, for good or ill.

If you've read this far, maybe you've already got that.
This is the story I wanted to tell, with all the
elements and structure that I wanted to include, and in
the playful way (what I consider playful, as an aside),
that amused me at the time.

So, "self indulgent novel?" What is that? Is that bad?
Is there any other kind?

Of course I haven't read them all, so I don't know.

My advice? If you decide to write a novel (and I don't
advise it), write the one YOU like.

That's what I did.

And look, I'm almost done.

(<o>)/(14.18)\(<o>)

Forest Lake, North Branch, Pine City, Hinckley, Finlayson/Askov,
Sturgeon Lake, Barnum, Otter Creek, Cloquet.

They went and went and went.

But they always stopped in Cloquet, the halfway point, to see the Frank
Lloyd Wright memorial gas station.

"I love this thing," Patrick said, "design for the proletariat. It's a cool
message."

They had all been there before, many times for some of them.

"Fuel to the people," Book said, "how are you ladies holding up?"

Annie was fine, but Carol looked uncomfortable.

"Should we rest for a while?" he asked.

"We should pee for a while," Carol jumped out, "don't get between me and
the bathroom, I'll knock you for a loop."

She scuttled away in a crouch.

(<o>).[].(<o>)

Grand Lake, Silver Spur, Canyon, Cotton, Eveleth, Virginia.

"Pit stop, Carol?" Book asked.

"I'm good," she said, "keep going."

Tower and Soudan, Eagles Nest, McComber, Burntside Lake.

They were tooling down the main street in Elysium by around 11:30 AM.
The whole trip had taken them well under five hours.

"Pull over, Book," Patrick said, "there's Calvin's van."

(<o>).[].(<o>)

Noon in the Portage Bar; a dimly lit, crummy little dive like so many
others.

Book parked the station wagon right behind the van. Then they looked in
the van and saw the groceries, and it didn't take Hercules Poirot* to deduce
where the group might be.

They breezed through the door of the Portage – Book, Patrick, Carol, and
Annie, just in time to see Calvin lose his temper.

321

"Gawd damn bastards!" Calvin shouted, "we drive all this way to sit in a bar! I'm telling you, THE BUS IS LEAVING. I spend my life in a bar, and didn't come all this way to do the same again."

"Just lemme finish my pitcher," Henry said, "then we'll go."

"Yeah, Calvin," Remo added, "you're not the boss up here, you're just the driver."

Calvin quivered.

"I'll tell you what," Calvin said, "I take off out of here, and you walk back. How's that?"

"Hey," Sutter said, noticing the new arrivals, "new blood. You folks want a drink?"

Book looked at Patrick who looked at Carol who looked at Annie.

"Not right now," Patrick said, reading the signals, primarily from the ladies "we'll go to Hack's and take it from there."

"Calvin's right," Sutter said, "it's time to deliver the food. Let's go Henry, drink up."

Henry stood up, clad in bib overalls with no shirt, a mass of humanity, and picked up his pitcher like it was a beer stein.

"Okay," he said, "green river."

Then he tossed the beer back in one swift draft and slammed the pitcher down on the table.

"Let's go ," Henry said, "it's almost time for lunch."

(<o>)/(14.21)\(<o>)

Noon at Lon's guard post.

Lon had been to speak with Hack, and now he was sitting in his truck, waiting with Hank. Soon, Jack appeared, shuffling down the driveway.

"Delmar up there?" Lon asked.

"Yeah," Jack shrugged, "he's still in the rack."

"Okay," Lon said, "hop in. It's the 4th of July tomorrow, and I'm giving you boys the day off. But first I need to get rid of Delmar."

"We need our truck," Jack said.

"That's where we're going," Lon said, "together."

(<o>).[].(<o>)

They crowded into Delmar's shed, Lon in front, with Jack and Hank behind him. It was a small shed, they filled it.

"Delmar," Lon said, touching his shoulder, "wake up."

"I'm awake," Delmar said, coolly, "what do you want, Uncle Lon?"

"It's time for you to go," Lon said, "you're fired."

Delmar sat up on his bunk, wearing nothing but camouflage skivvies.

"You thinking to get rid of me, Lon?" he said, his voice was hard and even.

"Yeah," Lon said, "you're out. Pack your stuff and be gone by tonight."

Delmar looked at Lon, murder in his eye. Then he looked past Lon and saw Jack and Hank standing behind him.

"You boys think this is right?" he said to them.

"The boss," Jack shrugged, "is the boss."

Delmar seethed.

He had his pistol under his pillow, but there was just too many of them. And they were standing there, armed and alert. This was not the time to start a firefight, and he was in no position to win it.

"Lon," Delmar smiled, "this is your mistake."

"Pack up," Lon was unflinching, "we'll take you to town."

"No," Delmar said, laying back down, "I'm sleeping now. I'll get up and go later."

Lon wavered.

"You're gone by dark," he barked, "no question."

"Yeah, yeah," Delmar said, "leave me alone and I'll be gone by nightfall."

"Alright," Lon said sternly, and then speaking to Jack and Hank, "you two make sure he packs up, and ride him out of here. Got it?"

Jack and Hank nodded, apprehensively.

"Come back after the holiday," Lon went on, turning to go, "after he's gone."

They crowded back out of Delmar's shed and stood in the clearing.

"Get him out of here," Lon said to Jack, "and then take your time off. Be back on Monday, the 5th."

Jack looked at Hank and then back at Lon.

"Okay boss," he said, "we'll see you Monday."

Lon got into his truck and drove away.

Jack and Hank waited until he was out of sight, then they quietly packed their stuff and followed him out the driveway. Neither planned to be back, and neither planned to deal with Delmar ever again. Certainly not to oversee his packing and hauling him to town. Delmar could go screw himself, which he already had, so far as this job was concerned.

Good riddance to bad garbage. They loaded their truck and left, no going back.

(<o>)/(14.23)\(<o>)

Ace was standing in the driveway, next to Hack's pickup truck, when the van and station wagon convoy pulled up.

He was still freaked out, not knowing the perimeter was secure, so he took a strident, safety first approach. He waved the van and the station wagon into parking spots just behind Hack's truck, and he gave the "freeze" sign.

Patrick got it. Book did not and was going to get out of the wagon, but Patrick put a hand on his arm.

"Everybody," Patrick whispered, "sit tight. Book, stay ready."

Patrick climbed out, leaving his door open.

Ace was already in Calvin's face to cut the engine.

Then he had Book switch off too.

"Annie, honey," Ace said into the back seat, "it is so good to see you. But I gotta go now. I'll be right back."

He wheeled around.

"Stay here," Ace whispered to Patrick, "and keep things quiet. Delmar is in the woods, and it might be serious. You get me?"

Patrick got it – Ace was on a mission. This could be serious.

Ace ran back into the forest.

Patrick leaned into the van, talking to Remo and Calvin, who were in front. "Stand by," he said, "quietly. Something's up. We wait here."

Remo nodded and gave the silent "freeze" sign. He hadn't heard everything, but he had heard the word "Delmar," and that was enough.

(<o>).[].(<o>)

Ace pelted back down the path until he was in view of the clearing. Then he stopped and crouched to collect himself before bolting back across the open space. He could see Rexee', still sitting on her crate, senselessly smoking the cigarette that might give them all away.

If the girl had ever played "guns" she would have known better.

Then he saw Hack and Skate, moving down the gully to a point directly above the truck. They were loose, he could tell by the way they moved. The coast was clear.

So Ace stepped into the clearing. He sauntered towards the truck, and was near the campfire about the time Hack and Skate had navigated to a point directly above Rexee'.

Ace locked eyes with Hack. Hack gave the high sign – all clear.

"You enjoying the smoke?" he said mildly, looking at Rexee', "a soothing break from the everyday?"

Rexee' looked at him archly, "what's it to you?"

"Oh, nothing," Ace said smiling, then added sharply, "except you're giving us away with every drag!"

Then Hack jumped from the top of the truck, directly above her, into the soft gravel behind the truck.

"Green River!" he yelled, as he pounded to the ground, just feet in front of her.

Rexee' bolted upright like she'd licked a 50 amp line. To Ace it looked like her hair stood on end, which it did.

But she didn't make a noise – just lurched in a cardiac spasm and landed back on the crate she was sitting on.

Then she saw the two of them, smiling in front of her.

"You bastards," she hissed, "I'll fucking get you, if I die trying."

(<o>).[].(<o>)

Ace and Hack went to the driveway to fetch the crowd. Skate worked his way silently down from the top of the truck and sat with Rexee'.

"You know we all love you, right Rex," he said, "all in our own way."

She looked like she might cry, which Skate had rarely even seen her remotely close to doing before.

"I didn't know, about the smoking."

"I know, it's no big deal. And we're safe here, otherwise they wouldn't take the chance to tease you."

"Torture me, you mean."

"You're our girl, we'd never let anything happen to you."

Rexee' stubbed out her cigarette, which was still lit.

"Last one for a while, I guess."

"Anyway, so you know, we made a sweep, and he's not out there, and there's no sign that anyone has been out there – nobody at all."

Rexee' just stared at him.

"We know what we're doing in this department," Skate paused, "believe me."

Rexee' sagged a little, "okay, good. But you know I'll get you back. You should know that."

"Hey," Skate protested, "it wasn't me, it was those guys. I'm not like the others."*

(<o>).[].(<o>)

Ace had been to the driveway, and collected the troops. He was still revved up, and had impressed on them, quietly but forcefully, that there was a situation brewing and they needed to walk QUIETLY up the path – no talking, no smoking, single file, follow the leader.

They were standing around the dead campfire at the back of the liquor truck, and it fell to Skate to try to explain.

(<o>)/(14.27)\(<o>)

A one act play in several scenes:

Scene Fourteen –

The lights come up on an outdoor scene.

To audience left there is a path leading into the brush. Center stage is a rough campfire, not lit. To the right is the backend of a truck, its back doors are exposed but the rest of the truck is buried under a slope of gravel. The printing on the truck door says "Royal Distribution Co." The truck doors are closed. There are a few liquor crates on the ground directly behind the truck and around the campfire.

There is knot of people huddled at center stage around the dead campfire: from left to right – Calvin, Remo, Old Man Sutter, Fat Henry, Patrick, and Carol – Skate at center stage – Book, Hack, Ace and Annie, holding hands, and Rexee' nearest the truck, sitting on a crate.

It is Saturday, July 3rd, 1976, at 1 P.M. in the Central Time Zone, near Unkafrank Lake, Elysium, Minnesota.

=#=#=#=

```
    Skate
Let me try to explain.
    Carol
(whispering)
Why are you whispering?
    Skate
Right now, we're trying to keep quiet.
    Carol
Yes, it is quiet here.
    Skate
(touching Carol on the arm)
We're safe right now. Hack and I made a sweep, and there's
nobody here but us.
```

Book
But he whose name shall not be spoken?

Skate
Yes, he's here.
(looks around at the group)
You all remember Delmar?

Calvin
Shit.

Skate
Right. Hack's neighbor was just here. Delmar is staying on his
property.

Ace
Which is where?

Hack
(points upstage)
That way, two properties over. Two driveways back the way you
came.

Calvin
With the guardhouse, and the chain across the driveway?

Hack
Yeah, that's it.

Calvin
I know where it is, I saw it from the road.

Rexee'
I saw him last night in town. He was watching us drive
through.

Skate
Yes, that's what Lon said too.

Carol
What does he want?

Rexee'
Short answer? Blood. Mine (pointing to Hack) and his,
(pointing to Skate), and mostly his.

Book
You don't think he followed you up here?

Skate
I think probably not. After the flap in Calvin's two weeks
ago, he's probably just jumping bail.

Patrick
That was two weeks? Seems like two months.

Book
Eighteen days (checking his watch) plus about three hours.

Patrick
Mr. Spock computes.

Book
Make that two and half hours, precisely.

Skate
So apparently Delmar has been working at the neighbors …

Hack
Lon. Lon Lowbridge.

326

Skate

… working at Lon's as a security guard and sentry. Last night
he tailed us here from town.

Rexee'

I told you I saw him.

Skate

And Lon says he was on the way over with a rifle, except Lon
stopped him.

Remo

That rat bastard sniper.

Hack

Yeah, Lon says he's got his sights on me.

Skate

And me, we would guess. But I doubt this includes any of you,
and probably not Rexee' either. I think he's got a torch for
Rexee'.

Rexee'

Maybe once, but not after I kicked his balls in.

Patrick

Good point. I still wince picturing that. That was good.

Book

Yes, excellent form, a 6.5 on the Richter Scale.

Rexee'

Yes, well it's back to bite me now. If I could take it back …
(pauses)
I wouldn't.

Remo

Me neither. I just wish I could still do it.

Skate

Meanwhile, he's out there somewhere, but we don't know where.
He might be at Lon's, or he might be perched overlooking
Hack's place.

Remo

Rat bastard.

Skate

But he doesn't know we're here. That's why we stopped you and
brought you back here. He doesn't know about this place.

Carol

(looking into the woods, fearfully)
How do you know?

Skate

Hack and I made a sweep of all the high ground here. There's
nobody up there, and there's no sign anybody has been up there
for a long while.

Hack

That's right. Skate's right. We're okay here for now.

Book

For now. I notice you qualify that. Safe for now.

Skate

Right. We don't know where he is, and he doesn't know where we are. But if he's on the move, or looking for us, he could stumble through here.

Book
My, yes, I see. Fluidity. The luck has been bad in this regard up until now.

Ace
And why expect the luck to get any better?

Remo
I never expect that.

Rexee'
Me either.

Skate
So there's where we are with that.

Ace
Orient me here. Lon's is that way (points upstage) and where exactly is the cabin from here?

Hack
(points downstage) That way, about a half mile.

Ace
Okay, so if he's moving from Lon's to Hack's or back again, he passes by here?

Hack
Yeah, we're pretty much in the middle, except he'd be off that way
(points stage right, towards the liquor truck),
most likely following the stream.

Ace
I see. How far?

Hack
Maybe another half mile, give or take.

Ace
So passing through here on the way would be a real detour?

Skate
Yeah, but a sensible detour if you were working the woods.

Ace
I see, yes, I get it. So if we stay here, we need sentries of our own.

Skate
Yeah, probably. Probably two, one on each side.

Remo
I can do that. I've got training.

Patrick
Me too, but without training.
(looking at Carol, who is still fearful)
You know, protecting the women and the children.

Hack
I don't know, Remo, this is a sentry job that requires you to shout and run. You up for the running?

Remo

Fuckin-A, I can run. I can't tie my shoes, but I can move it on down the road.

Ace

But, are we staying here?

Skate

Yes, for now, and as long as it's safe. We're all better off here than trying to run back to town or anything else.

Rexee'
(sarcastically)
Yeah, tell them how we've got the "advantage".

Skate

Well, we do. He doesn't know we're on to him. He thinks we're sitting unsuspecting ducks. We know he's out there, but he doesn't know we know that.

Book

Oh, my, I'm afraid to think where this is going.

Skate

Yeah, you got it. At some point soon, we start to hunt HIM.

Hack

But first …

Skate

Yeah, first we have to sweep Hack's place, to make sure he's not there either. Once that coast is clear, we can go to the lake and pack you all up …

Ace

But until we know where HE is …

Skate

Right, we don't dare move around much until we know where he is.

Remo

Yup. Rat bastard sniper could be pumping lead at anything that moves. The van, for example.

Skate

That's the fear. If he's decided to shoot something, he could choose the van, which he's seen.

Ace

Okay, first sentries, I can do that too.

Annie

I'm going with you.*

Calvin

Me too.

Patrick

Calvin (laughing) I think we're saving you for night sentry.

Ace

Yes, good, to each according to his talent. But then, I'm supposing, a sweep of Hack's place. Then what?

Sutter
(interrupting)
Then, or first, or right now preferably, somebody explains what the hell's up with this truck buried in the ground.

329

Doc Sutter, I'm glad you asked that. How are you on forensics? (Blackout).

(<o>)/(14.28)\(<o>)

They decided on what Book called the "rock and roll protocol".

Skate was to take Remo up to a vantage point to the south of the clearing. Hack would take Patrick up into the woods to the north. Each of them would be armed with a softball sized rock. The instructions were that, if they saw or heard anything suspicious at all, they were to throw their rock down into the clearing – and then hide. This would signal the people in the clearing to lock themselves into the liquor truck.

Rapping an S-O-S on the truck doors would signal that someone needed to be let in. Rapping a Beethoven "V" would signal the all clear.*

Rexee' insisted on taking the flashlight from Ace.

"If you think I'm sitting in the dark, in that fucking truck, waiting around for you stooges to knock on the doors – gimme that damn flashlight," she demanded, "we'll have light in there, or nothing doing."

"I think there's a lantern in there, too," Skate offered, "towards the back."

"We'll post the sentries," Hack explained, "and then we'll come back here. It's best if you all move toward the back of truck. You can't be easily seen from there."

(<o>).[].(<o>)

Remo could, indeed, move well through the woods, Skate was glad to see. The infantry veteran was crabbed in his hands, but he could, with a little bar oil to loosen his joints, slide through the brush like an Indian scout.

"About here, I think," Skate said, "you can see the clearing, and you can see movement down the slope."

Remo positioned himself on a fallen log which was exactly the spot Skate would have chosen.

"No heroics, right," Skate said softly, "you see him, or think you see him, just pitch your rock into the clearing and get under cover. Best if he goes by without knowing you've seen him."

"Fuckin-A," Remo whispered, "I know how to do this shit. I just wish I had my rifle, it's in the van."

"No rifles. Figure a couple hours," Skate said, "that gives us time to scout the lakeside, get back, and send up some relief."

"Ten-four," Remo said, "get going."

(<o>).[].(<o>)

Hack and Skate met the group back in the clearing.

Skate said, "The only thing we don't have covered is if he decides to drive in from the road. If that happens he'll see the vehicles, but you'll hear him in plenty of time, and you can get out of sight, like we talked about."

Rexee' held up her flashlight, defiantly.

"You know it," she said.

"Meanwhile," Skate said, turning to Sutter, "let me take a minute to explain the truck situation."

(<o>)/(14.31)\(<o>)

Delmar seethed.

Lon had called him off, but Delmar could not accept that.

He had a score to settle, and his opportunity for revenge had dropped into his lap.

Delmar went through his gear and found his camouflaged army fatigues. Then he dug through his bag of trinkets and found his camouflage grease sticks.

He laid everything out on his bunk: clothing, camouflage materials, and his best remaining weapons, a World War Two vintage M1 carbine and a bolt-action 30-30 Remington with a deer scope. The cops had taken his best rifle, the Manlicher, when he was arrested the first time. They had taken his short barreled Winchester when that witch had ballsed him. He also laid out his .45 caliber sidearm and the military surprise, a pair of live hand grenades he'd stolen from the Army before they kicked him out. He also had a flare pistol with three flares that he'd bought at a flea market, no questions asked.

It was time to get ready. He was going to do some damage, and then fade. But before he faded he would make his mark – he would smite his enemies. Of this, he was certain sure.

Delmar got dressed and armed, slowly and lovingly. It was the mission he'd waited for all his life. Death and destruction and waste them all, every one. That was the plan.

His eyes were focused, and his limbs were tight. He noticed his vision was especially clear in the tunnel directly in front of him. He could see the threads in fabric.

Delmar got dressed.

(<o>)/(14.32)\(<o>)

"We've only got a few minutes," Skate said, "here's what we know."

Old Man Sutter nodded, listening.

"First," Hack said, "this property has been in my family for over a hundred years. The Hackneys settled up here before the Civil War."

Skate looked around at the group. Remo and Patrick were up the ridge on sentry duty, which left Old Man Sutter, Calvin, Fat Henry, Carol, Annie and Ace, Rexee' and Book.

"I stumbled across this last Tuesday."

"We dug it out," Hack added, "which took us until Wednesday."

"We walked in, saw the scene, and then walked out, taking a few crates with us" he pointed to two crates by the door, both occupied by Henry, who was sitting on them, one cheek per crate.

"Today," Rexee' contributed, sensing the need for precision, "they took Ace and me in to see. We tried to walk in the same footsteps."

"And that's where it stands right now," Hack said.

"We think this might be a crime scene," Skate went on, "but we don't' know. Meantimes, we've kept it secret while we decided what to do."

"The other thing is," Hack said, "The license plate says 1936. This would be about the year, in the family stories, that my grandfather disappeared. When my dad was about six"

Sutter nodded, "I think I see."

"We've got to go," Skate said, "but the perimeter is secure, and there are sentries out."

"I see," Sutter said.

"You're a doctor," Skate went on, "and Calvin is the king of the mystery novel. So we'd like you both to take a look, and say what you think."

"But," Hack added, looking from Sutter to Calvin, "only if you can keep it quiet in good conscience. I want information, but I need Hackney family final say on what gets done. You understand? If you're conflicted by this, just stay outside, and pretend the truck isn't here. Got me?"

"I understand your parameters," Sutter said. "go and do what you need to do, and I'll think it over."

"Think it over, hell!" Calvin said, "I'm checking this scene, and I'm keeping my mouth shut. You've got my word."

"Let me have that flashlight," Calvin said to Rexee', "or lead the way. I'm gonna see this, no doubt, no how."

"Okay," Skate said, "work that out. Meanwhile, there's a couple more things."

Skate looked at Henry.

"Here's what you do if there's a calamity," he said, pantomiming the liquor truck doors open, "hoist everyone in here, and pull the lever. That locks the truck from the inside. Then get everyone towards the front, and sit tight. At that point, you're deep in the hillside, yards underground, and no bullet can penetrate. You're safe in there like Fort Knox."

"Got it," Henry said.

"The other thing is stay close, and stay together," Skate said.

"No smoking," Hack said, looking at Rexee', "and keep quiet. You're safe here as long as you lie low."

"Also," Book said, looking at Annie and Rexee', "you should know that Carol is pregnant."

"This is no secret, right," Book said to Carol, "so I want everyone to know. It's information I want everyone to have."

"I think everyone knew that, Book," Skate said.

"Well, nobody told me," Annie said, "thanks a hell of a lot."

"Sorry, honey," Ace blushed, "I guess I forgot to mention it. It's Patrick's fault."

"I've been in a car with her all day, I figured it out," Annie answered.

"Patrick," Skate said, "he's not here, I blame Patrick."

"Well, what ho," Book said, "let's not tarry. Who's scouting the campsite?"

"Book, you Henry, Calvin, and Sutter stay here." Skate said.

"Ace, you should come with me and Hack," Skate went on.

"Doc," Hack said to Sutter, "I'd like your opinion, because I still don't know what to do."

"Go do your business," Sutter said, "I'll talk to you later."

Hack and Skate moved away to the north, up the slope towards where Patrick was stationed. Ace gave Annie a hug.

"Stay safe," she said to him.

"You got it babe," Ace answered, "stick with this crew, and I'll see you soon."

"Henry," Ace said, looking to the big man, "handle it."

Henry nodded, and Ace turned and followed Hack and Skate up the hill.

(<o>).[].(<o>)

"Patrick," Hack hissed, "we're coming through."

Patrick had his back to them, but he heard them coming. He turned for a moment and gave the high sign, then turned back to his vantage.

"We're passing through to the lakeshore," Skate whispered on the way past, "to sweep the area."

Patrick only nodded.

"We'll be back in an hour or more likely two."

"Do the thing," Patrick whispered, "I'll be here."

"You got your rock?"

"Go, or I'll bean you with it."

(<o>)/(14.34)\(<o>)

"Calvin," Sutter said, "I think we should investigate, don't you?"

"Hell, yes."

"Miss Rexee'," Sutter said, "can we borrow your flashlight?"

"Like hell," Rexee' said, "follow me."

Henry stood, up from his liquor crates, and worked the door until it swung open. Stench wafted out.

"Yep," Sutter said, as Rexee' clambered up through the doors, "that's what it smells like."

Sutter struggled up with Henry's help.

"Here," she said, "is where we stepped."

She played her flashlight over the floor, showing footsteps in the dust.

"There's a passageway through these liquor crates," she intoned, like a docent, "and an open area at the end. Let's go."

"Henry," Calvin said, hopping lightly aboard the truck, "you're the man. If it rains rocks, you take action."

"You know it, " Henry said, "I'm here."

(<o>).[].(<o>)

Rexee' got a thrill sometimes from watching accomplishment. It was a weird tingling, that she never talked about. But every once in a while, seeing someone who displayed unhalting competence, she would feel a physical chill. It didn't happen often, and so it was a thrill on top of a chill. It was a rush.

One time she had watched, as her mother bustled around the kitchen baking biscuits. Another time it was that sculptor, Abel, brushing stone with an emory cloth. Once it was Hack, carving a piece of wood. The first time it was a glass blower, when she was a young girl visiting the World's Fair in New York, creating glass animals.

It was almost impossible to describe, and it happened with ever decreasing frequency as she got older, but there was a thrill she got from seeing someone who seemed to do something very, very well. It was a subtle tingling in the belly, that glowed out into her chest cavity and down her arms. It wasn't sexual, it wasn't cognitive, it was visceral. When she saw someone doing something that was difficult, or mysterious, and she was a more-or-less silent observer, it gave her a buzz to see it. It was a physical manifestation of admiration.

It was witnessing the behavior of someone who "knew what they were doing."

She had had this experience only a few times in her life, and she treasured every one. A baker rolling dough in Lansing, Ace changing her tire that one time, a bartender pouring heavy cream over a spoon into a hot drink in the Stockholm Bar one Sunday afternoon.

And now Old Man Sutter, as he worked his way through the scene at the back of the truck.

(<o>).[].(<o>)

"Stand back there," Sutter instructed Rexee', "and point the light where I tell you."

Old Man Sutter stood in the entryway for a long period, surveying the scene. Then he got on his knees and probed.

Sutter started with the skeleton closest to him, inspecting the remains while doing his best to leave things undisturbed.

"Calvin," he said, "have you got a notepad?"

"I do," Book said, having walked carefully behind them, "what do you need?"

"Write down what I say," Sutter answered, "and stop me if I go too fast."

"Go," Book said, "I'm on it."

"There is a body," Sutter intoned, "prone on the floor, and another apparently sitting, but more likely suspended on a hook or a nail against the back wall."

"The first body," Sutter went on, "prone on the floor, is desiccated into skeleton form. It lies face down, A cursory inspection reveals broken neck bones, presumably from a blow delivered shortly before and causing death."

Sutter turned back towards Book, "are you getting all this?"

"Go," Book said, "I'll let you know if I'm falling behind."

"Okay," Sutter continued, "the body appears to be laying on top of a weapon, probably a shotgun."

"Whoa, "Calvin said, "lemme see that."

"In a minute," Sutter said.

(<o>)/(14.37)\(<o>)

Quiet. Too quiet. You wish.

"There is great disorder under heaven, and the situation is excellent"*

Bard laying in his loft, lantern lit, snuggled in his bedroll, pen in hand, papers strewn on the floor around him. He props himself on an elbow and scribbles madly, fighting sleep.

Murder in the moonlight, almost.

Babes in the woods, dead to the world, belts after breakfast. Later.

The second wave, reinforcements on the way, the situation is excellent.

Put the kids in back.

A flashlight probes the black spaces of the vast chilly past.

The present intrudes – there is great disorder, and change is bad.

Stealth patrol, the boys on the quiet in the woods. Cage always takes the point.

Reinforcements. Rendezvous. Closure. Get gone.

Reinforcements. Rendezvous. Bivouac. Deployment. Sentries. The rock protocol. Winston Churchill meets Ludwig Van Beethoven. The beat, the beet, you can't beat the beet.

Man'O'War. Guys, mount up.

There's no place like home. We wish for our homes, and for safety, and security. Home is where the head is. If the stuff flies, lock yourself inside. Sure, lock homes.

(<o>)/(Endnotes 14.38)\(<o>)

90. Image, Blues (1969). Ride Captain Ride. ASCAP. "Be amazed at the friends you have here on your trip."

91. Uncle Sven's Comic Shoppe, 1838 St. Clair Ave. St. Paul, MN 55105

92. King, Stephen (2000). Secret Windows. BotMC.

93. Poirot, Hercule (1920-1975). Fictional Belgian detective, the work of Agatha Christie.

94. Eye of the Holy See (1975/2009). AHC Productions. http://www.imdb.com/title/tt1391059/

95. Morse Code - a system of communication developed for the telegraph

96. Mao, Chairman. The Little Red Book. Quotations from Chairman Mao Zedong, The most printed book in history after the Bible.

Chapter 15

Delmar poked his head out of his bunkhouse and surveyed the land. Jack and Hank and Lon were nowhere. He stepped out, in full battle dress, an American fighting man.

He was head to toe in army issue camouflage, from combat cap to canvas boots. His canvas belt had a holstered pistol, a flare gun, a set of grenades, and an ammunition pouch. He had a wicked clasp knife poking out of one boot. The Remington with the scope was strapped across his back. He carried the carbine in front of him.

He stopped in the clearing next to the picnic table and saluted Lon's flag. Then he turned towards the back of the property and started a brisk trot.

When he got to the stream, he crossed it this time. It was shallow and narrow, so he just splashed across.

Lon knew his path down the near side, but not the far side. He took the far side because he didn't want Lon catching him from behind, like before.

It wasn't that he wanted to shoot Lon, and it wasn't that he wanted to avoid it either. Lon was okay, but Lon was not a real military leader. Lon would be fine if he stayed out of Delmar's way, and Delmar was through taking orders from Lon. That ended the other night. Delmar was an army of his own from now on, on his own mission – nothing more to say, nothing more to think, nothing more to worry about.

Delmar went past the stream a few yards, into the brush, and then turned north towards Unkafrank Lake. He would follow the water down to the battle. He kept the stream on his right, but he didn't worry too much about keeping to cover. He was a heavily armed fighting man, and the evilest son-of-a-bitch in the valley.*

(<o>)/(15.2)\(<o>)

Terry and Traci had been at it all morning.

This was after they'd been at it all night.

Traci was a professional, so the first amorous moments had been with their usual detachment.

Terry had been a monk for years, and had a lot of pent up sexual energy. He had also had a lot of time to read. So he had a repertoire of things he wanted to do in bed, if he ever got the chance.

Terry was from a small town, and his relationship progression had been arrested by the draft, and the war, and his 'stranger in a strange land'* life for the last four years.

Terry had tons of fantasies to work through, and years of celibacy to make up for.

They had been at it all night, and then they slept. Then they woke up to the sound of vehicles leaving. And they had been at it all morning.

"Wow," Traci said, "where have you been all my life?"

"I've been in Canada," Terry answered, "and they don't have women up there."

"Well, I'm here now," she said, "and so are you, again."

"Yes," Terry said, rolling her over, "let's try this."

"Okay," she murmured, "I'm okay."

(<o>)/(15.3)\(<o>)

Delmar worked his way down the stream, and came out by the lake on the west end of the Hackney land. Then he moved along the shore, carefully, eastward towards the campsite. He had never been there, but he knew it must be in front of him, and it was.

When he reached a point where he could see the cabin, which was the nearest element of the campsite from that direction, he went inland, uphill, to get a vantage. Soon he was on the ridgetop, southwest of the clearing, looking down on the site.

There was no movement that he could discern. The vehicles were gone, and the land was abandoned. He had the run of the place.

Still, he was careful, as there was the chance of people in the cabin, or in the trailer, or in the little tent.

But he wasn't afraid. He was heavily armed and there was nothing in the clearing below that could stand up to his firepower – he was sure of it. Still, there were a lot of them. He was outnumbered.

He watched and waited.

(<o>)/(15.4)\(<o>)

They followed Hack over the ridge, Skate and then Ace.

After a short gentle walk they crested a low hump. The easy route from there was down a draw that ended in a gap between two high points, and then winding a curve that came out in the lakeside clearing just above the old homesite.

From that angle you would see a broad open semi-circular wedge of cleared land surrounded by trees and heavy brush, with land sloping up in all directions from the clearing.

Coming out of the trees at that point, you would see the driveway entering to your right, the ruins of the homesite directly in front of you, the trailer just below the homesite, the lakeshore spreading before you, and the new cabin far to the left, hidden from the shore by a thin line of trees.

(<o>).[].(<o>)

They stopped to talk it over.

"If he followed the stream from Lon's, then he came out on the lake in back of the cabin. He could climb a bit from there, and be up on that side with a pretty good view of everything."

Skate knew the terrain, and he followed this. Ace did not. He was at something of a loss. But it was time to listen rather than break in.

"We don't know if he's there," Skate said, "or if he's been there long."

"Right," Hack said, "If he's there, and being careful, he could have worked his way all the way around the campsite."

"Yeah," Skate said, "he'd be smart to take a position on the far side, the east side. We wouldn't expect him from that angle."

"So, here's what I think," Hack said, "one of us goes up and right from here, clearing the draw, and then going around to the east edge, like we were just saying."

Skate agreed.

"The other one goes up and left, moving along above the cabin and down to the stream. That'll be me."

"Ace, you give us exactly ten minutes, then go down this draw. Follow it around until you get to the edge of the clearing and sit tight. You'll be our eyes until we can make sure the area is clear. Just get to a point where you can see everything and not be seen, and stay put."

Hack looked at Skate, "You think?"

"Yeah, it's a plan. We stick together, which I'm inclined towards, frankly, and the whole thing takes twice as long. More time for something to go wrong."

"That's about it," Hack answered.

"You," Skate said to Ace, "are key here. When I get to the far end, I'm going to be looking for you. I'm not going to step into the clear until I see a high sign from you. So you've got to keep an eye out for sign from Hack."

Ace nodded.

"So check your watch, and wait here for ten full minutes. That gives me and Hack the chance to see that he's not just above us here. That will mean you're clear to move down to your position. Low and slow. Really low and freaking slow."

Hack locked eyes with Skate. They were worried about Ace. They were good at this game, Ace was only average.

"Don't worry about me," Ace said, "there is nothing lower, and nothing slower. But I'll be there."

"Good deal," Hack said, "ten minutes, then low, and slow."

For a goof, Skate slapped his fist to his chest, then raised it, like a Roman Centurion.

Hack laughed silently. Skate turned uphill, grinning to himself. Ace was too freaked out to smile.

They moved off.

Hack had taken the more probably treacherous job, and they both knew it. But there were a million things to go wrong, in all directions, and they both knew that too.

(<o>).[].(<o>)

Skate moved along the right-hand ridge top looking for Delmar, and looking for sign. There was nothing, as he expected. He turned east and followed the ridge line around the perimeter. He moved swiftly, keeping to cover, until he came to the driveway. This was an exposed point, no way around it. He moved up the slope, listened for anything at all, and then hustled across to the far side. No gun shots, no death. His heart was pounding, but he felt little fear. White boy raised in the suburbs, yet he felt in his element.

(<o>).[].(<o>)

Ace waited ten eternal minutes, hardly hearing a sound, and hardly knowing what to think. Finally, he started moving down the draw. He stayed so low, he practically crawled, and he moved so slow, moss offered to grow on his northside.

At long last he saw the clearing through the trees in front of him. He got down on his belly and crawled into an opening, inching forward by degrees until he could see the lakeside clearing. Ace looked to his right, to see if Skate was visible down by the lake.

He wasn't.

Ace looked to his left to see if Hack was signaling.

He wasn't.

Ace looked into the clearing for any signs of life. There were none, except the trailer, which was rocking slightly side to side.

Ace settled in to wait. He looked out onto the lake. There was a boat coming, a canoe.

(<o>).[].(<o>)

Hack had rougher terrain, and he was likely to find Delmar on the way, so it was slower going for him. Still, he was almost around his circuit when he heard the gunfire, ahead of him and down toward the lake. He hunkered into a crouch for a moment, until he was sure where the sound was from. Then he moved towards it as quickly as he could, keeping silent.

He counted one shot, then two more, quickly – then a pause, and then two more. Hack broke into a run.

(<o>)/(15.9)\(<o>)

Delmar surveyed the scene.

He had full oversight, and nothing could move that he couldn't hit if he chose to.

He had stayed on the west end of the campsite, near the stream, because it afforded him full view, and kept an escape route open behind him. He was crouched against a tree for cover.

But he bridled at the inactivity. He wasn't there to scout, he was there to fight, and surveillance was playing on his nerves. Where were they? He wanted to pick them off, one by one, but there was nothing to shoot at.

Were they on to him? Waiting for him?

Just then he saw movement in the clearing below him. It was subtle, but it was there. The trailer was rocking – someone was in there.

He sighted down the pinhole of his carbine, and pondered a shot. Maybe he could flush them out into the open. He removed the safety on his rifle.

Instead, he decided to work his way down into the clearing. He had the element of surprise, he was sure. He should keep quiet until he had a clear shot.

He got to his feet, but he had been crouched for long time, and his legs were stiff. Delmar stumbled as he was rising and fell back against the tree. He caught himself easily, steadied himself and didn't fall over, but the safety was off his hair-trigger carbine, and he was tensed. A round fired into the dirt. A sharp report in the morning silence.

"Crap!" he cursed, flinching at the sound.

Pissed at himself, he wheeled around to the campsite. The trailer was a likely target, and his position was blown, so he aimed and fired two quick rounds into the side of it.

"Hey!" Terry yelled from inside the trailer, "what the hell!"

"You!" another voice called, from out on the lake, "what are you doing?"

Delmar reversed himself. There was a woman in a canoe, just offshore, screaming at him. He had not thought to look that way, and he had not seen her approach.

"I see you," she shouted, "put that gun away!"

Delmar panicked – it was like a fire fight and he was suddenly surrounded. He ran towards the woods behind him, firing as he turned. Two quick rounds went towards the lake.

Delmar ran, just past the cabin, west towards Lon's stream, his escape route.

(<o>).[].(<o>)

Hack burst out of the woods behind the cabin, and saw Delmar running just yards in front of him. He came in low and cut Delmar at his knees. They fell in a bundle.

(<o>).[].(<o>)

Ace heard shots and plunged out of his position. He couldn't see Hack and Delmar from where he was, but it didn't matter. He sprinted across the clearing.

Terry came out of the trailer, just as Ace got there.

"What the hell?" Terry yelled.

"I don't know," Ace answered on the way by, "follow me."*

(<o>).[].(<o>)

Skate had not seen anything until the movement and the accidental shot, as Delmar stumbled from cover. Then Skate saw Delmar taking aim and firing at the trailer, heard Terry yelling, and saw Delmar spray fire towards the lake, only then seeing Sister Louise in her canoe.

For a timeless second he was frozen, not knowing what to do. Then he saw Hack caroming out of the woods and colliding with Delmar, falling out of sight.

Skate started running.

He pelted along the shoreline towards where Hack and Delmar collided. Sister Louise was standing in her canoe, shocked.

"What's going on?" she called to him.

"Stay there," Skate yelled, he was running full tilt.

Hack held Delmar who was writhing in fury. Hack threw a punch but it glanced off Delmar's forehead – hard enough to stun him, but not to stop him. Delmar broke away from Hack. His rifle on the ground, he pulled out a weapon, but not his pistol, his flare gun.

"Stand back," Delmar ordered, trying to get up, "or I'll kill you."

Hack rolled and leaped to his feet, confronting Delmar in a low crouch, but looking up the barrel of a gun.

Which is exactly when Skate arrived – barreling into Delmar at full speed.

Delmar anticipated the impact at the very last moment and fired his pistol wildly at Hack, as he was falling under Skate's weight.

The flare went over Hack and through the cabin's one north-side window, the little uncovered one with no glass.

Skate and Delmar were on the ground, ass over tea kettle. Hack jumped on Delmar. Ace and Terry were there by then and each grabbed a leg. That made four against one - they subdued him. The battle was over.

Terry handed a leg to Ace, then while Ace was unable to prevent it, his hands being full, Terry pulled Ace's belt out of its loops and, with two quick moves, used it to truss Delmar like a roped calf.

The battle was totally over then.

Delmar was still writhing and squirming against the restraints, there was spittle foaming on his lips and chin.

"FUCK...YOU...GUYS...I'LL...KILL...YOU"

Sister Louise walked up, and without a second of hesitation pulled a fat red bandana out of her hip pocket and stuffed it into Delmar's mouth.

"Shut the fuck up," she said in a low serious voice.

(<o>)/(15.13)\(<o>)

"Did you hear that?" Annie said to Carol.

A rock fell into the clearing from the north.

Then another rock fell into the clearing from the south.

"Ladies," Henry hissed, "get your asses into the truck."

The ladies got their asses into the truck.

Henry hoisted himself aboard with deceptive agility, and locked the door behind him. Then he turned into the darkness.

"Rexee'," he said, "a little light back here, please."

(<o>)/(15.14)\(<o>)

Hack produced some nylon rope, and they completed the trussing of Delmar. Ace was careful to get his belt back. They picked Delmar up like a slaughtered carcass and carried him over by the campfire near the trailer.

Terry went into the trailer to fetch Traci. He was gone for a long while.

"Now what," Hack asked, "do we haul him up to the truck, or go get the truck and drive it down here?"

"First thing," Ace said, "we better get up to the...the, uh, the..."

He stopped, suddenly mindful of Delmar and Sister Louise, and looking at Hack and Skate for an inspiration.

"...the other place, where the other's are," he concluded, lamely.

"Yeah," Skate laughed, "the other place. If they've been listening at all they're in lockdown."

"Exactly my point," Ace added.

"Our friends," Skate explained to Sister Louise, "they're hidden up the road. We've got to signal the all clear."

"So, okay," Hack said, "me and Ace will head up the road. You, Skate, sit on this situation until I get back with the truck. Then we'll dump this guy in town."

"You," he said to Sister Louise, "should probably come to town as an impartial witness."

"I can do that," she nodded.

341

"Okay, good. Ace, let's peel," Hack said, and then to Skate, "sit tight, be back in a snap."

"Nobody's going anyplace," Skate said, looking at Delmar, "until you get back."

Skate picked a short pole from the wood supply by the campfire, hefted it like a baseball bat, and sat down facing Delmar, laying inert.

"Take your time."

Hack and Ace raced away, up the driveway, their adrenaline still kicked in.

(<o>).[].(<o>)

Delmar was laying face down, into the dirt. He was squirming to get the ropes off, with no chance of success.

"So, sister," Skate said amiably, "how have you been?"

"Okay," she said, and sat on the log next to him, "what's the story here?"

"This," Skate said, pointing with his pole, "is Delmar."

Skate shrugged.

"Delmar is a murderer, convicted of manslaughter, out on parole. He violated his parole about two weeks ago. First, we think, by taking a shot at Hack – attempted murder in the first degree. But certainly by stealing food from a market, and also certainly by being found in a bar with a rifle on his person."

"What about that Delmar?" Skate said mildly, "that was you gunning for Hack, right?"

Delmar writhed and squirmed, screaming incomprehensibly behind Sister Louise's handkerchief gag, his face still buried in the dirt.

"Well, anyway," Skate went on, "today's attempted murder should seal his fate. With all and everything, Delmar should be back in the big house for a real long time, I think."

"So," Sister Louise said, "you two have history."

"Oh, sure," Skate whispered, "Delmar and I go way back. Don't we Delmar?"

Skate turned suddenly angry.

"I witnessed a murder, and testified to what I saw. Since then, not a day has gone by that I didn't flinch from the memory, and fear he would ..." his anger strangled him momentarily, "fear he was coming to kill me too."

"Fear every day?" Sister Louise asked.

"Yeah, every day pretty much."

"I know a little bit about what that's like," she nodded, "I do, indeed."

"But now," Skate slapped his stick into his palm, "rage is more like it. I'd like to take this club and beat his bones into jelly."

"His balls, too?" she asked.

"Yeah," Skate snorted, "his balls to jelly, right."

It was funny to hear a nun say that.

"But probably not."

Skate turned to her, smiling now.

"I don't know," he said, "he might try to escape."

"Well, then," she smiled back, "then it would be okay."

Delmar, squirming face down and unable to see them, quieted down.

342

(<o>)/(15.16)\(<o>)

Hack and Ace were up the driveway, by the vehicles, lined up three in a row.

"I'll go right back down," Hack said, "and pick up the package."

"Right," Ace answered, "and I'll go liberate the village, like Patton in France."

"Yeah," Hack said, starting his truck, "that's what the situation calls for."

(<o>)/(15.17)\(<o>)

"Whatever happened with that girl?" Sister Louise asked.

"You put it together, finally."

"There were hundreds of cases in those days, and those days were some years ago now. But yes, I think I remember."

Skate nodded.

"I saw her last winter," Skate said, "she had the baby, and it wasn't mine."

She nodded, "you were distressed, I remember, wanting to be a father."

"Not even so much," Skate answered, "but ready to do what was needed."

"Not at first, of course," he added, "I was flailing at first."

"And she was going to abort, right? Which you didn't want."

"Not really, no, but sort of, not knowing what was best, or right."

"And then?" Sister Louise prompted.

"And then she disappeared, and I was lost" Skate shrugged,. "and I didn't see her again for over a year, and then by chance, in a winter storm."

"She was part of this, by the way," Skate indicated Delmar on the ground, "she was also a witness. The dead man was actually the father."

"Wow," Sister Louise said, "that's some shit to handle."

"You could say that," Skate answered.

(<o>)/(15.18)\(<o>)

Ace swaggered into the clearing like Patton liberating a village in France.

"Remo, Patrick," he shouted, "can you hear me?"

Ace paused.

"Ollie ollie in free."

No reaction.

"The wicked witch is dead – short, short, short, long."

"Was that gunfire?" Patrick shouted down.

"Yeah," Ace shouted up into the woods, "Delmar shooting his wad. He's in custody, no casualties, come on down, it's over. Remo, you too."

(<o>).[].(<o>)

Ace swaggered up to the truck like Patton liberating a village in France and rapped on the back doors. Three short quick raps, a pause, and one more: Morse Code "V" for victory.

The door swung open.

Ace was expecting to see a crowd of detainees pouring out, but there was nothing to see in the gloom. Then he made out the low crouched figure of Fat Henry in the gloom, in a football stance, ready to launch himself out the door into the teeth of whatever he encountered.

343

"You alone," Henry growled.

"Easy, Henry," Ace took a step back, truly frightened, "the war's been won. Stand down."

Henry sagged.

Ace stumbled backward another step, downhill, and landed on his butt in the gravel.

"I was ready to rush you," Henry said, "if this was a trick."

Rexee' walked past Henry and clapped him on the shoulder.

"Henry," she said, "I saw you. You were coiled like a cobra. You were ready to do battle."

She hopped lightly down to the ground.

"In this totally fucked situation, you made me feel safe – like we had a fighting chance."

She turned and looked Henry in the eye, "Thank you, seriously."

"Now, Timothy" she looked down to Ace, "Let's hear it. What the hell just happened."

(<o>)/(15.20)\(<o>)

Hack returned with the pickup truck. They hoisted Delmar into the back (after taking their canoe out). Skate and Sister Louise crowded into the cab with Hack. The trailer was rocking, they did not go knocking.

They went back up the driveway, and stopped as Henry and Rexee' were coming out from the path, by the van and the station wagon. Ace and Annie were right behind, holding hands. Followed by Patrick and Carol, also holding hands.

"Everybody, you remember Delmar," Skate said, nodding into the back of the pickup truck.

For some reason, the men all took a step forward to peak into the back of the truck, and the women all took a step back.

(<o>).[].(<o>)

Skate was feeling plucky and euphoric. He had slammed into Delmar like a runaway freight, blind-siding him with a crack-back block. He could still feel the impact and the delicious feeling of knocking a man clean off his feet and flat on his ass. A hard body check – a clean hit, like meeting the high hard one in your wheelhouse with the sweet spot on red maple.

(<o>).[].(<o>)

"Delmar has been very bad, haven't you Delmar?"

Delmar lay face down, rigid as a lightening rod. You could practically see the steam rising off him.

"But Delmar is going away now, maybe forever, right Delmar?"

Hack came around and put his hand on Skate's shoulder to calm and silence him. Their eyes locked. Hack squinted. Skate took a breath, sighed, and nodded.

"Where's Book?" Hack asked Ace.

"Bound up, I guess," Ace said, "he's still back there with Calvin and Sutter."

"I suppose we should get them," Skate volunteered, "and drive in together. Hold on, I'll fetch."

344

Skate trotted off down the path towards the liquor truck.

"What's with him?" Rexee' said to Hack.

"He met the enemy," Hack offered, "and kicked his fucking ass."

(<o>).[].(<o>)

Skate ran up behind the liquor truck. The doors were swung open, and he could see a flashlight playing against the back wall.

"Hello this truck," Skate called, and hopped into the back.

"Come on back," Book said, "don't worry about footprints. We had the Mongol Horde in here a minute ago."

Skate once again encountered the macabre scene. The shrunken prone skeleton dressed in winter gear, laying on the floor; the larger shrunken skeleton sitting up on crates. He had not been back here since the first day they opened the truck.

The three of them, Sutter, Book, and Calvin, were clustered near the back wall, actually the front of the truck compartment, around the sitting skeleton. Calvin had the flashlight, holding it high above his head, and pointing it as Sutter directed. Book stood on the other side of Sutter with his notebook out, pencil poised, writing as Sutter mumbled aloud. He was inspecting the sitting skeleton by this time.

Skate was about to speak, when Sutter straightened from his stoop.

"That's it, I've seen enough."

Book shut his notebook, and Calvin said, "Solid, let's get out of this graveyard."

"You guys got it figured?"

It was Hack, who had come up so quietly nobody heard him.

"I think so," Book said, his voice flat.

"Yes," Sutter added, "enough to make a preliminary report."

"Okay," Hack said, turning to go, "we can talk about it in town. Somebody make sure the doors are shut, okay?"

Hack jumped off the end of the truck and walked swiftly up the path.

They helped Old Man Sutter down from the truck, and followed.

Skate made sure the doors were shut.

(<o>).[].(<o>)

They waited together as everyone finally filed out and loaded onto the van and into the station wagon. Then they drove to town together as a convoy, to deposit Delmar with the city police and make their various reports.

Behind them, forgotten, Delmar's flare fizzled away in Skate's bedroll.

(<o>)/(15.25)\(<o>)

Thirteen people is just about capacity seating in the tiny Elysium police station waiting room. They could have separated, since most of them had nothing to report. Nothing they were willing to report, that is. The principal witnesses were just Ace, Skate, Hack, and Sister Louise. But the rest of them stayed, reluctant to split up.

There was one other eye witness, Terry, but they kept his name out of it, for obvious federal fugitive warrant motivations.

It didn't take long to establish the first fact – that Delmar was a convicted felon and a parole violator. A single phone call to Minneapolis Police and Delmar was placed in custody.

The police insisted on being the ones to carry him in from the pickup truck. They removed Sister Louise's bandana, and Delmar started a feral howling. They tried to ask him his name, but he was unable to respond. They put the handkerchief back.

The police started to untie him at first, but Delmar started writhing and struggling, so they re-secured the knots, hauled him into a cell, handcuffed him, and then removed the ropes. In that process they discovered he was more heavily armed than seemed at first.

The guys had taken Delmar's flare pistol and his side-arm, and they had unhooked his deer rifle from his back. And they had picked up his carbine. But they had somehow missed the grenades on his belt, and it took a sharp-eyed policeman to notice the clasp knife in his boot.

"Survivalist," one cop said.

"Yeah," the other answered, "at least."

(<o>).[].(<o>)

The statements took a while.

The Chief was called in, and he gathered Skate, Hack, Ace, Sister Louise, and Rexee' into his office.

"Okay," he said, "I'm running this tape machine here, to record the conversation. Who wants to start?"

"The murdering bastard," Rexee' led off, "was going to kill us all."

The Chief nodded.

"Yes," he said, "but let's start at the beginning."

Skate became the spokesman. He told the story of the manslaughter, and the trial, but he left Effie out, and he neglected to mention Rexee's role in those events. Then he told about the scene in Doogan's where Delmar was arrested for petty theft, and parole violation, being in possession of a rifle. He left out the Constitution of the United States, the American Dream, and Rexee's well-placed balls-job punt.

Then he told what he knew about Lon, and the armed camp at his place. And he told about Lon's warning on the driveway. He left out the path from that point to the liquor truck. Then he told about the scouting, looking to see if the site was clear, and then his version of the firefight, including the struggle with Hack, and Ace being there too.

Skate only heard four shots.

"No," Ace said, "there were five. One, then two, then two more."

"Yeah," Hack added, "five."

The Chief wrote something on the pad in front of him.

"Lon met you in the driveway?" he asked Hack shrewdly.

The Chief watched Columbo* and loved it. He liked to ask unexpected questions.

"We were on the way out, and he met us on the way in."

The Chief nodded.

"And what's your version?" he said to Sister Louise.

346

"Not much, really," she answered, "I was paddling across the lake. I heard a shot, then I saw the guy in the clearing, firing two more shots into the trailer."

"Into the trailer? Why?"

"I really don't know. Then I yelled, and he started to run along the lakeshore. But he paused for just a moment and shot at me. He aimed in my direction and shot his gun."

"The rifle," the Chief asked.

"Yeah," Ace and Hack answered together.

"He took two shots at her, definitely, as he was running," Ace added.

"Then what?" the Chief said.

"Then I saw Hack jump on him," she said, "they struggled, and Skate ran up and knocked him down."

"It took me a bit," she went on, "to paddle into shore. He shot my canoe, it has two holes in it."

"He hit the canoe with both shots?" the Chief seemed skeptical.

"One shot, I think, near the water line."

"Ah," the Chief nodded knowingly, "a through and through. Then what?"

"They were tying him up when I got there. That's it." She shrugged, "I stuffed a handkerchief in his mouth, to quiet him – he was furious, and I quieted that."

The Chief nodded again.

"And why were you on the lake at that time?"

"I was coming across with an invitation," Sister Louise said, "to join us on the island for the Fourth of July. That's all."

(<o>).[].(<o>)

The Chief had mixed feelings about the nuns. They had been on the island for a really, really long time and he had known for years they were involved in various things. He didn't agree with them politically and never had. And they were a close-mouthed bunch when it suited them. You couldn't make them talk sometimes, when they decided they had nothing to say. But on the other hand, they didn't lie. It was either silence or truth with those ladies.

He didn't like it, but he grasped the rules they went by. The rest of these were strangers up from the city, with nothing to vouch for them, neither for nor against. The Chief did not know them, and had no reason to believe, or to disbelieve, any of them. Except for Hackney – he came from a family the Chief knew very well, and trusted very little.

But Sister Louise was the goods. He trusted her testimony completely. He even liked her a little bit, although he'd never show it or admit it. Whatever Sister Louise said was true, end of story. He had absolute faith in that.

(<o>)/(15.28)\(<o>)

They went to the bar.

The nearest was Powder's Tap, a dimly lit, crummy little dive like so many others. Larry presiding.

Ace, riding shotgun in the station wagon with Book and Annie, led the way.

"Innkeeper! drinks for my friends."

They piled in and took positions in the corner of the bar, at a range of empty tables. Larry hustled, drawing pitchers of beer and making drinks to order.

It was 7:30 on Saturday night, but Powder's Tap was practically deserted.

Only Hank and Jack were sitting at the bar.

Powder's was not much of a hot spot until near closing time. Larry was known to be lax about closing on time.

(<o>)/(15.29)\(<o>)

A one act play in several scenes:

Scene Fifteen –

The lights come up on the interior of Powder's Tap, a crumby little bar, the same as before.

Larry, as before, is standing at the audience-left end of the bar.

There are two men sitting at the bar with their backs to the audience: Jack and Hank.

The tables have all been pushed together, center stage, and the entire group of thirteen is sitting together. From audience left to right: Patrick, Carol, Sister Louise, Fat Henry, Rexee', Hack, Skate, Ace, Annie, Book, Remo, Calvin, and Old Man Sutter.

It is Saturday, July 3rd, 1976, just after Seven-Thirty P.M. in the Central Time Zone, in Powder's Tap, Elysium Minnesota.

=#=#=#=

```
    Skate
(looks left and right, counting, then raises his glass)
This is my blood, drink this in memory of me.

    Sister Louise
Oh, very funny.

    Skate
(laughs and puts down his glass)
So, here's the story as I saw it. We left you guys and hiked
past Patrick and down into the gully. Then we split up. I went
right, Ace up the middle, and Hack went around the left end.

    Patrick
It was all so serious, and yet I was trying not to laugh.
Nerves I guess.

    Carol
I was scared to death with you out there.

    Patrick
Yeah, me too I guess.

    Hack
We were looking for Delmar, or sign of Delmar. The idea was to
make sure the area was clear, and then get everybody out.

    Carol
It's the nerve that gets me. What qualifies you guys to be
Indian scouts?

    Hack
Riding a bicycle, right Skate?
```

Skate

Sort of, I guess. It's like driving millions of miles in bad
weather over bad roads. After a while you develop confidence.
That's pretty much it, I think.

Rexee'

What in the hell are you talking about?

Ace

Boyhood pursuits. A short lifetime in the woods before we
could shave. Boy Scouts from hell.

Hack

Green River.

Rexee'

Okay, the next person to say that gets killed, entirely.
(she punches Hack in the shoulder, hard)
Is that clear to everyone?

Skate

Meanwhile, to continue, we split up. I crept all the way
around to the east of the campsite -- low and slow. There was
nothing, and not even a bad moment until I had to cross the
driveway.

Hack

Yeah, I was wondering about that.

Skate

I went up the driveway pretty far, and then crossed.
(shrugs).
It wasn't too bad. Anyway, I got all the way to the lake and
there was nothing, so I hunched in and kept watch for you and
Ace.

Ace

How long?

Skate

Minutes, not long at all.

Ace

I thought so. Me, I was the lowest and freaking slowest
organism on the planet. But I was still in position for two
eons and an epoch, waiting and watching.

Skate

How many epochs?

Ace

One or two, I forget. I was just trying not to be the weak
link out there, and trying not to crap my pants while I
waited.

Remo

Waiting. That's the bitch. I hear that. Hurry up and wait,
that's what they say. But I say hurry up and wait, and keep an
eye out, and expect something bad is going to happen.

Sutter

(Nodding) The full text of the verse.

Remo

That's right. Wait around in the valley of death for the sky
to shit bricks. That's the full verse.

Book
So it is written.

Skate
And that's my preamble. I was crouching in the woods, I could
see Ace, but he hadn't seen me yet, and I was about to give
the high sign when I heard the shots and saw Hack and Delmar
fall out of the brush.

Patrick
The shots. That was the beginning and the end of it for me. I
heard the gunfire, and where I was, up on the ridge closest to
the lake, and they were LOUD. I waited about two seconds, to
see if there was an army coming. Then I threw my rock and hid.

Carol
Very sensible.

Patrick
Thank you. I still kept a watch, but I kept it from under deep
cover.

Remo
I heard the shots, and was waiting. You know, waiting for the
rest. But it was real, real quiet for a second.
(growing animated)
And then I heard this boy's rock hit the ground. That's how
still it was. I don't know what I was thinking, but I threw
mine too.

Patrick
And then very sensibly hid?

Remo
You fuckin-A boy. I was flashing back by that time. I was
getting ready to call in the Hueys. I was jumping out of my
skin and looking for a bunker. I wanted my rifle.

Sister Louise
Then, I guess, the next thing was the slow motion. The maniac
is in the clear -- shooting at that trailer. And Terry comes
out shouting. And then Hack appeared.

Skate
I saw Delmar firing, at the trailer, and I flinched back. But
then I heard Terry, and saw Hack was almost on him, so I
started running.

Ace
Me too, sort of, except I couldn't really see Hack. But I saw
Skate on the move.

Sister Louise
At some point he turned and shot at me. I always thought you
could duck if someone shot at you.

Book
We used to watch the same movies.

Sister Louise
But it's not true.

Remo
No, it's definitely not true.

Sutter
No, it's not.

Sister Louise

Those bullets whistled past me before I could even think of reacting. I heard them go by. At least I think I did. Then I saw water on my feet. He killed my canoe.

Ace

Slow motion? Did you say slow motion? Man, nothing like that for me. I see you on the lake, and I'm freaking out about what to do, and then there's the shots, and then I see Skate high-balling across the lakefront, and then Terry falls out of the trailer, and I'm running my ass past him. It was every second zen for me. Like my head was a speed bag.

Skate

I was halfway across the beach before I saw Sister Louise. I never thought to look at the lake, so it was funny and surprising to see you out there. I remember thinking that as I ran by.

Sister Louise

Do you remember what you said to me?

Skate

Said to you? When? Then?

Sister Louise

Sit tight, you said, as you ran by. I'm thinking, "I'm going to sit out here on the lake and wait? For the water to come up over my nose? Oh no, not likely"

Skate

Seriously? Well, it wasn't the worst advice. But you were wise not to follow it, I guess.

Ace

About then I was running past Terry. He was out of the trailer, and he says something casual, like "what's up?", and I ran past him like John freaking Wayne and screaming (deep voice) Follow Me! Except it came out like this (high squeaky voice) Follow Me!

Book

The most famous of the famous last words.

Annie

We heard those shots … one, two more, then two more, quickly, in a period of about five seconds. I didn't know what to do. I looked at Carol, and said something stupid. And then Henry -- thank you Henry -- Henry us moving.

Fat Henry

We were just sitting there. Then we were at war. That's how I felt. We had a plan, and all I could think was to follow the plan.
(he looks at Carol)
It seemed urgent. Meanwhile, it was good of you ladies to hop up into the truck. My adrenaline was pumping, and I was about to throw you in if I needed to.
(he looks at Carol again)
Gently of course.

Annie

Shots in the air, rocks falling from the sky. We were in there … where Remo?

Remo
You mean the valley of the shadow of death?

    Annie
You fuckin-A, shitting bricks with rocks raining down.

    Ace
(putting his arm around Annie)
Scary in the trenches, too, yes.

    Annie
(whispering)
You fuckin-A.

    Ace
(hugs Annie, and speaks loud enough for the group to hear, to
deflect attention from her)
You should have seen Skate, barreling across the beach, and
just as Delmar got loose to take a shot at Hack. Bam! Skate
was there and ploughed him down. It was like a bowling pin
meeting it's maker. Delmar flew! And then he crumpled like a
doll.

    Sister Louise
All in slow motion.

    Ace
Yeah, it's funny, that part was, sort of …
(looking at Rexee')
 … like that time in the bar, except with an explosive
horizontal component. You should have seen it.

    Hack
I looked up, and he had the barrel of that gun in my face. I
was about to go for his knees, but then he wasn't standing
there any more. He was flat.

    Sister Louise
I'm telling you, it was in slow motion.

    Hack
It WAS like slow motion. Delmar was there, drawing down on me,
and then he was flying, like an ice skater. Sideways like a
ballerina.

    Sister Louise
From my angle, it was like gymnastics. Delmar on a trampoline.
He just bounced, then hit the ground, and bounced again.

    Ace
But in slow motion, right?

    Sister Louise
Yes, actually, kind of.

    Skate
(shrugs, lowering one shoulder)
Hockey practice.

    (Blackout).

(<o>)/(15.30)\(<o>)
diaria -- 15.0 -- 10/29/77 -- minneapolis
A note on writing books. Damn! It takes a long time.

I don't know how the big boys do it, but me, I had an hour or two a day, and there were many days when I came away with less than a page. If I cranked out three pages, it was like sunshine. I'd go to bed feeling really satisfied with my work.

If you decide to write a book, and I don't advise it, be prepared to take the long view. It's a long project, and you need to keep chipping away. That's my advice. Figure a year or more, front to back, and more is more likely.

More books? I don't know. Joseph Heller* told about writing Catch-22* at night after work. He did that for 8 full years. After a while, he said, it got so he couldn't imagine another lifestyle and had trouble figuring out what other people did with their evenings. It might sound crazy, but after a few weeks of plodding along, it got the same for me. I became jealous of the two hours an evening I'd put into this, and there were times I looked forward to it all day.

The productivity started to rise too, once I'd finally realized where the story was taking me. There were nights when I'd stay up late and rip through ten or even twelve pages in a three hour shot. I've heard people say this, but never experienced it until this: but the book did indeed take on a life of its own, and did indeed seem to write itself. If you decide to write a book, and I don't advise it, my experience is the first two hundred pages are the hardest. If you're lucky, as I suspect I was, the rest is easy.

(<o>)/(15.31)\(<o>)

Powders Tap. Saturday, 8:30 PM.

After a while, Skate and Hack huddled with Old Man Sutter, Calvin, and Book: the forensics team. Rexee' saw them gathering and came to join them.

By this time, Patrick was huddled with Carol, and Ace was huddled with Annie. It turned out that Remo, Fat Henry, and Sister Louise had a lot in common. And they were huddled too.

"So," Hack said, "I guess you'd better spill it."

Book pulled out his notebook, but it was Old Man Sutter who started talking.

(<o>).[].(<o>)

"First, understand, this was a preliminary and cursory examination. The light was bad, the conditions were poor, no laboratory work was done, and the time was limited. Plus, I did not want to disturb things, should a real forensic scientist actually be called upon to evaluate the scene."

Hack was nodding.

"What I'm trying to tell you is I'm guessing. I'll tell you what I think happened, but you have to know this is just my professional impression. It won't, probably, stand up in a court of law, and I'd be at a certain amount of risk, as a medical professional, for even embarking on this investigation. Are you getting me?"

"Doc," Hack looked from Skate to Book to Calvin to Rexee', "I think it's safe to say that nothing leaves this table, and all we want is your best guess."

Hack looked from face to face. They were all nodding.

Hack squinted, "Let's hear it."

(<o>).[].(<o>)

"Alright," Sutter said, "here's how it looked."

"The smaller guy, laid out on the floor, was named …"

Book had his notebook out, "Dewey, Dewey DeWitt."

"Yes," Sutter said, "he was 29 years old and died of a broken neck from a blow delivered from in front, I think, from above and from his right. He had a shotgun underneath him."

"A twelve gauge," Book interjected, "sawed off, with both barrels expended."

"The other one, suspended on the crates by a nail caught in his clothing, was killed by a shotgun blast to the back left chest and shoulder area."

"We identified him from his wallet, Hack," Book said, "his name was Abner Hackney. Your grandfather, right?"

Hack nodded, "He wasn't talked about much as I was growing up – the story was that he'd run off. But yes, his name was Abner."

"Yeah," Book added, "I think I remember that too, from that one time we talked to your grandmother."

(<o>).[].(<o>)

This was a dim recollection, from staying the night as boys. Grandma Zelda was alive, and watching them, maybe eight years old, while all the adults were in town for some reason. Book was up for the weekend on a sleepover. They sat around the fire and Zelda had talked about the family, and told old stories. It had seemed odd to Book, how matter-of-fact and unemotionally she had gone through it, but he'd imagined her eyes were a little damp in the telling.

(<o>).[].(<o>)

"What it looks like," Calvin spoke up, "is this."

"They probably, Dewey and Abner, stole that liquor truck up in Canada and were hiding it. How they got it across the border is anybody's guess."

"Hackney family business," Hack said.

"Then Dewey tried to kill Abner, for some reason, by blowing him in the back with the shotgun. Right?" Calvin added.

Sutter nodded.

"Then, it looks," Calvin went on, "like Abner swung around and broke his neck, killing him totally dead."

"Possibly with a single blow – impossible to say definitively."

"But," Calvin continued, "Abner was fucked up, big time, and sat down on the crate. But he was weak, and got hung up on a nail, and couldn't get off. So then he died from the gunshot."

"Right," Old Man Sutter said, "it looks like an attempted murder, followed by a self-defense type justifiable homicide, followed by death as a consequence of the wound, and maybe the cold. It was obviously winter, and a really cold day, judging by how they were dressed. It is doubtful that he suffered much, if that's any consolation."

"Then," Book said, "there must have been a kind of cave in. So the truck was embedded under many feet of gravel and dirt, so the whole scene was preserved. And it sat there all these years."

"It was an insulated truck," Sutter continued, "and it was under several feet of earth. So the crime scene was untouched, and the temperature was kept pretty constant at around 55 degrees for all these years."

"A constant 55 degrees? How do you know that?" Skate asked.

"Book told me," Sutter smiled.

"Yes," Book said, "that's the ambient temperature of most places, year round, below the frost line. If the cave is deep enough, it stays about 55 degrees whether it's in Ecuador or Siberia. With the cave in, and the truck insulation, I think it pertains."

"This is going to kill my Dad," Hack sighed.

"But on the bright side," Rexee' chimed in, "besides the ancient family tragedy, you're sitting on about a million bucks worth of beer and booze, kept cool and dark for all these years."

"Good to go," Calvin said.

(<o>)/(15.36)\(<o>)

Powders Tap, Saturday, 11 PM. They headed back to the lake, it was dark.

For once Calvin didn't have to threaten homicide to get the van loaded. It was decided they would head back, and they quietly finished their drinks and got ready to go. The fleet included the van (with Calvin, Remo, Old Man Sutter, Fat Henry, Rexee', and Sister Louise), the station wagon (with Book, Ace, Annie, Carol, and Patrick), and Hack's pickup (with Hack and Skate). It had been an exquisitely long day for everyone.

"It seems like only eighteen hours ago I was opening the diner and letting Lily in," Annie said.

"Eighteen hours and three hundred miles ago," Ace added.

"Eighteen hours, three hundred miles, a homicidal firefight, and a crime scene investigation ago," Book proffered.

"Not to mention," Carol said, "I chipped a nail."

Patrick started giggling. He couldn't stop. He hugged Carol, sitting next to him in the station wagon. He continued to giggle.

Annie started to giggle too, "I mussed my hair."

For some reason, this was hilarious, and they all started laughing. The nerves coming out, as they will after a battle.

"We're losing it Book," Ace said, giggling, "get us out of here."

Book put the car in gear and said, "I mussed my hair too."

They dissolved laughing. It lasted almost all the way back to Hack's.

(<o>).[].(<o>)

County highway, blacktop, Township road, gravel, past Lon's driveway and the deserted guard post.

The convoy kept together and crept around the left hand turn into Hack's driveway.

"What's that?" Skate asked.

"That's a fire in the night," Hack said, "a big one."

He accelerated down the driveway, faster than was safe, towards the lake.

(<o>).[].(<o>)

It was an hellacious, unearthly sight.

The cabin was on fire, shooting flames high into the dark night.

There was to be no thought of putting it out. The entire thing was consumed with flame. They had used logs that were dry, and seasoned, and yet full of combustible pine sap. The fire was huge and cast light over the entire camp site – not as bright as day, but as bright as hell. The light was so bright, and the flames were so high, they could see the Nun's island across the lake, and they could make out the nuns gathered on their shore, watching.

(<o>).[].(<o>)

Hack and Skate parked and scrambled out of the pickup, but there was nothing to be done. The van and the station wagon pulled in shortly behind them, and everybody got out. The whole group was standing by the campfire, just staring at the flames.

Terry and Traci were waiting for them when they pulled into the camp site. Terry's shirt was covered in small ragged burn holes. Traci's face was black with soot.

"It was going full blast before I even saw it," Terry said, apologetically, "I was in the trailer with Traci and didn't notice anything until it was pretty far along."

"I'm really sorry, man."

Hack just nodded.

Then he looked at Skate.

Then Hack grabbed Skate and hugged him. It was like two old men consoling each other at a funeral.

"We did what we could," Traci said, "Terry ran in and pulled out everything he could. I took it all and hauled it out of the way."

"What?" Old Man Sutter said.

"It's all over there by Remo's tent," Traci said, "everything we could grab and carry. It's sitting over there."

"Yeah," Terry said, "I got the bags, and the luggage, and the crates, and everything, even the table and chairs."

He looked at Skate, "I just couldn't get up into the loft. Sorry man. I think the fire started up there, and it was in total flames."

Skate looked stunned. It finally hit him why Hack, after all these many years, was hugging him for the first time.

"The loft," Skate warbled.

"The loft and the roof were, whaddya call, engulfed, and I went under to get the foot locker, and I was dragging it when that part of the cabin collapsed. That was the last thing I got. The rest of the cabin was just too far gone after that."

"I was begging him not to go back in," Traci said, "it was like a furnace already. But he ran back for one last thing. Then that half of the roof collapsed, and I thought he was dead, I really did."

"Yeah, for second, I did too," Terry said.

"But he came back out", Traci said, fiercely, "and I wouldn't let him go back."

"I wasn't about to go back," Terry added, "by that time it was, whaddya call…"

"An inferno," Book interjected.

"Yeah," Terry said, "that's the word."

(<o>).[].(<o>)

Hack still had his uncle's compressor, and they hooked it up to draw lake water and spray it on the fire. Not so much to put the cabin out, which was far beyond saving, but to stop the fire from spreading into the woods.

The Elysium volunteer fire department showed up too. But there was nothing to do but mop up. The cabin was down to smoldering embers by that time. The bottom two runs of logs were still standing, that was it. The roof had fallen in, the A-frame poles had burnt to a point just above the two rows of remaining logs.

They squirted the contents of their tanker/pumper, and shoveled some dirt on it, to make sure there was no chance of the fire spreading. When it was safe, they left.

(<o>).[].(<o>)

They sat around the campfire, fifteen souls with a small trailer and a smaller military tent amongst them for shelter. That, and a van and a station wagon.

The embers from the remains of the cabin fire were mostly dead. They had a robust campfire roaring.

There wasn't much to say.

"It was a damn nice cabin," Ace offered.

"Yes," Patrick said, "it was. It was damned nice."

They sat in momentary silence.

"Terry," Old Man Sutter said, "Thanks for saving our belongings. That must have been hairy."

"I was scared to death," Traci said.

Terry shrugged.

"I just did what I could – it was little enough."

They looked at Skate, slumped silently.

"What did you lose, Skate?" Rexee' whispered, knowing the answer.

Skate didn't respond for a moment, and then he shuddered.

"Skate?" Hack said.

"I lost my cabin, my belongings, and my book, that's all."

Skate wept.

"Everything, that's all. Everything."

There was nothing that anyone could think to say.

"Wait," Terry said, "the motorcycle."

Skate bolted upright, "Aw, hell, it was back against the cabin."

357

"It was," Terry managed a smile, "I moved it."

"Terry," Hack sobbed, "I love you."

(<o>).[].(<o>)

Ace looked at his watch.

"Well," he said, "on the bright side, it's officially after midnight, making it the Fourth of July."

"There's nothing much to do," Old Man Sutter said, "except break out the liquor. Thanks again, Terry."

Terry shrugged, again.

"Somebody drag my footlocker down here," Old Man Sutter ordered, "the bar is open."

"And fireworks," Ace added, "let's see if we've got any fireworks."

(<o>).[].(<o>)

They fed the fire, and watched as Ace fired bottle rockets and Roman Candles over the lake. They sat up for a while, as Old Man Sutter dispensed liquor.

But soon the day caught up with them.

Sister Louise waited for Ace to finish his cannonade. Then she borrowed their canoe and paddled home.

"Sorry Skate. Tomorrow," she said, "we'll do the 4th."

Carol and Patrick picked through the pile that Traci had made, finding their sleeping bags and zipping them together out behind Remo's tent, just up the slope in the dark. Ace and Annie were next, following the same pattern.

Old Man Sutter squeezed into the little tent with Remo – two old crippled soldiers on bivouac. Book crawled into the back of his parent's station wagon. Calvin laid down in his van. Terry and Traci got the trailer, again.

An extra sleeping bag was retrieved from the trailer, and Hack and Skate laid out by the campfire under the stars. Neither of them slept much.

(<o>).[].(<o>)

Fat Henry was picking through the pile of stuff that Terry and Traci had saved, pulling out his blankets and his suitcases.

"Henry," Rexee' said, coming up behind him, "where are you going to sleep."

"I really don't know, Rexee'," Henry said, "I've never camped out before in my life."

"Come with me then," she said, "we'll find a spot out here in the dark."

"Okay," Henry said, somewhat stunned, "I'll just go with you, if that's what you're saying."

"That's what I'm saying."

She picked her backpack from the pile, and waited for him to collect his stuff.

"This way," she said, "away from the lake."

She led the way. Henry followed.

(<o>).[].(<o>)

"You've been with a woman before?" Rexee' whispered.

"Yes, but not like this," Henry said.

"You know this is just for tonight, right?"

"Yeah, but that's okay."

"Oh, Henry, it will be more than okay."

"I know."

"I'm going to want to be on top."

"I know."

And then Henry had what Skate always wanted, but would never have. All night long.

(<o>)/(15.46)\(<o>)

Sunday morning, sunrise.

They started a small fire and got coffee started.

"What do you think about just building it again?" Hack said, "same spot, same plan."

"We could," Skate said, "except ..."

"With the first one as practice," Hack went on, "we could do another probably faster."

"Except," Skate continued, "we don't have near enough seasoned logs left."

"True."

"And it's doubtful there's another big batch of plywood just laying around."

"Also true," Hack grinned.

Ace wobbled up, wrapped in a blanket like a Woodstock refugee.

"Plot's hatching?" he said.

"Working on it," Hack said.

"Let me get a cup of joe for Annie, and I'll be right back."

"Dinero is the problemo," Skate accented.

"Not with that gold mine on the other side of the ridge," Ace said, pouring.

Hack and Skate met eyes and bobbed their heads. Ace hustled away up the slope.

"I'd actually almost forgotten about that," Hack said.

"He's right, though," Skate said, "there could be gold in them thar hills."

Hack groaned, "I've still got to tell my dad."

"Yeah," Skate said, "that'll be tough. But your old man is likely to see the sense in capitalizing on the Hackney family legacy. Abner hijacked it for the family."

Hack laughed. Ace was back.

"There's a couple of pretty easy possibilities."

"You don't mean Calvin," Skate said, "I don't know if he'd be a good choice, for a couple of reasons."

"No, not Calvin," Ace said, "he probably wouldn't want the risk, plus it doesn't fit. This is high grade collectible stuff – twelve year old Canadian Whiskey in forty year old bottles."

"Black market, you're saying," Skate said.

"I'm saying," Ace countered, "you could move a few cases a year to collectors and live off it for a long, long time."

"Could be done," Hack said, gazing across the landscape, "it surely could."

(<o>).[].(<o>)

Remo dragged himself out of his tent, using his arms, and then slowly managed to stand. He hobbled down to the fire with one of Old Man Sutter's liquor bottles in his hand.

"Who wants a belt?" Remo said.

Hack held out his coffee cup, "Why not, it's the Fourth of July."

"What you guys discussing," Remo asked, pouring.

"Deciding what to do about the cabin," Hack said.

"Fuckin-A rebuild," Remo said, "otherwise the Nazis win."

They all nodded in agreement.

Except Skate.

"Trouble is," Skate said, "this was supposed to be my chance to hide out and write. But the writing is up in flames. Everything except the Triumph is up in flames."

They sat together and pondered that.

"Rebuild, yes," Skate went on, "that's the American way. But…"

Skate's voice trailed off.

"But what to rebuild first?" Hack finished for him.

"Yeah, pretty much."

By then the rest of the camp was coming to life. High up behind the home site Rexee' appeared through the trees. She marched across the camp site, past the little trailer and the parked vehicles, the very picture of bow-legged exhaustion.

"Who's got a smoke?" she said, slumping on a stump.

Hack poured a cup of coffee and handed it to Remo, who topped it off with a jolt and handed it to Rexee'. Meanwhile, Ace fished a cigarette out of his clothing and handed it to her.

"I thought you quit," Rexee' said, leaning over the fire to get a light, careful not to catch her hair on fire.

"These are yours, you left them on the table last night.."

"So, what's up with the beefcakes this morning?" she said, leaning back into the sunlight and exhaling bitter blue smoke.

"Well," Ace said, looking around the campfire, "it looks like Hack is going to get into the high priced liquor market, which will finance rebuilding the cabin."

"And," Ace went on, "it's looking like Skate is taking off."

Rexee' sipped her coffee and nodded, without surprise.

They sat together and pondered that, too.

"A writer's gotta write," she said.

(<o>)/(15.48)\(<o>)

Moe lived just down the street and knew my Da. He liked to joke wit me and spin me yarns. My Da would grin and tell me "pay no mind."

My Da knew Moe.*

Bard laughs. You save the dumbest gag til last?

Guess so.

97. The 23rd Psalm starts with "The Lord is my shepherd; I shall not want" and contains the line "Yea, though I walk through the valley of the shadow of death, I will fear no evil: for thou art with me; thy rod and thy staff they comfort me." which was very commonly corrupted by U.S. soldiers in the Viet Nam war to say "Yea, though I walk through the valley of the shadow of death, I will fear no evil: for I am the evilest son of a bitch in the valley." Remo had this engraved on a Zippo lighter, for example.

98. Heinlein, Robert A. (1961).Stranger in a Strange Land. Putnam Publishing Group. A best-selling Hugo Award-winning science fiction novel.

99. Words, Famous Last. Webster's Standard American Heritage New World Dictionary of Inert Phrases and Little Used Words (Minneapolis: Clean Jerk Curl Press, 1976), p. 1976.

100. Columbo (1971-1978), NBC Mystery Movie, starring Peter Falk as Lieutenant Columbo, a homicide detective with the Los Angeles Police Department.

101. Heller, Joseph (1923-1999). American novelist.

102. Catch-22 (1961). Simon and Schuster.

103. dénouement, [da-noo-mo'] get it? the events that follow, in classical narrative structure, to 'untie the knot' of the plot

Chapter Last

Okay, that's it. Book's over.

I know, you thought there might be more, but that's it. Sorry.

I was standing in a sod field in about 1975 on crisp summer morning with sunlight sparkling off the dew, and steam rising from the sod rolls, when I thought to myself, "Don't look at me, man, you said if first, it don't hurt to be well-versed."

I actually developed that to about sixty pages and submitted it for support to the Minnesota Arts Council, or some such.

They were not amused.

Or more likely they were – but not in the right way.

There was a period, in the fall of 1976, when I stayed home collecting unemployment and trying to write television scripts. My friends, the ones I've known long enough, still mock me for this. None of that stuff made it into this book.

I first read about meta-fiction while attending college, in La Crosse Wisconsin, in 1982 or so. I had a very understanding English professor, Mike Coulombe, who agreed to let me work on it for independent study credit. I hope he doesn't mind my mentioning his name. I think I finished the first sixty or so pages under that arrangement. In those days, the book started with the words,

"From fourteen thousand feet you see blue smoke and clouds, a chimney poking through the haze and herons circling in the west..."

That material is now about 20 pages in, the first example of the first dumbass gag.

Then I went to graduate school.

Then I got married and there were kids.

The book got put away – and although it was never far from my mind, it did not move forward except at extremely odd intervals.

I tried to pick it up in about 1994, after we bought our first house, but all I managed were a few notes about structure and plot. The next year I put a few hours into outlining the symmetry of the structure, part of it while hanging around my Mother's garage on a cold Thanksgiving weekend. In 1999 I went to a professional conference in Mexico (or was it Las Vegas?), and slipped away to write the story of Abner Hackney on a yellow pad.

I picked it up again in earnest during the Fall of 2001. I'd finally reached a point in my life, I guess, where I felt I could afford to spend the time. I'd reached my late forties, and had had some success in my career and, like I said, this book has never been far from my mind. So I began re-assembling my notes and drafts, and recovered my files. Then I made the decision to put an hour or two a day, whenever I could, to chip away as best I could.

I'm actually in that period now, as I write this, about 275 manuscript pages into it, and taking time out to write the epilogue now, with probably 200 pages left to write. Go figure.

A couple of stretches, to be perfectly candid, were imported from other, mostly earlier writing. For example Remo's story was originally a short story called "Otto's Malady" I wrote for an English class in the early seventies. Effie in the blizzard started out as a Christmas story, also written for a class.

This next bit is a diaria piece, originally in chapter nine, that I decided to save until now:

(<o>).[].(<o>)

```
diaria -- 12/5/76.
in case you haven't tumbled to it yet - one of the
themes here is vision, eyesight, perception, point of
view and that sort of thing. The idea was you can tell a
story a lot of different ways.
the cryptic chapter division symbols are supposed to be
a winking eyeball or an eyeball with a tear forming in
the corner
```

(<o>).[].(<o>)

That is actually one of the other dumbass ideas I had for writing this.
Once I took it up again in 2001 it was a secret project.
Nobody knows what I do.*

(<o>).[].(<o>)

A word on characters. Joseph Heller once claimed* that the characters in Catch-22 were all composites of people he knew in the military. There was nobody lifted directly from his life – they were all amalgamations of different people, sometimes many people. He didn't say it, but the idea I think is that they began as composites that he turned into types, not people, and then he fleshed them out, the types, into new people.

I have nothing to add to that.

Well, except this. If you've known me a long time and you think you see yourself in this book, forget it. And don't ask me about it either. I'll just refer you to Helling, that's it.

(<o>).[].(<o>)

A word on events. Some of the stuff in this book might have actually happened. But not to me. Mostly the events that someone who knows me might recognize are stories I was told and remembered and adapted: Terry under the train, the felony phone booth, the "free" building supplies. I was around at the time, but I wasn't actually there for any of it. Well, the felony phone booth was actually me, logging stolen long distance from England in 1971. I helped build a log cabin once, too.

But the rest of it, no, forget it. I made this whole thing up, and I deny everything. Don't ask. Once in a long while some young person will ask me about the seventies: what happened, what was it like? And I tell them all the same thing – don't ask me, I don't know, because it was the seventies and, unfortunately, I don't remember a single thing from the seventies.

(<o>).[].(<o>)

A note on writing books. Damn! It takes a long time.
More books?
Here's the only remotely off-color story my father ever told me.

(<o>).[].(<o>)

- A man was happily married for many years, but one day his wife died. After the funeral his friend found him sagging against a tree, crying his eyes out.

"Don't worry," the friend said, "you had a good marriage, and in a year or so you'll be over your grief and you'll probably get married again."

"I know," the man said, wiping his tears, "but what am I going to do tonight?"

(<o>).[].(<o>)

Indeed, I think to myself. Suppose I finish this book one morning. What am I going to do that night?

Here's all I have in mind about that. I might have two or three more books in me after this. I called this book "Chapters" to be self-referential: a book about a book. I've often thought I'd write one about a bunch of guys working on the railroad in the late 1970s. I would call that one "Sections." Then I'd like to write a sort of "One Flew Over the Cuckoos Nest" account of Artificial Intelligence research in the 1980s and working as a research scientist in a self-styled "top flight" research institution at a famous mid-western university in the 1990s. That one I'll call "Sentences."

You see the pattern.

If I write a book about my marriage and those crazy days in La Crosse, I'll call that one "Periods."

Kidding, just kidding.

I may never write these books – but hey! what AM I going to do tonight?

(<o>).[].(<o>)

A note on epilogues.

I love epilogues, where the author tells the reader what became of everyone, years later.

But I hate when the epilogue is screwy and makes no sense. For example, contrast the epilogue of "American Graffiti"* with the epilogue of "A Fish Called Wanda".*

I love "Wanda", I really do, but they go for low finishing. The epilogue of "American Graffiti" tells the story of how things really came out. That is far, far better in my opinion.

Ace got laid off at the factory, and got a good paying job on the railroad. He and Annie got married. They're doing fine. Ace is still the sphincter of the Web. The guys get together whenever he organizes it.

Hack lives up north. He guides a bit, and fights fires when the need arises. He does okay.

Rexee' got her PhD and lives the life of an academic vagabond – she teaches in Europe sometimes, or wherever the next job beckons. She never married.

Book hangs out at the library, doing his thing. He's still in the old house near campus, but now he owns it.

Patrick and Carol had a large number of kids, and slowly migrated up into the woods near Hack. They have no money, but they live nicely together and

Patrick scratches a living together doing odd jobs, and painting things, signs, houses, whatever.

Effie still lives in Silver Spur. She worked at the Silver Spur Tap for a long time, raising her half-white daughter in that all-white town. Later she trained herself into being a graphic artist and she was an early adopter of computer technology. She freelances now, you might have seen her stuff.

Terry was granted amnesty in 1977 by President Carter. He's still up in Canada with Traci.

And Skate? Well, Skate got on with it. And he has other book projects in mind. You'll just have to keep an eye on the bookstore, and see what's next.

(<o>).[].(<o>)

So, how to end?

How else, but with a story?

One I've never told before.

My grandfather was a World War I veteran. He was born in Ireland but he'd fought in the trenches in France for the English army, was gassed by the Germans, was captured and ended the war in a German POW camp, claimed he once fought a duel, and after a series of life events, ended up in the Deer Lodge nursing home in Winnipeg, Manitoba, Canada, in 1976.

I wanted to visit him. But there was a hang-up. I was a grimy long-haired motorcycle freak with a live-in girlfriend. He was a reprobate himself, a heavy drinker for one thing. But I was of a different type – I wore a headband, I rode a motorcycle, and I lived in sin.

I had ridden up to Winnipeg to visit, and resolved to go see him one afternoon, but something kept me from it. I was a little afraid he didn't want to see me, and a little afraid he'd be embarrassed by me, the grunge boy, in front of his Deer Lodge pals. I don't know if any of this was realistic, but I kept delaying the visit. I stopped for a couple beers. Then finally I showed up just minutes before 4 PM when visiting hours were over.

We were in the lobby of the lodge, a big waiting room filled with couches and chairs. The walls were mostly glass, and there were very few people there besides us.

We tried to talk, without too much success.

"I've decided what I want to do with my life," I finally told him, "do you want to hear?"

"No," he said.

I've thought about that answer a million times since, but at that moment I just barreled ahead.

"I'm going to tell you anyway," I said,. "I want to be a writer."

"That takes more than just brains," he answered, "I've read many a Western myself, and often thought I could write one. But I can't"

"Why not," I asked.

"It's not just writing," was the second to last sentence he ever said to me.

And when he said the next sentence, I bid him goodbye and left myself – visiting hours were over, and I had to go. He died shortly afterwards. I never saw him alive again.

He looked over his glasses with gunmetal grey eyes – eyes that had seen war and mayhem, the cruelty of man, and the death of masses in the trenches of World War I. After being gassed in the war, he suffered from lung ailments the rest of his life. He had been a prisoner of war. He had killed men, and seen men killed.

I think on one level he cared about me, but on another level he viewed me as a speck on his windshield – a pissant who had never faced a fact of life, the worthless son of his favorite son, who had little to contribute. He was probably right.

The last real sentence he ever said to me was this.

"It's not just writing, or wanting to write," he looked into my eyes, "it takes a knack."

(<o>).[].(<o>)

And that's it. End of book. Really. Go do something else.

(<o>)/(Endnotes L.12)\(<o>)

104. Hartford, John (1937-2001). Singer-songwriter, banjo player. His 1976 album was titled "Nobody Knows What You Do"

105. Heller, Joseph (1975). Playboy interview.

106. Graffiti, American (1973). Lucasfilm. Written and Directed by George Lucas.

107. Wanda, A Fish Called (1988). Metro-Goldwyn-Mayer (MGM). Directed by Charles Crichton, Written by John Cleese (story) and Charles Crichton (story)

Chapters

They sat around the campfire that fine sunny, Sunday, Bicentennial, 1976, Fourth of July morning, and said their goodbyes.

It would be a travellin' Fourth.

They packed the van for Calvin, Old Man Sutter, Remo, Fat Henry, Traci, and Rexee'.

They packed the station wagon for Book, Ace, Annie, Patrick and Carol.

Skate rolled his motorcycle out and checked it over.

Nobody wanted to be the first to leave.

While they lingered, Sister Louise paddled across to invite them to a bean feed. She was in a convent canoe, towing their borrowed canoe, to return it.

The invitation was declined, but Terry decided to go back across to get his car. He was going to try and sneak across the border with it, to be with Traci. But Traci decided to paddle across with him, and the two of them elected to head north instead of sneaking south.

Luckily, there were two canoes. They unpacked her stuff from the van and distributed it with Terry's stuff onto the canoes. It was a LOT of stuff, and both canoes settled deeply into the water.

Remo asked about staying around to help build the next cabin. Hack said okay.

They unpacked Remo's stuff from the van, too, and packed it into the little trailer.

Book tried to slip fifty dollars to Skate – Skate's stash was up in smoke. But Skate refused.

Book persisted, and the others heard them. A collection was taken up, and Skate was compelled to accept the gift. It was nearly $500.

"We should go," Ace said, "and beat the traffic. We can be back in town for the big fireworks spectacle at the fair grounds."

Ace was a nut for fireworks. But nobody moved.

Skate got things going, finally.

"It's time, I think," he said.

"I suppose," Hack answered.

"Where to, Skate?" Book asked.

"West," Skate replied, "in the great American tradition. Wind in my hair, bugs in my teeth. The American Dream, she's west of here someplace."

The station wagon and the van were quickly filled.

(<o>).[].(<o>)

Ace gets out of the station wagon and leans into the van window, whispering to Rexee'.

"I've got a copy of his manuscript, which he gave me, and I never read. Should I tell him."

Rexee' looked at him, coldly.

"You're his friend, right?" she asked.

Ace nodded in a sideways fashion.

"Then, no" she said, "No. Let him start over. Make him start over."

She paused for a second and met his eyes.

"He needs to start fresh. It's best."

She was serious.

Ace knew she was right.

They were lined up in a convoy, headed out. Skate started his motorcycle, and moved slowly past them to lead the way up the twisty unpaved driveway.

Rexee' leaned out the van window, she was riding shotgun.

"Hey, Skate!" she yelled.

He stopped by the van, "Yes, Rexee'."

"Goodbye," she said, "and don't forget to write."

He canned it, and zoomed away, spitting gravel and laughing.

=#=#=#=

Chapter Notes

Chap.Sub -- Date, Time -- Style -- Leading Text

1.1 -- Summer 1970 -- authors aside -- When the guys graduated

1.2 -- Wed. 6/19/1974, 6AM -- narrative - flashback -- Lily of the Alley stepped

1.3 -- Wed. 6/19/1974, 6:30 AM -- narrative - flashback -- Hack and I were

1.4 -- -- recursive bit -- He arrived home from the doctor's

1.5 -- Mid May, 1976, 12:00 PM -- narrative -- When the notice arrived

1.6 -- Early May, 1976, 7:00 PM -- narrative -- The evening was

1.7 -- Mon, 6/14/1976, 12:00 PM -- narrative -- It was a Bicentennial

1.8 -- -- authors aside -- A tangled mass of twigs

1.9 -- Mon, 6/14/1976, 12:00 PM -- narrative -- At ground level, Skate

1.10 -- Mon, 6/14/1976, 3:00 PM -- narrative -- A small crowd had

1.11 -- Mon, 6/14/1976, 3:00 PM -- narrative -- Across the way, this

1.12 -- Mon, 6/14/1976, 3:00 PM -- narrative -- Skate made his phone

1.13 -- -- definition -- Great Blue Heron: Ardea herodias Linnaeus

1.14 -- Mon, 6/14/1976, 9:00 PM -- narrative -- Skate walked out into

1.15 -- Mon, 6/14/1976, 9:00 PM -- narrative -- Of all things

1.16 -- -- authors aside -- I was just there to observe

1.17 -- Mon, 6/14/1976, 9:00 PM -- narrative -- Skate walked out front

1.18 -- Mon, 6/14/1976, 9:00 PM -- narrative -- The city crew was still

1.19 -- Mon, 6/14/1976, 9:30 PM -- narrative -- It was dark when Hack

1.20 -- Mon, 6/14/1976, 9:30 PM -- narrative -- Ace! Skate called

1.21 -- Mon, 6/14/1976, 9:30 PM -- narrative -- The stand-off had

1.22 -- Mon, 6/14/1976, 9:30 PM -- narrative -- Hack's move from house

1.23 -- Wed, 6/16/1976, 5AM -- Iambic cinema -- From fourteen thousand

1.24 -- Wed, 6/16/1976, 6AM -- narrative -- Patrick slid onto

1.25 -- Wed, 6/16/1976, 6AM -- play -- The guys turn up at Doogan's

1.26 -- Mon, 7/12/1976 -- diaria -- diaria get it

1.27 -- -- free association -- Mounds of debris on every point

1.28 -- -- endnotes -- Tom Robbins, James Joyce

=#=#=#=

2.1 -- Mon, 6/14/1976, 10:00 PM -- narrative -- The night seemed soft

2.2 -- Mon, 6/14/1976, 10:00 PM -- narrative -- Tiger felt hot and

2.3 -- -- recursive bit -- recursion, see recursion

2.4 -- Mon, 6/14/1976, 10:00 PM -- narrative -- The reporter approached

2.5 -- Mon, 6/14/1976, 10:00 PM -- narrative -- The first cameraman had

2.6 -- Mon, 6/14/1976, 10:00 PM -- narrative -- Clouds were gathering

2.7 -- Mon, 6/14/1976, 10:00 PM -- narrative -- And then several things

2.8 -- Mon, 6/14/1976, 10:00 PM -- narrative -- The Constitution of

2.9 -- Mon, 6/14/1976, 10:00 PM -- narrative -- To Skate, already keyed

2.10 -- Early June, 1973, 12:00 PM -- narrative -- It was three summers

2.11 -- Wed, 6/19/1974, 6AM -- iambic cinema -- What Lily of the Ally

2.12 -- -- authors aside -- I was aware of Effie long before we met

2.13 -- -- authors aside -- A place like Doogan's

2.14 -- -- authors aside -- The fraternity house around

2.15 -- Sat. June 1, 1974, 8:00 PM -- narrative - flashback -- It was one of those

2.16 -- Sat. June 1, 1974, 8:00 PM -- narrative - flashback -- The surf rat event

2.17 -- Sat. June 1, 1974, 10:50 PM -- narrative - flashback -- The three of them

2.18 -- Sat. June 1, 1974, 11:15 PM -- narrative - flashback -- Andy the sculptor
2.19 -- Sat. June 1, 1974, 11:30 PM -- narrative - flashback -- In those days you
2.20 -- Sat. June 1, 1974, 11:50 PM -- narrative - flashback -- What you mean by
2.21 -- Sat. June 1, 1974, 11:55 PM -- narrative - flashback -- You okay, Skate
2.22 -- Wed, 6/16/1976, 7AM -- play -- Book arrives
2.23 -- 7/20/76 -- diaria -- in real life rexee' was a grad student
2.24 -- -- endnotes -- Federman, Kellman, Johnson

=#=#=#=

3.1 -- Mon, 6/14/1976, 10:01 PM -- narrative -- The entire street began
3.2 -- Mon, 6/14/1976, 11:50 PM -- narrative -- They were sitting
3.3 -- -- authors aside -- This is the story of the guys
3.4 -- Mon, 6/14/1976, 11:59 PM -- narrative -- Skate had terrible
3.5 -- Tues, 6/15/1976, 12:15 AM -- narrative -- Rexee' had given Hack
3.6 -- -- recursive bit -- Hack had thought that he had shad
3.7 -- -- iambic cinema -- When Tiger thinks about himself....
3.8 -- Summer, 1970, 8:15 AM -- narrative - flashback -- That damn tree is dead
3.9 -- -- authors aside -- Annie's mother had planted the tree
3.10 -- -- authors aside/recursive -- Annie is a victim of the well
3.11 -- Summer, 1970, 10:00 AM -- narrative - flashback -- The next day was a
3.12 -- Summer, 1962 -- narrative - flashback -- She had gone to the pet store
3.13 -- Early June, 1973 -- 1st person -- I was aware of Effie long
3.14 -- Summer, 1972, 10:00 AM -- narrative - flashback -- Skate needed some
3.15 -- Summer, 1972, 10:00 AM -- narrative - flashback -- I been workin
3.16 -- Wed. 6/19/1974, 6:30 AM -- narrative - flashback -- ...I closed my eyes
3.17 -- Wed, 6/16/1976, 8AM -- play -- ...the baby boom...Rexee joins
3.18 -- 8/13/76 -- diaria -- one of the amusing gambits
3.19 -- -- free association -- Sucking his teeth
3.20 -- -- endnotes -- Thompson, Fielding, Vonnegut

=#=#=#=

4.1 -- Tues, 6/15/1976, 12:30 AM -- narrative -- When Ace and Book
4.2 -- Tues, 6/15/1976, 12:45 AM -- narrative -- Rexee' turned on her
4.3 -- Thur. 6/20/1974, 11:15 AM -- narrative - flashback -- Skate had been to
4.4 -- Thur. 6/20/1974, 11:30 AM -- narrative - flashback -- They were at
4.5 -- Thur. 6/20/1974, 11:45 AM -- narrative - flashback -- They had settled
4.6 -- Summer, 1970 -- authors aside -- By the time the guys moved into
4.7 -- -- authors aside -- In the fifties...cowboys
4.8 -- -- authors aside -- The general rules applying to gunfights
4.9 -- Summer, 1960, 3:00 PM -- narrative - flashback -- It was a rainy afternoon
4.10 -- Summer, 1960, 3:05 PM -- narrative - flashback -- Ace had a Mattel
4.11 -- Fall, 1968, 10:00 PM -- narrative - flashback -- It was the fall of
4.12 -- Fall, 1968 -- authors aside -- Skate had gym class with Tim
4.13 -- Summer, 1970 -- narrative - flashback -- Annie got up and made ready
4.14 -- Summer, 1970 -- narrative - flashback -- Annie grieved
4.15 -- Early June, 1974, 2:00 PM -- 1st person -- What'd ya make of
4.16 -- Spring, 1963 -- narrative - flashback -- For a second Skate was in the
4.17 -- Early June, 1974, 2:00 PM -- 1st person -- Ace was our public

4.18 -- Wed, 6/16/1976, 9AM -- play/iambic bit -- ...and the American
4.19 -- 9/1/76 -- diaria/recursive -- there's some standard themes in
4.20 -- -- free association -- Bard on a blanket
4.21 -- -- endnote -- Milton, Scholes, Thompson

=#=#=#=

5.1 -- Wed, 6/16/1976, 10:00 AM -- narrative -- Delmar felt an itch on
5.2 -- Wed, 6/16/1976, 10:30 AM -- narrative -- Delmar stumbled around
5.3 -- Wed, 6/16/1976, 10:30 AM -- play -- Rexee gets caught up, Delmar
5.4 -- -- authors aside -- By 1974 the sixties were almost over.
5.5 -- -- authors aside -- We were a sort of 'after school club'
5.6 -- -- recursive bit -- At Hallowe'en the kids go out
5.7 -- Thur. June 20, 1974, 12:45 PM -- narrative - flashback -- Skate and Effie
5.8 -- Thur. June 20, 1974, 8:45 AM -- narrative - flashback -- Thursday
5.9 -- Thur. June 20, 1974, 1:30 PM -- narrative - flashback -- We should go
5.10 -- Thur. June 20, 1974, 2:00 PM -- narrative - flashback -- By 2 PM
5.11 -- Thur. June 20, 1974, 2:20 PM -- -- Skate and Effie left Doogan's
5.12 -- Thur. June 20, 1974, 2:25 PM -- -- Ace was slack-jawed.
5.13 -- May, 1972, 1:00 PM -- narrative - flashback -- Skate sat down with
5.14 -- 20th Century -- authors aside -- Bill Sutter was a product
5.15 -- 20th Century -- authors aside -- After the war, Bill Sutter
5.16 -- May, 1972, 2:00 PM -- narrative - flashback -- You KNOW Castro?
5.17 -- 20th Century -- authors aside -- Bill Sutter moved back
5.18 -- Summer, 1963, 9:30 PM -- narrative - flashback -- Skate stepped away
5.19 -- Summer, 1963 -- authors aside -- We played guns
5.20 -- Summer, 1963, 9:45 PM -- narrative - flashback -- Skate had flanked Ace
5.21 -- Fall, 1968, 11:00 PM -- narrative - flashback -- Oteye and the Klang
5.22 -- Fall, 1968, 11:30 PM -- narrative - flashback -- The fight in the parking
5.23 -- -- iambic bit/authors aside -- When walking over to the dump
5.24 -- 9/15/1976 -- diaria -- tragedy is a literary concept
5.25 -- Sat. June 22, 1974, 10:00 AM -- narrative - flashback -- Skate was sitting
5.26 -- Sat. June 22, 1974 -- authors aside -- That was Friday
5.27 -- Sat. June 22, 1974, 7:00 PM -- narrative - flashback -- They did the usual
5.28 -- Sat. June 22, 1974, 10:00 PM -- narrative - flashback -- They were in the
5.29 -- Sat. June 22, 1974, 10:30 PM -- narrative - flashback -- I don't know
5.30 -- Sat. June 22, 1974, 10:45 PM -- narrative - flashback -- They talked
5.31 -- Sat. June 22, 1974, 10:55 PM -- narrative - flashback -- Hack draped
5.32 -- Sat. June 22, 1974, 11:05 PM -- narrative - flashback -- Later they were
5.33 -- Sat. June 22, 1974, 11:15 PM -- narrative - flashback -- They sat together
5.34 -- Sunday, 6/23/74, 7:30 AM -- narrative - flashback -- Sunday morning
5.35 -- Sunday, 6/23/74, 7:40 AM -- narrative - flashback -- Skate crept into
5.36 -- -- endnotes -- Miller, Williams

=#=#=#=

6.1 -- Sunday, 6/23/74, 8:00 AM -- narrative - flashback -- Skate met Effie on
6.2 -- Sunday, 6/23/74, 9:00 AM -- narrative - flashback -- They were on the
6.3 -- Sunday, 6/23/74, 11:00 AM -- narrative - flashback -- They made their
6.4 -- Sunday, 6/23/74, 4:00 PM -- narrative - flashback -- Shit, he said, and

6.5 -- Sunday, 6/23/74, 4:05 PM -- narrative - flashback -- That WAS weird, she
6.6 -- Sunday, 6/23/74, 4:30 PM -- narrative - flashback -- Boscobel Wisconsin
6.7 -- March, 1965, 12:00 PM -- narrative - flashback -- Ace and Hack worked
6.8 -- Early Sixties -- authors aside -- The nuns...(part 1)
6.9 -- Fall, 1972 -- narrative - flashback -- After Skate had taken ...sufficient
6.10 -- Sat. June 1, 1974, 9:00 PM -- narrative - flashback -- It was one of those
6.11 -- August, 1972 -- authors aside -- Remo was a veteran
6.12 -- August, 1972 -- authors aside -- That all changed after the
6.13 -- August, 1972 -- authors aside -- And it was a demanding job
6.14 -- -- authors aside -- The first few minutes of a rainfall
6.15 -- Fall, 1972, 3:31 PM -- 1st person -- I was enjoying an overcast
6.16 -- Wed, 6/16/76, 11:30 AM -- play -- author steps in
6.17 -- -- authors aside -- What happened at Doogan's bar that special
6.18 -- Sunday, 6/23/74, 6:30 AM -- narrative - flashback -- A pine cone
6.19 -- Sunday, 6/23/74, 6:40 AM -- narrative - flashback -- Look at this
6.20 -- 9/20/1976 -- diaria -- another function of the metafictionist
6.21 -- -- free association/recursive -- Laying back on the web sofa
6.22 -- -- endnotes -- Scholes, Dylan, Canfora

=#=#=#=

7.1 -- September, 1974 -- 1st person -- I had to testify
7.2 -- Sat. June 1, 1974 -- narrative - flashback -- It was one of those
7.3 -- -- authors aside -- The web was in a college neighborhood
7.4 -- Sat. June 1, 1974 -- iambic bit -- The closest frat house
7.5 -- Sat. June 1, 1974, 9:00 PM -- authors aside -- These guys were
7.6 -- Mid-Seventies -- 1st person -- The Web didn't do that well
7.7 -- Mid-Seventies -- authors aside -- Fast Eddie, now there
7.8 -- January, 1966, 12:30 PM -- narrative - flashback -- Lunch hour was fading
7.9 -- January, 1966, 12:35 PM -- narrative - flashback -- Ace was barely off
7.10 -- January, 1966, 12:40 PM -- narrative - flashback -- It was actually pretty
7.11 -- Fall, 1972, 3:35 PM -- 1st person -- I did not know Kenny
7.12 -- Fall, 1972 -- narrative - flashback -- I don't know, Skate was saying
7.13 -- Fall, 1972, 3:45 PM -- narrative - flashback -- Skate pulled up in
7.14 -- Fall, 1972, 3:55 PM -- narrative - flashback -- It was one of those
7.15 -- January, 1966, 12:45 PM -- narrative - flashback -- They looked at
7.16 -- January, 1966, 12:50 PM -- narrative - flashback -- Skate and Sister Joel
7.17 -- January, 1966, 12:52 PM -- narrative - flashback -- The boys waited
7.18 -- -- authors aside -- By 1976 the Revolution was over
7.19 -- Spring, 1964 -- narrative - flashback -- Patrick came out first
7.20 -- Fall, 1964 -- narrative - flashback -- In the Fall of seventh grade
7.21 -- Early 1960s -- 1st person -- The most profound philosophical
7.22 -- Summer, 1964 -- recursive bit -- Suppose we invented
7.23 -- Early Summer, 1971 -- authors aside -- Terry was the deserter
7.24 -- Early Summer, 1971, 6:30 PM -- narrative - flashback -- The boys were
7.25 -- Early Summer, 1971, 7:00 PM -- narrative - flashback -- The beer was
7.26 -- Early Summer, 1971, 7:30 PM -- narrative - flashback -- They scrambled
7.27 -- Summer, 1965, 3:00 PM -- narrative - flashback -- Ace and Skate were
7.28 -- Early Summer, 1971, 7:45 PM -- narrative - flashback -- Terry had rolled
7.29 -- Wed, 6/16/76, 12:30 PM -- play -- funny book story, record

7.30 -- 11/14/1976 -- diaria -- time frame is always a problem
7.31 -- -- free association/iambic -- Bard by the barges.
7.32 -- -- endnotes -- Hesse, Conrad, Clemens

=#=#=#=

8.1 -- -- street poem -- Well-Versed: first half
8.2 -- Late Spring, 1974, 10:00 AM -- narrative - flashback -- Wait a minute
8.3 -- -- project body -- Summer Dawns: People and Meetings
8.4 -- Late Spring, 1974, 10:15 AM -- narrative - flashback -- What is this shit
8.5 -- -- project body -- Fall Noons: Birth and Parties
8.6 -- Late Spring, 1974, 10:30 AM -- narrative - flashback -- So, now we're in
8.7 -- -- project body -- Winter Evenings: Death and Partings
8.8 -- Late Spring, 1974, 10:45 AM -- narrative - flashback -- You're kidding
8.9 -- -- project body -- Spring Nights: Infinity and Movement
8.10 -- Late Spring, 1974, 11:00 AM -- narrative - flashback -- She closed
8.11 -- -- street poem -- Well-Versed: second half

=#=#=#=

9.1 -- Late Summer, 1972, 9:00 PM -- narrative - flashback -- It was the Fall
9.2 -- -- authors aside -- Long tradition ... underground railroad
9.3 -- Late Summer, 1972, 9:00 PM -- narrative - flashback -- It's actually pretty
9.4 -- -- authors aside -- Unkafrank Lake is relatively small
9.5 -- Late Summer, 1972, 10:00 PM -- narrative - flashback -- Unkafrank Lake
9.6 -- Late Summer, 1972, 10:15 PM -- narrative - flashback -- The paddled
9.7 -- 12/5/1976 -- diaria -- anyway, one of the devices
9.8 -- Wed, 6/16/76, 12:30 PM -- play/iambic bit -- You should eat
9.9 -- Wed. June 23, 1976, 10:00 AM -- narrative -- Skate leaned over
9.10 -- -- authors aside -- Imagine a heavy, sharp, steel sword blade
9.11 -- Wed. June 23, 1976, 10:10 AM -- narrative -- Skate reached out
9.12 -- -- authors aside -- Here's the problem
9.13 -- Wed. June 23, 1976, 11:00 AM -- narrative -- Hack worked the
9.14 -- -- authors aside -- Skate had never felt better
9.15 -- Wed. June 23, 1976, 11:05 AM -- narrative -- They had two short
9.16 -- Wed. June 23, 1976, 11:10 AM -- narrative -- Hack works
9.17 -- -- authors aside -- The boys don't actually augur
9.18 -- Wed. June 23, 1976, 6:00 PM -- narrative -- Walls up, roof
9.19 -- Wed. June 23, 1976, 6:01 PM -- narrative -- Truth is, they went
9.20 -- -- authors aside -- Once the walls are up, you need a roof
9.21 -- -- authors aside -- Consider a triangle
9.22 -- Wed. June 23, 1976, 9:00 PM -- narrative -- Thirty two sheets
9.23 -- -- authors aside -- The math is a little harder on this
9.24 -- Wed. June 23, 1976, 9:00 PM -- narrative -- These will be green
9.25 -- Wed. June 23, 1976, 11:00 PM -- narrative -- The noise level in
9.26 -- Wed. June 23, 1976, 11:00 PM -- narrative -- Except for Lon
9.27 -- -- authors aside -- Elysium is a typical town
9.28 -- Wed. June 23, 1976, 11:10 PM -- narrative -- A matronly
9.29 -- December, 1936, 5:00 PM -- narrative - flashback -- Abner Hackney was
9.30 -- December, 1936 -- narrative - flashback -- Stealing the truck had been

9.31 -- December, 1936 -- narrative - flashback -- Normally, in January
9.32 -- -- authors aside -- The nuns…part 2
9.33 -- -- authors aside -- Hack was from around there
9.34 -- -- free association -- Bard bouncing.
9.35 -- -- endnotes -- Wolfe, Vonnegut, Frost

=#=#=#=

10.1 -- Thur. June 24, 1976, 7:00 AM -- narrative -- It was the morning
10.2 -- Thur. June 24, 1976, 9:00 PM -- narrative -- Thirty two sheets
10.3 -- Thur. June 24, 1976, 9:00 PM -- narrative -- Ace hung up
10.4 -- Thur. June 24, 1976, 9:10 PM -- narrative -- They'd been to
10.5 -- Thur. June 24, 1976, 9:20 PM -- narrative -- Do I know you
10.6 -- Thur. June 24, 1976, 9:00 PM -- play -- Thirty two sheets
10.7 -- -- authors aside -- The swiss approach to ridge pole
10.8 -- Thur. June 24, 1976, 9:30 PM -- narrative -- The geometry
10.9 -- Fri. June 25, 1976, 9:30 AM -- narrative -- By this point
10.10 -- Fri. June 25, 1976, 9:40 AM -- narrative -- Man! Skate said
10.11 -- Fri. June 25, 1976, 11:00 AM -- narrative -- They fixed
10.12 -- Wed. June 23, 1976, 11:00 PM -- narrative -- The bar was full
10.13 -- Wed. June 23, 1976, 1:00 AM -- narrative -- The bar
10.14 -- -- authors aside -- The guys were raised in a mostly
10.15 -- Sun. June 27, 1976, 11:00 AM -- narrative -- The squad was
10.16 -- Sun. June 27, 1976, 11:05 AM -- narrative -- It was a
10.17 -- Sun. June 27, 1976, 11:30 AM -- narrative -- Beat cheeks boys
10.18 -- Sun. June 27, 1976, 11:40 AM -- narrative -- They worked like
10.19 -- Sun. June 27, 1976, 12:00 PM -- narrative -- They went to the
10.20 -- Sun. June 27, 1976, 11:00 AM -- narrative -- Delmar was out
10.21 -- Sun. June 27, 1976, 12:00 PM -- authors aside -- It takes
10.22 -- Sun. June 27, 1976, 12:00 PM -- narrative -- Delmar walked
10.23 -- Sun. June 27, 1976, 12:10 PM -- narrative -- They pissed
10.24 -- Mon. June 28, 1976, 3:00 AM -- narrative -- Three in
10.25 -- 3/26/1977 -- diaria -- Another guy who fools with time
10.26 -- -- authors aside -- Like much of the lakeshore property
10.27 -- Mon. June 28, 1976, 11:00 AM -- narrative -- Monday…final leg
10.28 -- Mon. June 28, 1976, 11:30 AM -- narrative -- The ridgepole
10.29 -- Mon. June 28, 1976, 4:00 PM -- narrative -- Town tonight
10.30 -- Fri. Dec. 19, 1975, 7:00 PM -- narrative - flashback -- The blizzard that
10.31 -- Fri. Dec. 19, 1975, 7:00 PM -- narrative - flashback -- Elizabeth Vera
10.32 -- Fri. Dec. 19, 1975, 8:00 PM -- narrative - flashback -- The snow was an
10.33 -- Fri. Dec. 19, 1975, 9:00 PM -- narrative - flashback -- Skate was several
10.34 -- Fri. Dec. 19, 1975, 9:00 PM -- narrative - flashback -- Instant vertigo
10.35 -- Mon. June 28, 1976, 7:30 AM -- narrative -- Ace stopped into
10.36 -- Tues. June 29, 1976, 9:00 AM -- narrative -- Tuesday ... Hack
10.37 -- Tues. June 29, 1976, 10:00 AM -- one iambic line -- Skate was
10.38 -- Tues. June 29, 1976, 10:15 AM -- narrative -- Skate paused
10.39 -- Tues. June 29, 1976, 10:30 AM -- narrative -- He started
10.41 -- -- endnotes -- Vonnegut, Berra

11.1 -- Tues. June 29, 1976, 11:30 AM -- narrative -- What the hell
11.2 -- Tues. June 29, 1976, 11:45 AM -- narrative -- It didn't take
11.3 -- Tues. June 29, 1976, 8:00 PM -- narrative -- What the hell
11.4 -- Tues. June 29, 1976, 9:00 PM -- narrative -- Hack worked at the
11.5 -- Wed. June 30, 1976, 9:00 PM -- narrative -- Uncle Lon had
11.6 -- Wed. June 30, 1976 -- authors aside -- Delmar, Jack and Hank
11.7 -- Fri. July 2, 1976, 9:00 PM -- narrative -- Friday, and Lon was
11.8 -- Fri. July 2, 1976, 9:00 PM -- narrative -- Delmar could see
11.9 -- Fri. July 2, 1976, 9:30 PM -- narrative -- Friday, and Lon was
11.10 -- Fri. Dec. 19, 1975, 10:00 PM -- narrative - flashback -- Back at
11.11 -- Fri. Dec. 19, 1975, 10:30 PM -- narrative - flashback -- Skate was
11.12 -- Fri. Dec. 19, 1975, 11:00 PM -- narrative - flashback -- It was the usual
11.13 -- 4/28/1977 -- diaria -- There's a wrinkle in that point
11.14 -- -- iambic cinema -- Elysium is the last town
11.15 -- -- authors aside -- Elysium is the last town on the road to
11.16 -- -- authors aside -- Before it was an officially designated
11.17 -- Spring 1976 -- authors aside -- This set up the situation that
11.18 -- Fri. July 2, 1976 -- authors aside -- Against all predictions
11.19 -- Fri. July 2, 1976 -- authors aside -- It wasn't like Cal was
11.20 -- Fri. July 2, 1976 -- authors aside -- The Fourth of July was
11.21 -- Fri. July 2, 1976, 10:30 AM -- narrative -- Friday mid-morning
11.22 -- Fri. July 2, 1976, 11:30 AM -- narrative -- There was an
11.23 -- Fri. July 2, 1976, 11:30 AM -- narrative -- Ace walked into
11.24 -- Fri. July 2, 1976, 12:00 PM -- narrative -- Considering how
11.25 -- Fri. July 2, 1976, 12:01 PM -- narrative -- The luggage
11.26 -- Fri. July 2, 1976, 12:30 PM -- narrative -- Friday just after
11.27 -- Fri. July 2, 1976, 1:00 PM -- narrative -- They sat in the van
11.28 -- Fri. July 2, 1976, 2:00 PM -- play -- all we need now
11.29 -- -- endnotes -- Jack London, Sam Johnson, Tom Wolfe

=#=#=#=

12.1 -- Wed. June 30, 1976, 1:00 AM -- narrative -- Holy Shit
12.2 -- Wed. June 30, 1976, 1:00 AM -- narrative -- They were too tired
12.3 -- Wed. June 30, 1976, 1:30 AM -- narrative -- What the hell
12.4 -- Wed. June 30, 1976, 7:00 AM -- narrative -- Hack was shaking
12.5 -- Wed. June 30, 1976, 12:00 PM -- narrative -- Noon
12.6 -- Wed. June 30, 1976, 2:00 PM -- narrative -- There was still
12.7 -- Wed. June 30, 1976, 2:00 PM -- narrative -- Skate was laying on
12.8 -- Wed. June 30, 1976, 2:00 PM -- narrative -- The interior of the
12.9 -- Wed. June 30, 1976, 2:00 PM -- narrative -- It was a hallway of
12.10 -- Wed. June 30, 1976, 2:30 PM -- narrative -- Hack and Skate
12.11 -- Wed. June 30, 1976, 3:00 PM -- narrative -- What the hell?
12.12 -- Wed. June 30, 1976, 9:00 PM -- narrative -- They were sitting
12.13 -- Wed. June 30, 1976, 9:00 PM -- narrative -- That's not funny!
12.14 -- Fri. Dec. 19, 1975, 11:00 PM -- narrative - flashback -- Shorty had been
12.15 -- -- authors aside -- In the neighborhood, when the guys
12.16 -- -- authors aside -- Sometimes the tough guys would fight

12.17 -- -- authors aside -- After eighth or ninth grade, the tough
12.18 -- Summer 1961, 10:00 AM -- narrative - flashback -- Skate was playing
12.19 -- Summer 1961, 12:00 PM -- narrative - flashback -- To get home, Skate
12.20 -- -- iambic bit/recursive bit -- When Skate was learning
12.21 -- Spring 1975 -- authors aside -- Five years had passed
12.22 -- Spring 1975 -- authors aside -- Then the war ended
12.23 -- -- authors aside -- At one point he met
12.24 -- -- authors aside -- When he wasn't working, Terry
12.25 -- -- authors aside -- By this time he had his own car
12.26 -- Fri. July 2, 1976, 10:00 AM -- narrative -- Friday. They were
12.27 -- Fri. July 2, 1976, 10:30 AM -- narrative -- Friday. They were
12.28 -- Fri. July 2, 1976, 10:30 AM -- narrative -- Sister Louise
12.29 -- Fri. July 2, 1976, 1:00 PM -- narrative -- Friday. The van
12.30 -- Fri. July 2, 1976, 3:00 PM -- narrative -- The van ploughed
12.31 -- Fri. July 2, 1976, 4:30 PM -- narrative -- They were back on
12.32 -- Fri. July 2, 1976, 5:30 PM -- narrative -- The tire blew
12.33 -- Fri. July 2, 1976, 6:00 PM -- narrative -- They all piled out
12.34 -- Fri. July 2, 1976, 6:20 PM -- narrative -- The cop appeared to
12.35 -- Fri. July 2, 1976, 9:00 PM -- narrative -- The mutiny erupted
12.36 -- Fri. July 2, 1976, 10:30 PM -- narrative -- Tower and Soudan
12.37 -- Fri. July 2, 1976, 8:00 PM -- play -- How's that coming?
12.38 -- Fri. July 2, 1976, 11:00 PM -- narrative -- Elysium at last
12.39 -- Fri. July 2, 1976, 11:05 PM -- narrative -- They parked on
12.40 -- -- endnotes -- Sandburg, Wright

=#=#=#=

13.1 -- Sat. Dec. 20, 1975, 8:00 AM -- narrative - flashback -- Morning
13.2 -- Fri. Dec. 19, 1975, 11:30 PM -- narrative - flashback -- The men
13.3 -- Sat. Dec. 20, 1975, 12:00 PM -- narrative - flashback -- They brought
13.4 -- Sat. Dec. 20, 1975, 4:00 AM -- narrative - flashback -- Skate sat
13.5 -- Sat. Dec. 20, 1975, 7:30 AM -- narrative - flashback -- He was
13.6 -- Fri. July 2, 1976, 11:05 PM -- narrative -- Delmar sauntered
13.7 -- Fri. July 2, 1976, 11:05 PM -- play -- The gang gets together
13.8 -- 6/25/1977 -- diaria -- Cover the story, that's the gig
13.9 -- -- iambic cinema -- The thing he felt through out his life
13.10 -- Fri. July 2, 1976, 11:10 PM -- narrative -- Delmar worked
13.11 -- Fri. July 2, 1976, 11:25 PM -- narrative -- They boiled out
13.12 -- Fri. July 2, 1976, 11:25 PM -- narrative -- Delmar stood
13.13 -- Fri. July 2, 1976, 11:30 PM -- narrative -- The van
13.14 -- Fri. July 2, 1976, 11:31 PM -- narrative -- Lon was sitting
13.15 -- Fri. July 2, 1976, 11:32 PM -- narrative -- This is good
13.16 -- Fri. July 2, 1976, 11:50 PM -- narrative -- The road
13.17 -- Sat. July 3, 1976, 12:00 AM -- narrative -- Lon was in his own
13.18 -- Sat. July 3, 1976, 12:00 AM -- narrative -- Friday midnight
13.19 -- Sat. July 3, 1976, 1:00 AM -- narrative -- The fire
13.20 -- Sat. July 3, 1976, 5:00 AM -- narrative -- Lily, Anne said
13.21 -- Sat. July 3, 1976, 6:30 AM -- narrative -- Book had the keys
13.22 -- Sat. July 3, 1976, 6:45 AM -- narrative -- Carol was not huge
13.23 -- -- authors aside -- In the sixties it was more common

13.24 -- -- authors aside -- Go and go and go. This was an old Web
13.25 -- Summer, 1966, 11:00 AM -- narrative - flashback -- What the hell
13.26 -- -- authors aside -- The guys lived on the north side
13.27 -- -- authors aside -- There is a sequence of small forested
13.28 -- Summer, 1966, 11:30 AM -- narrative - flashback -- They paddled
13.29 -- Summer, 1966, 12:00 PM -- narrative - flashback -- There was another
13.30 -- Summer, 1966, 1:00 PM -- narrative - flashback -- Getting back took
13.31 -- Summer, 1966 -- authors aside -- They were back
13.32 -- -- free association -- He has taken the canoe and paddled
13.33 -- -- endnotes -- Kesey, Vonnegut, Bass

=#=#=#=

14.1 -- Sat. July 3, 1976, 1:00 AM -- iambic cinema -- It's quiet here
14.2 -- Sat. July 3, 1976, 1:00 AM -- narrative -- Delmar loaded up.
14.3 -- Sat. July 3, 1976, 1:00 AM -- narrative -- Let's go
14.4 -- Sat. July 3, 1976, 7:00 AM -- narrative -- Saturday morning
14.5 -- Sat. July 3, 1976, 9:30 AM -- narrative -- There were ten
14.6 -- Sat. July 3, 1976, 7:00 AM -- narrative -- Annie was waiting
14.7 -- Sat. July 3, 1976, 9:00 AM -- narrative -- They ate breakfast
14.8 -- Sat. July 3, 1976, 9:15 AM -- narrative -- Hack's uncle lived
14.9 -- Sat. July 3, 1976, 10:30 AM -- narrative -- Try not to touch
14.10 -- Sat. July 3, 1976, 10:35 AM -- narrative -- Far, far, far
14.11 -- Sat. July 3, 1976, 11:00 AM -- narrative -- They were back
14.12 -- Sat. July 3, 1976, 11:00 AM -- narrative -- Lon was waiting
14.13 -- Sat. July 3, 1976, 12:00 PM -- narrative -- They stood by Hack
14.14 -- Sat. July 3, 1976, 12:05 PM -- narrative -- They were sitting
14.15 -- Sat. July 3, 1976, 12:15 PM -- narrative -- Hack and Skate
14.16 -- Sat. July 3, 1976, 12:30 PM -- narrative -- Skate crouched
14.17 -- 8/7/1977 -- diaria -- Lots of writers write about writing
14.18 -- Sat. July 3, 1976, 9:00 AM -- narrative -- Forest Lake, North Branch
14.19 -- Sat. July 3, 1976, 11:30 AM -- narrative -- Grand Lake, Silver
14.20 -- Sat. July 3, 1976, 12:00 PM -- narrative -- Noon
14.21 -- Sat. July 3, 1976, 12:00 PM -- narrative -- Noon at Lon's
14.22 -- Sat. July 3, 1976, 12:05 PM -- narrative -- They crowded into
14.23 -- Sat. July 3, 1976, 12:30 PM -- narrative -- Ace was standing
14.24 -- Sat. July 3, 1976, 12:35 PM -- narrative -- Ace pelted back
14.25 -- Sat. July 3, 1976, 12:40 PM -- narrative -- Ace and Hack went
14.26 -- Sat. July 3, 1976, 1:00 PM -- narrative -- Ace had been to
14.27 -- Sat. July 3, 1976, 1:00 PM -- play -- Skate explains
14.28 -- Sat. July 3, 1976, 1:30 PM -- narrative -- They decided on
14.29 -- Sat. July 3, 1976, 1:30 PM -- narrative -- Remo could, indeed
14.30 -- Sat. July 3, 1976, 2:00 PM -- narrative -- Hack and Skate met
14.31 -- Sat. July 3, 1976, 12:30 PM -- narrative -- Delmar seethed.
14.32 -- Sat. July 3, 1976, 2:00 PM -- narrative -- We've only got
14.33 -- Sat. July 3, 1976, 2:30 PM -- narrative -- Patrick, Hack
14.34 -- Sat. July 3, 1976, 2:40 PM -- narrative -- Calvin, Sutter said
14.35 -- Sat. July 3, 1976, 3:00 PM -- narrative -- Rexee' got a thrill
14.36 -- Sat. July 3, 1976, 3:00 PM -- narrative -- Stand back there
14.37 -- -- free association -- Quiet. Too quiet. You wish

=#=#=#=

15.1 -- Sat. July 3, 1976, 1:00 PM -- narrative -- Delmar poked
15.2 -- Sat. July 3, 1976, 2:00 PM -- narrative -- Terry and Traci had
15.3 -- Sat. July 3, 1976, 2:00 PM -- narrative -- Delmar worked
15.4 -- Sat. July 3, 1976, 2:30 PM -- narrative -- They followed Hack
15.5 -- Sat. July 3, 1976, 2:35 PM -- narrative -- They stopped to talk
15.6 -- Sat. July 3, 1976, 2:40 PM -- narrative -- Skate moved along
15.7 -- Sat. July 3, 1976, 2:45 PM -- narrative -- Ace waited ten
15.8 -- Sat. July 3, 1976, 2:50 PM -- narrative -- Hack had rougher
15.9 -- Sat. July 3, 1976, 3:00 PM -- narrative -- Delmar surveyed
15.10 -- Sat. July 3, 1976, 3:00 PM -- narrative -- Hack burst out
15.11 -- Sat. July 3, 1976, 3:00 PM -- narrative -- Ace heard shots
15.12 -- Sat. July 3, 1976, 3:00 PM -- narrative -- Skate had not
15.13 -- Sat. July 3, 1976, 3:00 PM -- narrative -- Did you hear that?
15.14 -- Sat. July 3, 1976, 3:15 PM -- narrative -- Hack produced some
15.15 -- Sat. July 3, 1976, 3:30 AM -- narrative -- Delmar was laying
15.16 -- Sat. July 3, 1976, 3:40 PM -- narrative -- Hack and Ace were
15.17 -- Sat. July 3, 1976, 3:40 PM -- narrative -- Whatever happened
15.18 -- Sat. July 3, 1976, 4:00 PM -- narrative -- Ace swaggered
15.19 -- Sat. July 3, 1976, 4:00 PM -- narrative -- Ace swaggered up
15.20 -- Sat. July 3, 1976, 4:15 PM -- narrative -- Hack returned
15.21 -- Sat. July 3, 1976, 4:15 PM -- narrative -- Skate was feeling
15.22 -- Sat. July 3, 1976, 4:15 PM -- narrative -- Delmar has been
15.23 -- Sat. July 3, 1976, 4:20 PM -- narrative -- Skate trotted up
15.24 -- Sat. July 3, 1976, 5:00 PM -- narrative -- They waited
15.25 -- Sat. July 3, 1976, 5:45 PM -- narrative -- Thirteen people is
15.26 -- Sat. July 3, 1976, 5:45 PM -- narrative -- The statements took
15.27 -- Sat. July 3, 1976 -- authors aside -- The Chief had mixed
15.28 -- Sat. July 3, 1976, 7:30 PM -- narrative -- They went
15.29 -- Sat. July 3, 1976, 7:30 PM -- play -- The last supper
15.30 -- 10/29/1977 -- diaria -- A note on writing books.
15.31 -- Sat. July 3, 1976, 8:30 PM -- narrative -- After a while
15.32 -- Sat. July 3, 1976, 9:00 PM -- narrative -- First, understand
15.33 -- Sat. July 3, 1976, 9:30 PM -- narrative -- Alright, Sutter
15.34 -- Summer 1960 -- authors aside -- This was a dim recollection
15.35 -- Sat. July 3, 1976, 10:00 PM -- narrative -- What it looks like
15.36 -- Sat. July 3, 1976, 11:00 PM -- narrative -- They headed back
15.37 -- Sat. July 3, 1976, 11:15 PM -- narrative -- County highway
15.38 -- Sat. July 3, 1976, 11:30 PM -- narrative -- It was hellacious
15.39 -- Sat. July 3, 1976, 11:30 PM -- narrative -- Hack and Skate
15.40 -- Sat. July 3, 1976, 11:55 PM -- narrative -- Hack still had
15.41 -- Sun. July 4, 1976, 12:00 AM -- narrative -- They sat around
15.42 -- Sun. July 4, 1976, 12:30 AM -- narrative -- Ace looked
15.43 -- Sun. July 4, 1976, 1:00 AM -- narrative -- They fed the fire,
15.44 -- Sun. July 4, 1976, 1:30 AM -- narrative -- Fat Henry was
15.45 -- Sun. July 4, 1976, 1:45 AM -- narrative -- You've been
15.46 -- Sun. July 4, 1976, 7:30 AM -- narrative -- Sunday morning

=#=#=#=

=#=#=#=

ISBN 978-0-9859947-1-6

=#=#=#=

About the Author: Brian M. Slator

Brian M. Slator was born in Winnipeg, Manitoba, Canada. The oldest of four, he broke a leg, had his tonsils out, and survived spinal meningitis, all before the age of five. He was raised in the Minneapolis area, educated in Catholic schools until the 8th grade, participated in track and field through high school, and was a hockey player until trying out for a high school play. He hitch-hiked through Europe, lived in London for a while, and hitch-hiked all over North America. After buying the first of a series of English motorcycles, he rode all over North America, including Sturgis for the Bicentennial . He worked various places through his 20s, attending the U. of M. in a desultory and part-time fashion, then got a job on the Soo Line Railroad as a linesman on a traveling crew living in a railroad car. After that he registered at the UW-L, where he met his future wife. He has remained married to the same woman since 1984, and participated in the raising of three children. He has owned the same motorcycle since 1973, which still starts on the first kick.

Professional Biography:

Brian M. Slator was raised in Minnesota and eventually earned a B.S. in CS (second major in English), from the UW-L in 1983 – the English major focused studies on contemporary American fiction. He attended graduate school at NMSU where he studied with Yorick Wilks and received a PhD in Computer Science in 1988. After serving six years as a research scientist at the Institute for the Learning Sciences at Northwestern University he joined the CS department at NDSU in 1996 where he is currently a professor and engaged in research dealing with learning in role-based simulations. He has co-authored two non-fiction books, the thematically titled "Electric Words" (ISBN: 0-262-23182-4) and "Electric Worlds" (ISBN: 0-807-74675-4), as well as dozens of technical articles in professional journals, conference proceedings, and book chapters.

Artistic Biography:

Brian M. Slator was a creative liar as a child, telling carefully plotted tales of innocence to his parents, and implausible tales of adventure to his friends, who all eventually learned to mistrust his every word. The first written stories were produced in long-hand as a 7th grade assignment, and featured a character named Percy who was an English attaché to an American PT boat during World War II. Luckily, none of these stories have survived the ravages of his mother, who liked to keep a clean house. He tried out for a one-act play in high school, which led to a succession of high school and college productions, culminating in a memorable turn as the tragic MacDuff. He began to keep a writers journal, crafting a cycle of stories eventually woven together into an unpublished experimental novel. He has always been a sucker for the 'band of buddies' story line. While a college student he wrote theater reviews for local and student newspapers, and co-founded an ad hoc film cooperative, AHC Productions, writing screenplays and acting in short features. These productions have recently appeared at various Film Festivals and are represented in the Internet Movie Database (http://www.imdb.com/name/nm3352650/).

Other Books by Brian M. Slator

Coming Soon!

~~~

Sections: a Novel

Brian M. Slator

Copyright Brian M. Slator

https://www.smashwords.com/profile/view/bslator

~~~

Section A. Back in the Saddle Again

Ace pushed open the door.

"Wake up, boy," he said, parroting his father, "we're burning daylight."

Skate groaned. Another 5 AM reveille in the hall of the mounting developments.

"I'm not working today," he implored, "I lost the job yesterday, remember?"

"Yes, and we celebrated with many beers. Hmm. But that was yesterday. Old news. The last day of the first part of your life."

"You know how often I'm inclined to kill you, right?"

"Yes, yes, yes, once a day at about this time. You know what today is, don't you?"

Skate simmered.

Skate was slow to wake up, and Ace knew that. This was the usual ploy – test him with trivia until his brain started working and to the point where there was no point staying in bed. So Skate'd get up, and they would go to breakfast. It worked every time.

Skate sat up, the blood rushed to his head. He had always been like that. A heavy sleeper who woke up grumpy, but not one to crawl out of the sack. He was either lying down, complaining, or he was upright, grumpy.

"What month is this?" Skate stalled.

The answer was usually useless trivia, like Bastille Day, or Edison's birthday, but it typically took a lot of banter and cajole for Ace to give it up. Half the time Skate could wheedle it out of him.

"We're well into Gemini," was Ace's answer.

He liked to answer the questions with another oblique reference.

"Well, then," Skate pulled on his work boots, "this must obviously be the day of John Glenn's lift-off."

"Not even close."

They heard heavy footsteps approach in the hallway. Book was on the way to the bathroom.

"You fellows mind if I tag along to breakfast?"

Book did not always get up this early, but it was not uncommon. He worked in the University library, a straight 8 to 5 job, and could sleep a lot later if he chose.

"Yes, yes, but chop-chop," Ace answered, "we need to be there when the doors open, or we wait in line."

"And that," Skate said, standing up to pull on his shirt, "would burn daylight."

He looked out the window at the gray pre-dawn and turned balefully to Ace, "and we wouldn't want THAT."

(<o>).[].(<o>)

Annie's diner, in the alley, opened up at half past five. A diner counter with 12 stools, and four two-place tables against the wall. That was it – total capacity of 20.

She'd made the place into a hot spot with snappy friendly service and an interesting morning menu. She offered coffee, of course, but also a range of breakfast foods from Blueberry Pancakes to Eggs Benedict. And she did it on her own.

The door would open, she'd glance over her shoulder, and work the kitchen and the counter at the same time. You found a seat, if there was one, or you'd wait for a spot to open. When you were settled, she pointed at you with her spatula, and asked what you wanted. You called out your order, reading the menu on the wall above the grill, and she made it up for you on the spot.

Plates of food were handed to the counter, and handed back from there to the wall-side tables by cooperative counter customers. Or you might, on a bad day, have to stand up and get your own plate and wait on yourself.

Prices were cleverly calculated, bill, tax, and tip, to even dollar amounts. So you paid by leaving dollar notes on the counter by the door. There were no tickets, just the honor system, and nobody working the cash register. Annie would ring it up when she could take a minute away from the grill.

Nobody piked. Annie had too many friends in there, and there were too many sets of eyes.

It was chaos, it was chatty, it was noisy, it was lovely. A great way to start a day, with people lined up on the sidewalk in nice weather, schmoozing and waiting, and no seat left unoccupied for more than a few seconds between 5:30 and about 8 AM.

This wasn't a place you came for a leisurely breakfast and a smoke and political discussion – not during the rush. It was understood, you got a good breakfast and you got your ass going. This was the model, the modus operandi. After 9 AM or so the crowd thinned, and you could sit in there and talk, but not before.

Then Annie would close the place at 10 AM and spend the next several hours doing clean up and prep for the next day. And so it went, seven days a week, all year long. She closed for a weekend off, once every two hundred years.

(<o>).[].(<o>)

"Ready", Book said, "let's go."

They were sitting on the front steps of the Web house, waiting for his nibs to descend and join them.

"Did Ace mention," Skate said, pointedly, "We are burning daylight?"

Book rumbled down the stairs, in the warm grey morning light.

"Yes, my yes, we'd better get going then."

"Book, what day is it today?" Skate asked.

Book pondered, "May 2nd? Several deaths, I guess – Leonardo da Vinci, Joe McCarthy, Caryl Chessman, J. Edgar Hoover."

"Crap." Ace said, his riddle blown, "I suppose you know it's Bianca Jagger's birthday, too."

"It's also the day the Early Bird satellite was used to transmit television to Europe, back in 1965."

"Really?" Skate said.

"I could be wrong," Book said, stepping past them onto the sidewalk.

Ace and Skate exchanged looks and leaped to their feet – following his most royal majesty down the sidewalk towards the diner. They walked briskly.

"Still at the tablets?" Book asked.

"Yes, a daily event, like Rexee' prescribed."

Book nodded, "something to share?"

"Maybe by the end of summer," Skate answered, "we'll see."

They were dancing around the question of Skate's writing, which he did for fun and not, so far, for profit. Book was a supporter, in a vague way. Ace was a critic, in a fatalistic way. Rexee' was too, succinctly. Skate was defensive about it, in a diffident way. Nobody wanted to scrap so early in the morning. Ace moved on.

"So," Ace said, "the job tanked?"

"Yeah, it was bad. I wasn't ready for some of the boss crap, and we got into a shouting match."

"You defending the rights of the working man, I'm sure."

"Well," Skate shrugged, "you eat shit on any job, is my experience, and that's just part of it. I don't know what happened, really. I'm doing my stuff, he's giving me crap, and suddenly we're nose to nose exchanging views."

"Exercising your first amendment right to free speech?" Book offered.

"Yeah, well, it's not like that exactly, is it?"

"On the job?" Ace said, "No, it's not like that. The boss's ideas are automatically good ideas. You've got to figure part of your pay is just for packing that down."

"Yeah, I know," Skate shrugged, "like I say, I don't know what happened. He was being a boss prick, and I stopped what I was doing to face him. Suddenly I was shouting, he was shouting, and just as suddenly I was fired."

They walked a few more steps, "Thus endeth my sodball career."

They hiked in silence.

"Unemployed," Book said hopefully, "whatever shall you do now?"

"Now?" Skate paused, "Now I'm going out to eat breakfast."

Book could get him a job in the library, and wanted to, they all knew, but Skate didn't really want that back.

"I've heard they're hiring on the railroad," Skate went on, "I'm going to look into that. A friend of my mother's said she read in the paper Amtrak is looking for cabin boys."

"Union job," Ace interjected, "good money."

"Yeah, that and riding the rails," Skate said, "That could be cool. There will be stories in that."

They had katty crossed their intersection, hustled past the Surf Frat, and hiked past the House of Rip-Off to the next alley. There they found the door of Annie's diner, right where they'd left it. There was a small knot of people on the sidewalk. The door swung open at exactly 5:30 AM. They were in.

The old lady, Lily, was already sitting on her usual perch at the end of the counter. They occupied the middle of the counter space.

"What'll it be, boys?" Annie, lovely lady, knows the answers.

"Blue cakes," Ace said, and settled onto a stool.

Annie was looking at Ace with a smile in her eyes. They were a couple.

"Me too," Book added.

"Blueberry pancakes," Skate said, "And a railroad job."

"You got it," Annie said, turning to the grill, "Coming right up."

At the end of the counter, Lily stooped. It was her way to nod.

"Aye," she said quietly, "Thet'll bay naxt."

Section A.4. Blinded by the Light

Ward Michaels slid onto a barstool and rested his weary head on his hands. Straight brown hair poked through his fingers as he pressed his corroded eyeballs into his palms. Calvin slipped a double Screwdriver between his elbows and beneath his nose, saying nothing. Ward meditatively stared into the glass, admiring the pith speckled ice cubes with the canine calm of the thoroughly exhausted man. He was dog tired at seven A.M., happy hour at Doogan's.

He said, "Thanks, Cal" knowing another stroke had already been noted on his tab, and Cal could give a damn whether he was grateful or not. The score got settled on payday, twenty six times a year.

Old man Sutter was sitting in his personal booth, blindly surveying the Racing Form and chewing an unlit stogie. He made occasional notes on a tally sheet, sipping a tumbler of brandy and hawking up lungers into a Styrofoam cup with emphysemic violence.

The next booth contained the bloated girth of Fat Henry who peered disinterestedly at a well worn copy of the morning paper. Henry slurped from a shell of beer that he ponderously refilled from a private pitcher. Dressed in the soiled white uniform of an hospital orderly Henry looked like nothing so much as the great white whale with his face tinged pink and his blubber heaving as he delicately drank from the ridiculously small glass and filled and refilled it. Henry moved with the casual grace and studied indifference of the resignedly obese person.

Calvin resumed his usual station at the far end of the bar. His sleek, thin, black back gently rippled as he dealt a hand of gin to young Remo, who was gathering the cards into his arthritic claws when the back door opened and the big guy walked in.

The morning sun was to his back and the natural gloom of the tavern was cut with a dazzling glare. Ward Michaels barely turned his head to observe the big man, with precious little interest, only mildly curious because an unfamiliar face was rare in Doogan's, and because Calvin usually had the back door locked during the morning.

The guy verged on huge. He strode up to the bar and sat midway between Ward and the end where Cal and Remo were standing. He wore nothing but leather; buckskin pants, a shirt that was loosely tied in the front with thong and moccasins with incongruous gold colored brooches holding them on. His belt buckle was heavy and golden and he carried a big leather pouch on his waist.

"Innkeeper," he said, basso profundo, dropping the pouch on the bar, "drinks for any that wants'm and keep'm coming, it's my birthday."

(<o>).[].(<o>)

At exactly the same moment, Alan "Easter" Crowley, at the wheel of a stolen Pontiac, pulled into the mostly empty parking lot of the King Super Marquette on the corner of Marquette & Franklin Avenues. Clad in a dark suit and overcoat, overdressed for the warm May weather, he casually sauntered up to, and quietly entered through, an inconspicuous back door marked 'office'. The room was deserted except for a man sitting at a desk, punching at an old-fashioned mechanical adding machine.

Crowley smiled coldly to himself and slipped a dark ski mask over his head.

"Excuse me," he said.

The man at the desk, startled, spun around.

"Hello," said Crowley before the man could speak, "I've come to rob your store."

(<o>)/(A.6)\(<o>)

Skate walked into the Amtrak office in downtown Minneapolis and addressed the receptionist.

"I'm sorry," she said, "we're not accepting applications right now."

"You sure?" Skate said, leaning on the counter, "my mother sent me down here, on the advice of her friend, and my mother is very, very seldom wrong."

He beamed his warmest smile, and she liked him.

"Your mother was right, about three weeks ago," she consoled him, "we were hiring cabin boys."

She was over forty, nice looking, and a veteran of receptionist warfare. She appraised him with unblinking calm. Skate was tanned and hard from laboring in the sod fields. He was ready to work.

"You wouldn't want that job anyway," she said, "it wouldn't suit you."

"My mother," he said, "will be very disappointed."

"You should try the Soo Line," she answered, "I've heard they're hiring."

"The Soo Line?"

"They're just around the corner. Make your mother proud."

Skate turned to go, half pissed. When would things just open up for him, so he could step in, like they seemed to for other people? Here was another blow off.

"I thank you," he said, still smiling, and turning, "and my mother thanks you, too."

She stopped him, and then, kindly, wrote the Soo Line address for him, which was, indeed, just around the corner.

(<o>).[].(<o>)

Skate sat in the Soo Line offices with a clipboard on his lap. The application was simple enough, and they let him use the phone book to specify his references. People he knew at his last job in the library, and reliable Web friends, and not the people he knew, so briefly, at his last job in the sod fields.

"Here you go," he said, handing the clipboard across the counter.

"Okay," the secretary said, getting to her feet, "follow me."

She was young with dark hair and an olive complexion, and she was desperately thin, a walking skeleton. Her skin seemed painted on her skull, and her legs were so thin they were lucky – lucky they didn't break. Skate leaped to his feet and obeyed without question. She led him around the counter and through a door into an office.

"Mr. Nelson," she said, and handed the clipboard to a businessman behind a desk.

Craig Nelson was an assistant director of personnel. It was his job to fill vacancies as quickly as they came open. There were often long periods without vacancies, where he had little to do but look out his office window and admire the weather.

He actually enjoyed looking out his office window and admiring the weather, so when it was time to fill vacancies he liked to get that over with as Soon As Possible, so he could get back to his main pursuit.

Craig wore a checked suit and a loud tie. He stood when Skate walked in and extended his hand to shake. He had this salesman's habit of extending his hand high, almost at eye level. It was weird, and Skate, not knowing what to expect, clasped and shook.

"Sit," Craig Nelson said warmly, smiling and pointing to a chair, "let's get started."

Skate was dumfounded. He had come in expecting to fill out a form and leave. He was wearing yesterday's clothes: a dirty work shirt, blue jeans, and muddy work boots. He hadn't showered or changed his clothes since yesterday, and here he was in an interview situation.

"Sorry," he mumbled, looking down at himself, "I'm not really dressed."

"You look like you're ready to work," Craig Nelson answered, "that's the main thing."

Skate nodded. Craig was right about that. The boss's thoughts are automatically good thoughts.

Craig went through the usual questions, although he'd already decided the job was Skate's.

Had he ever worked on the railroad? No.

Did he have relatives on the railroad? No.

What was his last job? Working on a sod farm.

"That's hard work," Craig observed.

386

"I was an athlete in high school, but I'm in better shape now than I've ever been."

"What sport?"

"Cross country, Hockey, and Track."

Mr. Craig Nelson nodded, not really listening.

"Why did you leave the sod field?" Mr. Nelson asked.

"They were going out of business," Skate answered, only half lying.

Craig nodded. The questioning continued.

Did he know how to run heavy machinery? Mostly driving truck, 12 forward gears, and a little tractor work.

Chain saw? Oh, yes, plenty of chain saw experience.

Any history of back problems? No, Skate lied again.

Was he available to start right away? Yes.

"That's it," Craig said, standing.

He held his hand out at eye-level again, and they shook.

"We'll check your information," he added, "and get back to you one way or the other."

Skate, on his feet, was jazzed from the rapid fire questioning. All he wanted now was to find an exit and flee.

He stood, trying to form a farewell sentence that would communicate his willingness to work and his desire to have this job. Instead he wisely kept it simple.

"Thanks," he said, backing away.

Craig was already in his chair shuffling papers.

Skate fled.

(<o>)/(A.8)\(<o>)

Skate left the Soo Line office and spent Tuesday running around town. He still had paperwork from the sod job, and he returned that. He needed parts for his motorcycle, and ended up hanging around the motorcycle shop shooting the skip. He rode down the river road on his Triumph, enjoying the breeze in his teeth. He stopped here and there for a beer.

It was a nicely unemployed day, with no income, but no commitments, and enough to keep him occupied. He ended up on the West Bank, patrolling old haunts, and checking in. He shot a few games of pool, dollar a game, at the Triangle Bar, and then across at the Viking Bar, and he broke even – a good outcome, considering the venues.

He was hoping for a woman, but he found none – a bad outcome. He cruised home on his bike, tipsy, and fell into bed, after midnight, still wearing the clothes he had worn to work on Monday – his interview outfit on Tuesday, still dirty from his sod job.

(<o>)/(A.9 Diaria)\(<o>)

Diaria, get it? My notes, cranked out on my trusty electric corolla, blown ass-wise. I think of it as hindsight. Har, har, har. An old gag.

"What now?" my roommate asked, "can you collect unemployment?"

"What now," I said, "Right now I think I'll go get breakfast. And no, I don't think I can collect after that farm job. I didn't pay in."

I was suddenly between jobs again. I'd been working on a sod farm for pretty good money -- but that had suddenly blown up in my face. My roommate was worried about the rent. I think. But I wasn't. I had enough to last the month. Barely.

"I've been thinking about the railroad," I said, "do we know anybody?"

My roommates pondered a bit, "I don't think so."

"Too bad," I said, "let's eat."

(<o>)/(A.10)\(<o>)

In the 1860s grain and other produce from the upper Midwest (northern Wisconsin, Minnesota, and the Dakotas), traveled through Minneapolis to Chicago and from there to the east. There were multiple railroads that covered this distance, but shipping costs remained high because they were all more or less in collusion, and guilty of shameless price fixing. It was essentially a monopoly situation, healthy competition did not exist, and costs to the consumer were exorbitant.

The Minneapolis, Sault Ste. Marie & Atlantic Railway was founded in 1883, aimed at linking Minneapolis with Upper Peninsula Michigan (and to Canadian railroads from there), as an alternative route that would provide competition and, it was hoped, a way of driving down prices. Seventy-five percent of the stock was owned by flour milling companies in those early days, Pillsbury among them.

(<o>).[].(<o>)

Pronunciation note. When you see " Sault Ste. Marie" or " Sault Sainte Marie" you should say in your head, "Soo Saint Ma-ree." This is how it's pronounced, and that's why this railroad eventually came to be called the Soo Line, because "Sault" rhymes with "Soo".

On the same subject. Everyone who reads from an early age has got words they mis-pronounce in their heads before they learned how it is said aloud. A friend of mine tells how he said "tee-toe-tailor" in his head for years before he leaned the word "teetotaler" was pronounced "tee-toe-taller". Similarly, the word "depot" which you will see many times in this document, is pronounced "dee-po" or "deep-oh" and not the "dep-ought" that I still say in my head at first.

(<o>)/(A.11)\(<o>)

Four hours later, Ace pushed open the door.

"Wake up, boy," he said, parroting his father, "we're burning daylight."

Skate groaned. Another 5 AM reveille in the hall of the mountain developments.

"I'm unemployed," he implored, "please go away."

"You know what today is, don't you?"

Skate simmered.

"Haven't I killed you yet?"

"It was on your list, but you lacked on the follow through."

"Remind me to do that today," Skate said loudly, "Wednesday!"

They heard heavy footsteps approach in the hallway. Book was on the way to the bathroom.

"Skate, did you get your phone message?" Book said.

"No, what was it?"

"Cramer, he said was his name, and he wants you to call him. He was calling from the Soo Line."

"Huh?"

"That's all he said. To call him about your job."

"You mean I've got the job?"

"He wouldn't say any more. He just said to call."

"What day is it today?"

"My, I don't know," Book said, "can I go to breakfast with you fellows?"

"Yes, yes, but chop-chop," Ace answered, "we need to be there when the doors open, or we wait in line."

"And that," Skate said, standing up to pull on his shirt, "would burn daylight."

(<o>)/(B.1)\(<o>)

Sunday night, dark. Skate loads his car, a black 1969 Ford Fairlane 500. He puts his luggage in, a duffel bag and some other stuff. He needs to be in Michigan by 7 AM, and he has a map. That part is good.

Trouble is, he's been celebrating his departure with friends – first at the Stockholm bar, which offers free snacks on Sunday, and then at other joints around town. It has been a nice party, but now everyone else has gone home to bed, and Skate has got to drive through Minnesota, across northern Wisconsin, and into Upper Peninsula Michigan.

Skate is half-buzzed and he's got about 300 miles to drive on 2-lane US highways and narrow county roads before reporting to work in the morning. It's a long road, and he knows it. What he doesn't know is, this is the first in what will be a long sequence of such drives.

(<o>).[].(<o>)

Considering he was raised in Minnesota, Skate knows remarkably little about Wisconsin. Green Bay Packers, cheeseheads, Badgers. Not much else. Capital? Madison. Milwaukee? King of Beers. Also a baseball team. Not the Braves any more. Which? Slogan? The Dairy State (Skate guessed), State Bird? Who could say? Other data?

Nope, that was it. After living virtually his entire life within 50 miles of the Wisconsin border, that was all there was.

At Our Lady of the Snows, when they were kids, they went on a field trip every year. The seventh and eighth graders were loaded onto a rented orange school bus and driven to St. Croix Falls, Wisconsin. It was a beautiful site and a day of clambering around on rocks, picnicking, and swimming and boating for those so inclined. It was invariably a bright sunny day when they took this trip, through some meteorological miracle

The other miracle was nobody was ever killed on these trips, as the students, full of hormones and uncontrolled energies, were set loose on arrival and then left completely unsupervised after that.

(<o>).[].(<o>)

Skate settled into a nice light driving rhythm, crossing Wisconsin from left to right, angling northeast as he went. It was the first of many such journeys. He would learn over time how to keep his body still, to minimize aches after a long drive, and how to wedge his foot so as to avoid accelerator pedal fatigue in his right leg. On later trips he would pack sandwiches and learn the trick of opening a sandwich bag and eating while hardly taking his eyes off the road. It didn't take long to discover where the late-night gas stations were located, and to develop a routine for buying fuel.

... the Interstate, I-94, east into Wisconsin, to the Highway 63 exit, then north through Clayton, Comstock, Cumberland, Barronett, Shell Lake, Spooner, Trego, Springbrook, to Hayward....

The first night he reckoned he needed six hours for the trip, to be safe and on time. He was due at 7 AM and left slightly after midnight, so allowed to be there a little after 6 AM and maybe catch a nap in the morning – if he got there in plenty of time. He calculated that he could stop for coffee, suffer through a flat tire, and still get there before 7 AM. He had his map open on the seat beside him, and the route was fairly simple.

He was halfway across Wisconsin, stopped in Hayward for gasoline, coffee and a doughnut, and studying his map, when he noticed the little dotted line on the map.

A time zone!

He cursed.

Upper Peninsula Michigan was in the Eastern time zone, Minnesota and Wisconsin were in the Central. He had lived most of his life in the Central Time Zone. You could drive from Minneapolis to Chicago and remain in the Central Time Zone. But the pointless tip of Upper Peninsula Michigan operated in Eastern Time. He cursed again.

His nap potential was down to nothing, and if he was unlucky he'd be late. He cursed again, paid up and left, heading north and east into the night. His hour of cushion time was gone before he got it.

Just as suddenly, his coffee breaks were over – and a flat tire would be a disaster. He tried to push the speed limit to get some cushion back, but a speeding ticket would also be a disaster. And not knowing the way, he was fearful of missing a turn or getting lost. Either of these would now also be a disaster. He pressed on, less lightly, and more grimly.

... leaving Hayward on Highway 63 through Seeley, Cable, Grandview, Benoit, and then east on Highway 2 to Ashland, and a spectacular drive by view of Lake Superior in the half-light, then east through Birch to Hurley and Ironwood....

(<o>)/(B.4)\(<o>)

He drove through wooded gloom. The last leg of the trip is on US highway 2 from where Hurley, Wisconsin turned into Ironwood Michigan, east in a more or less straight line. Frequent farm fields and houses along the road side gradually gave way to ever increasing stands of brush and timber.

Long stretches of road were dead east, which put the sun in his eyes at a shallow and disconcerting angle. Not for the last time, he found himself blinded by the light.

This became a theme on the railroad: blinded by the light. He started every week that way, east into the sunrise, and ended it the same, as he drove west into the sunset at the end of the week.

About fifteen miles east of Ironwood, Highway 2 veers southeast towards Watersmeet, and he needed to jump onto Michigan State Highway 28. He was alert to the change, and did not miss it, although had prolonged anxiety as he kept expecting the turn off, and it didn't appear, and he started fretting he might have missed it. Once on 28 he passed through Tula, and Topaz and Matchwood, and then just faced the last five miles to Ewen.

He'd been carefully counting down the miles, and doing a new "estimated time of arrival" calculation after every road side mile sign. He was going to be a few minutes late, but not many, and he was looking for another sign when he saw a towering pile of lumber off the road to his right. In the morning light he could easily read the sign, "Ewen, World's Fair Load of Logs."

"Must be the place," Skate said to himself, suddenly feeling nervous after a night of concentrated voyage, and took a right at the light marking the intersection with the highway and the main drag – Cedar Street.

(<o>).[].(<o>)

As Skate turned the corner, a brown mid-sixties Chevrolet pulled up to the light on the cross street. The driver had long red-brown hair under a baseball cap. The passenger seat held a big dark haired man wearing a tan welder's cap, opening his door to vomit on the street. He spewed red bile, while leaning out the car window, with the door half open supporting his weight.

Skate hardly caught it out of the corner of his eye as he drove past, intent on his job. But he saw the results in his rear-view mirror. The dark haired man blew chunks to the east, supporting himself on the car door as he retched, and then swinging himself back into the car as it started its right-hand eastward turn down the highway.

The passenger fell back into his seat, bouncing the springs, but by then Skate lost sight of the car, as he moved into town to find his own future.

(<o>)/(B.6)\(<o>)

Ewen Michigan.

From the highway to the railroad tracks and the Soo Line depot is two "city" blocks. On the right, a motel, real estate office, lawyers office, some empty store front, and the grocery store, followed by an open patch and the tracks. The local fuel oil distributor, Maki's, is just across the tracks. After that you are into the residential area, and the elementary school beyond that.

On the left side of the main drag, a bar, a line of brick buildings with stores and such, and the old three story hotel, with a bar on the first floor. Right against the hotel is the Soo Line depot, and then the tracks.

(<o>).[].(<o>)

The Soo Line tracks, a single set of rails, run east and west, parallel to the highway and perpendicular to the main drag. Every little town along the way has a siding where rail cars can be stored to wait to be added to a train. Ewen, a slightly bigger operation than some, also had a second siding for crew cars. When Skate pulled through town, he saw the depot at the end of the street to his left, and a short line of dilapidated rail cars opposite. Not a soul on the street, no train at the depot, and no workers in sight.

There were cars parked in the open spot area past the grocery store, just short of the tracks. He pulled in and parked. Skate checked the time: just after 7 AM. He'd beat the start time deadline, but missed the "report in" time by a few minutes. A bad way to begin, he feared, and the wrong footing, but probably not a disaster.

(<o>).[].(<o>)

Skate got out and stretched. It had been a seven hour drive, although he had only aged six hours. Like a beam of light he had collapsed time – perhaps Einstein's Theory just all about time zones, despite all the relativity fuss. Must remember to ask Book about this. How long must a particle move at the speed of light to make up an hour? Is that even calculable?

He sat back into his car, as anxious as he was to be "on time" to his job, and pulled out his journal to write this question down. It might make a story element some day.

He got out and looked around.

Behind him was the town, such as it was. In front of him, a neighborhood of wood frame houses.

To his right was a line of very dilapidated looking railroad cars. A Pullman "open platform" coach car, then what looked like a converted freight car with windows and a chimney sticking up, then a water car, and a really worn down looking wooden freight car. The whole thing looked badly in need of maintenance and a coat of paint. Except, it looked to Skate, a coat of paint would only put a sheen on a wreck.

Across the road was a single set of railroad tracks, stretching through town in each direction and disappearing into the forest.

To his left was the depot, another dilapidated monument to time and neglect, except for the Soo Line sign, looking large and red and white and freshly painted.

(<o>).[].(<o>)

The funny thing about railroad depots is that no two are the same and yet they are all alike. Wood frame, single story buildings, usually, with a platform for passengers and freight to be loaded on and off. They usually have a shallow pitched roof, with a waiting room, and an area inside behind a counter where the dispatcher and ticket sellers work. Usually, in a small town, this is the same person.

Behind the public areas, with the hard inhospitable benches, there is always a warehouse area for storing freight, and a workshop of some sort with an area (sometimes a 'break room" but sometimes just a table with some chairs with an ashtray), where the working men congregate, sometimes to prepare for work, but often to linger, smoking cigarettes and avoiding work or, more fairly, smoking cigarettes and waiting to work, or smoking cigarettes and recuperating from work.

The type of shop will differ, depending on the function and status of the depot, but there is always a break room. A savvy railroad man, on a new assignment, knows to go and find this room. It is here he will learn who his new crewmates are, and possibly many other things, like where to eat, and where not to, where to stay, and where not to, who the bosses are, and how bad they are – all the simple railroad man survival information that each new assignment demands.

Many men travel on the railroad, working different jobsites as the railroad needs their specific skills. Anyone who's worked on the railroad knows to look for the break room, and from there learn where to report. This is the way it's done.

Skate knew none of this stuff.

(<o>).[].(<o>)

As he stood there, by his car, he saw a man in coveralls and a white hardhat step out of the depot and walk away from him down the platform. The man was short and square-jawed, and looked in Skate's direction only briefly. Skate was about to gesture, but the man turned away before he could act. They were separated by a shouting distance: the length of the parking area plus the main drag, and Skate couldn't bring himself to yell across that gap. So Skate stood there, cool, acting as though he had no questions to ask, and watched the man disappear into another door of the depot.

He thought he should check into the depot, and find his assignment, so he walked over and pushed his way into the waiting area. He suddenly realized, as he did, formulating his main question, that he could not remember his foreman's name.

Mr. Cramer had told him when they spoke, and he had written it down, but that piece of paper, he suddenly apprehended, was on the table by the phone, in the house, in Minneapolis, about 300 miles behind him.

As he pushed through the door, he realized he had a fall-back. All he needed to do was ask for the "line crew", and let the steerage arise from there.

But there was nobody in the depot.

"Hello," he said awkwardly, feeling foolish and out of place.

It was an old-time waiting room, with slatted benches around the room, and nothing else – minimum hospitality. Passengers might sit down to wait for a train, and that was it. No vending machines, and no accoutrements, not even a water fountain.

His voice echoed in the void, but nobody answered. He was on his own.

He stood there for a moment, thinking to shout louder. He could see there was a door behind the counter leading into the bowels of the depot, but he didn't want to barge into what could easily be an off-limits area. So instead he pushed his way outdoors into the gray morning.

Looking down the tracks, he could see the main line stretching around a long curve. To the right of that was the siding, with the short line of rail cars parked on it. To the right of that was his car. To the right of that was the town.

When he looked back at the main line, he could see a teen-aged girl who had miraculously appeared from out of nowhere. She was walking right to left, having already crossed the main line, and she was moving away from him: fifty yards and more. It looked like she might have been coming from the rail cars, or cut through them on her way to wherever she was going.

She was small, he could tell, but perfectly formed. Her long straight honey blond hair fell halfway down her back and swayed with her hips when she walked. She wore a simple green and yellow dress that stopped mid-thigh and revealed short, perfectly shaped legs. She wore tennis shoes, with no socks, and her arms and legs were tanned to a golden brown.

Skate took a step towards her and hollered softly, "hey!"

He was desperate for information, about his new job, naturally. But he was not opposed to learning more about this creature in the mist.

She turned towards him without breaking stride, and for a brief moment he saw she had surprisingly large breasts for a girl her size, and she was carrying a bra and panties in her hand.

She saw him, and smiled and waved with her other hand. But she did not pause, and turned away as she half walked and half skipped out of sight around a corner.

Skate hoped this was an omen, a look into a future of sylph sightings at dawns early light, with visions of beauty before breakfast every day.

He watched her disappear and then made his was back to his car, near the tracks. As near as could be told, he was the only living being for miles around. The man with the white hardhat having disappeared, the girl was gone, and he was it, the lone entity on the planet. He looked at the short line of cars on the siding, wondering what to do.

(<o>)/(C.1)\(<o>)

This is the story of a railroad, and the precise point at which it turned from being a provider of jobs, and a way of life, to becoming just another desperate and failing American institution. It's a story about people and places, about history and folklore, about friendship and teamwork, about conflict and death. In a lot of ways it's a sad story, it's Skate's story, about a time that passed before his very eyes, and which will never be back this way again. It's also a human story, about what the railroad meant to people, about what those people meant to each other, and about what that railroad life was like. And in many ways it's a tragic story, about the passing of an era, the squandering of human potential, and the power of the human spirit in the face of suspicion, waste, and greed. In short, it's an American story, with all the capacity for nobility and for shame that every real American story has in it.

When Skate started on the railroad he was sent to the Upper Peninsula of Michigan to help restore a pole line. It was during the 1970s and he worked on a traveling crew of 4-6 men (it varied). They spent the summer, fall, and winter of that year refitting the infrastructure that supported telephone communications between all the depots from Ironwood to Sault Sainte Marie, a distance of three hundred miles. They set new poles, hung new cross-arms, and strung new wire. When they were done, the line was in first class condition.

Later they were sent back to the Upper Peninsula. But this time the job was much different. The pole line was abandoned, and they were sent to take it all down. They had a larger crew for this job, and worked fast. The entire system was dismantled, and the valuable copper wire recovered, in the course of one summer – undoing an onslaught of building and a century maintaining in 90 days.

At the same time, other events were unfolding in the world. In a tough economy, thieves would steal copper wire to sell for high priced scrap. This created a break-down of communication that paralyzed the railroad and endangered railroad workers. The government of the United State was in a 'Cold War' with the Soviet Union resulting in an arms race, the famous Strategic Defense Initiative, and nuclear weapons proliferation. This created an atmosphere or fear and mistrust around the world. Meanwhile, sun spots were erupting at unprecedented levels, causing breakdowns in communication around the world and further fueling the fear and mistrust among nations.

Here we go.

(<o>)/(C.2)\(<o>)

Well, almost.

This is the "up front" section, where the stage is set in the preamble sense of "up front," and where the writer is "up front" about what's going on here – revealing the artifice and the gears of the machinery. This is where the "cards are laid on the table," the "curtain is lifted," the inner workings are revealed, and the "truth" is told.

The truth is, this is a story, a fiction, but based in reality like every fiction is. And yes, it's a story about the guys, in all their different guises.

As I've explained elsewhere, this is the story that I want to tell about these times, in the way I want to tell it – in the way that's fun for me, and that I'll enjoy reading later. That's me talking.

As foretold in the epilogue of the first volume of this epic -ology, the Web has scattered in a way, while remaining together in another.

(<o>)/(C.3)\(<o>)

By this time ...

Hack is full-time up in the woods, living off his land, in several senses. Book is entrenched in the University library system, and moving up the ladder of responsibility. Rexee' has completed her degree training and moved to Europe where she lives the life of an academic vagabond. Patrick and Carol are raising their kids and working on getting out of the big bad city and into the countryside. Annie's diner is a big success. Ace is Ace, doing his thing and toiling in the factory/warehouse trade as little as possible. They are together, Annie and Ace, and Ace keeps his Web address, but lives with Annie in every other sense.

Lily is still hovering around. Tiger is gone, far gone. Calvin and the barflys do their deed every day. Remo stayed the Bicentennial summer with Hack, and helped him rebuild, as best he could – but it wasn't really the life for him, and he moved back to the Cities. Terry and Traci are working on Canadian citizenship. It turns out that Traci can't have kids, and they're talking about adopting – but they have pretty much faded from the scene – neither of them writes or calls. Effie and Margie are both working in the Silver Spur Tap at this point. Sister Louise is on and off the island, as duty demands.

Delmar is in the slam. Hank and Jack pulled a workhouse stretch and now they're back in town. Lon is no better off than he was before.

And Skate? He's been on the road. He went and went and went.

He did not forget to write.

Now he's back.

Here we go.

(<o>)/(C.4)\(<o>)

Well, almost.

I want to be "up front" about a few more things. First, I'm writing this top-down, from an outline, so the general parameters of every chapter have been decided. You will see this at the top of every chapter. I know already what each one is supposed to be about. Thing is, I find the story writes itself, within the outline, and the writing doesn't always follow the outline very well. You'll see what I mean as we go along. I use the outline as a guideline, but then the writing extemporizes from there.

I don't apologize for this. It's a book after all, and the books tend to go and go and go. We're all along for the ride, and we just have to see where this takes us – maybe not where was planned, but that's okay and not too surprising. Planning is highly over-rated anyway.

Second, you may as well know, Skate actually worked for the Soo Line, starting in May of 1978, and quitting in August, 1980. And yes, he worked on a line crew that reconstructed a pole line one summer, and then turned around two summers later and dismantled the whole thing.

Third, I'm not thinking of playing with time so much. In other opii there was a lot of time management going on – which was fun – but this go-around I don't think so. This is a story with a beginning, a middle, and an end, in that order. Like a river that runs from source to destination, or a rail line that goes from the first depot to the last, we move on down the line. We go and go and go.

But, I might change my mind about all this as it goes along.

We'll just see what happens.

Here we go. Really, I mean it this time.

=#=#=#=

www.ingramcontent.com/pod-product-compliance
Lightning Source LLC
Chambersburg PA
CBHW051441260626
47162CB00001B/193